Praise for Lystra Rose and *The Upwelling*

'It is amazing to read a fantasy novel that draws on ancient original knowledge systems and their understandings. It's fun to read a book you can identify with.'

**Dr Bronwyn Bancroft, award-winning
Bundjalung artist and author**

'Lystra Rose writes with a fresh and compelling voice, seamlessly marrying meticulous word craft and storytelling with a deep connection to her Indigenous culture. This is uniquely Australian storytelling with purpose and a poetic sensibility.'

Tim Baker, bestselling author

'A deeply immersive young adult fantasy and an enthralling debut. It's a privilege to walk this new path into the oldest of stories.'

Amie Kaufman, *New York Times*-bestselling author

'Not a surfer? Me neither, but I felt like I rode the waves with Kirra, feeling the salt spray on my face. Not Indigenous? Me neither, but I felt like I walked, and at times ran, amid the rich Yugambeh culture. There are so many things I am not, but that's why I love to read. *The Upwelling* is a cultural education by stealth.'

**Bern Young, award-winning radio
presenter, ABC Gold Coast**

THE UPWELLING

LYSTRA ROSE

LOTHIAN

State Library of Queensland

 Queensland Government This manuscript won State Library of Queensland's black&write! Fellowship.

LOTHIAN

Published in Australia and New Zealand in 2022
by Hachette Australia
(an imprint of Hachette Australia Pty Limited)
Gadigal Country, Level 17, 207 Kent Street, Sydney, NSW 2000
www.hachette.com.au

Hachette Australia acknowledges and pays our respects to the past, present and future Traditional Owners and Custodians of Country throughout Australia and recognises the continuation of cultural, spiritual and educational practices of Aboriginal and Torres Strait Islander peoples. Our head office is located on the lands of the Gadigal people of the Eora Nation.

 A catalogue record for this book is available from the National Library of Australia

ISBN: 978 0 7344 2025 1 (paperback)

Cover design by Astred Hicks, Design Cherry
Chapter opener images by Ray Bisschop
Cover art, N'gian symbol and dinkus art by author, Lystra Rose
Typeset in Adobe Garamond Pro by Kirby Jones
Printed and bound in Great Britain by Clays Ltd, Elcograf S.p.A.

 **MIX** Paper from responsible sources **FSC® C001695**

The paper this book is printed on is certified against the Forest Stewardship Council® Standards. McPherson's Printing Group holds FSC® chain of custody certification SA-COC-005379. FSC® promotes environmentally responsible, socially beneficial and economically viable management of the world's forests.

To my husband, Ray, who, in our twenty years
of marriage, has always helped me turn impossible
ideas into realities

And to my grandmothers: Nan (Anne with an 'e'
Thompson, nee Rose), who gave me the love of reading,
which led to writing; and Nanny (Marjorie Wallace),
whom I followed as a two-year-old, eating oysters off the
rocks like our ancestors did, where Yugambeh-speaking
people once traded, danced and feasted

CHAPTER 1
KIRRA

Can't trust friends.

Can't trust counselling sessions.

Most importantly, can't trust who this secret is forcing me to become. I trudge along the path to my high school admin block – thanks, Nan, for ruining my life with therapy.

'Kooky Kirra,' a classmate sniggers from behind. I stick to my usual plan: keep my head down and motor away. 'Kook Kirra has no –'

'She can't be a *kook*,' a male voice interrupts. 'You seen her surf? She rips.'

I'm tempted to check who's sticking up for me but then he adds, '*Cracked Kirra* works better – 'specially if she needs weekly therapy. My brother doesn't go that much and he's suicidal.'

'Shut up, Shawn,' the first voice says. 'Suicide's not funny. And you can't surf for –'

'Cursed Kirraahhh,' booms down the path, and my foot Falcon hits the accelerator. Don't want to cop another insult from the school's loudmouth. Wish Mel hadn't chucked a sickie; she would've given them a mouthful, spiced with a few F-bombs. My heartbeat increases with my pace, but Loudmouth's words bail me up.

'Whatever she touches is cursed. Her mum: dead. Brother: dead. And her father works in the mines to get away from her. Watch out, Granny, you're the last one left.'

Loudmouth used to be my friend. Used to live across the street. Used to be puppy-eyed shy. I swing open the office door and launch inside, hoping to avoid her Rottweiler aggression. A waft of air-con collides with the clinging heat and cools the beads of sweat on my skin.

Squinting to stop the fake breeze from plastering my contacts to my eyeballs, I kinda freeze. The door shuts. I'm too late. Their insults flood in.

'Cursed Kirra will get you killed!'

'Careful,' the *kook*-caller says, 'she might put a blackfella curse on you.'

Loudmouth roars with laughter, 'Nah, her granny was fostered by whites. I'd know more about her culture than she does.'

And I gulp back two hundred years of genocide and White Australia policy and Stolen Generations and every town's segregation line marked by 'Boundary Street' and government law banning us from speaking language and practising culture, and a slippery, hollow truth that she's probably right about Nan.

'Truth!' they snarl as if they're mind readers, and a *slap-slap-slap* repeats as Loudmouth, no doubt, hi-fives her siccable bitch-pack. Their carry-on rings through the admin courtyard, then seeps under the office door. When their taunting ends, it somehow still haunts me.

The school administrator, with a phone pressed to her ear, swishes her hand for me to take a seat. I slouch into one in the corner away from the goldfish-bowl windows.

If my plan works, today's session will be different: life-changing different. And if the truth can't convince them, I'll surrender to their lies.

The receptionist covers the end of her phone. 'Kirra?' A smile pops on her face like an emoji on a screen. 'You can go in now.'

'Thanks,' I lie. I'm as thankful as a vegan winning a meat tray, but I keep my head down and scurry to the counselling room.

Mrs Furroway cradles a coffee cup. There's nothing wrong with her (no warts or broomstick). She's a clichéd career spinster: bottle-blonde hair shaped into a not-one-strand-out-of-place bob, French-manicured nails, and smothers awkward silences with porcelain-veneered smiles.

'Hello, Kirra. Please come in, close the door and have a seat.'

I slump onto a plastic chair opposite her ridiculously large desk. The air-con rattles, so does the wasp nest inside me. The stinging and swarming has begun.

'Kirra, your hair looks lovely. Did you colour it?' She places her mug down, thuds my file onto her desk (real old-school), and sports a synchronised-swimmer's smile – perfectly held throughout her whole routine.

'No, it's always been brown.'

Nothing changes in my life: brown hair, brown eyes, brown skin. I stare at my hands, which can't stop fidgeting. Well, lighter brown than Nan and Dad 'cos of Mum's European genes, but I'm the brownest in this room.

Mrs F slurps coffee, and I can't help smirking at the tacky lipstick smeared across her front teeth. I want to tell her but she's slurping more coffee, adding red marks to the rim of her *World's Best Counsellor* mug. Seriously?

Furroway opens my file, orders her wad of notes, then checks out my hair again.

'I never wear it out,' I blurt, as my fingers comb my knotted waves.

'Ahh – that's what it is. It suits you.'

I smooth the strands into a ponytail, secure a hairband 'round it and wait for Mrs F's next predictable question: surf-related.

'Did you see that surfer on the news with that horrible fin chop?'

There it is, I think, before I mutter three octaves below an old person's hearing range, 'He was a bodyboarder.' Wanting her to feel as uncomfortable with small talk as I do, I add, 'I'm surprised you know what a fin chop is – you seen one up close?'

'Yes, yes, ghastly thing.'

She squirms through her reply at Melbourne-Cup-race-caller speed: 'My brother had a terrible fin chop when he was about your age. I drove him to hospital. He had thirteen stitches across his forehead to the top of his head in the shape of a "C". I'd tease him that the ocean had tattooed the first letter of his name on his head.' She giggles – a kid's laugh, not a woman who's ready for retirement – then, between cackles, says, 'He couldn't grow hair there again.'

Never heard Furroway laugh. What is in that coffee? Never thought of her having a brother either, 'specially one that surfed. Figured Furroway was more of a loner surrounded by cats she'd rescued from hessian bags. Might've misjudged her.

'Your brother still surf?'

'Wouldn't know,' she replies, and switches into therapy mode with her well-enunciated words. 'Let's just say, *people* are not his forte.'

Another gulp of coffee and her pen's in hand. It's time for business: 'How can I help today?'

I shift in my seat and hope Furroway, with her gaudy red lippy, can somehow help me. If I could talk to anyone else, I would. Tried talking to Nan six months ago, and this is where 'truth' got me. I have no-one else. Even Mel would bail, like everyone did when Great Nanna Clara was alive. If the world wasn't gonna end, I wouldn't be here. And I can't go head-to-head with Nan about this again. Where would I live if she threw me out? Maybe I *am* cursed.

Furroway places her pen on her pile of notes. 'Something on your mind, Kirra?'

'No ... well, actually yes. But you can't tell anyone, 'specially not Nan, 'cos I promised I wouldn't talk about it.' Fear's long icy fingers pincer-grip my vocal cords.

'Kirra, anything you tell me is confidential.' Another smile appears, muscle memory without emotion. 'You have my word, it will not leave this room.' Furroway waits, her face parked in 'neutral', except gravity – more like negativity – tugs on it.

Each awkward second expands the inevitable. And my secret is bursting every sensible seam in me. 'Um ... don't know how to say this, so –'

My words accelerate, so does the *bzz-i-zzing* in my belly.

'Remember you suggested I keep a dream journal because you thought it would help deal with ...'

I can't say it.

My eyes yo-yo between a stain in the carpet and her eager face. Minutes pass before Mrs F says, 'Your brother.'

I slouch into the belly of the chair. 'Thought I handled it pretty good for a six-year-old.'

'Of course, Kirra. It's not unusual for repressed emotion to manifest years later in other ways, like dreams. Tell me, has the journalling helped?'

I nod. Since I turned sixteen and these strange dreams began, Nan made me promise not to tell anyone the real reason for these weekly visits. And if my own grandmother won't believe me, who will?

'It's helped me confirm my dreams come true. A few weeks ago, I told you about a dream with my friend, Mel – that red sports car and how I saved her. Well, it happened.'

'Yes. But Kirra – remember we also talked about coincidences. And how our brains make sense of trauma. Take your dreams about your brother, Byron, for example.'

I wince at the mention of Wuz – no-one called him Byron – and veer back to the point. 'I know you call them coincidences. What if they're not?'

'Okay, we'll play the "what-ifs". What if your dreams come true? Does it really matter? Does it change life as a sixteen-year-old?'

'My latest one does,' I fire back in a bulletproof tone.

'Really? Please go on.'

'It's at Jellurgal Point.'

Mrs F scribbles ferociously, then power-clasps her long fingers. 'Yes. What happens?' Maybe this old croc isn't so bad.

I force myself to relax by drawing a deep breath, the kind you take before you ditch your surfboard and dive under a massive, surging wave. 'The world is destroyed. Everyone – everything – dies from a huge explosion.'

She probably thinks I don't notice the extra blinks or the way her smile is held in place, like bookends at the end of her lips, but I do.

'What exactly are you saying, Kirra?'

My throat is dry; the air feels stuffier than ever. 'I think the world is going to end.'

The room is still. Uncomfortably still. Unnaturally still. And I've got fifty-one minutes to prove I'm not lying.

Furroway's thin lips spasm. 'You said, "I *think* the world is going to end." What did you mean?'

Her ploy is obvious, a blind pimple could see it. She's trying to trap me into talking more so she can twist my words, and prove I'm wrong. It'll never work. Not when she's emphasised 'think' that way. Like the wi-fi's on but there's no internet.

My diary proves my dreams come true. If I can make this know-it-all *migalu* believe me, there's a small chance I could convince Nan as well.

I grab my dream diary from my bag and clutch it with both hands. 'It's all in here: three dreams, their dates and deliveries. It's easier than explaining.'

After flicking to the page that proves my point, I pass my diary over. I'm exposed and alone, a joey thrown from its mother's pouch.

The air-con rattles. Her office chair squeaks. Nothing can distract me from Furroway. She reads on in poker-faced silence. I know exactly what she's reading. Wrote it three days ago, when that dream woke me in a sweat-fest.

THREE DREAMS — DATES & DELIVERIES

1. <u>Dream Date:</u> 15 Nov. Dreamt Dad rings me to take me for a belated birthday brekkie. Pancakes. He works in the mines, never makes birthdays or Chrissy. Dad hasn't taken me out for a meal, or eaten pancakes (that I know of), since Wuz's funeral. He used to cook them for Wuz and me every Saturday.

   <u>Dream Delivery:</u> 16 Nov. Woke from last night's dream, rolled over to write it down, and there's a text from Dad: he's picking me up for brekkie at Pancakes in Palmy. We went. I drenched a fat stack of pancakes, fresh strawberries and coconut yogurt with maple syrup, but all I kept thinking was, *Funny how silent meals are our new norm.*

2. <u>Dream Date:</u> 11 March. Dreamt Mrs Drew screamed in pain. Then she stopped and the pain disappeared after she was stabbed in her left side.

   <u>Dream Delivery:</u> 11 March (found out later when we had an art sub teacher because Mrs Drew was in hospital). Mrs Drew had her appendix removed that same night I had the dream. THE SAME NIGHT!

3. <u>Dream Date:</u> 13 April. Dreamt a flash red car drove up on the curb and hit Mel while she was waiting (with her surfboard under her arm) for the little green dude to light up so she could cross the Gold Coast Highway and go for a surf. Woke up, wrote it down.

   <u>Dream Delivery:</u> 15 April. Met Mel for a surf two days later, and saw it playing out in real time like I'd dreamt. Except I pulled her away from the

curb, and the reckless driver in the red convertible just missed us.

Finally, *finally* Furroway peers over her narrow frames. My mind's racing with a million ways we can dissect this: the dreams are getting more serious, even dangerous. The delivery date is soon after I dream them. We'll need to move quick if we want to save millions of lives, 'cos three days ago, I had the 'Jellurgal Point world-ending' dream, which means it could happen soon.

'Kirra.' Mrs F slides her glasses up the ridge of her nose, and it's not a short trip. 'First, I want to thank you for allowing me to read your very, very private diary. It's extremely brave of you. But –'

Every muscle tightens.

'– these diary entries don't prove anything. As we previously discussed, they're coincidences. Dreams are our mind's way of dealing with emotion. Fear of death. Death is a common underlying symbol in many dreams, especially in your Aboriginal Dreaming stories.'

I tremor, cracks breaking my volcanic crust – *my* Aboriginal Dreaming stories – like there's one Aboriginal tribe or culture, not hundreds. And she calls herself educated.

'The brain is such an interesting piece of machinery, processing everyday life through dreams. Remember, this started with dreams of your brother.'

Mrs F blabbers on and on about an upcoming surf comp, a fundraising event at Jellurgal Point I should enter as a way of moving past my brother's 'accident' – code for DEATH.

The hell? That's where and probably *when* the world will end.

Furroway's smug, stuck-up voice makes me wanna dive across her desk, snap her scribbling pen, and RIP that file into shreds. Then I'd take that mug, it's about the size of her –

'That symbol you've scribbled on your diary. Is it from one of your dreams? Or is –'

I lunge across the desk and snatch my diary out of her hands.

'– Kirra, I was hoping to borrow that for a bit.'

'No!' My eyes duel with hers. 'You can't. I need it.'

'Oh?' Her lips pull tight like a cat's butt, then her face relaxes. 'Can you tell me about that symbol?'

This whole counselling routine is at a stand-still.

I shove the diary into my bag, and zip it tight. 'I'm sorry, Mrs F, I mean Mrs Furroway, gotta see a teacher.'

She jumps to her feet. 'Right now? Kirra, you've only been here sixteen minutes.' She feigns disappointment.

I feign innocence. Ignoring her, I move towards the door. 'Sorry, I have to go.' I rush out of the room, but the red-lipped jabberer's voice chases me into the corridor.

'That's very disappointing, Kirra.'

Really? I don't give a flying kickflip.

'This conversation isn't over. We'll discuss this and those drawings at our next session.' Her voice singes the back of my neck, and I scurry off.

As soon as the final bell sounds, I speed away on my beach cruiser. Wish I could leave the Gold Coast – been here my whole life, and I'm tired of GC people and places. The wind's blowing in my face, sunnies in place. I pump my legs hard. It's easier today without my surfboard: the rack on the side of my bike is empty.

The world will end. And no-one will believe me. I throw my bike against the house; it clatters as it hits the wall. Who cares? It's all gonna burn anyway. I push through the back door and charge towards my bedroom.

'Kirra?'

Pretending I didn't hear Nan, I march into my room and slam my door.

There are footsteps down the hall, then a knock. 'Kirra, you okay?'

'I'm fine,' I say, and hope she'll leave me alone.

Nan pushes the door open, and I can tell by her stern brown eyes that we are in for a long chat whether I want to or not.

'Why ya stompin' and slammin' doors?'

'You wouldn't understand.' I open my bag, the diary tumbles to the floor.

'Try me,' Nan says, and taps an annoying beat with her shoe, which forces her grey curls to spring up and down.

'You made me promise never to talk about it.'

'Oh, yer still wild 'bout those dreams and counsellor stuff?'

I say nothing. I'm tempted to stand and make her look up at me, but I know better.

'Kirra, ya don't think that counsellor is helpin' you?'

'No.'

'Why not? Don't mind ya sayin' "no" if you 'splain yerself.'

'What's the point of counselling?' Session after session. Mind-numbing questions, robot responses. No real answers. No real progress. No real anything.

Nan shuffles closer. 'I thought it was goin' well.' Her voice softens. 'Ya told me it was helpin'. What changed?'

'I can prove my dreams come true, but Furroway thinks it's a coincidence.'

'Kirra!' She sucks in a breath, then smooths the creases on her dress with her palms, the calm before the storm. 'Firstly, it's *Mrs* Furroway. Secondly, you think yer dreams coming true is a good thing?' Her voice picks up speed and intensity. 'Believin' dreams come true is far, far, far from the worst.'

I grab the diary and thump it on my bed. 'This diary proves they do. The world's gonna end, Nan. I dreamt it. At Jellurgal Point – that place is cursed.'

'Kirra. No. I can't.' I've hit every nerve in her body, and centuries of therapy won't fix this. 'I won't let you destroy your life like my mother did. You think you're the first one to believe your dreams come true?'

My mouth is unable to move, let alone answer.

'You're not. Mum reckoned she received the "gift" when she turned sixteen. She ranted and raved 'bout the world ending. I ended up in foster care so she could get help. Well, Mum died twenty-four years ago, and the world never ended.'

So that's why Great Nanna Clara was sent to that psychiatric hospital.

'You wanna be like that?' Nan's hands move as fast as her lips. 'You wanna live like that? I tried the nice way. Sent you to a counsellor. But now, this is worse than I thought.' She holds out her hand. 'Kirra. Give me your diary.'

I pass it to Nan.

'No more dream diaries. No more talk of the world ending.' Her volume dials down to an almost whisper.

'Mrs Furroway phoned 'bout you running out in her session. You owe her an apology. She – we – believe you should surf in the comp at Jellurgal Point.'

Flippin' Furroway. Wish she kept far away – far, far away. I take a few yoga breaths to shift the vibe. Nan points at a drawing on my new, white, six-foot surfboard leaning against my wall, which happens to be my first single fin ... and swallowtail. 'What's that, Bub? It looks beautiful with the sun and the wave wrapped in that circle.'

'It's a symbol from my dream.'

Her expression hardens.

'I drew it the other day after my dream.' More like a nightmare. 'Nan,' I grab my board to convince her I'm telling the truth, 'this symbol is linked to Jellurgal Point.'

'Kirra.' Nan's eyes – if looks *could* really kill, there'd be a massacre.

'The comp's at Jellurgal Point. I don't think I should surf there. My dreams –'

'Stop ... this is for yer own good.' Her frown's fading. 'You'll surf Jellurgal Point with that symbol on yer board.' She heaves in a breath so loud, I'm not sure there's any air left in the room. 'Then when nothin' happens, we can end this whole dream-come-true and world-gonna-end business forever.'

She's waiting for my response. Wanting me to face Jellurgal Point, when she's been a home-bod since Wuz died.

'Okay, Nan. I'll surf if you come watch. It'll be good to see you at the beach again.'

What I wanna say is: If I have to face my nightmare, you should face your fear and leave the house – get out in our community. Catch up with your cousins and Elders, who've been asking you to join their beach walks, or take me to Yugambeh Choir and yarn with the aunties there.

'Deal,' she says, and patters down the hall.

I put my surfboard back, careful not to bang my shiny new baby, then collapse onto my pillow and grab my phone to check the date of the comp. *Gunang!* It's next Saturday, a full moon. And if a full moon makes everyone wild, I'll have no chance of 'calm'.

What if Mrs F is right about our brains processing life through dreams?

The dream could explain how our family's world ended at Jellurgal Point when Wuz died, while everyone else's continued. Maybe that symbol, a barrelling wave and a sun made from a 'meeting place' sign, is Wuz's last barrel, and it's trapping me in the past. I need to let him go.

Guess I'm surfing Jellurgal Point.

CHAPTER 2
NARN

Tarni is frustrating. Life used to be simple. We'd hang.
Talk. Laugh.

Now, it's different.

It doesn't matter what I say or do, it's wrong. And always
my fault. As a *jarjum*, I'd notice the things she disliked,
then make sure I didn't do any of them.

Now we're fully grown, but lately, another day is
another argument pushing us further apart.

A butcherbird's on the roof of our *ngumbin*. It calls,
pauses, and calls again. My father, Birrabunji, doesn't stir,
and every now and again, a mangled whistle escapes from
him. Songbirds, near and far, tell me to get moving because
the sun's outstretched arms have burst through our charcoal
ocean. I slip past Dad, grab my gear and wander to the water's
edge. I'm at my favourite bay below the headland where our
dolphin friends visit. The light seeps into our sea-bound land,
and I skim the surface for signs of their movement.

The pod swims past. No acrobatic show this morning;
it's all business as they chase fish further up the coast.
I check the dorsal fins hitting the dark blue surface for the

pointiest one. Is she here with her baby? I puff out a long breath, not realising I was holding it. Spinner and her calf are alive and well.

Yesterday, I dived my deepest by carrying heavy rocks and saw an underwater sea cave. Today's conditions make it easier to explore. The swell has dropped. North winds have stopped overnight, and the bay is a lake.

I swim to where the headland dips beneath the sea. Filling my chest with air, I dive down, reminding myself that calmness will make the air last longer. I swim towards the sea floor, grabbing the large thick columns of rock that form the base of the headland. When these columns were melded together in the beginning of time, little pockets and uneven shelves were formed. I grab a large rock I'd stashed on one of these ledges yesterday and squeeze it to my chest. Relaxing my mind and body, pretending I will never need air again, I descend deeper and deeper. Dropping the boulder as I reach the cave's mouth, I push with both arms and legs, frog-swimming through its jagged entrance.

I should turn back.

I'm running out of air, but there's a shaft of light in the darkness. I ignore my doubts and use the last of my breath to push through.

No air. NO AIR.

I swim up, up, up.

Following the light, I break the surface and flop onto a rock ledge, gasping, heaving in each lungful of air … until my breathing evens out. I'm in a small cave above the tideline with a narrow beam of light seeping into it. It's low tide so there's enough time to recover 'til I make the dive back, and before my dad worries that this latest obsession will distract me from my never-ending responsibilities.

As the ray of light brightens, faint markings appear on the cave walls. My fingers trace over them.

'What is it?' My question bounces off the cave walls.

I crouch to the height of the etchings.

Something else is scrawled into the rock. It's vaguely familiar. Dad'll know.

A new-found energy surges through my muscles, as I dive deep down and out of the darkness. I swim to the surface, then to the shore, with so many exploding thoughts.

Dripping with excitement, I run home to tell Birrabunji about my discovery.

'Dad.'

There's a gleam in his eyes. 'Narn. Didn't expect you back so soon or happy this time of morning. What happened to helping Aunty at first light? You said you'd do it yesterday, the day before yesterday, and the day before that.'

I've no time for his playful teasing or feeling guilty about another broken promise. 'I found a sea cave. There's a strange –'

'Not here, son.' Birrabunji grabs my arm. 'Let's go to the headland, where unwanted ears aren't listening.'

Is that fear in his eyes? I've never seen it there before.

We head over the dunes. I grab some *nyulli* – a creeper-like plant with bright pink flowers – squeeze the sweet-salty fruit out of its succulent maroon pod and munch on it. Following close behind Birrabunji, I worry about his reaction.

We walk in silence past a large flock of silver gulls. They're sitting on the dark-coloured rocks halfway up the headland. We clamber to the top, a special place for us, and stare at the shimmering sea.

I can't wait any longer. 'There's a sea cave below the headland.'

His eyes snap from the ocean to mine. 'That's a sacred place. A secret place. A place not just for anyone.'

I ignore his reprimand. 'In that cave are symbols.'

Birrabunji raises his voice. 'Narn. Stop.' The force of it vibrates through the air and the flock of gulls squawk and fly away.

My thoughts stop. My heart does too. I'm shocked into obedience.

Dad grabs my shoulder. His eyes puncture mine. 'Vow to me, under our lore, what I tell you will never be brought up again. Not now. Not ever. Listen, son. Really listen. This may be the only thing that will save you.'

My heart speeds up like two boomerangs clapping together, faster and faster as the dancing ceremony comes to an end. I'm more afraid than when I faced my first shark.

I grip Dad's shoulder. 'I promise, Dad. Under our lore, you have my vow.'

Dad taught me how to listen. Listen to understand. No discussions. No debates. No disobedience. There is time for questions and time for silence. And I understand what I need to do. A vow cannot be broken. If it is, you get speared in the leg by the men of the clan led by our hunter-Elder, and the last thing I want is to be speared by Minjarra, the fiercest hunter in these parts.

Dad squeezes my shoulder tighter. 'Our vow is a lore between us until death,' he says.

This is serious business. Life and death business. Business that scars me with more unanswered questions.

We face the sea and sit side by side.

'That symbol you saw in the cave is N'gian's.'

'N'gian?' I mumble.

He nods. 'He's known to work magic – proper powerful and respected by all.'

'Must be good to be N'gian … be liked by everybody,' I mutter.

'Being liked means nothing. Respect is balanced with responsibility – comes when love and courage help you choose to do the right thing. And be willing to put in the effort and be trusted.' He points to a nearby bush. 'Like that *midyim* we planted.'

Dad doesn't get it: he's never been mocked or called empty-headed, and if people don't agree with his decision, at least they respect it. When Dad's hair was black, we planted that *midyim* seed. He promised my future would bring growth and change. Now, that seed has grown into a mature bush.

But me. I'm still the same Narn.

Dad stares at the *midyim*, covered in small white berries speckled with tiny blue spots, and shakes his head. '*Tsk-tsk-tsk.*'

'What's wrong?'

'It shouldn't be fruiting this time of year. Another sign the balance is off. This could mean a shift in the spiritual realm. Got to gather the Elders and let them know.'

Birrabunji stands, ready to leave. 'Be careful, son. I trust you'll know what to do with these words: there may be a traitor in our tribe.'

'What? Who? How?' I swallow, then shoot another question: 'Is he from our clan or a neighbouring one?'

Dad glances at me, his eyes drop to my chest. 'You wear the marks of a man, yet question like a boy: they pour out of your mouth as they pop into your mind.'

I gather my thoughts and pick the most important one. 'Which clan is the traitor from?'

'Not sure, but time will tell if I'm right or wrong. One person can make a difference in the balance of things: if they're for or against us, it won't be decided until a choice is made.'

I wait, probably not long enough for Dad, and he's right, I am impatient, the same way I was as a boy. 'If a traitor hasn't made his choice, how can he be one?'

'Didn't say it was a "he" or a "she".' Dad stares at the horizon. I copy him. When he's ready, he'll share his thoughts.

'Women are missing from our clans. N'gian united our clans under one tribe with one shared language, long ago. Looks like someone's trying to ruin that.'

'Who would steal our women?' My hands form fists, itching to punch something, someone. I should be worried about our grannies, aunties, cousins, but only one long-legged woman fills my head. 'Who are they taking, ones of joining age?'

He strokes his white beard. 'Women with special gifts.'

I'm breathing faster. 'Gifts?'

'N'gian ones.'

'But they're ancient fireside stories. Who has N'gian gifts in our clan?'

'I'd hoped you did. And they're not stories. N'gian healed you as a *jarjum*. That means his life poured into you. You done anything powerful?'

'All the time.' I flex my biceps. 'Just don't think N'gian had anything to do with it.'

Dad sighs, its force could blow those berries off the *midyim* bush. 'You'd know if you had it. Never mind, when there's an imbalance, strange things reveal themselves. I fear the lore may be broken. Our connection to everything feels wrong.'

The agitation in Dad's eyes is enough to stop me mucking around. He often talks in riddles, and asking more questions won't help.

'Son, this is part of our vow. Do not repeat this, but I've only seen N'gian's symbol twice in my lifetime. Two people in our tribe have drawn it.' His voice drops to the bottom of the ocean, mournful like a whale's call. 'It's not my knowledge to tell.'

With a quick shake of my head, I hope the confusion will fall out. It doesn't.

'You can never join with someone who has a N'gian gift,' Dad says, as if he knows something miserable, and I'm not sure I want him to explain. 'Too much power is dangerous for everyone. The Elders have discussed these matters. If you want to be joined to someone, and you find out they've been given N'gian power, you must tell them you can no longer be joined. You understand?'

'Yes,' I say, struggling to free myself from his tangle of words. Because as soon as Dad mentioned 'joining' I think of Tarni.

Could she be in danger?

Not that she'd listen to reason. Or forgive me. But Tarni's of joining age and is the cleverest woman I know. Our clan, her mother's clan, all the clans that make up our whole tribe, respect her.

Do I need to warn her? Are N'gian gifts a way to say you're clever? But N'gian's magic healed me, and there's no way I'm clever.

I can't remember what I told Dad, but I'm sprinting down the track searching for the tallest woman in our clan.

Racing to the *wudjuru* swimming hole and ignoring the nagging thought that I'll be clipped around my ears by my grannies if they find me here, I arrive out of breath. I'm unsure what to say to the most beautiful woman in the world. My pulse is racing, not just from sprinting over here.

Tarni's motionless. Streaks of old tears stain her cheeks. She doesn't turn when I sit next to her. Shoulder to shoulder. Skin to skin. The way we did when we were *jarjum*.

I glance at her again. She death-stares straight ahead.

'Are you sick?' It's the only thing I can come up with to start some sort of conversation.

Tarni doesn't move.

I let the edge of my hand brush hers and a warmth expands from that tiny touch to every part of my body. Wish I could scoop her up and carry her away from all of this – whatever *this* is.

A 'don't touch me' growls out of her, and her eyes don't shift.

'Tarni. I should've listened to you and never gone to Shark Bay to challenge your father. I've said it so many times: I'm sorry.'

Her expression is granite, a hardness formed from our many feuds.

Sorry doesn't fix it. It used to.

If sorry were a star every time I apologised to Tarni, there'd be a whole galaxy out there, shining with my sorrys. Sorrys aren't good enough.

And neither am I.

'He cheated. Hid the crayfish in the shallows,' she says, and the edge in her voice shreds my courage. 'You

22

would've spent the night in Shark Bay and been eaten if it wasn't for me.'

'I know. Thank you.'

She still won't look at me. It feeds my dread.

'I'm sorry I said you ran and looked like an emu the other day. That emu-feathered decoration covered half of your body. Can't you just forgive me so we go back to how things used to be?'

'Things will never be the same.' The warmth we shared has been snuffed out, a winter's night without a fire.

Has someone thrown a mind-spear at Tarni? No-one survives that. I kneel in the thick, muddy sludge to force her to look at me. 'Tarni, let me help you. What can I do?'

Her gaze creeps over me. 'It's too late.'

'What do you mean? I don't understand. Are you dying?' A shiver leaves icicles along my spine, while I wait for her reply.

'If only I was,' she whispers. 'Death would be better than what I'm facing.'

Tears tumble over her high cheekbones and slip down her smooth brown skin. And I wish I could kiss them away. A curl swings in front of her eyes, and I tuck it behind her ear. I stroke the tears away with my thumb, as if I've done it a hundred times, except it's the first. And it feels so normal.

She pushes my hand away. 'Please, Narn, don't.' Her trance is broken with eyes that could torch me alive. 'Don't be nice to me. It'll only make it harder.'

I'm spinning. Days ago, she was upset because I was mean and uncaring. Now, she doesn't want me to be nice. Her words muddle my mind. 'What will be harder? What's going on, Tarni?'

I wrap her tiny hand inside mine, and she lets me. 'I'll sit here until you talk. If you don't, I'll sit with you forever.'

Her brown eyes widen. 'What will people say?'

'Who cares?' My voice is soft. I stare at her long wet lashes: dew stuck on the tips of dark river reeds. I love her more than I let myself believe. Tarni is the one for me. I've been waiting for the right moment. Is this it?

I place my hands on her wet cheeks, cup her face towards me, and let four important words flow out. 'I love you, Tarni.'

She gazes into my eyes, and I wish she'd give me some hint of how I make her feel. Those icicles sharpen. What's wrong with me? I've fought with myself for ages about telling her. And now it's out. My heart is naked, and I've risked everything.

Tarni seems surprised but not shocked.

This triggers a boldness. 'I've loved you for as long as I can remember. I didn't want to spoil our friendship. And I never thought I'd have a chance with you.'

The sun emerges from behind the clouds. Beaming on Tarni, lighting her up. Her hair and skin glows. She smiles. And I realise, it's not the sun that makes me grin and the world glow … it's Tarni.

'Do you like me? Do I have a chance?' I'm that clumsy, lanky kid before he grew into his feet, tripping over words. The questions hang in the air. My head's feeling light, and I'm glad I'm sitting down, waiting for this clever woman to give me some kind of sign.

She glances sideways, a tiny smile surfaces then disappears.

'I love you, Tarni,' I say to the rhythm of my racing pulse.

When I'm rewarded with a genuine grin, I stand and yell, 'I love Tarni!'

I shout it to the *wudjuru*, to the squawking birds, the sky, to anyone and anything. She springs up, covers my mouth and pulls me next to her. When she folds her hands into her lap, I stare at her lips. And she's staring at me staring at them. Maybe Tarni's not as confident as everyone thinks and wants me to make the first move.

I lean in to have our first kiss, the one I've thought about for ever. My eyes gently close, ready to feel soft warmth, but something pushes me back. Flinging them open, Tarni's hand covers half my face.

'Narn, what will we do?'

I chuckle at her innocence. 'We'll have a joining ceremony, then make a little clan of our own.'

She elbows me. She's done it a million times before, except this time it's different.

'You don't know, do you?'

I'm confused. I thought falling in love, not that she's admitted it yet, and adding a few *jarjum* seems obvious. I mean, what else is there?

'Narn. Father has gone –'

I cut her off. 'I know. We'll ask for his blessing when he gets back, and I'll sit with the Elders. Don't worry, it'll all work out.'

She squeezes my hand. 'He left to arrange my joining to another. And said I'd live in that tribe for the rest of my life.'

'*This* is why you were crying,' I mutter. My legs wobble and my gut swirls with sickness.

'What am I going to do?' Tarni's eyes pool with fresh tears.

'Nothing we can do till your father gets back.' My croaky voice betrays me, and I force a brave smile.

I wrap my arms around her slender frame.

She pulls away. 'You can't, I'm betrothed. You know our lore.'

I grab her left hand, rubbing the joint below her littlest fingernail. 'Where's the string –' I circle around her finger and add – 'that forms no end or beginning to show a joining for life?'

She blinks. 'Never happened.'

Hope lifts me up, along with an encouraging smile. 'Well, by our lore, that string shows you're betrothed.'

Her curly long hair bounces and sways in the breeze. I want to twist strands of it around my fingers. All the women in our tribe have short hair, except Tarni. She grew it after her secret meeting with her mother a couple of whale migrations ago.

'When Minjarra comes back, I'll make it known how I feel about you … if you want.'

Tarni is silent.

'But if your father doesn't give us his blessing and demands you be joined with another, we'll run away. I'm happy to live anywhere as long as I'm with you.'

Tarni's free-flowing hair doesn't match her feelings. 'I can't run away with you, Narn. You know our lore. If the Elders banish any couple, there'll be no future for them or their *jarjum*.'

I smirk. Has she thought of us together with *jarjum* and all that it means?

'Narn. The lore is for a reason.' The old Tarni is back. Confident and not wanting or needing guidance.

'Uh-huh.' It's all I can say. I breathe in her hair. She smells so great: a mixture of a salty, sweet scent. I want to kiss down the side of her long, smooth neck – remembering why I teased her the other day, calling her an emu.

'Narn?' I hear the tone of her voice. Her smile seems sweet and generous, but now it shields her. When Tarni needs to talk, talk is what will happen.

'If you want to be more than friends I need to know I can trust you. You need to know all of me, and I need to know all of you.'

What does that mean? If I keep silent, she might think I understand.

'You've kept the secret of my mother and our yearly meetings when everyone else believes she's dead. We can't have secrets. I couldn't be joined with someone I didn't trust.' She shivers. 'My father is like that ... It scares me.'

'Me too. Not your father scaring me but having secrets.' If I'm honest, her father does scare me, but I'm not telling Tarni that.

The tension releases in her voice when she asks, 'I have a secret to share. But first, do you have anything to tell me?'

I laugh a little too quickly. 'No secrets. You know everything about me.' And when she doesn't believe it, I add, 'There's a traitor in our tribe ... women with N'gian gifts are being stolen away.'

Something flickers across her face.

'What's wrong?'

'*My* secret. Promise you won't tell anyone.' She speaks softer than the flutter of feathers. Not a gliding-peacefully-on-the-wind type. More like the I'll-fly-away-if-you-don't-take-me-serious kind.

'I promise,' I say, coating each word with extra reassurance.

'Mum, me, most people from Mum's rainforest clan have a N'gian gift. We're language unweavers.'

'Tarni, that's no secret. You're the cleverest at language – our best interpreter at the last *buhnyi buhnyi* gathering … dancing, trading, storytelling with all those different language groups. Doesn't mean you have N'gian's –'

'Narn, listen. Unweaving languages is a gift N'gian gave our ancestors when he walked among us. We call ourselves "language experts" to keep that knowledge safe.'

No, not Tarni. Dad must've known. My palms feel itchy. Worry spreads from a thought-spore into prickly moss, irritating the skin all over my body. He can't have meant *my* Tarni.

'I haven't heard from Mum in a long time. I'm worried something terrible has happened to her …'

The louder my panic grows, the quicker her voice distorts and blends into the background, along with the creek and birdlife. No wonder Tarni gets on with everyone. N'gian's magical gift has made it easy for her.

'Narn?' I stare at her soft, full lips. 'You talked to your dad about joining with me, right?'

'Yes,' I almost yell, then adjust my tone to calm and confident. 'Dad'll help me convince the Elders.' The churning in my gut increases.

What choice do I have? I just have to persuade Dad later.

If I haven't received N'gian so-called powers by now, I'll never get them. They don't call me 'Dolphin Boy' for nothing. That's the extent of my skills.

Our chat ends with Tarni giving me a friendly squeeze, then she saunters along the track that leads deeper into the women's area. As I leave the swimming hole, I try to shut off my swarming thoughts. Except one attacks me: at no stage did Tarni say she loves me.

Hope she doesn't find out I fibbed, because some things she takes too seriously. Life isn't meant to be about rules. Tarni needs to relax, and that's what I'll teach her: how to have fun and bend the rules just enough so they won't break. Who wouldn't love that in a future spouse?

CHAPTER 3
TARNI

Shaggy-barked trees hug the bend in the creek. A huge pool of water snakes around to lead the fresh water out to sea. The brown *wudjuru*-infused pool is deceiving; its clean water is soothing with an earthy-mint scent. On these lethargic days, a few cousins gather here to swim. No longer girls but waiting in a stage of life we call 'in-between'. Familiar with the secrets of women's business but not yet joined. This doesn't stop us nattering about future husbands, most joinings already arranged by Elders, others arranged by fate.

Lounging in the shallows, my head's resting on a smooth boulder. I close my eyes to block the mid-morning sun, take another deep breath and think about what Narn said to me yesterday. He loves me. We've been friends for so long, I can't imagine it any other way.

It's Narn. So he has facial hair – thick and black – but that doesn't change the truth. This is the same Narn I've flogged in races when we were *jarjum*. The same Narn I've climbed trees with, sticking our big toes in the dug-out grooves of the trunk to reach that special spot to collect *gudje*.

My cousins giggle and gossip as they swim towards the bank, and I'm glad for the solitude.

Lia rings out her black hair. 'Tarni? Why haven't you been joined? You're old enough.'

I shrug and let the water steal my gaze so the flinch won't show.

'It's because her dad wanted a son so bad he raised her as one. Think of those poor fellas: why would you join with a woman who hunts better than you?' Jedda says.

'Nah, being so tall makes her a better hunter 'cos of her big feet and hands.' Lia pauses to let the cousins have a real good laugh. Then continues, 'That's why she's the best eugarie digger. She's taller than most of our men. Might make them feel a little "short".'

'And a little "shame".' Arika emphasises her words exactly like her elder sister did, and the whole lot of them snigger again.

I can't answer. Can't relax as their toxin paralyses me. Alba appears at the edge of the creek and pushes past the cousins.

'What's happening?' she says, her grin widening. Alba's never afraid of arguments. No-one answers her. She fires more questions: 'You talking about joinings again? No surprise. Who you setting up now?'

Alba eyeballs the elder sister, Lia.

'Tarni. She's had three to choose from since birth,' Lia says, 'and no string on her finger.' Her once-fiery voice now a pile of ash.

'Well,' says Alba with a hand on her hip, 'at least Tarni's got a choice. I heard you only have one – a hairy fat fella with no teeth. You gonna have real fun chewing his food for him.'

Lia's bottom lip quivers a little, and Arika rubs her sister's back. The other girls muffle a giggle. Lia glares at them.

'Now leave Tarni alone, and go make yourself useful. Granny Alkira's looking for you girls to help fix your *ngumbin*. She says the roof needs more bark from the *wudjuru*.'

The girls don't question Alba but rip me to shreds with their stares.

'No,' Alba booms in their direction, 'Tarni worked all morning with Granny Alkira, so she can stay and swim.'

They scamper along the track away from our hidden pool, muttering between themselves: 'Of course, she helped the Elders this morning.'

'Tarni loves to please the old people.'

'Ha – *please*? She's been greedy for their attention since her mum died.'

The cascading creek drowns out the rest of their criticisms.

Alba dives in and water splashes over me. I love how Alba speaks her mind, doesn't care if anyone likes her or agrees with her. Those girls might be wild with Alba today but they'll be laughing and hugging her tomorrow. A chance I can't take. Being a language expert means keeping the peace with everyone. It's an esteemed position, and I won't let gossiping cousins mess it up. Besides, Alba and I have an unspoken understanding. She keeps those girls in line, so I don't have to deal with a scolding from their mothers.

My blunt-talking cousin surfaces and swims closer; her smile glides across the water's surface.

'*Jingi wahlu*, Tarni.'

'*Jingi wahlu*, Alba,' I reply before arching backwards, dipping my head and letting the water smooth out my long hair. Unlike the previous conversation, this one I've been expecting but don't let on.

'Are you and Narn … you know?' Alba's boldness dwindles to a mumble. It's adorable – a side of her I haven't seen since she was a chubby-cheeked *jarjum*.

'Alba. You know how to talk straight.' It's hypocritical of me. Alba's done my straight talking for years – intercepting those cousins wasn't the first time. I know what Alba's trying to say, but where's the fun in making it easy? I've seen the way my younger cousin tries to be anywhere Narn is.

Alba's acted like Narn is the moon and she's the tide for so long. Who can blame her? He's fun, has a great smile, and that laugh of his always cracks us up. Narn has grown into a good-looking fella. Those brown eyes, with flecks of golden sun rays, are always full of passion. I mean *life*. Full of life.

My cousin squeezes her hand into a fist, pumps it open and closed, making water squirt into the air. Playing in the creek and averting her eyes, she asks, 'Well, *do* you like Narn?'

I don't answer – been asking myself the same question last night and all morning. Water trickles over the smooth stones, gains momentum and tumbles along larger mossy rocks. We duck under the small waterfalls, receiving nature's massage, before it flows into another deep pool.

Near the water's edge, rainbow lorikeets squawk like children fighting for attention. Dressed in blue, green, and reddy-yellow, they flap and bob on the skinny branches of grevilleas. The parrots lick nectar from the large pink-orange flowers.

'That's a big flock of lorikeets. You know what that means, it'll be a good mullet season soon.' Alba changes her approach. 'Rainbow lorikeets are always found in pairs. I love how they're partners for their whole lives. I want that.' They squawk louder, their feathers flap furiously.

She lowers her voice. 'Saw Narn racing here yesterday.' Then sneaks a look in my direction – waiting, hungry for my response.

Alba and I have a special connection. Like a lot of cousins, we're as close as sisters.

'Yep, he came here. Said he loves me and wants us to be joined. But you know Narn. Not sure if this is real or one of his tricks he does for a laugh.' My answer sounds unemotional and overly prepared, but Alba doesn't seem to notice.

'Thanks for telling me the truth, Tarni. Might go help those girls.'

With a quick goodbye, Alba climbs out of the water. I watch her with Narn in mind, and I'm a little jealous of my cousin's well-shaped body. What man could resist? She's certainly no longer a *jarjum*. Are those girls right? Am I too boyish? I'm tall and straight and don't have curves like them. As Alba leaves, I realise something. Something both disturbing and exciting. Is it even possible?

But … I think I like Narn.

I really think I like Narn.

Could this be love?

It's as if my head and heart haven't talked in years. Half of me can't believe it, and the other half accepted it a long time ago. A summer storm of emotion rolls through me. Its electric energy excites me, but I purposely ignore its other well-known trait … the trail of destruction it leaves behind.

I've left the waterhole with one person on my mind: Narn. Though he's got the body of a man, most times he doesn't act the way he should if he wants to be joined. Narn keeps busy laughing, joking or finding some new obsession to focus on. When we were kids he was hilarious, but even spontaneity can become predictable and tiring.

Love is deeper than wanting someone's attention or catching an easy laugh. It's about trust, respect – and after yesterday's yarn about secrets, he's showing potential. Should I have been more encouraging when he confessed his love? He made my head spin. Haven't ever felt like this. Think I smiled while I slept last night.

So, why's there a niggle instead of a tingle? Probably because Dad left yesterday to arrange my joining to one of my promised ones. Elders and parents choose them after you're born – give you a few options. Wise, as death isn't something we can control.

I duck into Dad's *ngumbin*. It's empty, like I expected, but that niggle is still irritating me. I scan his home for clues and stop at his ochre pots. There's a gap. Two large coolamon: one holds a clump of white sandstone, the other, yellow. But the third is missing. The niggle in my guts now ricochets. The coolamon that holds the colour of death is missing. One tribe wears it daily. A person I vowed I'd never be joined with, no matter if he was chosen by our Elders.

This is worse than I thought. I need to tell Narn. And if it feels right, maybe I should tell him I like him … like, a lot. We need to have a solid plan, so we can convince Dad and the Elders that Narn is the best choice. Wish Granny

Yindi was alive – could use her help with this mess. I walk over to Narn and Birrabunji. Narn is in the water with the littlest dolphin of the pod; it's as long as my arm span. I sit under palm-like leaves of the *jambinbin* to give them time with their totem before I talk to Narn. Alba, Narn and I would hide under these clumps of stilt-rooted trees when we were *jarjum*. Today, with the east wind blowing, clear conversations at the beach are carried to my ears.

Birrabunji stands on the grassy sand dunes below. He's shielding his eyes from the midday sun. Narn dashes to him, water and sand spray off his legs.

'Did you see?' Narn yells, still running towards Birrabunji. 'Spinner introduced her young one to me.'

Birrabunji smiles at Narn, and he sticks out his chest further. He's adorable. *How'd I not see this before?* Narn's wearing a light brown fur *tabbi-tabbi* with strands of kurrajong string wrapped around his waist. Other men would hang boomerangs or extra tools off it. But Narn's not like other men.

'Well, I missed her being born tail-first into the sea. And I missed her mum pushing her to the surface for her first breath. So, I'm glad I didn't miss her first meeting with a person.' Narn grins and my worries disappear for a bit. 'She waited a while, but she chose me.'

'Well, son, she's probably cautious with this youngster after losing her first one.'

Both of them stare further up the beach at the sandy spot where Narn buried Spinner's firstborn. Almost four whale migrations ago, Narn told me how Spinner pushed the tiny carcass across the water towards him. And that it was the kindest thing Narn could do, because Spinner had stayed by its dead body for days – mourning – the way we all do when death shocks us with an unexpected visit. I'm deciding whether to join in, leave or wait for a better time to approach Narn.

Birrabunji passes his son water and asks, 'Did you name her?'

Narn gulps the water and wipes his dripping mouth. 'Yep. Spinner brought her six-week-old to meet me, so she deserves a good name.'

Birrabunji grins.

'Echo,' Narn says.

'Echo,' Birrabunji repeats. 'That is a good name.'

'Spinner calls and that baby copies. When I splash, that little one splashes back. So "Echo" is her name. And she looks like an echo of her mum.'

'Spinner will be busy. That Echo's a lively one,' Birrabunji says, and they watch the wiggly little dolphin.

'True, but as you know, she'll stay real close to her mum, being only on mother's milk – will be for months.' Narn points at the water, 'Look. Echo swims all over the place, but wait, she'll flop over Spinner for a rest.'

Moments later, Echo slumps across her mother's body.

'Speaking of rest, time to get back to it. Your Aunty Lowanna told me to tell you she wants your help near the big fire.' He turns to go, but pauses. 'What's wrong, son?'

'Nothing.' Narn nods towards Echo. 'I just hope she makes it.'

'Me too.' Birrabunji pats Narn on the back, and says, 'Spinner's more experienced now. Don't worry, son.'

'I got to tell Tarni. 'Specially since I confessed my love yesterday.'

I stand to leave, but Birrabunji's words bind my legs. 'Narn, did Tarni tell you anything about N'gian?'

Narn stares at his feet, his guilt indicator hasn't changed since he was a boy.

'Tarni has N'gian's gift.'

'I wondered. She drew N'gian's symbol on the beach as a *jarjum* right where and when you almost died.'

My heart slams into my rib cage over and over as though it's trying to escape.

Then Birrabunji asks, 'Did you do as instructed?'

'Dad, I couldn't tell her you and the Elders don't want us to join. Not when I have no N'gian gifts. But I promise I didn't tell Tarni about the vow we made yesterday.'

Liar! Narn lied about permission for our joining. Lied about having no secrets. A vow with Birrabunji counts. And he lied about keeping his promise – told Birrabunji my N'gian secret one day later.

This isn't love. Love doesn't change with every wind, tide and swell.

'Son, you knew what –'

I'm cracking my knuckles. Leg muscles are shaking. I jump to my feet to gain control.

Narn.

Lied.

To.

Me.

Birrabunji glances behind, stops talking, and gawks at me. Narn does too. My thoughts feel hot and pulse in my temples.

Instinct takes over: my walk turns into a jog, and when Narn yells my name, I bolt to my *ngumbin*. I scramble to pack food, a stone knife, kangaroo water container, and some inner-bark string, and shove them into my woven bag.

Slowing my breathing, I pretend not to be in a hurry or that panic is threatening to spew out of me. I approach Granny Alkira and my other grannies and aunties who are yarning and stripping *jambinbin* leaves into long fibres. With their expertise, they'll be turned into baskets or dillybags in no time.

'I remember when my granny, your sister Yindi, first taught me and I made this,' I say to Granny Alkira, as I tug on the bag hanging from my shoulder. 'Miss her.' And I'm surprised at my calm surface.

'Me too, love. Me too.' Her hands keep a rhythm: rolling and pressing the long wet strands on her right thigh with her calloused right palm. 'Yindi made the work go quickly when she told her stories.'

I sit next to Granny Alkira. 'Alba and I always said Granny Yindi turned everything into an adventure.'

I remember our wet seasons with Granny Yindi: me and Alba and the other girls from our clan would collect *jambinbin* palms. We'd use a long stick to hook the younger leaves. Then sit in the shade and chat as we stripped the leaves into long fibres by digging our fingernails into the end of each leaf and separating it into lots of thin strips.

We'd follow Granny Yindi into the scrub, and she'd show us a special tree. At the time, it looked more scraggily than special.

'See this tree?' she'd say.

We'd nod and wait, knowing an explanation would follow.

'If we dig up its root, we can get yellow dye for our bags.'

We'd all dig with Granny Yindi. We'd take turns to wash the root, strip off the bark and crush it with a heavy rock. Then we'd chuck the *jambinbin* fibre in with the crushed root, and let it boil in a piccabeen basket. Granny would find berries that made purple dye, and we'd boil it with *jambinbin* fibres.

'If you want a dark colour, girls, boil it for longer,' Granny said. 'And if you want a lighter colour, dip it in for a short time.'

So we did.

Then after the shredded *jambinbin* were dyed and dried, women and girls sat under the shady trees laughing and chatting, while our hands rolled the fibres over our smooth thighs into long strands of string. These pieces of string were woven into colourful dillybags.

'Tarni, you alright?'

Granny Alkira wakes me from my memories, and I choose my words carefully so truth coats them. 'I need to follow Minjarra – I mean Dad. He's meeting my promised one to arrange our joining, and I was meant to journey with him. Can I catch up with him? He won't be too far ahead, and I'm fast.'

With Granny Alkira's permission, I'm walking away from the beach towards the *wudjuru* groves. I'll follow the creek into the rainforest, teeming with bird and animal life. This kind of noise calms me.

'Tarni.'

I don't turn. Don't stop. I hold my head high. Narn catches up. He's walking by my side. 'Tarni, please, let me explain. You owe me that.'

I freeze. 'I owe you that?'

'No, I didn't mean it that way. Just let me explain … please.'

'Depends.'

'On what?'

'If your explanations are lies. As far as I can tell, everything so far has been one big fat lie followed by another.'

'Tarni. I'd made a vow with Dad.'

'I heard.'

'So I couldn't tell you. You know our lore.'

'You didn't have to tell me what the vow was, only that you had one. You broke your promise and told Birrabunji about my N'gian gift. But that's not the worst one: you lied about permission for our joining.'

My legs are primed to run. This conversation is going nowhere.

'And is there even a traitor?' I say with such force that it would strip bark off the trees. 'Or did you tell me that to shut me up – maybe thought you could steal a kiss before my father or Elders gave their permission?'

Narn looks guiltier than when my little cousin Birri raced through the women's work and knocked over the smoking fish rack, and the dingoes gobbled up everyone's dinner. I quicken my step, hoping he'll take the hint and turn back. This solo journey will sort these feelings, so I can make sense of which path I need to take: joining with a man I don't trust or a man I don't like.

'I'm sorry.' Narn's rumbling voice snaps me out of my thoughts. 'If you stop pretending you're more perfect than the rest of us, I'll tell you four truths.'

'What? So saying I'm perfect makes you feel better about your lies?'

I'm ready to explain I don't pretend to be perfect – I work hard at it, when he says, 'Truth: there is a traitor in the tribe, but I don't know from which of our clans. Truth: I made a vow with Birrabunji. Truth: I'm sorry I broke my promise and lied; it'll never happen again. Truth: you are the most beautiful woman in all of the clans in our tribe and all the tribes in Wallulljagun ... and I love you.'

I search his eyes for a flicker of guilt. He seems truthful. But he seems to lie as quick as he says 'sorry', so I'm not sure if this is a virtue or a fault. At least with my promised one, he didn't hide who he was. What you saw was what you got – can't believe I'm sticking up for that orange-ochred snake.

The trouble with Narn this close, and his salty-spicy scent, is I can't separate feelings from thoughts.

'Do you love me?' There's desperation in his voice that traps me.

I can't breathe. My lack of choices and words and thoughts press hard. A gust of wind blows along the path. I want to feel its freedom. Without warning, I sprint down the track to the edge of the creek and rock-hop across it, the way I've done since I was a *jarjum*.

Narn is slower; he's racing on the opposite side of the creek, yelling, but I'm ignoring him. Some time alone will help me work out the difference between what's real and the lies he spits out to get what he wants. I run and run until my chest burns, and heave in cool air. Running full pelt, leaping over logs, launching across creeks makes me feel powerful again.

When I'm sure he'll never catch me, I slow to a jog, then a stroll. And I find a clue to Dad's journey. It's an emu egg full of water with a short stick to seal it. And it's buried in the dirt on the edge of the track. He would've put it here for his return trip. We do this for long journeys away from our water supplies. It shows me the direction he took. I keep walking along the shared corridor following a trail of buried emu water containers towards the country of my promised one, Jiemba, and his orange-ochre-painted tribe.

The first and last time I saw him, we were *jarjum*. People can change, right? When Wanjellah was a boy, he was a nose-picker. He's not anymore. Don't think my cousin Nyrah would've been joined with him. Maybe Jiemba was just going through an evil phase when we met.

What's more important: love or trust? You can learn to love a stranger – Granny Yindi did. But I've never heard of anyone trusting a liar.

CHAPTER 4
KIRRA

Today is it. Saturday, May the fourth. I hope, pray, cross my fingers, toes – anything to cancel the comp. Forever. Not just postponed. And, no, it's not my flight-*not*-fight mode. Everyone's been scrolling weather reports.

Despite the northerlies blowing all week, the comp's not cancelled. It swung overnight. With the southerlies blowing, the online cam shows live footage of waves piled high, symmetrically moving, like the swagger of corduroy jeans on a barefoot hipster swigging on a home-brewed bottle of organic kombucha. And no-one can take their eyes off our point break, our famous saltwater celebrity.

Jellurgal Point is already covered in bright-coloured beach towels. Nan is among them, slouching in her sling chair, both hands hugging a cup of coffee I bought from the local espresso van. No-one would guess my grandmother struggles with crowds and leaving her old weatherboard home 'cept for necessities: doctors, grocery shopping or the odd parent-teacher meeting.

After days of torrential rain, I soak up the sun's warmth – eyes closed, face pointing at the liquid horizon, taking deep, salt-infused breaths. The sky is cloudless with stain-glassed tones of blue. It has more of a cathedral feel, not the world-ending kind of weather I was expecting.

Why did I even think my dream could come true?

Up the beach, the school's faded blue marquees fill with competitors, commentators, judges and all kinds of surfboards and gear.

A blonde teen, a little younger than me, nudges her friend. 'That's her, the one I was telling you about,' she says.

They smother their sun-bitten skin in tanning oil and continue their loud conversation. 'Her brother died here in a surf comp.'

I trudge through the squeaky sand towards the marquees to escape the gossips, grab my single-fin and prep for my heat. Ten years on and I'm still the girl whose brother died in the surf comp at Jellurgal Point.

Mr Harris, my PE teacher and surf coach, strides across the sand. 'Kirra?'

I squint at him while rubbing wax on the deck of my board. 'Yeah, Coach?'

He throws me a blue rashie and flashes a confident grin. I stare past his thick mask of white zinc cream. 'Remember, be patient. Wait for the right wave, don't just catch anything.'

I pull on the one-size-fits-all rashie and tie the excess fabric into a knot on my back. I'm stoked the shirt's not red. Wuz's last comp rashie was blood red.

'Two decent waves, Kirra,' Coach's voice echoes behind me. 'May the fourth be with you … go have fun.'

I roll my eyes. He, and every *Star Wars* fanatic, recycles this joke every year. 'Fun is what it's all about,' I chirp over my shoulder. Fun and not focusing on Wuz or the world ending.

Glassy waves roll down the point. One after another, parallel walls of water forming to a constant beat. I crouch to wrap my leggie 'round my right ankle, fastening it to feel firm but comfortable.

The siren blasts and the comp kicks off. I sprint into the cold water with three other surfers, boards tucked under our arms. A wave rolls in at waist level. I leap over it, hold my surfboard next to me, and push down on it as hard as my lean frame can, to force the board over the peak of the crashing wave. I don't want to smash my new baby in the dumping shore break.

There's a lull between sets. I'm belly to board, back arched so I can paddle long, strong strokes 'til the next crest reaches me. When it rears above me, I duck-dive under its molten guillotine.

Perfect power. Trained timing.

The bigger its height, the deeper I push down my board with my arms and foot. Swooping under waves with my board makes me feel like I'm the only one out here. I power-paddle between breakers, progressing further and further past the impact zone 'til I'm out back with the other competitors in the line-up.

We're sitting on our boards, legs dangling in the water, watching and waiting for movement on the horizon.

A chill rattles through me and ends with a violent clashing of teeth. Had I'd known the water temp plummeted in the last couple of days, I would've worn a wettie … maybe a steamer.

I grin at the girl in red, and say, 'Never thought I'd surf Jellurgal Point, let alone pumping and only four people out.'

Her eyes stay glued on the lines forming in the distance.

'Yep,' she mutters and paddles away with her chest flat on the board and legs floundering: terrible style.

A well-known feeling rises: flogging that kook.

Love you, Bro. I'm gonna make you proud today.

A set wave forms, and I paddle-battle against the red-rashie rookie to get the perfect position, right of the crest.

It's mine. I paddle fast, hard strokes. No hesitation. No stopping. Hard. Fast. Hard. Fast. As if it's the last wave I'll catch and leave nothing in reserve. The tail of my board lifts, and I slam out two more strong strokes, then snap to my feet and scream down the face at invigorating speed.

An oceanic curtain cascades overhead, and I tuck next to the rising backlit wall. I'm inside a giant glass jar of honey with sunlit syrupiness spinning 'round me. Its deafening sound silences my world.

Here, time is an illusion: the tube ride feels longer, though it's never long enough. And life's distractions are muted by the barrel's thunderous roar.

I'm alone.

And I don't think about winning or Wuz. Seconds feel like minutes. I'm crouching, leaning forward, speeding along a glossy wall – cautious not to get caught in the rotating ceiling. Adrenaline's pumping. It fills my void. All the money in the world couldn't make me feel the way I do now.

In a split-simultaneous second, turquoise turns into a thrashing of white speed bumps. I'm spinning out of control in a gigantic washing machine. Forcing myself to relax, I pretend I'm a ragdoll and let the ocean's spin cycle twizzle me at an ear-piercing speed.

Relax. Just relax, I think, to save the little air I have left in my lungs.

I'm pulled deeper into the wave's vortex. Sand whips around me. Then the sunlight underwater vanishes. I'm surrounded by liquid black. If I panic in the dark, I could swim to the bottom of the ocean instead of the surface. I must wait and hope the air in my lungs lasts.

Fear can be a friend or foe. It depends how you treat it.

I play dead like those docos tell you to when facing a grizzly. And this beast is blue-black and ready to eat me alive.

CHAPTER 5
NARN

It's no secret Granny Alkira favours me. She told me which track Tarni took to catch up with Minjarra, and it's obvious Granny Alkira doesn't know Tarni's secret, as no N'gian-gifted woman would be allowed to travel outside our borders alone.

'Let her go,' Dad had warned at the beach. 'Give her time to think. You can't change fate: the river will bend in time without our will, plans, or lovesick intentions.'

Should've listened. If I hadn't chased, she might not have run.

And I've got to stop thinking, *It can't get any worse.* What's worse than 'bending the truth' to the woman you love? Her finding out and running into the arms of another man.

Tarni's long legs rock-hop the creek at roo-speed. I sprint after her. By the time I run through the *wudjuru* grove, Tarni is long gone. One wrong footing when a scrub turkey catches my eye in the distance, which I mistake for Tarni, makes me tumble off the track. My left leg lands in a soft, moist dirt burrow. A soft landing is good, *right*? Wrong!

I lift it out, and all the way to my calf is covered with baby brown snakes. They look like giant leeches: ten – twenty – of them biting my leg. Tiny fangs stab into my skin over and over. What are the chances of me landing in their pit the moment they all hatch? Baby snakes are the worst. They're scared of everything, so they put those tiny fangs to good use. Venom is venom whether it's from an adult or a baby.

I grab them by their heads, one at a time, and toss them away. Snake bites are rare, but we're taught to be prepared. I take slow deep breaths to stay calm and move away from the nest, back onto the bare track.

Wherever a plant or animal lives, within two big steps is nature's remedy. I need to stop moving. Our old people train us well, so I scan around. Then I grab some *wudjuru*, and the bush lore works again. Instead of searching for vine, I use the kurrajong string from around my waist. I'm propped against a thick trunk; calf and foot is wrapped in a sheet of bark. And tied tight with the string. Wish I'd found shelter beneath a *bilang* instead of a *wudjuru*. Not because its thick bed of pine needles make the best sleep … but because it'll keep away those snakes and their relatives.

No-one knows this droopy-eyed dolphin caller is on the shared corridor. Could be years before it's used. And Tarni will think I stopped chasing her … stopped caring.

I didn't – haven't.

My groin aches. When I open my eyes, there's two of everything. I'll be desperate soon, when the vomiting and fevers start, and my urine turns a reddy-black.

Dad warned me of the imbalance. And if I live to tell this tale, it'll either be added to my other disasters or taken as another strange sign for the Elders to ponder. It's normal for brown snakes to have a cluster of white oblong eggs. And for them to hatch and leave at the same time: safety in numbers is a survival instinct that many animals have. But for someone to fall into a viper's nest at the exact moment they all hatch is just creepy. Eggs in a nest can range from eight to thirty, but I've never heard of fifteen to twenty baby brown snakes biting someone over and over. Hope some of these punctures are dry, venomless ones.

I don't always follow Dad's advice. Didn't tell anyone I'm out here. I think about what I want and chase after it. The snake pit has stopped that. Just hope I get a chance to learn this lesson and prove to Tarni, Dad – everyone – I can change. If I survive this, I'll love lore, listen to my Elders, and put the needs of the tribe, particularly one of its long-legged members, above my own.

I hurl, and chunks of vomit thud next to me. I cough up more. My eyelids droop. Closed is easier than double vision. Sweat trickles down my face and back. I'm losing control of my muscles.

And I can't tell if I've been asleep, awake, or unconscious. My head burns and I must stay still even though there's writhing snakes around me. They can't be real or the birds would be causing a racket. Birds and animals continue their normal movements, ignoring me and my mess.

A coolness strokes my forehead. It's on my face. Immediately, I picture a snake's tongue. Nah, this one's thicker. Is a dingo licking me? My eyes won't budge. Every time I blink them open, they snap shut. Half my face has melted and is sliding down my neck.

'Narn, it's Aunty Lowanna.' She sounds as soothing as the water she's cooling my head with. 'Lucky our women were collecting more *wudjuru* to add to the single women's *ngumbin*.'

I move my lips. Nothing comes out.

'Don't talk. Don't move. You did well, Narn. That string slows the venom. Just rest. We'll look after you. There'll be someone with you the whole time.'

She dabs my forehead again. 'You'll probably be here 'til that moon becomes big and round. Plenty of empty leathery eggs in that brown snake pit.' Aunty shakes her head and sucks her teeth the exact way her brother Birrabunji does. 'Your name shouldn't mean *sea*, it should mean *trouble*.' And she chuckles in soft waves.

'I was brave,' I mumble. Can't people focus on what I do right, instead of my mistakes?

'You are brave, Narn. Remember: no talking, no movement.'

Shadows come and go. I can't remember who's with me. Words slip out of my mouth even when my brain tries to hold them back. 'Told her I loved her … didn't matter.'

There's a giggle. It's not Aunty's. But I don't react because staying still is saving my life. Different carers sit and talk to me. And as each night passes, the moon gets rounder and I haven't moved. All I can think of is that I can't chase Tarni to prove my love, can't train to gain Minjarra's respect.

One thing is sure: if Tarni returns when the moon is round and fat … I will be too. Lying here day after day, while every aunty, cousin and granny is feeding me up.

CHAPTER 6
TARNI

'Tarni, stop wasting time.'

And I'm talking to myself again. My father's mother – Granny – did it too. I'm not sure whether to be pleased or annoyed. She was my favourite among the grandmothers, and it wasn't because I was her son's daughter either, because she held a special place among all my cousins too. Granny Yindi was what we all called her. She was in the generation of our parents' parents, which means everyone of my generation called her Granny Yindi.

I should've *just* called her Granny because she's my direct line, but I wanted to be like everyone else and use her name. She let me get away with it. Father said my grandmother spoiled me.

Granny Yindi would laugh and ignore him, or say, 'The best thing about getting old is knowing which rules to keep or break.'

I thought she would tell ancient stories and sing songs for much longer. Those stories lead me to the edge of our boundary, and I hum the songs Father taught me the last time we took this trail. It was our first big journey, not long after Granny had passed. Back when we enjoyed stories around our small fire outside our *ngumbin* and knew how to share a laugh.

A soft breeze plays among the leaves; there's a familiar whistling in the air. I search for grey-green foliage of a small-coned tree. Its soothing fragrance wafts in.

There it is. I walk under its shade and happiness pinches my cheeks. It's my old babysitter, *bilang*; the safest spot to place *jarjum* while mothers work nearby.

I crunch across the ground, covered with brown layers of pine-needle-like leaves and remember that no snake will slither across this. Not that I've been bitten by a snake, I'm too clever for that. And I wasn't born clever, like Narn – I mean, everyone – assumes. I work hard at it. Practise, practise, practise. Watching, waiting, working. Listen-to-learn-to-listen-to-learn. Cleverness doesn't spring up out of nowhere.

A quick whiff of the crushed leaves settles the tumbling inside. Rummaging through my dillybag, I find my stone knife and dig away an outer chunk of bark. Then I add perfect smaller chips of inner bark, exactly the same size, to my bag. You never know when you'll get a toothache or a sore mouth.

I press my palm on its trunk. Lucky Father's not here, he'd take more than I have and turn them into woomera pegs and spears. I close my eyes and sniff in the deepest breath. My shoulders rise and loosen. Its pine-needle fragrance reminds me I'm safe.

A few days have passed, and I'm in no hurry to arrive there or return home. I cross inland, into red-dusted boulder country. The moon is bright, almost a full circle. And my suspicions are confirmed. My father is here, covered in red ochre. He sits shoulder-to-shoulder with another fella, who's obviously Jiemba, and they cackle like best friends.

My promised one looks nothing like the *jarjum* I met years ago. He's uglier, and I wouldn't have thought that was possible. Can't see his beady black eyes, but his skin is covered with thick layers of red ochre. His long hair is rolled into chunky strands and coated with red mud. Looks like a giant octopus sits on his tiny skull.

For every clan in our tribe, this colour means one thing: death. We wear it for burial ceremonies, not every day. Has Jiemba grown at all since I last saw him? He's stumpy, his head wouldn't reach Narn's shoulder. I'm probably taller than him, and he'll need to stand on tippy toes to kiss me – *eeeek*. A bad tang fills my mouth. I gag, then bite my fist to stop myself from puking.

Jiemba shrieks with laughter and slaps my father on the back, as if they're the same age. Narn, nor any young men in our clans, would never treat Father this way. My fist still guards my mouth, as I rustle up a plan. If I confront Father and refuse Jiemba, I'd shame him in front of these people, and it won't end well. There won't be a Narn and I, if that's an option anymore. Tucked behind a small crop of boulders, I wait while the red-ochred tribe eat, dance, and yarn.

The celebration stops when the air crackles with a stormy liveliness. There's no leaves showing their undersides or low flying birds or dark looming clouds or any other sign of nearing rain.

Jiemba's on his feet, spear clenched in his hand.

Children tuck under their mothers. No adults move, let alone sing or dance.

A yellow glow dangles around Jiemba's neck. The crystal pulses. Not like the sun or fire, but a strange yellow light that chills your spirit.

Jiemba yells and thrusts his spear into the air. 'Our powerful Elder, my father, the Malung, approaches. He is here tonight to form an alliance with Minjarra and his saltwater people. It will be complete when Minjarra's daughter joins with me.'

Adults and *jarjum* huddle with their heads tucked in the soil – an echidna's defensive position.

The ground trembles a little, a chattering of the dirt's teeth, and chilly air whips around. Ten or twenty spear-lengths behind Jiemba, a cloaked man appears. The long possum fur covers his head and drags along the ground. Red-dusted males with sharp spears surround him. A larger, more-powerful, putrid-yellow glow exudes from the cloaked being. And a thick fog moves in waves towards the group, as if it is alive. The possum fur faces away from his skin. What painted stories does he keep hidden?

The octopus-haired fool ends each statement with a spear-thrust. 'Minjarra will represent my father and become the saltwater clan's only Elder and leader. Anyone who questions this or who does not follow our ways will be put to death.'

People remain with their heads dipped to the ground. Except it feels more like fear than respect. A shiver spreads across my skin. The dark threat slinks closer. An evilness craving to feed.

'Our tribe will grow stronger. Our numbers larger. We will become the strongest in all of Wallulljagun.' Jiemba's voice grows louder and stronger. Each time the spear stabs the sky, red dust flies off his arms and fills the air.

When the yellow vapour creeps over the clan, each member stands and cheers. The hidden shadow-spirit is a few spear-lengths from Jiemba and my father. The closer he gets, the brighter Jiemba's stone glows.

'We follow you, Malung, into victory, in the past, in the present, in the future. Wallulljagun is your land. We are your people.'

The crowd, led by Jiemba, cheer each time the Malung's name is said. My father grins so wide it stretches into a crazed grimace. He's the traitor. No wonder he wanted this joining.

'Malung. Malung. Malung.' In unison, they yell.

One flat voice.

One cursed tribe.

One constant chant.

I cover my ears, not wanting to catch what mind-disease they have. The eerie mist is an arm's length away. I wiggle back into the safety of the scrub, then scramble away, clawing through the bush, not caring about the cuts and scratches left on my body.

Soft treads turn into a furious run.

The Malung is Jiemba's father.

No matter how fast I pump my arms and legs or the closer I get to home, that ghost-scared shiver doesn't leave me. I need to warn our peaceful clan before we lose everything we've ever known and loved.

An intense hate for my father ignites. It drives my legs, as I stampede through the bush, while the moon lights the way home. And I'm thankful Granny Yindi isn't alive to witness her son destroy our people.

Our Elders have always worked together to reach the best outcome for all the clans in our tribe. Never one leader but many Elders, with their variety of personalities keeping us safe. Minjarra traded his only daughter for unity with a shadow-spirit who plans to conquer every tribe of Wallulljagun.

Vomit hurtles upwards but I shove it back down. Acid rises again. There's no relief for my queasiness. Joining with Jiemba will make the Malung my father.

Never will I become his daughter.

Daughter to a murderer.

This is much bigger than me, Narn and our clan. Every clan cares for its country, wildlife, trees, sea, and there's no way Jiemba or his father will care for these simple things. How could they, when they're intoxicated with power? Poisoned by lust. Driven by evil.

CHAPTER 7
KIRRA

My head bursts through the surface, I heave in a breath and another tumultuous wave thunders above me. I dive through the churning sea. Grenade-like turbulence explodes around me, causing my teeth to clatter.

I resurface and grab my board before the next wave hits. In the turmoil, I've lost my blue rashie and I'm stoked my board and bikini are intact. An amped happiness tingles through me as I remember my barrel ride.

What's happening? Where is everyone? Everything is blurry. The hooter must've gone while I was underwater. Can't hear the commentator or the cheers of the spectators on the beach.

I blink, then open each eye. One at a time.

Dang it! I've lost both contact lenses in the forced acrobatics. It's happened before, just not in a comp. I'll catch a wave in, so I can grab a spare set of contacts from my bag. My heat should be finished anyway. Squinting at the texture on the blue horizon, I guesstimate the next set of waves and hope to catch a free ride with my limited depth of field.

A shape surfaces a few metres away. I jolt from left to right … panic stabs while I stare at the water and wait for confirmation. Is it the sun reflecting on a few odd waves?

Nah, there it is again.

Fins. I count three, maybe more.

They're fuzzy and I'm not hanging around to see if they're sharks or dolphins. I dig my arms into the water and paddle hard and fast, harder – faster. I ride the white-water brumbies, with their flowing manes, to the shore. They'll be calmed into submission when they stampede the powdery sand.

As the foreshore comes into focus, so does one desperate thought: *Get out fast.*

The foam smacks my legs. I regain my balance, scoop up my board, rip off my leggie with one hand and clamber through crunchy wet sand 'til it becomes soft and thick and warm. Sprawled on the beach, the fins are nowhere to be seen. I'm panting, puffing and my limbs are trembling. I'm alive.

But my vision's whacked and I have a jackhammer headache. Even with my short-sighted blurriness, I sense something is wrong. I scramble to my feet. Can't make out any cars or roads or buildings or crowds. My brain and eyes attempt to communicate when my ears tingle.

What is that?

I stop moving. An energy ripples through me, rising and falling. My step quickens over the pumice-stone-covered beach towards the sound, like the lure of a mermaid singing to a drunken sailor. 'Cept, I thought I'd be the mermaid, not the drunk.

Gliding over the crunchy sand in a trance, the air seems purer as I breathe in and let the saltiness calm my lungs. Is this a dream? Maybe I'm unconscious and my imagination's running amok? Or am I somehow stuck in an augmented reality? I rub my hands together, and grains of sand scrub my soft skin. It feels real. Somehow losing my contacts while tumbling around the solid waves has swept me further along the coast to an untouched piece of shoreline I don't recognise.

That unfamiliar noise entices me along the empty beach 'til I reach a rocky headland where dark basalt rocks form a natural jetty, which extends into the sapphire sea. My shoulder aches and I shift my surfboard, the way my cousin plonks her baby from one hip to the other.

The sound pauses then surrounds me again. I place my board on the sand and follow the low-pitched lilting. It leads me higher along the headland and I flit from rock to rock. The air is so clean: each breath is moreish. The deeper I inhale, the faster I ride a natural head-spinning high; surfing has the same effect.

Shivers lap my skin in little waves.

'Cos what I see is intoxicating.

CHAPTER 8
NARN

I wake to the sound of a low hum. *Bunngunn* beat far in the distance. Eyes fling open. Birds, yet to sing their morning song, stay silenced by the darkness. Still, the hum grows louder. Vibrations are small at first. Their strength pulsates through me. In my gut, down my back, across my skin. I sit up and realise it's not coming from outside, but within.

I leave my *ngumbin*, hobbling down the beach in the moonlight, humming the whole way. I'm thankful I am no longer forced to lay still and be handfed. Aunty Lowanna would be wild I didn't ask one of the lads to help me.

But I follow the music. It feels as important as the thumping in my chest.

By the time I climb the headland, the deep drone turns into song. Louder and stronger, louder and stronger, it gains momentum at hair-raising speed. The air feels thick and livelier than a thunderstorm.

The sea is silvery and restless. And the song surrounds a ghost-like girl trapped in a dark watery grave.

I sing. The darkness releases its grip, and she struggles free.

I sing. She swims across the waves.

I sing. She wanders over the sand.

Waves of tiny shudders roll from my head down my body. They don't stop. Ripple after ripple, quiver, shiver, prickle.

People tell me I have a strong voice. I need it for my full moonset role. But this is different. I'm not scared. It's the calmest and most confident I've felt. Little bumps form on my skin, and it has nothing to do with feeling cold. The song isn't like any I've sung or sensed before.

Standing on the rocky point with hands cupped around my mouth, I let the lilting sound form in my stomach, race through my throat and boom out. The song shifts. My voice trickles in quiet hummings before bellowing with fierceness, then softening into a soulful warble. The salty breeze keeps my hair out of my eyes. I follow it, rising and falling, while the full moon sets as the sun rises. Rays of light lead my song.

The hum gives power to every word I sing. A duet with a potent force. Unity of body and spirit. Was this what Dad was talking about?

Is this you, N'gian?

The song thunders within. There's no time to think. My instincts must follow as the hum leads. It climbs again. From the height of the sky to the depth of the sea.

At full strength, everything within me yields to the song. And I'm smiling, then serious, then delirious as the song moves through me.

There's a breaking point. I hear it. Feel it. Something releases. Three dolphins from our pod come bolting from a distance. The hum fades. It's carried on the breeze. And the song is done. I don't understand why, but I feel different. Strength surges through every muscle, as if the snake saga never happened.

I enjoy the leftover sensation of the song, and I won't let that ghost-girl distract me, even though she's scaled the headland, ducked behind a cluster of boulders, and is peering between a gap. She acts like a shadow, hidden away. But with her lighter skin and the way she stomps through the land, we heard her long before we saw her. And she's not tricking anyone. Our Elders will decide how we approach her; they're probably discussing it now. No need to rush or worry.

Laughter echoes below and a small group of *jarjum* wait at the edge of the water. Their bodies dot the beach, not far from the stranger's flat white canoe. Women, young and old, arrive with eyes on the sea. I cup my hands around my mouth and let my usual song fill the headland.

Five or six men with spears walk down the beach and wade into the shallows. Other young men slap their spears on the sea's surface, while I sing and search the blue-grey waters for our friends.

Something's below. My song ends. 'Yip. Yip. Yip,' I yell, then skip across the top of the rocks, my toes barely touching the surface. I peer into the dark blue waters.

A splash explodes and my clan cheers from the beach. Spinner jumps out of the water, and I greet my favourite dolphins, '*Jingi Wahlu*, Spinner. *Jingi Wahlu*, Echo.'

Seconds later, the dolphins dive over and under the waves.

The women and *jarjum* race into the water, some cheer, others clap.

A wave washes in flailing fish. The dolphins chase more, and another wave rolls in, then out, exposing loads of flapping fish. Men are spearing in the shallows. Women and young ones scoop handfuls of silvery fish and fill their dillybags.

People laden with fish stride up the beach and over the dunes.

I glide from rock to rock in a fluid motion 'til I land on the beach. Then I stroll through the helpers on the foreshore, scoop a fish and wade out to waist-deep water. The sea temperature has plummeted. Doesn't happen often, but when the northerlies blow, the cold water, from the deep, rises. It chases the warm water far away.

Our old people call it *dugan djulung waring gwong*.

Big Boi, the lead dolphin with a white fin, swims to me and I hold the fish by its tail and feed him. Our gathering is finished, and fins skip across the waves out to sea.

Birri, the most curious *jarjum*, peers into the stranger's hideout, his dark brown hair flaps in the wind and with a cheeky grin, he says, '*Jingi wahlu.*'

'*Jingi wahlu,*' she echoes. I didn't expect her to speak our tongue. She stands and her odd clothing is made from no skins I've ever seen. Her coverings are the same colour as red ochre. I flex my hand to calm an unwelcomed urge. She doesn't look like she's mourning, so why would she wear the colour of death? And the way she looks, stands, walks, smiles – all feel wrong.

The stranger rubs the sides of her head. And squints. Her eyes are weak.

Four or five *jarjum* swarm her. Each one says, '*Jingi wahlu.*'

And she repeats their greetings.

The *jarjum* speak non-stop, at the same time. Instead of answering, she grins with a smile too big for her face. It's stuck there, like she doesn't know how to pack it up and put it away.

Birri's younger brothers, Jehr and Jankum, sprint down the dunes near our *bora*. They race along the beach, and chat to the women carrying the fish.

'Bring her over,' the mothers yell to the *jarjum* surrounding the stranger. 'Gentle. Don't want to scare her. Everyone's been called up the sandhills.'

Jehr and Jankum join the other *jarjum*, and herd ghost-girl and her shiny flat canoe along the beach. She has no idea who's standing on top of the sandhills, or she still wouldn't be wearing that overstretched smile.

CHAPTER 9
TARNI

I never sleep in, but I wake to an empty *ngumbin*. The single women, along with everyone else, must be helping Narn with the fish gathering, and I'm thankful my knees won't be weakened by his mesmerising singing voice. Days have slipped away since I discovered my father's secrets. Last night, I arrived home to the soothing sound of the sea, and Birrabunji said he'd organise the circle of Elders.

I amble along the sandy path. Birrabunji collects kindling while other Elders sit, their quiet yarns waft in the air along with the smoke from the fire. I haven't slept much. It wasn't because the moon was glowing all night. Secrets of this size niggle at you – day and night – until you give them to those who have the strength to carry them. This is why I'm here.

'You ready, Tarni?' Birrabunji says, and he re-stokes the big fire in the shared space.

He points to an opening in the Elders' circle, and I sit in the gap.

I've never addressed the Elders before, and I remember what Birrabunji told Narn about bravery – doing what needs to be done while we feel the fear. Even if it burns in my belly. In my head. And in every breath while I wait to tell them about my father: the one Granny Yindi and I shared a *ngumbin* with when I was a *jarjum*, the respected hunter who should be part of this Elders' circle. The traitor.

Birrabunji addresses our circle of Elders, then nods at me. 'Tarni, thank you for your courage.'

I scan the calm faces knowing they'll distort when I share my news. Facts with no fixes. I hesitate to deliver the death sentence to my people.

'Tarni, it's alright, love. You're not in any trouble, just talk.' It's Granny Alkira. Her soft voice is comforting.

I gulp back my hesitation. 'No, Granny Alkira, we're in a quicksand of trouble.'

Their eyes don't stray from mine as I detail every part of my journey.

Granny Alkira is the first to speak. 'Jiemba's father, does he call himself another name?'

Nunnjahli scratches his beard and asks, 'Isn't his name Coen?'

Most of the Elders look at Birrabunji, who shifts in his seat, then he says, 'Yes, his name's Coen, but I think Alkira is talking about his new name – to do with magic from the shadows.'

Granny Alkira sends an encouraging nod my way and the rest of the Elders gawk at me. I wish I were a hermit crab, so I could retreat into my shell and hide at the bottom of an empty rockpool.

'I think his name is … from what was said … they call him …' I struggle to say his name in case it gives him more power. In the quietest way, 'the Malung' rushes out.

Their gasps and bulging emu-like eyes tell me they understand. This isn't going to end well.

Uncle Gukuji gestures as he speaks. 'Did he wear a thing around his neck made of unusual bones?'

I manage to nod. 'I didn't see his face or body. It was hidden under a long possum-fur cloak.'

'The stories say no-one's seen his face,' Birrabunji says. 'Makes sense he hides his body; he is a shadow-spirit.'

Gunggin, a senior fisherman, adds, 'But our stories say he died a long time ago, before our grandfathers' time.'

'That's what my grandfather told me too. That he'd been defeated, banished into the belly of a rock – that forbidden place – and the bone necklace burnt to ash,' Uncle Jarli adds.

'Looks like someone has brought his shadow magic back.' Birrabunji's serious eyes reflect the fear in all our hearts.

'This won't be easy to fix.' Granny Alkira rocks as she talks. 'Didn't that fella who guarded the forbidden cave say he saw someone enter and leave alive?'

Before I'm excused, so the Elders can discuss the clan's future, I say, 'Jiemba had a tiny glowing crystal, the same kind as his father's.'

'Another glowing crystal, that's the imbalance,' Birrabunji mutters to himself.

How can Jiemba's crystal be connected to the imbalance? Why not the Malung's? At least *now* I won't be forced into that evil family.

'Tarni?'

'Yes, Granny Alkira?'

'We will need to discuss all options.'

I cringe. Too nervous to hear more, I gaze at the ground.

'You were promised to Jiemba for a reason.' She waits for our eyes to meet. 'Are you willing to save us and keep that alliance?'

'Yes,' I lie, and regret it straightaway. Not that I lied to my Elders (which I should feel guilty about), but they wouldn't want the truth: I care more about what people think, or what they think I should think, than being honest.

Besides, what would they say if my answer were 'no'?

Guess I'll never know. And I was furious with Narn for lying.

It's tiring and lonely trying to be the best. There's no escape, not if Jiemba is the Malung's son. If I don't marry Jiemba I will die, and Narn – I mean the whole clan – will be punished. The Malung's punishment is death ... by the bone-pointing, or as we call it, a mind-spear. Or he could use a real spear. Doesn't matter because the outcome is the same. Death!

They're about to excuse me when two *jarjum*, older boys close to initiation, bolt over the dunes and stop on the edge of the Elders' circle.

Birrabunji shuffles over to the brothers. 'Jankum. Jehr. Why you boys running through here?'

'There's a ghost dolphin rider,' Jankum, the elder brother, says. 'She moved over the waves right onto the beach.'

'How is she a ghost?' Birrabunji asks and he crouches next to them.

'Her skin is lighter,' Jankum answers.

'And she was *on* a dolphin?' The way Birrabunji asks makes me wonder if he believes them.

'No,' he says, shielding his younger brother. 'On a flat canoe with a big dolphin fin underneath.'

Some of the older ones chuckle. And there's a sparkle in Birrabunji's eyes when he asks them to explain – maybe they're playing a game?

Jehr launches forward, and he speaks so fast it's hard to understand him. 'Was a shiny white fin. Birri saw her first. We followed her along the dunes – she never saw us. Birri wants to talk to her.'

'Where's Birri?' Birrabunji asks and his tone shifts. 'We should speak to him.'

'Not sure. Said after he talks to her, he was getting *gumburra* from his uncle,' Jankum replies.

And another Elder chuckles and says, 'That *jarjum* would do anything to eat those creamy nuts.'

Birrabunji sits on the sand beside the boys. 'You know this circle is serious business, not for games.'

'We're not playing,' Jehr says, and hides behind Jankum again.

'Boys, where's your mum? Is she on the beach?' one of the Elders asks.

'Nope,' Jankum says, with fresh worry-lines crowding his brow. 'She gone to stay with an uncle.'

'Well, tell us about this flat canoe. You boys tell the truth in this circle. No playing games – ah?' Birrabunji reminds them.

Jankum's face brightens, a comet in the night. 'She had this symbol on her flat canoe.' He draws a circle with a wave and a sun in the sand with his finger.

Birrabunji is solemn. 'You seen this symbol before?' His eyes swing to each boy.

'No,' Jankum says, and Jehr shakes his head so hard, it looks like it could twist right off.

Birrabunji ruffles their hair. 'You sure? You're not in trouble but it's very important.'

They continue shaking their heads, and he stands and says, 'Thank you, boys. See if the dolphin rider will follow you over the dunes. We'll speak to her there.'

They dash away, sand flinging into the air.

'Tarni, we'll need you at the dunes too,' Birrabunji says, and I know it's his polite way of asking me to leave.

I'm slow to rise and shuffle away, eager to eavesdrop.

'That N'gian symbol's been hidden for generations. Now it's seen two times by two different people in one moon cycle. A strangeness is stirring,' Birrabunji murmurs. 'His symbol should be revealed in the right place, in the right order and for the right person.'

'I agree,' Granny Alkira says, 'and N'gian's message stick is lost. No-one's seen that glowing stick since my grandmother's granny's hair went grey.'

Sometimes old people think they're whispering, but for younger ears, it's easy to catch – even if you're obediently dawdling away.

'Need to be clever. Need to uncover if this ghost dolphin rider is spirit or flesh,' one old fella says. 'Is it a messenger of the Malung pretending to be N'gian's chosen, or is it N'gian preparing to help?'

Birrabunji's voice carries on the breeze. 'We must be careful who we trust – not be caught in the mind-trap of the Malung. Yet, we cannot forget: a shadow is only cast by light.'

It *has* been a strange moon cycle: Narn loves me. My father's a traitor. A ghost dolphin rider glides along waves. The Malung has returned. And I could be joined to the evil shadow's son.

What will our Elders decide? My fate is in their hands.

CHAPTER 10
KIRRA

Should've known spying on a shirtless stranger is never a good idea. It's obvious I learnt nothing from bingeing those rom-coms. The snooping chick always gets busted.

Is this a Captain Cook re-enactment? The singer wears ochre, but no-one seems to be performing. And their clothing seems too 'well-worn' to be pre-colonial costumes. Blurry vision or not, a whole film crew would stick out like a shark in a wave pool.

I reach the dunes, secure my board under my arm, then clamber up the thick powdery sand. The kids surround me, their mums follow a few metres behind.

Breathe. My advice is useless. Nervous energy tightens my chest.

My dark-tanned skin has been a proud feature. Here, I'm the odd one out. I remember Nan's tea analogy: some Murries, Goories, Koories or First Nations people have a bit of milk added. Some have more milk. Some have none. But we are all tea. Yet, this place looks as though milk has never arrived, a different Australia to the one I know. Where the heck am I?

My head throbs, and massaging my temples doesn't seem to help. I need my glasses. As we near the sandy hilltop, I'm ready for the 'you've been pranked' hype. Or the big reveal that I'm part of an Australian Indigenous *Survivor* series, but there are still no cameras or lighting or any sign of modern things.

Instead, a group of gnarly men stand in a row, armed with long spears.

Should I run?

Their spears are by their sides with the sharp tips in the air, used as walking sticks, not weapons. At least they're not aiming at me. Everyone watches a white-haired, snowy-bearded man. I'm not afraid of him – not sure if it's 'cos he isn't carrying a spear or that his eyes are kind. He points to the drawing on my surfboard. The focus shifts to me. Am I expected to say something? Do something?

I crouch and draw the symbol in the sand with my finger. When I stand, the white-haired man grins and reveals a large gap where a front tooth used to live. He talks for a long time, not to me, but to the crowd, in a language I don't understand. Wish this were a TV show, I'd switch on the subtitles. My vision's stuffed, head pounds, and I wanna go home, have a long hot shower and raid the fridge 'cos I'm starvin'.

A tall girl, who looks a bit older than me, weaves through the mob. She's the kind of person who'd be the lead singer of a rock band or sport's captain or the alpha female of the 'it' crew at school. Black curls dangle past her shoulders, almost reaching her waist. '*Jingi wahlu*,' she says, the same greeting the kids used down the beach.

'My name is Tarni. What is yours?'

My brain glitches. She speaks English! It's the first time

74

I can understand anyone. A quick scan confirms there are still no white fellas or Western lifestyles.

'My name is Kirra.' Then I say, 'Kirra … Wonda … Wallace.' There's a murmuring when I say *Wonda*, and my stomach plunges like I've dropped in on a ten-foot wave over reef.

I want to launch a full-scale attack of questions. Where am I? Can everyone speak English? Why is that symbol on my board important? And a million more.

The white-haired man speaks, and Tarni says, 'Birrabunji asks where you came from.'

'From Jellurgal Point,' I answer.

They don't respond.

'Burleigh.'

Still no response.

'I'm from the Gold Coast,' and when that doesn't work, I point to the sea, tap my board and say, 'I caught a wave on this.'

Another string of unknown words leave Tarni's mouth, and the man she calls Birrabunji nods before speaking.

Tarni seems to focus harder. 'We have three tests.'

I cringe. I hate tests.

'Okay.' The word sticks in the back of my throat.

'Are your family saltwater people, mountain people, rainforest people …' she gulps, glances at Birrabunji before she finishes, 'or inland people?'

I throw back my shoulders and hold my chin high. 'My family are saltwater people,' I say, before remembering it's a test, which often have trick questions.

Tarni smiles and I cross my arms to cover my bikini. With so many sets of dark brown eyes staring, I wish I had a towel to hide behind.

A grey-haired woman, holding cooked fish wrapped in a large green leaf, steps forward and signals for me to eat. Every eye remains on me. I'm guessing it's the second test. She passes me the leaf. I'm blowing on the hot fish and switching the leaf between my hands.

Is this my last supper? Hoping it's not poisoned, I sniff it and peek at the faces surrounding me. It smells delicious, my tummy gurgles – I think, *The hell?* and gobble it all. I don't puke or drop dead but lick my lips, wishing for more of that sweet smoky fish.

Birrabunji speaks and there's noisy chatter. Tarni interprets: 'In the last test, you must choose the ochre you will wear tonight.'

Three women, older than me but younger than Nan, step forward. Each carries a coolamon, a wooden oval-shaped bowl, with different ochre: white, yellow, and red – well, more of a burnt orange.

The murmurings stop.

How do you pass a colour test? Do I just go with my favourite: earthy orange is in and matches my bikinis.

I'm about to grab that coolamon, when I remember our mob usually wears white during ceremonies. So I switch at the last second.

Everyone talks and Tarni yells over the racket, 'You passed, Kirra. We welcome you tonight. Follow me.'

She grabs my hand and leads me through the crowd. By the way the kids and women stroke my skin and hair, I reckon they've never seen anyone like me before. We walk along the dunes towards several bark shelters. This can't be a dream. I've never seen anything like this, and my brain couldn't make this up. Have I time-travelled? Like, hell.

'Tarni, do you have a phone?'

She tilts her head to one side; two creases settle between her eyebrows.

I form a shaka (a fist with my pinkie and thumb extended) and hold it up to my ear. 'You know – phone. I need to call my nan.'

'No. What is a phone?'

'What about a car? Computer?' I stare into her eyes as I say each word, hoping for a flicker of recognition.

'I do not understand.' And her expression, not her words, tell me it's true.

My arm's bruised from pinching it. A million sci-fi movies fill my head. Has my past been erased and now I've been thrown into this reality?

'Later we will talk,' Tarni says with a convincing cover-girl smile.

Later seems to come and go, while my brain bulges with more and more questions. And as the day ends, small fires appear at the end of each paperbark dwelling – the opposite end of the dome's large opening. And Tarni's tour ends too. There's a small village of round huts scattered in three rows. Children weave through the homes in the middle one. Tarni and other young women occupy the dome-shaped homes on the line closest to the beach. And the young men with initiation scars on their chests live in the round structures closest to the rainforest.

These dome homes stand between the dunes and the edge of the rainforest, sheltered under the shade of pandanus palms, paperbarks and groves of banksias. On one side of this small village, beyond the dunes, the beach seems to go forever. On the other side, about a football field away from the homes, is a shelter with a few dingoes resting. What I can't see, Tarni fills in with details.

A large group of people, maybe the whole clan, gather in a wide-open circle, around a big bonfire. This seems routine, as if it happens every night. White- or yellow-ochred bodies huddle around the flames. I'm stoked I didn't pick the red one. Would those walking sticks have become weapons?

The breeze whips around and a dingo howls in the distance. The apparently tamed dingoes howl in our camp, and heebie-jeebie bumps rise on my arms. I rub them but they don't disappear.

'Kirra, wait here. I have something for you in my *ngumbin*.'

Tarni dashes off, ducks into a nearby hut and hurries back. 'These are for you.' She drapes a grey fur blanket around my shoulders. 'You can borrow this possum-skin cloak. It will get cold tonight.'

Then she hands me a stringy, woven thingy.

'Thanks,' I say holding them in my hands.

She's expecting me to do something, so I smile.

Tarni points to her skirt. 'You wear it. See?' And I copy her actions 'til she's happy with my outfit: dressed in my bikini, a possum-skin cloak, and a string skirt. Tarni smears white ochre on my face, then leads me through the people gathering around the fire.

Birri, the boy who spotted me earlier, sits on the other side of the fire with thick yellow stripes covering him. He pats the ground beside him. 'Kirra. Kirra.'

I accept his invite and sit on the paperbark mat beside him.

Tarni and the dolphin caller sit next to me.

'This is Narn,' Tarni says. 'Birrabunji has made him your protector.'

It makes me more uneasy than safe. 'What do I need protecting from?'

I think Tarni tells Narn what I said but neither reply. Instead, she points to an older lady brushing a little girl's hair with a banksia pod. 'That is Granny Alkira, our cleverwoman. She looks after the women and will also watch over you tonight.'

Before I can answer, Birrabunji walks towards me carrying an ancient coolamon. It's filled with smouldering gum leaves, and a white-grey trail of thick smoke follows him. He crouches opposite me and swishes silvery eucalyptus clouds over me. My hands gently play in the billows, inviting the smoke to waft over and around and through me. I love smoking ceremonies. Time feels different here, more fluid.

Everyone else moves through the grey swirls, cupping the smoke over them. Even my surfboard is cleansed with it. I'm calmer. But the truth is, Nan's gonna be stressed out when I don't come home tonight, and there's nothing I can do.

The flames rocket up the stacked tree branches towards the stars. I wiggle back, the hot glow overpowers me. I take off my possum-skin cloak and roll it up.

Coolamon of all different sizes are passed from person to person. Each one is filled with delicious food: roasted fish, crabs, eugarie, fruit, a salad made from native spinach leaves, flat bread and heaps more. Some I've never seen before. I place a small handful of food on my big leaf plate as each coolamon is passed to me. Both Birri and Tarni are eager for me to taste each dish. There's plenty of food, but I eat slowly 'cos there's a lot of people to feed. And like my family – my large extended Goori family – during big gatherings, the children eat first, then the old people, and because I'm a guest, I'm one of the first to eat as well.

Birri scoffs down his macadamia nuts, and now he's eyeing mine. So I slip him a few and am rewarded with a hello-new-favourite-person grin. When the light fades, the dancing begins. Some older women sneak into the edge of the circle. They are the last ones to arrive, shielding something with their backs.

'What are they doing?'

Tarni whispers in my ear, 'Secret women's business. The Elder and married women come in last and will leave first. The men cannot see the possum-skin drums. After, they will hide those skins in a sacred place.'

The grey-haired women pull the possum skin tautly across their laps and between their thighs. They start each song by thudding out the rhythm with their palms on their right hand. Their left hand holds the woman next to them, which makes them keep exact time. The younger girls beat their bare thighs, linked by their left hand to the row of women. All sing into the sea breeze. Two boomerangs are clapped together by two tall men with white hair and full beards.

First the men dance – every move is powerful and proud. The younger boys join in, clouds of dust rise from their fast-moving feet. The women and girls dance next ('cept the older women playing their lap-drums), all together in one row, hips and legs move in rhythm. Then everyone not playing instruments joins the dance. I was taught our dances during culture class at school by uncles and aunties from our community, but here, it feels more than just learning culture. I'm glad I ignored my splitting headache and joined in, 'cos a fire ignites inside me that I didn't know I wanted or needed.

I'm welcomed to this beautiful place, their home: I can stay as their guest. No-one else speaks English. They use my translator, and when Tarni speaks, it's as if she enters a special zone that helps her understand.

I unravel my borrowed cloak and rub the thick warm fur.

'You wear it with the fur warming your skin,' Tarni says. And when I turn the grey fur over, twenty or more rectangles the size of a laptop are neatly stitched together. Each piece is painted with different tints of ochre. Some have intricate designs engraved on the leather side.

'It's beautiful,' I say, as I touch a panel painted with a long row of hairy caterpillars.

'Mum painted that one,' she whispers. 'We will see those itchy grubs soon. They come when the mullet breed on the waterways. Here, see this one?' She points to a patchwork piece that has lots of fish the same size and shape. 'I painted those mullet with Mum when I was a little girl. Our clan lives here for early winter and the mullet run.'

'Where's your mum?'

Tarni stares past my shoulder without answering.

'Whose cloak is this?'

I'm about to ask again when she whispers, 'It's my mother's.'

'Won't she need it?'

'No.' The way she says it stops me asking about her mum.

Everyone is shushed. The kids stop playing and form an inner circle, their eyes glued on Birrabunji. Six or seven tame dingoes lay between the fire and the kids. Birrabunji is as dramatic as a Hollywood star. His speech is melodious, then he says, *Jarjum.*

My ponytail flings from side to side when I whip 'round to Tarni and then Narn, who sit each side of me.

'*Jarjum*. Child,' I say, bouncing to my knees. 'I know that word from Nan, my grandmother.'

Both reward me with a nod and grin.

These must be my people, speaking Yugambeh from Nan's lineage.

Birrabunji's voice jolts Tarni back into action. 'He's asking the children what story they want. He's suggesting the dolphin one, but Birri is convincing everyone to pick the one about a trapped evil shadow-spirit, which isn't good after this morning.'

A cool breeze plucks hair after hair from the back of my neck, and I shuffle closer to the fire. Ghost stories around a fire in a place I don't know surrounded by strangers. I try to relax, try to hide the fact that I hate horror movies and dark nights and places that summon the worst of my imagination. 'What happened this morning?' I whisper.

Narn says something to Tarni. She snaps at him. By the looks on their faces and the tone of their voices, I'm thankful I don't understand. So, I focus on Birrabunji, who seems hesitant at Birri's suggestion.

Tarni catches me up: 'Birrabunji's grandmother told him the Gowonda story when he was a boy.'

The fire lights the Elder's face; it's the children who seem to love his stories the most. Birrabunji speaks, pauses for Tarni to translate, and his story unfolds.

'Gowonda was a tall, strong, clever hunter. He had long, white hair that matched his white, woolly beard. He was resourceful and patient, and not many people know this, but he had a powerful singing voice.'

Birrabunji's deep voice with the background noise of the roaring fire and tumbling waves makes this outdoor performance even better.

'Everyone loved Gowonda: the children,' Birrabunji ruffles Birri's hair, then adds, 'the hunters, the singers, the old people and the women. One day, he asked our skilful women to weave a big net using the inner bark fibres of *mungulli*.'

He stands and mimes the enormous size of the net. 'He wanted a net large enough to hang across the bush, low on the ground, and be strung from tree to tree.'

Birrabunji gathers some twigs, and throws them into the flames. 'The women spent days making the big net. They wove it finely.'

Our storyteller crouches and pats a dingo that a kid is using as a cushion. 'Gowonda taught the wild dingoes how to be our friends,' he says. 'He trained them to work together and follow his instructions. His whistle would tell them different things. Three high, short whistles: run hard, run fast. One low, long whistle: circle behind, get ready to chase them towards us.'

Birrabunji whistles low and long; it blasts through the air. A little boy purses his lips and only noisy air blows out. We chuckle and he ducks under his mum's fur blanket, which makes us laugh harder.

Birrabunji says, 'Gowonda would burn off patches of scrub near the waterhole on the mountain, to get fresh green grass to grow. And when the grass was thick and lush, he'd sneak in before sunrise and tie the big black net in place, on the opposite side of the grass and the waterhole.'

Birrabunji moves around the fire acting out each part of the story. 'Gowonda took the hunting men and his pack of dingoes up the mountain. All the wallabies and kangaroos were in a big group, munching on the sweet grass. The men hid near the net, while the dingoes rounded them up. Those animals were trapped by water on one side and with the dingoes behind them, there was only one place they could go. One low whistle,' and Birrabunji rips out a loud long whistle that makes all of the kids, and me, jump, 'and the dingoes chased them straight into the nets. Gowonda and the men had *jabir* ready.'

Tarni mimes to explain a *jabir* is a long pointed stick with a long handle. Then snaps back into interpreting mode. 'They used *jabir* to hit and collect plenty of food, enough for the clans. We sent out smoke signals with an invitation to other clans to join us in a great feast with singing and dancing.'

I smile. It must've been similar to tonight.

'Gowonda grew very old … One day he died. All the clans mourned for days.'

Birrabunji pauses, and I hope no little kids cry.

'Their tears dried when a group of youngsters raced into camp. They were playing on the beach, when they saw a large dolphin swimming in the shallows. It had a white fin, the same colour as Gowonda's long, white hair. Gowonda, the white-finned dolphin, taught the dolphins to chase fish into the shores, the same way he taught the dingoes to hunt together.'

Birri sits tall; the happy ending lifts him higher.

'That's why, when there's a big mob of fish, the men slap their spears on the surface of the sea and wait in the shallows with their nets and spears. Gowonda hears us: the spears slapping the water, the songs we sing, and the *jarjum* cheering him on.'

Birrabunji stops in front of Birri and says, 'And that's why in our language, the word we use for dolphin is …'

He points at the young fella, who yells, 'Gowonda.'

Birrabunji sits. Children clap and story time finishes.

Later, most of the kids are asleep, using dingoes as a pillow or a blanket. Narn, doesn't say much, just dishes out the odd smile, the kind you offer in an elevator when you accidentally make eye contact.

'Narn,' I say, using Tarni's help to chat to him, 'how did you learn to call the dolphins?'

He draws circles in the sand with his little finger. And it's obvious my protector doesn't want to talk.

As I shrug off my disappointment, he speaks and Tarni repeats in English: 'The previous dolphin singer, Birrabunji's first-born, had passed.'

I lean in. You'd never guess he was the powerful singer from this morning.

His eyes stay on the sand. 'I was trained by my dad,' and Tarni makes it easy to converse with him.

'Is Birrabunji your father?'

He nods. 'He used to be the dolphin singer, before my brother and me.' Even though I wouldn't understand him without Tarni, Narn's voice is so quiet, his words are whisked away by the breeze.

The three of us stare as the flames glide over its embers. The singer may be quiet, but he's answered more questions than Tarni.

Narn's deep voice crackles like the fire, and I wait for Tarni to interpret. 'Where did you come from again?'

How do I explain? One minute I was surfing, then I was here. I rub the tension out of my neck. 'I'm from the Gold Coast.'

He scowls and mutters and Tarni says, 'He said, "Never heard of it."'

My eye twitches. 'Where am I?'

'Wallulljagun.'

Wallull – what? Where the heck is that?

It's been a long, chaotic day. My eyes and head are sore. It's easier to deal with the pain if I curl up, close my eyes and attempt to relax. And ignore those weird wild animal cries and focus on the familiar sound of the waves. The fire crackles and a warm softness covers me. The faster I sleep, the faster tomorrow will wake me from this freaky dream.

CHAPTER 11
NARN

Flames leap along the thick branches of the fire. The women collected this wood before nightfall and the dance ceremonies. Orange and yellow flames stand proud, not blown about by the wind. I'm sitting, my eyes resting on the fire. And for the first time, the flames don't calm me. They should. I faced a pit of snakes and survived, and recovered in time to call our dolphins and gather their generous scaly gifts.

My insides writhe: Tarni's back and we haven't had a proper talk. We've been busy. Kirra arrives with N'gian's symbol marked on her flat, shiny canoe, which is made from something that no-one has seen before.

Now she's curled up not far from me, fast asleep on layers of *wudjuru*. And she'll be tired tomorrow from staying up half the night questioning common animal noises: 'What was that?' 'Did you hear that?' 'Is it getting closer?'

Once Kirra finally fell asleep, Tarni was no longer needed and bolted to her *ngumbin*. I was hoping she'd yarn with me, but it's clear Tarni only sat next to me to perform her new role for our unusual guest. Our clan's older members have scurried off to their *wudjuru*-covered homes as well. Even the mothers, who were yarning on the other side of the fire and watching their sleeping children, are now snoring. Kirra shivers and she snuggles back under the possum-skin cloak Tarni lent her.

Granny Alkira offered to look after our clan's guest. She's sleeping next to Kirra. And Tarni's Aunty Marlee is here tending Granny Alkira. Half the clan is snoozing under the stars caring for loved ones. Dad nominated me to keep watch tonight, which includes protecting everyone around our shared fire. Ears are listening. Eyes are alert. No idea if there's a traitor, but there'll be no missing women on my guard. I glance over to where Tarni's sleeping.

My almost-but-failed promised one is a few spear-lengths away in her bark home with all the unmarried women. Her father, Minjarra, our powerful and proud hunter-Elder, is still away on his secret business. Business that may ruin my life.

Thought I'd have a chance to prove myself. But being the son of a wise and well-respected Elder doesn't mean much to Minjarra. Every time I hunt with him, I'm not fast enough, quiet enough nor good enough in any way.

A lot has happened before Kirra arrived that Tarni and I need to discuss: snake pits ... possible promises of joining ceremonies. There's no string around her little finger. It was the first thing I checked.

My left leg twitches as though it's battling my frustrations.

'What you thinking, Narn?' Granny Alkira sits and sips some water.

I remember my snake-pit vow – never tell a lie – well, not an obvious one. 'Minjarra. He's been gone a long time ... Left Tarni alone.'

'My granddaughter is only ever alone if she chooses. She's got plenty of family around here.' She swishes her arm at the sleeping bodies. 'Is that what you're really frowning at?'

I shrug, then add more wood to the fire, careful not to disturb the tall wooden structures that store wrapped smoked fish and other food, high off the ground so the dingoes don't help themselves to a midnight snack. Some of the women have been drying and smoking these fish all day in a hollow tree trunk.

When I sit again, I'm relieved Tarni's granny has nodded back to sleep.

'I'm not asleep, just giving my eyelids a rest.'

'You should sleep; the sun won't rise for a long time.'

'At my age, I sleep when I can and wake when I can. Simple – I'm not going to fight an incoming tide.'

I hold in a chuckle. She sure is related to Tarni.

'You heard why Minjarra left?'

A 'yeah' sighs out, deflating me of purpose and possibility.

'Tarni's promised to Jiemba and his evil family.'

She rolls over, and that heaviness thuds back on. 'What?'

How can she fall asleep that quick? 'Granny – who's Jiemba? Who's his family?'

I'm tempted to shake her, but she answers with her back to me. 'His mother was a good woman, a keeper of N'gian magic. It was terrible when she passed. Not as terrible as who Jiemba's father has become ...'

I suck in a quick breath, in case what she says snatches it from me.

'... the Malung.'

'No, that's a ghost story to keep *jarjum* from wandering at night or going in forbidden caves,' I say, thinking they're too young to read those warning paintings on the rocks at the mountain's boundaries. Paintings of people with giant lumps covering their bodies. It's there the Malung remains trapped.

I cringe when I remember when Wanjellah first showed me them. On that empty mountain track, a much younger, tormenting Wanjellah screeched the Malung's last known words at me: *I will escape. I will return. A rock cannot hold me forever.* And I left him there and sprinted all the way home. That same eeriness creaks inside me again.

'Granny Alkira' – I call her Granny out of respect and not because we're related – 'how did he escape? And how can a spirit become a man?'

But she snores again. A soft *phuff-phuff-phuff, phuff-phuff-phuff* fills the air.

I don't know what to do. Tarni's the only one I've loved, and I'd hoped she could learn to love me too. My shoulders slump into the shape of a dome *ngumbin*. I add more wood to the fire and bright flames swarm the dry branches. Do coincidences exist or does life just happen in spite of what I want?

A yawn takes over my body, followed by two more. I've stayed awake through the night stoking the fire, and as the darkness invites the new day, my duty is over. Blinking open my sagging eyes, I drag myself away to grab a few hours of sleep. Ducking my head under our bark shelter, I remember when I was short enough to stroll right in. Now I have to hunch to get through the entrance.

'Narn?'

I can tell Dad wants to yarn, but I haven't come here to talk. I need a quick nap before I find Tarni. Not that I'd ever say that to Dad. Who would? A grind-stone-like pressure thuds onto my chest as I tell my foggy mind to come up with a plan.

I let out a loud, long yawn. 'Yes?' And hope he gets the hint.

'Where's Kirra?'

I rub my eyes and another yawn escapes. 'Still sleeping. I left Birri there to keep an eye on her.'

Tarni's voice is nearby, and I step towards the opening. I'm desperate to talk to her. Sleep can wait.

Dad grins. 'Where you going in such a big hurry?'

'To talk to Tarni. We haven't spoken since she got back.' And I mumble, 'From what I've heard, there's a lot to catch up on.'

He nods but has other plans for me. 'First you need to take Kirra's flat canoe and hide it in the sea cave.'

'Why?'

My head drops. I should know better than to question him.

'That symbol is N'gian's. You need to hide it, while the tide is at its lowest. Don't forget, not everyone is N'gian's friend these days, especially after what Tarni discovered.'

'What did she –'

He gives me a look, and I know there's no use fighting it. I race off with the shiny, smooth flat canoe, which is lighter than it looks. The quicker I do this, the quicker I'll see Tarni. My toes touch the chilly water. I forgot *dugan djulung waring gwong* happened yesterday.

The ocean is a glassy lake, making my task easier. I check the beach and headland are clear before I swim across the water, dragging Kirra's canoe behind me. I reach the columns of rock and hover at the surface. Below me, the sea cave's entrance is hidden by the dark ocean. This sacred site is now guarded by two – the previous and the present – dolphin callers.

I pull Kirra's canoe beneath the surface, but it pops up. With Kirra's buoyant canoe, Dad's request is going to be more difficult than I'd realised. The tide's at its lowest. I need to move fast – can't miss this opportunity. I fill my lungs with air and swim along the columns of rock, hauling the canoe deep enough to scrape it through the sea cave's entrance.

Heaving and spluttering, I sit on the flat rock inside the cave thankful I made it. Inside the dark basalt walls are blurs of thin white lines marking the high tide level. A sliver of light from the headland reaches into the cave.

Birrabunji's contradictions are confusing. First, he didn't want me to come here. Next thing, he demands I return to stash Kirra's flat canoe high above the salty white lines. My fingers run over the symbol she's drawn, then over the etchings on the cave wall.

It's identical.

How is this N'gian's symbol? I thought N'gian was a famous cleverman who'd died years ago. Maybe he never died or he's come back from the spirit realm.

Standing and staring, I'm hoping for a revelation to jump out and jab me in the face. Tarni said 'N'gian' means 'sun' in one of our neighbouring tribe's languages. Tarni's mother's mother came from there. Dad says that there's always layers of hidden messages, but I only see two things: a sun and a wave.

Maybe there's no secret message. Though my instincts tell me differently. This N'gian sign is important, even dangerous. And I don't know why.

What did Tarni discover that's got Dad making me hide this unnatural canoe?

A good reason to talk to Tarni.

I chew the inside of my cheek. I need to prove she can trust me.

She's right, if we ever stand a chance, I need to be completely honest with her. About anything she wants to know. I'll tell Tarni my two vows with Dad: the first one before I was initiated, when we planted the *midyim* together. And the recent one, when I found out about N'gian's symbol in this cave. Dad said two people in our tribe have drawn it. Tarni and someone else.

What's the worst that could happen for breaking my vow? A few spear holes in my leg.

I remember talking to Tarni when we were younger. I was showing off and said, 'I'll sing a dolphin in for you.'

She replied, 'But would you kill a shark for me?'

At the time, I was confused. I never understood females. Wasn't singing to a dolphin far better than killing a shark? I thought women wanted men to make them feel special.

Now I understand. Fighting for her shows love. And real love is protecting her from a shark, the one that's circling her, ready to attack. Doing that shows more love than impressing her with my dolphin song.

I suck in air and relax my muscles. Not because I have to time my dive and hold my breath long enough to leave this underwater cave but because I need courage. Courage to hunt a shark. A shark called *Jiemba*.

CHAPTER 12
TARNI

The sun's been up for some time, and Kirra's the last to wake – strange behaviour for a guest. She yawns and stretches. I'm helping my cousins smoke fish in the hollow tree not far from last night's gathering at the edge of our *bora*, while I wait for our sleepy visitor. Been keeping busy to stop thinking about the Elders' decision, but it's not working. Need an excuse to get away.

'*Jingi wahlu*, Kirra,' Birri says, sitting next to the girl the waves brought in.

Kirra staggers to her feet and Birri follows her. 'I'm still here? This isn't a stinkin' dream?'

The wind carries her words, and everyone can hear: 'Tarni. Where's Taaarniii?'

Doesn't matter how slow or loud Kirra speaks, my little cousin won't understand. I swipe some fish, wrap it in a leaf, grab my roo-skin water carrier, and hurry over. Young fella has been minding our guest all morning.

Kirra sits under a grove of *jambinbin* with her knees tucked under her chin. When Birri sees me, he scampers to the nearest aunty cooking food over the fire. Kirra's eyes are shut. Both hands grip her head.

I touch her shoulder. 'Kirra? Were you looking for me?'

She opens one eye, then groans and buries her face back into her hands.

I crouch next to her. 'What's wrong?'

'Need to leave *Wullull*-something. Gotta see Nan. My head aches. Lost my contacts surfing yesterday. Left my glasses at home.' She grips her belly ready to heave.

I'm too busy weeding her words to say anything.

'My eyes are blurry. My head hurts. And I can't see.' Her face turns *nyulli* pink from the force of her voice.

I hand her the smoked fish wrapped in a leaf to calm her, and realise her pain could benefit us both. 'Eat first. Then, we will go to Nungarrii.'

While she gobbles the fish and washes it down with water, I tug handfuls of leaves growing along the vine-covered dunes. Then pull Kirra to her feet and lead her back to our gathering place.

'Where are we going?' she says, walking with one eye open.

'To see a healer. I will get food for our journey.'

'Journey? How far are we walking? Doubt this healer can fix me unless an optometrist lives in the middle of nowhere.'

I don't have time to explain, so I sit Kirra near the fire, next to Birri, scorch the leaves over the flames. Then I give Birri his instructions, because I need permission from Granny Alkira to see the healer from the rainforest clan.

'Wait, what did you tell him?'

'When it blisters, take it off the fire. After it cools, he'll place it on your forehead. It will ease your pain. I will be back soon.'

'You can't leave, Tarni. You're the only one who understands me.'

'Don't worry,' I say in my calmest voice, even though her questions are wait-a-while vines that hook in and never let go. 'Birri will take you to the small creek and I'll gather supplies and meet you there.'

'Tarni, wait. You're leaving me with a little kid?'

Birri passes Kirra more food and I race away. He's a helpful *jarjum*.

Granny Alkira said not to go far but to use medicinal herbs nearby. Our rainforest clan is within our boundaries; we're the same tribe. And I was careful not to get too specific – to stay truthful but still do what I need to do. With all the strange things going on, I need to find Mum or at least ask our rainforest relatives to make sure she's alright.

Birri's chatting in the distance, leading Kirra away from the beach and into the shadows of the rainforest.

'Birri? Birri? Where are you going? What are you doing? Don't leave me.' Our guest's voice chases the birds out of their homes and into the sky.

Although Birri listens well, he's easily distracted – probably following something up the creek. And he's left Kirra sitting alone.

'Kirra, I'm here. We will journey to our neighbouring clan in the rainforest,' I say, thankful no-one can understand her language.

The further inland we walk, the cooler it gets and the heavier the rain falls. If Kirra wasn't wearing the possum-skin cloak I gave her yesterday, she'd be drenched and shivering. A whipbird calls, its partner responds from the green undergrowth, and the creek along the rainforest floor turns from a trickle into gushing waterfalls.

Though the rain stops, walking with Kirra is a slow process. She looks young and agile, but the soles of her feet are newborn-soft. Her ankles don't seem strong either, as if she's been carried everywhere in her life. Then there's her weak eyes. I must lead her around vines, mossy rocks and everything else.

I fight the urge to sprint along the creek and hop from rock to rock. I could do it with my eyes closed. Kirra is different from any girl I've met. It's not just her clothes or hair or skin colour.

'You reckon it's gonna rain again?'

I ignore her — doesn't make a difference.

'Tell me it's close. We almost there? Didn't get much sleep last night,' Kirra says, unaware of the spiky vine I steer her past that would've clung to her soft skin.

'Less talk, more walk,' I grunt. If her legs were as fast as her lips, we'd be there already. I wish Alba could understand Kirra, then I wouldn't have to deal with her whinging and not sound so bossy. Alba would handle all of that, so I could get my job done proper-like.

'Sorry,' Kirra says, and we trudge along surrounded by the songs of the rainforest and the creek gaining speed.

About fifty steps later, Kirra asks, 'How do you know this healer?'

I ignore my twinging muscles — slowed by another question — and say, 'She's from my mother's clan — my mum's cousin — and was given magic from the most powerful magicman that ever lived.'

'Magicman?'

'You know, cleverman. Spiritual loreman?'

Kirra nods, a frown crowds her face. 'Why are you whispering? What's wrong?'

'We could be in danger. We're too slow. I want to reach the boundary of my mother's clan before nightfall.'

'Danger? Does anyone know we're out here?'

'Granny Alkira gave us permission.' I throw the words out quick to hide that I sort of got approval. And a tightness wraps around my chest, as we leave our clan's borders.

Can truth be stretched? She didn't say which borders: our tribe's or our clan's.

'What happens if we don't reach there before dark?'

'Shoosh,' I say, and I pull her along faster.

Granny Alkira also said Kirra passed their tests but the Elders are waiting and watching for more confirmation: whether she's sent by N'gian or the Malung. His name makes me shudder. I'm out here alone with her. What if the shadow-spirit sent her?

Kirra grips my shoulder and I jump a little. Determined to quicken our pace, we walk along the edge of the creek towards the base of the mountain. At first, small drips splatter, then rain pummels everything. Normal, for the end of the wet season. Days are shorter and cooler. Squelchy thick mud is trickier for Kirra, and we've already stopped more times than I can count for rests, drinks, food and questions. Kirra claims to be from a saltwater clan, near mountains and rainforests, yet she acts like she's grown up in the open plains.

My gut tells me it's more than that. We learn from watching and listening. For Kirra, questions seem to be how she learns. Lots of them, pelting me more than this heavy rain.

The Elders' decision could take days. I thought this distraction would be good. Now I'm not sure. I must take Kirra to Nungarrii, get her eyes healed and be back at the beach in a couple of days. At this rate, it'll be weeks.

I yank Kirra's arm again. 'Move faster.'

She pulls back. 'I need to stop.'

'You told me you climbed a mountain.'

Kirra's got one hand on her side, panting. 'Not like this.'

'It's tricky for old people and little ones to climb through vines on a steep incline. And this is a small journey.' I want to say she's old enough to be joined and ask how she managed in her last tribe. I know her sight is bad. But if it were me, I'd be jogging, not plodding.

'Kirra. You need to try harder. We can't stop every few steps.' Birds dart away, no doubt other animals too, and I'm thankful my father, the hunter-Elder, isn't here to witness this.

She swipes away my hand, and yells, 'With no glasses and the rain stinging my eyes, I can't see!' Kirra rubs her eyes, then clutches my cloak again.

We shuffle through the rainforest at the speed of a baby snail who ran out of slime. A hundred questions later, we reach the shared corridor. A path many tribes use without going through ceremonial greetings. It leads to and from other neighbouring tribes, and allows you to pass other territories. Every three years many tribes use the main corridor to go to the *buhnyi buhnyi* festival, but this one is used mainly by the rainforest clan, beach clan and some of the inland clans. And this time of year, it's usually empty.

Darkness is coming. We will need to find shelter and prepare for nightfall. A few more steps and I should see the waterfall flowing from the mountain and feeding into the creek. It marks the boundary of my mother's people, the land of the rainforest's clan. I find the section that's easy to cross. There's movement further up the creek, near the cascading water. It's the silhouette of a woman.

Don't want to give anyone a fright this close to nightfall. I whistle to let the person know we're here: two long sounds, a short high one, followed by another long low one, like Mum taught me for when we meet in secret, so everyone in Father's clan will still believe she's dead.

'Who's there?' the woman says, her voice a little too high.

'It's me, Tarni, daughter of Merindah.'

She steps into the open.

'Nyrah.' My tone delivers an I'm-so-relieved-to-see-you quality.

My cousin's dark curly hair bounces on her shoulders when she moves. She not as tall as me, but way taller than Alba.

'Jingi wahlu, Tarni.' Her voice returns to normal. She gives me a small squeeze, then faces Kirra. Nyrah's bright brown eyes match her shiny dimpled smile. *'Jingi wahlu. Ngulungmal waringan gahla.'*

I explain Kirra speaks another language by using it. 'Yes, Nyrah, it will get cool. This is Kirra. Nyrah is joined with Narn's older brother Wanjellah.'

Nyrah checks behind, then hugs Kirra. 'Welcome, Kirra. Any friend of Tarni and Narn is our friend too.'

'Wait, how can she speak my language?' Kirra's eyes bounce from mine to Nyrah's.

My cousin shoots me a does-she-know? glance before answering, 'We are from the same people, it's a part of our –'

'Skills,' I quickly answer. 'She's a cousin from my mother's clan. I'll explain later.'

I'm ready for Kirra's onslaught of questions.

Instead she only asks, 'Narn has an older brother?'

'Wanjellah and Narn became brothers when they went through initiation,' I reply.

Nyrah is fidgety, glances behind for the third time. 'I'm sorry but I've got to keep moving to our new camp.'

'We came to see Nungarrii. Kirra needs her help.'

'Is your Granny Alkira alright? She's a good healer.'

'Yes,' I say, slowly figuring out how to word it right. 'She may need special magic for this one, and I wanted to check on the healer's helper too.'

'Well, Wanjellah has gone to get Nungarrii. When they return, she'll be able to tell you about the woman you seek.' Nyrah moves through the forest, every foot and hand finding the best spot to pass easily. We follow behind until we reach a *gunyah*, and I'm thankful the rain has eased.

'Tarni, Kirra, come sit. I'll start the fire and make some tea.'

We sit at the open entrance and Nyrah lights the small fire. She moves quickly, filling a piccabeen basket with water and herbs – it's shaped like our bark canoes with the ends of the basket folded and tied together with string. Nyrah places it on the fire. The water will always boil before the basket could ever ignite. A lemony scent fills the air and will soon warm our bellies.

After we've had tea, food and more tea, Kirra lies down, wrapped in Mum's fur with her hands covering her eyes.

'How's Narn these days?' Nyrah's eyes have a twinkle I wish I could dim.

I pretend she isn't hinting at anything, and I'm thankful she's not talking in Kirra's language.

'Wanjellah will want to know how his little brother is.'

'You know Narn, he's always around his dolphins. Sometimes, I think he prefers their company to mine – ours, I mean – people's.'

My cousin's expression tells me she knows what I'm talking about. 'Wanjellah was the same. Thought he only talked to me because we watched and protected the western shared corridor around the forbidden place.'

'How did you know he loved you?' I lean in and whisper, 'In the joining kind of way. Not just told you the words but you knew he meant it and would live by it for the rest of his life.'

I ignore her enormous grin, her giggling about Narn confessing his love, and focus on her explanation: 'Those two fellas are alike. It's in the little things.'

I steady my voice – don't want to sound too eager. 'Little things?'

'Does he show up in places you are?' Nyrah asks.

'He always has a good reason …' My voice drifts off with my thoughts. Does he? It's hard to tell because, back home, Narn is everywhere I go.

'They always have good reasons.' Nyrah shifts position. 'But does he show up unexpectedly, and when you think about it, it makes no sense?'

I grapple with her words. 'Nyrah?' I'm quiet in my approach. 'You know when we're promised to be joined, our granny or female relative, who's an Elder, weaves the string and wraps it around our little finger?'

'Uh-huh,' she says, and there's no teasing or giggling now.

'You ever heard of anyone being joined without that happening?'

'Never. Why?'

I'm about to answer, when Kirra sits up and rambles in one long breath, 'Had the weirdest dream someone dies and he ties a boomerang to his side – so, did I miss anything?'

'Nothing,' I say, careful to use her language. 'We better go make camp.' And I ignore her dream nonsense. Everyone has dreams. No need to blabber on about them.

'You two want to stay the night?' Nyrah switches language so Kirra understands.

'Thanks, but what about Wanjellah?'

'He'll probably return tomorrow. Like I said, he's gone to find Nungarrii and bring her back. And that's who you want to see anyway.'

I scan Nyrah. 'Are you sick?'

'Wanjellah worries too much.' She lifts her fur coverings and a strange red rash is across her skin.

'Never seen this kind of a rash. Have you?' I say, staring at her.

She drops her head. 'My father had this, then large lumps on his arms and legs. He said it was from the evil lurking deep underground in that forbidden cave. But it was his duty to guard that place. That duty passed to me.'

'Nyrah. We know how –' I can't finish, it's too sad to say aloud.

'What's wrong?' Kirra asks.

'Nyrah's father died with a strange sickness, which started with rashes.' I turn to Nyrah and place my hand on her back. 'Nungarrii will know how to fix it.'

What else can I say or do to make Nyrah feel better? This ends our conversation, and we prepare for sleep. Should've listened to Granny Alkira.

No men. No weapons. No way I can sleep.

Nyrah, Kirra and I wake to a warm morning sun, mindful that those distant rainclouds will soon be on us. Wanjellah rushes towards us. His hair is longer. It's kept off his face with a long piece of woven string that's wrapped around his head. Emu feathers dangle from his wavy hair. He's filled out. Ignoring us, he grabs spears, boomerangs, axes from a hollow tree, while he speaks in quiet phrases. I would've slept with one of those weapons last night had I known.

'Nyrah. Pack up. Time to go.' Wanjellah's speaking in our language, the one Kirra calls Yugambeh. 'You got to go, Tarni,' he says, then towers over Kirra. 'Who are *you*?'

She stares at me, waits for me to interpret.

But Nyrah jumps in front of him, her red skin obvious now, and I don't know how I missed it yesterday. 'Wanjellah, don't be so rude. This is Kirra. She's Tarni's friend.'

He steps around her.

'Did you even say hello to your brother's *friend*?'

The way Nyrah says 'friend' makes my cheeks feel like ants are scurrying over them.

He stops. 'Hello, Tarni, sorry, I'm not being rude. I'm in a hurry, even though my wife thinks politeness is more important than staying alive.'

Nyrah's staring at him. 'What?'

Wanjellah places both hands on her shoulders. 'We need to go!'

It's awkward. I look at Kirra and mutter, 'I'll explain later.' Then say to Narn's rude brother, 'Sorry, Wanjellah. We'll leave. Just came to see Nungarrii and ... and ... check on my mother.'

Wanjellah glares at me. 'Your mother's been dead since you were little. Everyone knows this.' And he's right. The rainforest clan vowed never to say her name or reveal she's alive.

'Wanjellah!' Nyrah slaps him on his left shoulder, the one decorated with rows of raised straight scars. Narn has similar markings on his same shoulder. And instead of thinking of Mum, I'm remembering when charcoal filled Narn's wounds on the top of his muscular arm.

'They are no more,' Wanjellah says, still staring at me. He ties a boomerang to his side.

'Where's Nung –'

'Do not say her name.' He's in my face with nostrils flaring. 'She's dead.'

My tongue is lifeless and dry. 'What about Mum – I mean, the woman who helps the healer, the one I meet every season when the humpback whales return with their young?' I say it the way Mum taught me, to get information without exposing who she is. 'Where is she?'

'Been missing a while.' I hear it in his voice. Danger. Like when an animal senses it's being hunted and is skittish. 'But the healer's remains,' he clears his throat, 'were placed in the sacred spot early this morning. Nyrah, let's go. I still need to find you another healer.' He turns back to us. 'You two should leave. It's dangerous. Tell Birrabunji an evilness is killing N'gian healers.'

Wanjellah scurries into the bush, his back burdened with water and weapons and worries.

Narn said there's a traitor in our tribe. Maybe it's not Dad, because he wouldn't kill a healer ... would he?

Nyrah squeezes my arm; her eyes are moist with sorrow. 'Sorry. I must go. Never seen him like this. Take care, Tarni. If we find our other healer or the one you're worried about, we'll send word.' She hugs me, then gives Kirra a quick embrace. 'Keep safe.' My cousin bolts away and rain drenches us again.

Nungarrii is dead.

I gulp back tears. Mum may be dead too. We're not safe. My impatience destroys my level-headedness. Should've listened to my Elder. Kirra leans on me, we shuffle towards the corridor and retrace our tracks. This time I answer every question about Wanjellah and the healer. A heaviness presses in.

'We've got to hurry.' I grunt as we clamber up the hill.

Kirra complains less today, even though she moves with her eyes squeezed shut. I'm on all fours, clawing our way through the thick mud to the top of a slope, with Kirra tugging on my back.

In one blink, she shifts backwards and stumbles before I can grab her, trips over a rock and crashes on the ground. She groans and her hands no longer shield her eyes.

I scramble to her. 'What hurts?' After pestering her to move faster, I'm in brown sludge comforting her.

Tears camouflaged by raindrops roll down her wet cheeks. She looks young, innocent, and there's a thickening in my throat but I must stay tough or we'll never make it. We're not even halfway up the mountain which will get us back on the shared track.

Kirra's covered in mud. I wrap her arm around my neck and ask, 'Can you walk?'

She shifts her weight slightly and moans but convinces me she'll be alright. The rain pounds heavier. The sun isn't descending, yet desperation and darkness press in. Unable to wipe my eyes, I blink away the heavy rain that stings my face.

I should feel sorry for Kirra. She falls again and slumps against a large, slippery boulder.

'What's wrong with you?'

Kirra's eyes stare at the slushy ground. 'Sorry,' she mumbles. Then as quickly as she thudded down the hill, she snaps. 'I told you before we climbed this *gunang* hill, I needed a rest. If you'd listened to me, *this*,' and she points to her mud-covered body, 'wouldn't have happened.'

'Needed a rest?' I sneer. 'All you have done is rest since you came here. Rest and whinge. Because you are weak. Our grannies walk faster than you. Start. Stop. Start. Stop. You know that makes you more tired and your legs ache worse? You should walk at a steady rate.' I throw my head back, and yell into the heavy downpour. 'Arrgh!'

She looks confused. And I don't really care. I can't tell if I'm speaking her language or mine.

I slouch against a slippery log away from Kirra to let my anger dissipate. We need to find shelter, and I can't carry her all the way.

She thinks I don't know she's been crying. 'Kirra.' My voice has lost its strength. 'We need to find shelter.'

'Shelter? I need an optometrist. No, what I really need is to go home.'

I ignore her useless words, wrap her arms around my neck and trudge upwards. Every muscle aches. I struggle to breathe, her body presses me further into the thick muck. Little by little, we edge our way forward, stop every few steps to try different techniques while the rain hammers our soggy bodies. Kirra drapes her arms across my side, but the slope of the mountain works against us. The light is fading, our rainforest darkens, yet one thing is consistent: the torrential downpour.

It's hopeless. I can't guide Kirra and collect food and water, much less carry her all the way home to the beach.

I release my grip. 'It is almost night. We have to find shelter and make camp.'

Kirra steadies herself. 'Okay.'

I point to an overhanging rock further around the mountain. It's no cave, but it's better than nothing. 'We will camp there.'

No-one knows we're here.

No, Narn, I'm not the cleverest.

CHAPTER 13
KIRRA

Later, we sit around the warm fire Tarni has made and stare into the dancing flames. There's no conversation. I said sorry. Tarni did too. I'm not sure she meant it, but at least she's trying.

'Kirra, how is your headache?' She sounds patronising.

'Fine.' I slam the word into her, before remembering I rely on my translator. 'Better now that I can rest,' I say in a softer, more tactful tone.

'Better is good.'

A joke might change the vibe, so I say, 'At least it made me forget about being hungry.'

Tarni doesn't laugh or smile. 'I am sorry, Kirra. I should be more patient,' and her apology seems genuine this time.

'It wasn't your fault. Nan says, "Things just happen. You got to look for the good in a bad situation and focus on that."'

'Good water,' Tarni says, has a swig, then passes it to me.

I gulp a few mouthfuls and pass it back.

'Good fire,' I say, pick up a twig and aim for the flames. It totally misses. We giggle for no good reason and can't stop. It feels great to belly-laugh.

Tarni shuffles back to lean against the granite, and changes the topic. 'Do you speak any other languages?'

'No, just one,' I reply. 'How can you speak English?'

Tarni stretches out her legs. Peers at me as if she's sussing me out.

'You heard of N'gian?'

'The symbol I drew on my surfboard, you called it N'gian's symbol. I sometimes have dreams that come true. That symbol was in one of them and why I drew it on my board.'

I grab a twig, dip it into mud and draw N'gian's symbol on the rock behind me. 'I think this led me here.'

'Kirra, you dreamt about someone dying, and a fella tying a boomerang around his middle. Wanjellah did that. It came true.' Tarni's speech slows and her eyes light up. 'N'gian's gifted you with truth dreaming or future seeing.'

'Okaaay,' I say, and thought I'd be more excited, 'cos she's the first person who's believed my dreams come true. Tarni doesn't notice my hesitation to continue this conversation, 'cos 'truth dreaming' hasn't helped anyone.

'This proves you're N'gian's helper and not the shadow-spirit's spy. I need to tell the Elders, because this could shift the balance. We should've never left the beach. You could be stolen like those missing women Narn warned me about.' Tarni's panic is contagious.

She's hyperventilating.

'Breathe with me,' I say. 'In through the nose for one, two, three, four. Hold for one, two, three, four. Now out

110

through your mouth for one, two, three, four.' We do this a few times 'til she settles the hell down. 'Better?'

Tarni nods, takes a sip of water, then says, 'My aunty, Mum's cousin, the one who passed, was a great healer. She'd been given more than one gift. I thought she could restore your sight. Now I don't know what to do.'

'I don't get it. How can I be a spy when I've never heard of a shadow-spirit. And what missing women?' A clanking gets louder and louder in my chest, too loud to be my heartbeat.

'I'll smuggle you back to the Elders at first light,' she says, and I don't want her — nor me — having a panic attack, so I redirect the conversation away from spies and balance-shifters.

'Tell me more about this N'gian fella.'

'My grandfather's grandfather's grandfather passed down the story of N'gian, the great spirit who came down from the sun to walk with the people and live among the animals and trees and things he loved looking on. Clans along the coast, in the rainforest, and further in the sandy soil countries were all intrigued by this glowing man, N'gian.'

I absorb every word, and Tarni adds a little flair the way Birrabunji does: 'The people loved him. He was thought to be one of the greatest clevermen to have ever lived. They brought him the sick and he healed them. They came with problems and he solved them. But when the people came to see his power, N'gian surprised them. He wanted to share it. He gave different ones little parcels of his power to help with their natural abilities.'

She wavers a little, so I give her an encouraging smile.

'Well, N'gian gave me a gift. Mum thinks I'm the youngest to receive one. She has it also. Ours can unweave languages, so we can understand and speak others.'

Tarni pauses. Normally, I'd fill this gap with questions, but her gift is blitzing my mind.

'I think N'gian shares his power with those who share his purpose, you know? Those who want to use it to help others. I don't think it works if you want the power for yourself.'

She leans in and whispers. 'It's dangerous to talk about N'gian, especially if he has given you his magic. There's another who hates him and is trying to stop him, his followers and his magical gifts.'

'I believe you,' I say. Don't know why I said that. My brain is questioning but my instinct isn't.

'I wasn't going to tell you, but my future husband is in a clan that hates N'gian.'

'What?'

'That is the reason I left with you. The Elders are deciding my fate … whether I'm to be joined to Jiemba.' She shivers, and a cool breeze drifts around us.

I tug the fur tighter.

'When I was a little girl, my father promised me to Jiemba's parents. Only met Jiemba once. Thought he was evil then.' Tarni dry retches, then stuffs her fist across her mouth, probably to stop her hurling.

'Why? What happened?' I lean forward. 'Pleeeassse tell me. I promise I won't tell anyone. No-one understands me, anyway.'

I feel closer to Tarni. With our N'gian gifts, we're connected.

She guzzles more water. 'When I first met Jiemba, I had night terrors for a long time afterwards.'

The rain pours and our conversation flows.

'Birrabunji gave me *nguran*, a dingo. Was his way of thanking me for helping Narn after his accident. You see, Narn almost died. People call him empty-headed because of it. Not when his dad Birrabunji is around, because no-one's meant to discuss it. It was a beautiful golden pup.'

Listening to Tarni yarn is as relaxing as watching the flickering flames.

'I knew my father didn't like Narn. You haven't met Minjarra yet.'

I shake my head *no*, keen to hear more.

'So when he asked how I got the pup, I left out a few details. Said Birrabunji gave it to us. Well, my father thought it'd be the perfect gift for Jiemba. And what Father says, goes. No use fighting about it, so I took care of the pup until we gave it to Jiemba.'

I lean my back against the rock, close my eyes, and listen to the rise and fall of Tarni's voice.

'I wanted to name him but knew that was Jiemba's privilege. Father and I walked for many days and camped many nights. It was the longest journey I'd been on. We arrived at these giant trees – parts of the trunk had been used for a canoe, and carved patterns decorated this inner layer.'

A loud crack makes me wide-eyed. Tarni's snapping wood into smaller pieces and stacking them on the fire.

'We waited there until we were welcomed into Jiemba's country by the Elders of his clan. I hid behind my father for most of it. I was shy back then.'

'What happened to the pup?' I ask, wondering when we get to the 'Jiemba turns villain' part.

Tarni swallows more water, passes it to me, and I have a small drink.

'After we gave Jiemba the pup, he wasn't grateful.'

'Little *gunang*,' I mumble.

'You mean big, stinky *gunang*,' Tarni says, and we snigger.

'You know, first he seemed polite.' Her voice is super serious again. 'Thought he got bored with the pup and with me. Jiemba made an excuse to leave our fathers, so I ...' Instead of talking, Tarni stares through the fire.

'What? Tarni, what?'

'I followed him, crept through the long grass. He was playing with the pup.' She stiffens. 'A darkness covered his face like a shadow. And my body went numb.'

I sit taller, lean closer, urge her to spill everything.

'It was a look I'd never seen before and hope I never see again,' Tarni murmurs, then she inhales the longest breath and the truth gushes out. 'Jiemba picked up a huge rock. That poor pup didn't know what was about to happen. Neither did I.'

I swallow, worry baking the back of my throat. 'What happened, Tarni?'

'It gave the tiniest little yelp. And it was over.'

Tarni's fists are shaking, and a shiver ice-skates down my spine.

My friend's energy has been sucked away. Her scratchy voice kind of huffs out. 'I covered my mouth and bit my tongue so I wouldn't scream. I shut my eyes, but the thudding noise of rock hitting fur over and over and over made me curl up and cover my ears.'

What can I say? Her parents set her up with a psycho-killer.

'Every tribe knows the lore. We only kill animals to eat. And no-one kills a dingo pup for pleasure.'

Tarni chews her bottom lip and says, 'Blood pooled around its little limp body. My shaking wouldn't stop. I couldn't move.'

'Then what happened?' A tug-of-war of wanting and not wanting to know battles within.

Tarni rubs her hands over the fire. 'Jiemba got up, wiped his hands on his *tabbi-tabbi*. And he strolled over to the others, as if he'd woken from a nice afternoon nap.'

We stare at the fire; even the dripping rain stops to soak in the silence.

'I loved that pup. It would have made a perfect hunting dog … could've been my best friend.'

I massage my temples. 'I'm sorry, Tarni. Why don't you just say "no" or run away?'

'I'm hoping the Elders will say "no". And where would I run to? It's dangerous to leave your family. Life – one life – depends on the help of everyone else's.'

I don't understand lore here, so I ask, 'Does your father know about this?'

She nods. 'At the time, I cried and cried, then I dug a small hole with my hands and buried the pup. Don't think my father even noticed I'd been gone.'

'That's terrible.' I almost yell over another sudden shower. 'I thought I had dad-problems, but mine are nothing compared to yours.'

'That little pup didn't live long enough to get a name, and that's the man I'm meant to be joined with.'

The wood turns to pulsing embers, and as the flames dwindle, so does our conversation.

Eventually I say, 'I'm sorry about your dad. Mine's not as bad as yours. He'll never force me to marry anyone – just doesn't want anything to do with me. When my brother and mother died, it's like his love died with them.'

'I'm sorry about your mother and brother … and your dad,' Tarni says in a way that shows we have a new respect for each other. The rain eases and the nocturnal animals howl and screech and chirp and flap. Reckon it'll be another sleepless night.

'Am I late for school? Five more minutes,' I say refusing to open my eyes, hoping Nan will stop shaking my arm. Her grip tightens.

'Wake up. Got to move now,' she whisper-growls.

My heavy eyelids open. 'Tarni?'

'Don't talk.'

How the heck did I fall asleep under a rock ledge on the side of a mountain? I blink at the blurry view. Right on cue, my head throbs, pain is screaming between my temples, echoing through my skull. My fingertips automatically massage the pain in small circular movements. Not a great start to the day.

'Tarni?'

'Shoosh!' She looks like she's gonna crack me in the head if I make another noise. And her whisper is quieter than mine.

'Men are on the track.'

Tarni slips the dillybag over her shoulder. I roll the possum-skin cloak up and tie it 'round my waist, the way she showed me.

'You think they killed Nung –'

She slaps her hand around my mouth and my face stings a little. 'You can't say her name this close after death. Call her "the healer".'

I nod, letting this new lore sink in, and give myself a mental uppercut 'cos I always seem to say the wrong thing.

Tarni checks the track, then lays her head on the ground. My foot slips and when I regain balance, a few pebbles scamper down the hill. I freeze, not wanting to cause a landslide and give away our position. My interpreter signals and I hook my arm into hers, as we scramble from our hidden overhanging rock and onto the shared track in the valley.

Tarni stops abruptly and I slam into her. Before I can apologise, I see them too. Tall, well-built men surround us; their dark brown faces are covered with red ochre. All have long spears pointing at us with their sharpened barbs.

A string of words spray out of their mouths like a verbal machine gun. They jab our backs with the wooden spear handles.

Tarni's hands are two stop signs in the air. I copy. She screeches the same words over and over, which I don't understand.

The tallest hunter bellows. I scowl at him, then at Tarni. Her eight words stop my questions.

'N'gian symbol. N'gian followers. The penalty is death.'

CHAPTER 14
NARN

Rain never bothered me before. I'd get on with it whether it poured or not. Today it's annoying. Slows every step, every thought.

Why am I out here? One reason.

Tarni.

She left with Kirra two days ago. Did I learn anything from the snake pit? Nah, I'm living up to that empty-headed name again.

After all, I'd be out here if Kirra were lost, but if I were honest, it'd only be to please Birrabunji. In the end, it doesn't matter what secrets you keep or tell – can't please everyone. Still, I'm determined to make things right with Tarni. Problem is, I'm not sure if they aren't right, which makes me as irritated as a canoe-swallowing sea.

I'm at the edge of our western boundary, where the rainforest meets the mountains, the one with large yellow-ochred boulders at its base. The night-fire stories our old people share and the songs we dance to give us knowledge of our country, its landscape, and our boundaries. I hum the song, and a musical map in my head navigates me through.

Around the creek, through the rainforest and towards the yellow-rock mountain, I walk where the ancient giant once filled his stomach with dark, sweet gooiness before he fell asleep.

My stomach grumbles and I lick my dry lips when I think about *gudge* that our friendly bees make. I'm about half a day behind Tarni and Kirra, so I hurry to Tarni's mother's country.

The rain slows to a light sprinkle. The trees and branches drip while I power through the rainforest, following Birri's vague directions. Something doesn't feel right. And it's not being alone in the dark undergrowth with possible snake pits or, as Aunty Lowanna claims, that I attract trouble.

I launch over fallen trunks, evade thick vines and scoot around slippery boulders. Then I slow my stride, adjust the string around my waist, and pretend to collect something off the ground so I can spy behind. My skin prickles. A presence is watching and waiting while I walk through a fog of uneasiness.

Prey: hunted by a predator.

I lean back against the trunk of a towering pine and wrestle every urge to move except for my eyes. I glance left and right, up and down.

Why would someone be following me? Is it Birri? I'd have known by now. He can't keep quiet and would be bored before I'd reached the first creek-crossing. The rain stops and there's no wind.

Should've brought my spear or *jabir*. I'm too close to our outer boundary – could be outside it, and I'd be in trouble.

Think, Narn!

If I climb a tree, I'd be trapped. I should backtrack – draw them away from Tarni and Kirra, then hide somewhere with an easy escape. There's a sacred cave on the other side of the creek near our northern boundary – was taken there after I drowned.

N'gian's cave.

Birrabunji showed me its secret entrance when I was young, after I was healed there. If I knew I'd have needed it again, I'd have paid more attention.

I plod through the undergrowth and take a less direct route over rocks, under vines and around large fig trees. As I near the cave, I sprint through the mud. I stumble. Legs are covered in muck but I don't care. I jump up and run again. A yellow boulder is high above. It's the key to the position of the entrance. I glance over my shoulder and hope no-one sees me.

Birrabunji's story directs me as I scramble along a granite wall between rock and moss-green undergrowth. Both hands feel for the narrow opening. Both feet edge along the slippery ledge. I find it and pull myself inside. Then I step past a small circle of rocks that once held a fire. N'gian or someone has lived here. In one corner is a pile of gear: coolamon, fire sticks, grindstone, bark from the *wudjuru* and a woven bag. There's a spear tip – not attached to a spear – and no *jabir*, so nothing I can protect myself with.

We don't take someone's stashed tools – that'd be stealing. I could leave a small thank-you gift and borrow a tool or two ... if it belongs to someone living. But these things could be those gifts left for N'gian from long ago. That Malung had heard stories of N'gian and wanted the people to love him, follow him and bring him presents. His jealousy is why he hates N'gian and his followers.

Ignoring those old stories, I search for openings along the side that faces the rainforest. Two peepholes formed by gaps in the rock are in two different places in the cave. One on the ground. The other is high up on a rock-shaped platform, giving me the best vantage point. I'll spot anyone coming from the rainforest track towards the mountain.

Lying on my stomach, the cold hard rock's beneath me. Confident I'm not imagining things, I slow my breathing. My instincts are normally sharp, but I see nothing.

No movement.

I wait longer, as Dad taught me. Patience requires focus, strength and time – refusing to quit. Not willing to blink or scratch the mud itching my legs, I stare straight ahead. My stomach grumbles and although this cavern is dry, there's a distant dripping I'm tempted to investigate. Instead, I wait.

Was that a flit of movement?

I focus on the trees. Something blurs past. A tall, agile woman with grey hair moves like a sugar glider from trunk to trunk. Is she following me? She stops where my view of her is the clearest and sits, as if she's waiting for someone.

That prickling feeling creeps over me again. I wait, keen to see who she'll meet. She whistles. It echoes into the air, through the cavern and shoots tiny spears along my spine.

What if *I'm* the someone she's waiting for?

I slip out the leafy entrance, and loop behind her to hide the cave's opening, except I'm suspicious she knows this secret place.

Circling around, I approach her from behind. 'Who are you? Why are you following me?'

The grey-haired woman remains seated, turns and says, 'I was sent to meet you here.' Her brown eyes hold a confidence.

'Who sent you?'

'Doesn't matter. Do you know whose cave this is?'

'Yes. Do *you*?' I sound like Birri when he's huffy, and I'm tempted to cross my arms the way he does too.

'Yes,' she replies, quieter than I expect. 'Do you follow him?' She glances around before she says, 'Or his enemy?'

I've never been asked that. Thrown off balance, my words tumble out: 'Don't know if I "follow" anyone.'

The older woman springs to her feet, a frown dominating her face.

'Wait. Yes. Yes, I do.'

She pauses for me to explain.

'His magic healed me when I was a boy. I'm Narn, son of –'

'Birrabunji,' she says, her frown flipping.

How can a person change so much with a smile? She's far less scary and I relax a little.

The woman sits, pats the ground, and I join her. She's a lot older than I realised, but I'm not sure if she'd be as old as my grandmothers or aunties. It's hard to tell with some – most – women I meet.

'I remember that story,' she says. 'People call me Silverbird. You need to stay in his cave tonight,' she glances over her shoulder and mutters, 'to prepare for your future.'

I was so focused on Silverbird, I almost forgot my reason for being here. 'Have you seen two women, Tarni and Kirra?'

'Yes,' she says, as she stands and rattles off commands. 'Go in the cave. Meet me here at first light, then you'll be ready.'

'Ready for what?' I ask, the urgency rising in my voice.

'Timing. Right people. Places. I'll tell you tomorrow.'

She gives me some dried food wrapped in outer layers of the *wudjuru*, before she vanishes into the wet greenery.

What a strange woman. I walk back to N'gian's cave. Should I follow her instructions? She seemed certain. Was that knowledge or made-up? Why didn't I ask Silverbird if Tarni's alright? Or if Kirra's eyes have been healed. If she wasn't in such a big hurry, I could've. No, she wasn't in a rush. She's waiting for me or 'the right moment' to be ready.

When the yellow-rock marker comes into view, my thoughts are still on that odd visitor. For a woman who spoke with such confidence, she seemed troubled. I'll convince her to tell me about Tarni and Kirra first thing tomorrow.

I scrounge the area outside the cave, gathering berries, water and dry firewood to prepare for a night of solitude. I ease through the greenery at the mouth of the cave and pile the wood next to the old fireplace. The air is cold and musty. And I miss the smell of the sea.

Tarni standing on our headland floods my thoughts, her long hair blowing in the breeze. And how I felt – feel – jealous that the wind can tussle and play with it and never need permission.

I collect two fire sticks from the pile of tools tucked in the corner of this enormous rock amphitheatre. One is a drill stick – long with a rounded end. These are gifts from afar, because our clan uses flint rock to make fires. I grab the other piece of dry light wood – the one that's flatter and wider – and make a furrow in it. The smell of cedar is released. Then I kneel on this flatter piece and push the rounded end of the drill stick into the hollow.

Dad never taught me this, so I must've learnt it before the accident replaced my memories with emptiness.

Pressing hard, I move my open hands back and forth, past other – almost to my fingertips – without stopping the strong downward pressure. My hands move down the spindle and when I reach the lower end, I quickly switch back to the top without shifting the drill from the hole or stopping the fast spinning motion. Small powdery dust forms in the hollow. There are a few hiccups of smoke. It's almost there. Fine char-dust drops into the dry leaves, and I don't relax till a few more form. Then I blow gently. More smoke swirls. I blow harder this time and the red glowing embers ignite the tinder. I nurture the flames, blow long soft breaths, then feed the hungry fire with twigs and branches until the hardwood starts to crackle and burn.

With the fire cranking, I take a quick dip in the creek to wash off the thick, dry mud. Sunlight evaporates out of the rainforest. The cave is well hidden: no fire or smoke can be seen out here. I'm about to leave the fresh water, when a shadow rock-hops across the creek further down. Two more shadows follow it. They're moving along the creek, and I'm thankful darkness conceals me.

'She's here somewhere.' The deep voices sound agitated.

'We can't go back without it. He'll kill us. You sure you can still trust our new friend?'

'He better not be lying. He said we could find her here and she'd lead us to –'

Drawing in a quiet breath, I sink into the water as they pass the bank next to me. Are they hunting Silverbird or searching for Kirra and Tarni? My cave-diving training is paying off. I lay motionless at the bottom of the creek, unsure of how much time has passed. Air is running out, so are my choices: either remain underwater, push it too far, as I obviously did when Dad rescued me from drowning, or risk being captured by three angry shadows.

CHAPTER 15
TARNI

It's the first time the spears aren't pointing at me, with their sharp ends prodding me along an unfamiliar path. It's the first creek-crossing the hunters have stopped at to fill their water holders. And it's the first opportunity Kirra has to ask her never-ending questions.

'What did you tell them that stopped us getting killed?'

Not wanting to add to the welts on my back, and to keep Kirra safe, I keep my head down and mumble, 'I'm Jiemba's promised one and we were on the way to our joining ceremony.'

Kirra's hungry for more information, so I add, 'Said you were helping me prepare for the joining ceremony as part of our clan's customs.'

'Is there anything I need to know?'

The red-dusted hunters seem agitated. 'No talking, you two,' the tall one yells. And when a noise in the distance distracts them, I say, 'No. I said it to keep us alive.'

'Leave the creek now or I'll show what'll happen if you don't,' one of them sneers, as he thuds a thick branch into his large, calloused hand.

We scramble away from the water and onto the track. Kirra is frog-eyed and I pretend to relax by stretching my neck from side to side as we trudge along.

There's a stampede of thudding sounds ahead. Two men, different from the ones who captured us, speed our way. My response doesn't change: I shield Kirra, hold my breath while I check their faces. No Jiemba. Relief whooshes out, and I breathe again.

The men step aside. A cloaked shape skulks along the path behind them. I blink, hoping it's an illusion, because I recognise his stride: slithery slow, yet precise. The dark cloak covers his entire body, except for long claw-like fingers that curl and straighten when he walks. I swallow hard but a lump the size of a *buhnyi buhnyi* cone re-forms again. I hold Kirra's arm – make sure she's hidden behind me.

That yellow eerie mist billows over the track. I heave in a lungful of untainted air, which doesn't last long. The closer he gets, the more he reeks. Part shadow-spirit, part human form. He's right in front of me secreting a putrid yellow fog.

The Malung.

His men slam their spears across our shoulders. We stumble onto uneven ground. Knees burn with fresh grazes.

Then they drag Kirra along the track by a fistful of hair. She kicks and screams.

The shadow-spirit passes me.

He towers over Kirra. She's whimpering. The Malung's men pin her down, and the cloaked creature grabs her arm, scratches at her skin until she bleeds. Kirra shrieks and my muscles spasm. I lurch to save her. Something slams my head. And a spear presses against my throat, so I submit.

'Where's the magic canoe?' the shadow-spirit rasps.

I yell to translate but can't be heard over Kirra's cries.

The Malung grips her throat and lifts her so she dangles in his face. 'Where's the thing you used to break the time barrier?' he sneers.

Her kicking slows to a hanging limp, and he's losing patience.

'Kirra … Kirra …' I shout. She can't give up and die. What have I done?

I yell to save her, but his men yank my hair and force me down.

Kirra hasn't breathed or moved. He releases her. She thuds to the ground and heaves in air.

I hold back a tidal wave of tears and tell her his words. 'He wants your magic canoe.'

'Dunno where it is. Narn took it,' she says with a hoarse voice. Her face lightens to the shade of a *wudjuru* trunk. 'It's not magic.'

They ignore me when I translate Kirra's words.

'Search them,' a captor says.

His men snatch my bag, rummage through it, then chuck it in my face. I slip it over my shoulder.

'Nothing,' the red-dusted rock-head answers.

The Malung bellows, 'Find it or you join their fate. If they carry N'gian magic, they must know where he hid his things.'

He points to me with a long decaying fingernail that should belong in a tomb. 'Take this one.' Then he snarls at Kirra, 'Leave the time-breaker.'

'NoKirraNoKirraNoKirraNo.' It's all I get out as they drag me away. My legs scrape over every sharp rock on the track. Then a thick-necked man ties my arms in front of me. I launch to my feet to run back to Kirra. His huge paw cracks the side of my face; pain buckles my legs and my cheek smashes onto rocky rubble.

Bright spots float around me. I strain to hold one eye open and ignore the bloody taste in my mouth.

The shadow-spirit wraps his necklace around his fist. It's made of bones, and not like bones of any animal we've hunted and devoured. In the middle is that shining crystal similar to Jiemba's, only bigger.

The yellow glow hovers and vibrates through the air; the ground shakes so violently, my teeth chatter and my tense muscles lose control.

A sound begins. A language I've never heard, but I understand it clearly.

And wish I didn't.

His drone intensifies to a repulsive yawl. It judders out of him and chokes the air. If my hands weren't tied, I'd block my ears. And nothing comes out when I strain to shriek.

He chants.

Kirra crumples to the ground.

He's killing her.

Her deafening screech becomes silent, and it's scarier than her screams. It was my idea to find the N'gian healer from my mother's clan. It's my fault we're here. And now I know who she is, I can't let her die.

I plead with his men. 'Please help her.'

The Malung snaps at them. My scalp burns as they use my hair to drag me further away.

'She doesn't understand. She doesn't know N'gian,' I yell. '*I* put his symbol on the rock. I'll tell you anything you want.' My words fall to the ground, are trampled and ignored.

Kirra lays crumpled in an awkward heap.

The Malung arches his body towards the sky. He twists forwards, spewing a poisonous curse with the authority that thunder and lightning and lava command. He heaves a mind-spear, an evil curse – some call it the pointing of the bone. No matter its name, it leads to one thing: death.

My friend's body is left on a barren track in the territory of our enemies. A path no-one will visit for months. She won't have a proper ceremony. And by the time this corridor is used, there'll be nothing left of her.

Tears sneak down my face, and I hide their tracks with my restrained muddy hands. I won't show weakness.

They lead me away from Kirra's lifeless form.

No doubt to my death.

Never to see Narn again … never to tell him how I feel.

CHAPTER 16
KIRRA

There's a creepy silence and a weird smell. Dust? No, dirt. The kind you get during a life-long drought with no hope of rain. The kind they bury you with. Hovering over a teenage girl – by the smell of her, she's been dead for a while – I scan the wasteland for help to turn over her ballooning body. 'Cept this place is a barren dust bowl. The only living thing out here is me. With an urgency, I grunt and haul her on her side, but her hair is plastered over her face. I claw the ash and hair away, and I'm thankful I don't dry retch. Her face is bloated and distorted.

I recognise her. My heart doesn't race, and my hands don't sweat, which makes sense.

It's me. *You're dead.*

I cover my ears, not from the loudness but its force.

You're dead. You're dead. You're dead.

'Who's there?'

A yellow vapour sweeps around me. 'I said "die" and you did.'

The dust talks to me, and I know it's true.

This is what my end-of-the-world dream meant: I would die. It did come true. My world has ended. And I blew the time I'd had to make a difference. Thoughts and feelings, past and present, are a tangled mess.

Have I failed everyone?

Or do I get a second chance to save the world as a spirit?

CHAPTER 17
NARN

Rising to the creek's surface, I draw in a soundless breath. The men's voices are distant, so I creep onto the bank in the darkness, then slip inside the hanging vine entrance of N'gian's dry cavern. The blazing fire warms my body, but with those prowling men, I let the fire burn out and hide deeper in the cave.

Tiny lights are glowing at the back of the dark cave. Haven't seen them since I was a young fella. I follow the glistening beads through a narrow passage into the depths of the cave's belly. The glow-worms lure me further. Mini galaxies of tiny green twinkles cover the walls and ceilings. Some shine brighter and bigger than others. Something glimmers on the far cave wall. Painted in bright white ochre, the drawings jump out of the wall. I move past the moist tunnel to another, drier region of the cave.

The shining symbols span across the cave wall. It's the mind-spear story, the one Birri almost convinced Birrabunji to tell around the big fire when Kirra arrived. And N'gian's sunlight reminds me of these glow-worms. There's no loud performance. Instead, they quietly do their light-shining job … except everyone knows where glow-worms shine from.

Their *kumo*. And if Wanjellah were here, we'd snigger like small boys.

My humour disappears when a humming begins. Each deep, soothing sound calls a word into existence.

The music asks questions.

Can 'giving' be more powerful than 'taking'?

Something or someone is planting melodic seed-thoughts: What if mind-spears are used to stop people believing in their magical gifts and prevent them from doing their glow-worm jobs, stopping them from quietly bringing light to dark places?

A warm tingling fills me, a sweet sticky *gudje* settles deep within. What if I can learn how to shield people from mind-spears?

I touch the glowing ochre. It seeps into my fingers and a bright glow throbs under my skin. It matches the song's vibration and spreads inside me from my fingers to my arms, to my chest – everywhere.

Then the glowing stops. The symbols aren't surface patterns on a cave wall. There are layers and layers of meanings. Deep knowledge. It's as if I've chopped across the belly of a giant ancient tree and the circles of life, formed there, speak to me.

It's our 'Gowonda Dreaming' story of how the dolphin caller began. I thought I'd been taught everything. Been training since initiation to take care of and work with dolphins, understand tides and swells and wind and waves. Except Dad hadn't taught me everything.

The hum thumps in the core of me. I know it was not an accident Kirra arrived during the calling of the dolphins. I drag my fingertips across the wall, processing the symbols. Layers are often shadows of things to come. The lead dolphin and the rest of the pod have always chased in fish to feed our clans.

In the past, they've rescued our people from starvation; tomorrow's children were saved. And as certain as the tide is connected to the moon, the light-skinned dolphin will save our future. That tingling grows stronger, as does an unexplainable peace ... a belief in unseen things.

'I call the unseen when we need them, and they come.' When I say those words, the white ochre shines over my body again. And a layer of knowledge awakens a depth in me. The *midyim* shrub, a reminder of my first vow with Birrabunji, has fruited. I'll keep my oath of silence, like I promised Dad.

A speck of memory escapes the void.

I scratched those symbols in the sea cave as a boy.

Dad said two people in our clan had drawn N'gian's symbol. Tarni drew it on the beach when she was a little girl. But I never thought I'd be the other one. Now our future relies on Kirra, who painted that sacred symbol on her flat canoe. N'gian called her through my song. And he's gathered the three of us.

'I know who I am,' I say aloud; it echoes three or four times through the caverns.

And the hum stops.

Its tune is powerful, so I continue to belt out the notes.

The N'gian symbol on the cave's wall juts out in pulsing layers. First, a woven circle. Next layer is a curling wave – the opening of a watery cave. The last layer, which sticks out the furthest, is a meeting-place symbol: a sun. The melody flows out of me. I touch the glowing symbol; it's sticky and stringy like *gudje* from our bees.

The sun picture is as big as my fist. It's rippling slightly. I poke it with my finger, but instead of touching a gooiness, it sucks my arm in right up to my elbow. It happens so fast my hand feels numb.

When I look at my hand again, I'm standing in the same spot but holding an old clay pot with a sealed lid. The N'gian symbol is no longer on the wall; it's etched on the vessel. And I know in my head and heart and gut, the song is complete.

I meander through the maze of wet tunnels with long straight strands of sticky webs that hang from the cave ceiling and walls, and past the small cave pockets, back to the large open cavern.

After peering through the peepholes in the rock, I'm certain the men have gone. My eyes have adjusted to the dark, so it's easy to rebuild the fire. I strain to break the seal of the vessel with my hands. It doesn't budge. I search the pile of sticks nearby, then try to pry it open with a sharp one.

Still doesn't move.

Then I sacrifice the spear tip to break the dark hardened resin. The seal crumbles a little, so I work my way around the entire edge. When I lift the lid, an invisible coolness scampers over my skin leaving behind a trail of tiny bumps.

Inside the pot is fine white powder.

Is it food or a medicine with N'gian's magical powers?

After a few sniffs and a tiny taste test, my body slumps. It's just ground ochre. Ordinary ochre we'd find in every tribe. The same kind we paint ourselves with for ceremony.

I gorge on the food Silverbird gave me.

The clay lid has a carving on it. I run my fingers over it: a dolphin pushing fish towards a person. Was N'gian a dolphin caller and was this ochre meant for dolphin callers?

I mix some ochre powder with water in a small coolamon, then smear it over my face. Nothing happens. I paint my arms and legs. Still nothing.

N'gian was a spirit, glowing like the sun.

No, don't think it has made me into a spirit. I'm not invisible or glowing either. I shove the lid back on, grab the *wudjuru* from the pile, wrap it around the pot, and secure it with string. Silverbird told me to stay here, which means she'll probably be fine with me borrowing a few things – if she hasn't been captured. So, I place the pot in the woven bag. Might as well take it with me.

Dread digs deeper, a tick paralysing every movement and thought.

Tarni will never know my secret.

Silverbird said 'first light', and I've been waiting most of the day. Did those men take her? When the sun shines high above the yellow-ochred rock, she appears in the same spot she sat last time. At least my bag is packed with water, string, *wudjuru* and the ochre.

'*Jingi wahlu*,' I say. She ignores my greeting and gets straight to the point.

'Finally showed up, Narn. I checked the cave the day we were meant to meet and you weren't inside. This is the first time I could make it back. It's been four days,' and she doesn't give me a chance to think or respond. 'Walk with me. Need to keep this place safe,' she says, leading me away from N'gian's cave.

Silverbird makes her own unmarked path. And similar to my dolphin friends, Spinner with little Echo, I follow her every move. She weaves around a thin spiky vine. 'Did you get it?'

'Get what?'

She looks over her shoulder with that motherly you-know-what-I'm-talking-about face. 'His magic?'

This woman probably won't tell me if I ask her how she knows, so I keep my mouth shut and nod.

'We call it the unseen gift,' she says, her eyes flicking from mine to the trees around us. There's more panic in her eyes today. But this old girl knows about my encounter, which gives me hope for a new life with a real purpose.

'Unseen gift. What does that mean?'

'I can speak and understand many languages, but my most powerful gift is "seeing tomorrows". Days ago, I had a vision of you in N'gian's cave. Saw you receive a gift, which is why more time probably passed than you realised. You have an ability to shield others from mind-spears.'

I know she's right.

'This means you can strengthen other people's gifts too.'

My mouth goes dry. 'What? How?'

'Maybe it's making them believe in N'gian or encouraging them in their gifts? I don't know exactly. I've seen you do it in here.' She taps her temple.

I shake my head and say, 'Doesn't make sense.'

'Rarely does. Do you feel different?'

'I guess so.'

Silverbird tugs on my arm. 'Was something revealed … that glows?'

'You mean the glow-worms in the cave?'

'Doesn't matter,' she says, as though she'd caught a no-good fish and was tossing it back into the sea. 'You're not the one. I've got to go,' and she darts into the forest.

'Wait,' I yell. She can't leave now, and I chase after her calling, 'You've said nothing about Tarni and Kirra.'

Silverbird glares at me. What isn't she telling me? My heart becomes two fire sticks rubbing together, faster, harder, faster, harder, until they catch alight.

'Tarni's been captured by men who are influenced by the Malung.' Her eyes shift from mine to her feet.

'No. Not Tarni.' I can't say any more, in case I confess that I've lost the only woman I've loved.

The older woman studies me before she says, 'And Kirra has been captured by death.'

Heat rushes to my head, and I clench my teeth and fists to stop me from exploding. By failing to protect Kirra, I killed her. Is there any point facing the Malung and saving Tarni when Kirra, our much-needed helper, is dead? But it's Tarni, my Tarni. I'm a river, she's the sea. I'll gorge mountains and valleys to find her ... to be with her. Without Tarni, I have no purpose, no path.

Silverbird stops next to a large hollowed-out tree trunk. 'Beyond this ridge is a path with two directions.'

All around me is dense with rainforest – no gaps for paths.

'Stay here tonight. Tomorrow you can tell me your answer.'

I open my mouth to unravel her riddle, but she says, 'N'gian brought you back from death's ditch, so there's always hope.' Then all certainty is stripped from Silverbird's voice. 'You must choose: Kirra or Tarni.'

CHAPTER 18
TARNI

The Malung's men keep a fast pace for two days. When they move, their red-ochre dust doesn't fall off. It's easier to focus on pointless things than the truth. It's my fault my friend is dead. Mossy trees and thick undergrowth have disappeared. Orange-rock mountains tower ahead of us. We've left rainforest country and the lore of our tribe's land.

The taller one yanks me to a stop. 'Which one are you? A truth dreamer, a symbol teller or a language expert?'

I say nothing.

The other man, the one with a tree trunk for a neck, nudges me with his spear. Warm blood oozes from my thigh. I clench my teeth, pretend there's no pain.

'We know you follow N'gian. We saw the symbol at your overnight camp.'

I can't remember the words I hollered while attempting to save Kirra's life.

He talks slow to emphasise each word. 'Unless you tell us your gift, we will kill you here and now.'

Holding my chin high and hoping they can't tell I'm lying, I say, 'I am Jiemba's promised one. You would kill his future wife when I'm to be joined with him tomorrow?'

'Anyone can say they are Jiemba's promised one.' He sticks his face in mine. 'People will say anything to avoid death.'

His spit sprays me when he speaks.

'Tomorrow?' he snarls, and his offsider roars with laughter.

A tremor begins at my knees and shakes through my body.

'See these.' He rubs his fingers over the six or seven raised scars on his upper chest. 'I earnt these initiation marks. And you can tell I didn't get them yesterday.'

He swings his hand through the air. I wince. He smacks my face. My jaw jolts sideways. Pain radiates through my cheek, and I taste blood again. His hand is ready to strike once more, but men thud down the track from where we left Kirra, and I'm thankful for the distraction. I dab my puffy lip with my fingertips.

The men march over. The Malung's not with them.

'Confirm your gift,' they say at the same time, same pitch, same creepiness.

'Where's *my* friend?' The swelling makes my words collide, so I space them out, even though my cut tongue and swollen lips won't work. 'She ... needs ... help.'

The taller one doesn't laugh or hit me, but something flickers across his eyes. 'It's too late for help or choices,' he says. 'Confirm.'

He's right, Kirra can't be helped and I've no choice.

'I speak and understand languages.' It sounds empty-headed but it's the truth.

He drags me along the ground to the tallest man and reports, 'She unweaves languages.'

'Put her with the rest of them.'

They shove me along a dirt path towards a cluster of rocky cliffs. I stumble and fall, they yank and shove. I stumble and fall, they yank and shove. It's not the kind of treatment expected for Jiemba's intended.

Escaping is my only hope. I run, more diagonally than straight, because my battered head aches. A hunter swipes my ankles. My face and body whack the ground.

Someone covers my head with wet-dingo-smelling fur and chucks me over his shoulder. 'Move and it'll be the last time you do.'

I give in, for now. My body aches, thudding and bumping with every movement. And I struggle to breathe.

He stops. There's a strange scraping sound before I'm thrown to the ground. He tugs the cloth off my head and says, 'We'll let your promised one know you're ready to be joined.'

Muffled voices gather in the dark. I've no idea how long it's been since Kirra died – three, maybe four days. I blink, desperate to make sense of where I am. My knees and palms scrape over pebbles wedged in the hard dirt. 'Who's there?' I ask, as I stagger to my feet and secure my dillybag.

'You're safe for now,' a woman's voice replies; she takes my hand to lead me. 'I'm Yindari.'

'I'm Tarni.'

Behind us are grunts and that strange scraping sound.

'What's that noise?' I say, as I scramble away from it.

'A large boulder blocks the entrance,' she says.

'Entrance?'

'We're trapped in here.'

142

In the darkness, not far from us, are murmurs. Yindari takes my arm, the way I led Kirra. She directs me so I know where to step, who's there, and what to do. It's comforting in an unfamiliar place, and my chest tightens when I remember how unkind I was to our clan's guest. And how I treated her in the last days of her young life.

We edge closer to those noises and there are fuzzy outlines of more people. Sitting together, I chew the *bilang* bark I'd collected to sooth my cut mouth.

A cool breeze whips at our skin. Yindari huddles closer.

'Tarni, I've heard about you,' she whispers. 'Your father is the greatest hunter-Elder along the coast. Your mother was a skilful language expert. And you were the youngest to receive – I mean, become – a language expert too.'

I ignore her hint at my N'gian gift and want to say, Dad is the greatest hunter-Elder *traitor* plus Mum wasn't dead but she may be now.

'Where are we?' is all I manage.

Her small silhouette answers, 'Jiemba's men call it "the ending".'

Dawn reveals women of all ages, more than I expected. The bark has healed the inside of my mouth. We're in an enormous bare space with no roof, surrounded by slabs of smooth, orangey-brown cliffs. A few scraggily shrubs survive in here with us. Water trickles out one of the rock walls. There's no grass, only the remains of where a giant tree proudly stood. Three granite cliff faces loom, one lower than the other two. Boulders are piled to make it taller.

'There's no escape. They'll kill you if you do.' It's Yindari. She shared food with me last night. We huddled to keep warm but sleep evaded me.

'Joining with Jiemba is a death wish,' I say, and tilt my head to study a small divot in the smooth rock face on the shorter third wall. 'And once they find out I lied about *when* our joining ceremony is, they'll probably kill me anyway.'

'You're promised to Jiemba?'

I nod without taking my eyes off that hole. Maybe if I take a big run up, I could grab it and pull myself up.

'We all are.'

My focus shifts from escaping to giving her my full attention. 'Everyone here is promised to Jiemba?' I say, shaking my head.

Her eyebrows lift when she nods. 'That's another thing we have in common.'

I force a smile and hope it passes as encouragement. 'What?'

'We are linked to N'gian by his magical gifts. Tarni, I don't think there's going to be a joining ceremony.'

I remember imagining this moment: when my promise to Jiemba ends, and how thrilled and relieved I'd feel. But this? First, I'm part of a mass joining ceremony. Sounds more like a mass execution. Unless Jiemba is planning to hold us as captives, so he can use our magical gifts whenever he needs them.

Yindari speaks as though we're discussing the best weaving technique or our favourite food. 'Jiemba and his father hate good and everything to do with N'gian. You know, he could be serious about joining with you. Might be something in your saltwater country he wants.

And with your father, he could control the coast: all those trading routes, who can enter and leave. It's a clever plan. Evil but clever ... Don't forget you were the youngest to receive N'gian's magic. Maybe he thinks you're the most powerful of us.'

I don't know how long she talks, but I nod, slip in a respectful smile or two, while I focus on the tiny hole high in the cliff.

All this Jiemba talk: I work best angry.

I run full-force at the wall and lunge into the air – not even close – then smack feet-first onto the ground. I rub both hands over the flat surface to try and get one small handhold or toehold.

Nothing.

I jog back to Yindari.

Everyone watches me. I run my fastest at the rock slab again and fall short. After another six or seven attempts, my palms sting and knees bleed.

I sprint again. And again. And again. Every muscle aches. I pant and flop on the ground. Though my head spins, the hate hasn't faded: for Jiemba, my father, and being so naive.

The spinning eases. I stumble to my feet, wander to the wall and slump against it. Yindari comes over. I'm too angry to talk or listen.

She speaks.

'I can't understand you,' I grunt in her direction.

Is she confused? I talk. She does too. There's a clatter in my ears. It can't be true. I listen to everyone and focus hard, but the racket gets louder. And confirms my worries.

It's never happened before.

My N'gian gift is gone.

I don't understand anyone. I'm alone and useless. There's no escape or rescue. Granny Alkira said to stay nearby. I gulp. Kirra's dead body sticks in my mind … Me and my empty-headed ideas. I seal in the anger to use its strength.

Another dawn, another day to escape. I circle the enclosure in case I've missed anything that could help. I climb part of the wall to a point that's double my height, then my muscles fail and I slip. Somehow, I land on my feet.

Yindari watches me for most of the morning. When the sun's above us, she signals for me to stop.

'I won't sit around and wait to die,' I growl, knowing she won't understand me. Then I climb and fall. Climb and fall. I'm worse each time. I dust my grazed hands to prevent them from slipping, and my legs have bloodied knee caps, as well as the cut thigh from the Malung's men.

My muscles and joints ache. But what I can't accept is the ache inside that whispers, *I am nothing and have nothing.*

What's happening to me? Did the real Tarni, the one everyone thought was clever, disappear with my gift? Turns out I'm not special. Everyone here has magical gifts.

I grind my teeth so I don't say it, but my thoughts are too loud: *I hate who I'm becoming. And I've only been here three nights and three days.*

I slump into the orange dirt. Beyond these rock walls, the sun slips behind the horizon. And everyone's lives in Wallulljagun continues, unaware of what we face.

Yindari plonks next to me. She doesn't say anything. A gecko runs up the rock, and I eye it jealously. The older woman picks up a stick, draws two faces in the dirt, one with a frown and one with a smile, then passes me the stick. There's little light, but I circle the frowny face.

She touches her heart and makes an angry face. Then points to her heart and makes a peaceful face. Yindari pretends to sleep, then points to other women and mimes climbing.

I nod, though I don't agree. If I can't climb out, they can't. And I've tried for days. Yindari mimes some more, and I'm too tired to argue or understand. My magic has gone. And I tell myself I don't care.

The large boulder moves and two men enter, grab two women and yank them out. They kick and scream. Moments later, the whirring dust settles and deafening shrieks cease, and we're alone in our desert deathbed.

After another restless night, the sky becomes more blue than charcoal, and I wake to find a new plan. Yindari has the younger women forming a human hill. Four strong women stand, linked together, while others climb onto their shoulders. Our men perform something similar during our ceremonies. They lean against the rock wall to balance. Two more climb on top of them. They tumble and thud, sprawled in awkward positions with a fine dust clouding the air.

The pain of scratches and bruises from previous failures fade. I misunderstood Yindari: they're helping me climb out. I lighten my dillybag: give my stone knife to Yindari, share out the last of my water, then hang my woven bag across my chest.

This time they hold their positions, and it's my turn to climb. I hope I make it before they tumble again. They grunt; it gets louder when I crunch their bodies to clamber higher. I'm standing at the top. It's wobbly and ready to collapse at any moment but I move quickly and launch upwards.

The mountain of bodies crumble. I'm hanging with one hand gripping a rock protruding from the cliff face – three fingers squashed inside the divot. Both feet are on the flat rock wall. I need to move and find another handhold or foothold, so I can climb skywards.

My eyes search for holes, cracks, anything. I wedge part of my body in and haul myself up. Tiny little edges hold tips of fingers and toes. Little by little I move towards the top of the cliff. My feet climb into the spots that once held my hands. My muscles scream at me to rest, but I focus on the next foot placement. Then hand position. Foot. Hand. Foot. Hand. I must keep moving. And not fall.

My foot slips and the women gasp.

Two secure handholds save me. I pull with all my might and regain my footing. A moan escapes, as I climb higher and higher.

The summit is within reach now. Large, grippy, granite boulders form the last section, and it's easier to find places for my limbs. I jam feet, knees, arms, elbows into gaps in the rock. My muscles cramp. Cuts and grazes sting my body.

Wish I was back at our creek gulping the cool fresh water. Blinking to regain focus, I urge my body to push through the pain. I groan and ascend. Groan and ascend. Leg muscles jitter and spasm out of control. I stare at my last move. It's a high reach. If I fall, I'll probably die.

I break my first rule and glance down.

A sea of faces watch. Their strength reaches me.

I will finish this!

My eyes snap back to the most difficult part of this climb. One more move. It's a rock bulging out of the smooth slab. I heave in a breath, pull up with both arms and push with both legs. The women murmur below me. I dangle over them, swinging upwards with my arms, while my legs hang in the air. Both forearms are pressing on the rock edge. I'm squirming and wriggling, my chest reaching the ledge. I haul my body one bit at a time, in a lizard-like motion, until my belly is on the edge.

I roll over the rock shelf. And I'm safe.

My mouth is dusty, frantic for water. I'm sprawled on my back against the warm rock, heaving with nostrils burning.

With eyes shut, I focus on breathing. The burning in my chest eases. It's time to search for a way to escape, because I don't have the strength or skill to climb down that rock.

This valley is not full of green grass or flowering shrubs. There are no birds, butterflies, wallabies or waterholes. Instead, it's dry and bouldered, with the odd spiky plant. If only that was all. My chin and lips tremble and legs and arms shudder.

There's a mountain – no, a mountain range – of human skeletons. Dry bones and skulls for as far as I can see. And right at the back are rotting bodies, all at differing stages of decomposition. A few steps away, a red-bellied black snake slithers over a brittle rib cage, then slips through the eye socket of a sun-bleached skull, and I clamber backwards.

Something is digging into me. When I check, it's not a rock.

I cover my mouth to stifle a scream and scramble away.

There's no escape.

I sit and stare at my future.

CHAPTER 19
KIRRA

You're dead. You're dead. You're dead.

A funeral dirge thumps my temples. I yank my hair to feel pain ... to tug it away from those words.

You're dead. You're dead. You're dead.

I groan, move my head as rattling bone-tipped spears jab it from every direction. Slamming my eyes shut, softness cocoons me. Feels like the satin interior of a coffin. The passing from the physical to the spiritual realm is a one-way solo trip; there's no manual or meditative voice to follow.

Did I live my best life?

I wish I'd done more about 'life being a journey, not a destination'. 'Cos it's over. I've arrived and not in the way I thought I would. The universe has taken a giant dump, and I'm a turd, floating in its raw sewage.

The end replays. Full moon sets. An enormous eruption is tinted with yellow – not happy-field-of-sunflowers yellow – a radioactive, fluoro-urine yellow. Grey snow falls. No, ash blankets everything. It blocks the sun. Tsunamis the size of mountains trigger earthquakes. Sea levels drop. Oceans freeze over. The earth's crust rips open. No-one lives to see it.

Life, defeated by death.

I tunnel away from the light. Moans interrupt the silent darkness.

'Hush now.' Her face is blurry; there are feathers, lots of them around her chest layered like an angelic breastplate. 'Pain is a wave, don't fight it. Flow with it.'

Seriously? Trust me to nab the weird angel.

I shiver and for one microsecond the fog clears. 'The light's too bright,' I say, and force her face into focus.

'Concentrate on the light, Little One. On good things. Push away darkness. It's a bad fear. Fight it. Resist it.'

'Can't see.' My eyes are open, but my mind and vision are fragments choked by yellow fog.

'Push past the yellow, it's another form of the shadow-spirit's fear. We don't fear shadows, because they cannot exist without the light.'

I'm confused about the gross yellow stuff, her words, and that she knows my thoughts and feelings without me telling her.

'Focus on good things: love.'

'Pfftt.' That's lame, even for an angel.

Her voice trickles into my thoughts. 'Love is powerful, so is a strong mind. Fight darkness and fear with light and love. And never believe the lie.'

'The lie?' I mutter, curious at how she says it. Is it the key to life's mysteries, or am I stuck between worlds like in those space opera shows, waiting for ascension into my spirit form?

'That he's won,' she says, disrupting my sci-fi debate, 'and your mind is broken, and who you are and are meant to be is splintered – unrepairable. It's the lie.'

I don't know if my eyes are opened or closed, doesn't make a difference. Creepy voices won't stop taunting me.

You're dead. You're dead. You're dead. It's louder, more agonising.

'How?' is all I can push out, and I lick my cracked lips. And in perfect angel mode, she pre-empts my thirst, lifts my head so I can sip water from a furry object.

'Truth,' she says matter-of-factly.

'Truth,' I mumble. 'Different people tell different truths.' Too weak, I surrender to the fog, her voice and my expiry date.

You're dead. You're dead. You're dead.

'You need his glowing ochre or you'll pass over to a dark place where you'll never see your ancestors again. Fight the lie, Little One.'

What lie: Am I human or spirit, living or dead, switched on or off? My head feels volcanic, my fingers are icicles, and I convulse as jolts of yellow smog suffocate me.

CHAPTER 20
NARN

I can't decide if Silverbird is a help or a pain in my 'hind. We avoid the shared corridor to evade people. And our pace is slow because, according to my guide, we can't leave any tracks to show we've been here or even exist.

Tried to tell Silverbird my answer but she's avoiding the subject. Instead, she's asked question after question about N'gian, his cave, Birrabunji's stories. I sense she's withholding information. Tarni's taken and Kirra's captured by death – whatever that means. Dad's going to kill me!

I cross my arms over my chest, and give her my best stare-down, not willing to walk any further till she answers my questions. The rainforest, oblivious to our stand-off, is loud with birdlife, and wind rattling through a million leaves.

'Where are you taking me?'

Silverbird sways side-to-side, unable to stand still.

'You knew Tarni was captured and said nothing until it was too late. And what's wrong with Kirra?'

'A mind-spear.' The words thud on the ground between us.

'How? Who threw a mind-spear?'

Silverbird glances everywhere except at me. 'A death curse from the Malung spears more than your mind … it takes everything.' She doesn't look sorry or guilty. What's with this woman? I need details now.

I clench my fists, my arms tightening in their crossed position. 'Kirra's dying from a mind-spear.' I say it aloud and hope the meaning will penetrate.

Silverbird winds through the undergrowth again, and I shadow her.

'It takes time to bring her mind back if I can find –'

'I've been following you all over this rainforest and only now you tell me you know where Kirra is.' I'm muttering, like Birrabunji does. 'We've been wasting all this time, chatting about N'gian and his glowing cave symbols.'

She stops and grips my arm. 'You never told me about glowing cave symbols.'

'Kirra can't die,' I say, and pace back and forth. 'I need to tell her who she really is; she must understand.'

Silverbird loosens her hold, and I whisper, 'The white-finned dolphin gets them working together to bring in the catch, so tomorrow's children will flourish.'

I pause, her expression doesn't change, and it's the first time since I've met her that she's focused on me, not flicking her eyes here-and-there.

'Kirra needs to know it's not a coincidence that she came,' I say, and I need Silverbird to catch the seriousness of this. 'Gowonda Dreaming has layers within our stories. It's more than dolphins gathering us fish. It's always bigger than ourselves … today's wave starts as a ripple elsewhere.'

I place a hand on Silverbird's shoulder. 'Kirra's important. I have to find her and bring her back to the dolphins and our saltwater people.'

'Well, it's decision time,' she finally says. Her arms point in different directions. 'Kirra or Tarni. And remember, each choice has a consequence.'

'Tarni.'

There's a thickness in my throat. I've chosen with my heart, not my head. Again. Last time it led to a snake pit. Where will it take me this time? But there's nothing I can do for Kirra, not if she has a mind-spear.

'This is your path. You have what it takes to do what needs to be done.' Her riddles sound as cryptic as Dad's. She passes me food and asks, 'What will you do now?'

'There's only one thing I can do. Save Tarni … I love her,' I mumble, and there's a smile in the older woman's eyes. 'Dad instructed me to protect Kirra. But I don't know how to save someone from a mind-spear.'

'N'gian's glowing ochre,' Silverbird says. Her bright eyes are anchored by wrinkles. 'It saved me when I lived in his cave, but we only are given what we need. Mine ran out long ago and Kirra needs it now. I thought it'd be revealed to you.'

'It was.' I gulp. 'But it doesn't work – look,' and I show her the ochre on my arms and head. 'Doesn't glow.' I pull out the clay pot and hand it to her, 'You can have it.'

She jumps back and glares at me. 'Are you empty-headed? Never give it to anyone. When it burns in your belly to share, give them a tiny portion. You are its custodian. It will work when it needs to, how it needs to. Just trust and believe.'

Silverbird unties a small leather pouch and I scoop ochre dust into it.

'Water, please,' she says. I pass her my roo-skin container. 'Now cup your hands.' She pours a tiny portion of powdered ochre in my hands then sprinkles in water.

'Let your instinct guide you.'

I rub my hands in circular movements. With liquid white clay, I smear it across her and my forehead at the same time.

'Practise your gift,' Silverbird says. 'It grows stronger with love. Fear kills it or, worse, distorts it, so you are too blind to choose wisely. And one more thing.' She whispers, 'They're killing N'gian followers. Killed our healer. Tarni might be dead because of her gift. You may be killed too. Be careful who you trust.'

A pain stabs my chest when I think of Tarni dying.

'After I save Tarni, I'll find you and Kirra. Saving them is what matters.'

Silverbird blends into the bush surroundings and is gone. I walk beside the track and repeat her earlier instructions over and over aloud. 'Look to the stars to follow the Dark Emu until you reach giant scarred red gum trees each side of a creek. That's where the welcoming ceremony is performed. It's the boundary to their dry-season camp. Their wet-season camp is further inland, with orange rocky cliffs and big grassy plains.'

Except I won't be welcomed at the scarred trees. I come as a challenger, not as a friend. If I had a message stick, I could approach as a diplomat and be protected by our lore. As the sky darkens and fills with a thousand shining lights, I miss Silverbird and her strange ways.

The Dark Emu is my favourite skylore. It's the darkness between a cluster of stars, and its long neck and legs trail behind it. Dark Emu extends all the way across the sky and later, we'll look at him and know when it's time to carry our emu callers and collect those night-blue eggs. But only one from each nest, unless Uncle Gukuji says we can take two. It's his totem, he carries the knowledge of the emu, its breeding season, nesting season – everything about them.

I grin at that old emu in the sky, guiding me to Tarni.

There'll be no ceremony – with Elders and dances and blessings. I'm breaking lore and Dad can't save me if I get caught. I need a plan, a clever one, to trick a tribe and an evil Malung into giving me my childhood friend, the woman I love.

My memory of the glowing cave symbols return.

'I can save Tarni. I will save Tarni. I'll fight her shark.'

CHAPTER 21
TARNI

There are bad days. And there are unspeakable ones. I'm living one of those days now. High on the rocky ridge, I sit and stare at the mountains of dry bones blocking my path to freedom, while the women are trapped below, unaware of what this place really is.

My chest hurts and the ache spreads to my throat. There were no ceremonies. No goodbyes. No respect. Lives stolen and forgotten. Like Kirra's and now mine.

Tears rush down my cheeks, and I don't bother to wipe them away. There's no point. I don't have to be anything for anyone anymore. Every lie bubbles to the surface.

Being promised to Jiemba.

Mum abandoning me to Minjarra and his horrible plans.

Narn. And the truth that he doesn't really love me.

Sobs heave out of me, and I mourn my life: what it could have been. What it has become.

Shafts of light beam into the valley and my tears dry. Brightness pushes away shadows. It reminds me of the ceremony my mother performed when I first received my N'gian magic. She called it 'waiting in the light' and taught me to sit in the sun with my eyes closed to empty my thoughts and let pictures float in. It was how she chased away those dead-puppy nightmares. It gave me peace.

'N'gian, do you mourn this valley of bones?' I speak to the sun.

Then I close my eyes, so its brightness warms me, and shades of orange and yellow form colourful spots in my mind. It's happening, the way it did when Mum helped me as a girl.

There's a blurry face.

Mum?

I relax my eyes, my body, and the image in my mind sharpens.

It is Mum. I breathe slowly and wait … Something surfaces and I know what to say.

I'm sorry, Mum. I forgive you. I was angry at you for not wanting to live with me and not protecting me from Dad, Jiemba and all of this.

Light whirls around, it sparkles and spins and Mum's face disappears. My body tingles from head to toe as if a million butterflies have landed all over me. Then another face appears. One I'm not ready to face yet.

My father.

Guilt fights my hatred. Like seven-foot grey kangaroos standing on their hind legs, my emotions box each other. And a memory floats in. I'm a little girl, my father's carrying me on his shoulders, and my anger melts a little. In that split second, I promise I'll try to make things right between us.

Pressure builds in my head.

Again, the light floods my mind and I'm glad it's enough for his face to fade. Another replaces it.

It's Narn.

Within moments I understand.

Narn, I'm sorry for blaming you. And judging you for not doing what I wanted you to do.

I wished you were like me and would fix the problems … not that it worked for me. I rub the end of my snuffy nose.

The next face appears. I freeze.

Jiemba.

How can anyone expect me to forgive this maggot face?

Please. I can't forgive him. Even if I wanted to, which I don't … I wouldn't know how.

I wait. Mum and Granny Yindi said unforgiveness will choke away life. And that hate will consume it all.

I know I must choose: Narn or Jiemba.

Love or hate.

It's both the simplest and most difficult choice. Forgive Jiemba or lose the ability to love Narn when hatred changes into unforgiveness, and then into bitterness, till it poisons love and life and happiness and everything I want.

I'd forgiven Jiemba in the first light ceremony years ago, but now he's an enormous carpet snake wrapped around my middle. With every breath, it strangles tighter and tighter until I can't exhale.

I remember waves rolling onto an empty beach. And just like my name means 'breaking wave', I let the light roll over every thought. In and out, I breathe to the rhythm of those waves. In … I release it. No longer will I cling to the darkness. Out … My body relaxes and mind empties its worries.

There's one more face. Didn't realise it's so hard to forgive and the trickiest to love. I'm on the beach, the sea sucks back the tide, and leaves a pool of water on the sand. I peer in.

Me?

I cringe at the lanky legs and straight-shaped figure. I've never stopped long enough to see me … love me. Instead of splashing away my reflection, I gaze into it, and I'm smiling a thousand different smiles, secured into one.

I let it all go. The perfect daughter who keeps her mother's secrets. The perfect offspring who hunts the best. The perfect language expert who does whatever the Elders ask. And trying to please aunties and grannies without the guilt-soaked worries.

I'm surrounded by bones and death, covered in bruises and scratches, and I have no power over life or loss.

It'll unfold whether I try to control it or not. I have my life to live, magic or no magic, joining or no joining, parents or no parents. Whatever my life is, I might as well live it with peace, rather than fear. Because death will visit us all.

As the sun slips past the valley, shadows creep over everything. A grating noise turns to shouts. I lean over the ledge but the overhang stops me from seeing the women below.

'Where is she?' a deep voice booms.

'Who?' one of the women answers.

'The woman we last brought in – the language unweaver.'

'No-one knows.'

'Wrong answer.'

There are screams, which are muted by a cracking sound, and I'm scared they've murdered someone, and her body will be added to this pile.

'We'll do this again tomorrow. And every day until you tell me where she is.'

There are sounds of the boulder being returned. I grit my teeth and vow to save them. Down the valley of bones, something catches my eye, it's carved in the rock.

The symbol of N'gian.

I scan the trail of bones that should lead me out. Is N'gian's symbol glowing? And I shake the idea out of my head: How can ochre glow, not glow, then glow again? It happens again. My thirstiness must be making my mind play tricks.

And to prove it, I stare at the rock for a long time and think, *It's not glowing. It's not glowing. It's – eeeeek!*

I rush over. Forgetting about snakes, bones, and trapped women, I'm at the rock running my hands over the ochre. My palms don't glow. The ochre shines brighter. There's a crevice in the rock and I shove my hand in there – go against everything my father taught me – and pull out a possum skin wrapped around something that's tied with string. I'm tempted to unravel it there in the middle of bodies and bones, but I retreat to the mound of dirt I sat on before.

My tummy spasms and my tongue feels numb. This is important. I'm meant to be here and find this. A message stick falls out. It's almost as long as my forearm and as thick as my wrist. All kinds of carvings cover it and the wood is old. I turn it over, feel the grooves and texture of its messages. Why would someone hide it here? In the middle of the message stick is N'gian's symbol, and my hands stiffen.

Is it his – the one that's been lost for generations?

And if I've found it, is that a good or bad sign? I tighten my grip and need to remember the old people's stories. N'gian's symbol: the wave, the sun, and the shape around it looks like the full moon. I rub the edges of the shape.

No, it can't be the moon. There's another fine line inside it and it looks familiar. And by habit, I roll the string – that held the possum skin in place – between my hands and along my upper thigh. It's not a moon; it's woven string. String that more length can be added to, and my mother taught me how languages are woven tight, so there's no beginning or end ... passed on and on forever.

I should be finding a way out, saving those trapped women and exposing this terrible place, not worrying about a stick.

'N'gian's message stick glows,' I say. Message sticks protect its messenger – lets them enter any land to deliver a message without needing a welcome ceremony or permission, which by the looks of it, didn't work for its carrier. And this one won't help me. An Elder writes a message on it before it's given to the bearer. I stare at the rock, but it's too dark to see.

My eyes must've tricked me. It didn't glow – it's not magic.

I'm tempted to biff the carved stick into the pile of bones, but our Elders might want to read it. So I wrap it in the fur, tie the string around it, and tuck it into my bag.

Wait ... I've heard about this place.

Secrets whispered late one night around the fire by two Elders. They'd yarned, not knowing I pretended to sleep. The Malung murdered these innocent followers of N'gian.

Plenty of people would want to find this place, honour their relatives with a proper ceremony. Wish I found N'gian's message stick instead of this valley of bones. And the teeniest part of me is happy I didn't, because all kinds of trouble come with N'gian and his glowing things. Like Granny Alkira says, shadows only exist when there's light.

And this place those Elders called 'the end of light'.

CHAPTER 22
KIRRA

Snake-like vines twist and ascend higher. My eyes venture up the giant ancient trees guarding this dewy rainforest. How long have I been here: days, weeks … months? Dunno.

My carer, Silverbird, wears an emu-feather necklace. It cascades over her chest to her waist and matches her hair in texture and colour. She shuffles out of a bark hut that's smeared in clay and is nestled in the middle of this leafy space. Silverbird prods a sleepy fire. 'Hungry?'

'A bit,' I say, and wrap Tarni's grey fur around me.

Hundreds, maybe thousands, of vertical fig roots descend from its giant trunk high in the canopy. These curtain-like walls form our natural rainforest haven with no obvious entrance or exit. A thick layer of leaves and stones, smeared together with clay, covers the dirt floor surrounding the hut.

'The light doesn't fall short anymore,' the older woman says, as I sit and stare at the green battle-rope vines anchored on the ground surrounding us.

'I get it,' I whisper.

The light reaches this place. Reaches my eyes. My eyesight is sharp. And the headaches have stopped. Everything has detail – far away, up close – in a way I've never seen. My eyes flick to the tallest tree and back at her.

I repeat her words: 'The light doesn't fall short anymore.' And smiles linger on our faces, the way the dappled sunlight warms those mossy vines. Her training has worked.

A delicious smoky smell of something roasting wafts through the air, and I'm thankful my carer has taken advantage of the fire's embers.

She passes me my morning meal in a small, shallow coolamon, a warm rice-like thing with fire-roasted yam and flat cakes, always sweet and pancake-shaped.

'Eat it all. Need you at full strength.'

'Thanks, Silverbird.' I nibble at them, and she sits opposite me with a small pile of macadamia nuts.

'Macadamias are my favourite,' I say.

'We call them *gumburra*.' She shells them, gives me a few and tucks the rest away in her dillybag. 'Got them from your little friend Birri one day near the creek. He loves talking about you. Said he was the first one to meet you.'

'He's a friendly kid,' I say, munching on the creamy nuts, a little surprised he parted with what's obviously his favourite food. 'I dreamt about eating these near some giant old trees. Their branches were interwoven, so it grows into one massive trunk.'

'Sounds like a sacred tree, like a birthing place. Knowledge, direction, change can be birthed there too.'

My tummy tightens. 'Well, Tarni ran past me there. Hope she's okay,' I mumble. 'Wherever she is.'

'Want to trade?' Silverbird asks, ignoring my concerns. She holds a dark, reddish possum-skin cloak that's twice the size of the one Tarni loaned me.

'It's not mine to trade. I borrowed it from my friend. It's important to her.' And I hope my dream is right, that Tarni's alive and safe.

'Better trade for you than me.' The silver-haired woman pats the grey fur draped over me. 'It could be a thank-you present.'

Doubt Tarni would agree, if I see her again. But I'm sitting in Silverbird's home, eating her food, after she saved my life and nursed me to full health.

'Okay,' I say, and hope Tarni accepts my apology and this thick reddish-brown blanket now piled on my lap.

Silverbird wraps the grey fur over her shoulders, spins around a few times, and when she stops, a seriousness returns. 'You battled his mind-spear and won.'

A wave of familiarity rolls over me.

'Now, the Malung called you the time-breaker. He wanted your magic canoe.'

'Magic canoe?' My shaper called that surfboard a magic sled, but how do I explain it's not magic? Her words mean nothing, yet they make me shudder.

'He has no power over you. Remember our lessons,' she says, then smears wet white clay across my forehead. A ritual she's done every day.

Somewhere deep inside, words rise and fill my mouth, 'I control my thoughts. These control my emotions. He has no power over me.'

A calmness washes my worries away. I close my eyes and a cool breeze swoops in and around us. I draw in and out, *iiiiin* and *ooooout* in a meditative-guru kinda way, 'cept how can I find peace, when I don't know why I'm here or how to get home?

'Wear this each day. Never stop, unless you've conquered the mind-spear completely.'

Silverbird hands me the pouch containing N'gian's ochre.

'I can't take this.'

'It was given for you,' and she passes me a dillybag to carry it in, along with a roo-skin water carrier. 'It'll protect your mind. Could help you find N'gian's message stick. We need it to restore order. It'll only get worse until we do.'

I place the ochre in my bag. 'Not sure I wanna find N'gian's message stick. Sounds too important for me to find. I've enough trouble with the odd dream coming true.'

'Your gift is strong. Your mind is strong. Narn says you're important and we need you.'

I cringe and want to tell her expectation gives birth to disappointment. And in my case, it's world-record size.

On second thought, I stand, straighten out the string skirt Tarni gave me, wrap the reddish-brown fur 'round me, and say, 'I'm ready for whatever I need to do.'

'Good. You didn't say "feel" ready. Feelings will control your thoughts if you allow them.'

'Yes, I remember.'

Silverbird breaks a clay seal of a large stone vessel, grabs handfuls of rice-like grain, and adds it to a small woven bag.

'N'gian's message stick will show itself to the humble. Hidden things will be revealed in plain sight.' She stands and her silvery hair drapes past her waist.

Flocks of squawking birds speed overhead. Something or someone chases them. The sky's thick as a mass of different species flee together.

Streaks of fire whiz above.

Silverbird freezes, then signals to me – I think she wants me to stay. She sneaks between the thick vines, weaves through more and disappears. I tuck food and a water carrier into the bag, except for the blanket, which I roll and tie the way Tarni taught me. Was I meant to follow Silverbird or hide in the hut?

Our fire's embers have gone grey. Someone else's smoke clogs the air. Flames engulf one green wall, and it's weird that green moss would burn that fast. Should I run, scream 'help' or do something? My feet cement to the ground.

Silverbird appears from behind that smoke screen, tugs my arm and gestures me to follow. Male voices rumble in the background. Spears stab the ground behind, beside, and we race into the rainforest's undergrowth. Dodging, weaving, sprinting, this has a video-game surrealness, the augmented-reality kind without a mask or screen or extra lives.

Greying hair disguises Silverbird's speed and agility. She moves fast and smooth in a swooping motion and refuses to use the shared corridor or any well-worn tracks. I'm panting and ignoring a stitch 'cos we can't stop. We haven't heard any voices for a while, yet we're stuck on repeat: duck and swerve, jump and launch, duck and swerve. After running for most of the day, Silverbird slows to an Olympic power walk.

All of a sudden, my new mother-warrior figure is interested in our tracks. We pounce from rock to rock, under vines, over fallen mossy logs, and I endure grilling after grilling to tread invisibly.

'Sorry,' I say for the thousandth time.

'One more thing,' she says, ignoring my apology, veering left and motioning me to follow. 'The mind-spear attaches to a truth. It's usually a lie cloaked in "truth".'

'Huh?' I say, pressing the pain in my side.

'The mind-spear attaches to something so deep, you believe it's a part of you. You think it makes you who you are but it doesn't. When your mind accepts it's a lie, it'll set you free to become who you're really meant to be.'

'And what if I can't find it or break it?'

'If you don't break the cycle, you relapse, repeat, return to its death sentence and spiral physically, emotionally and spiritually. Everything is connected to your mind.'

'So I'll die?'

'Not sure. But you don't want to carry it around your whole life. It'll suck the life out of you. Takes some deep thinking.'

'Silverbird?' I chew the inside of my cheek. 'You came when I needed you. Never knew my mum, so –' my voice fades so much I hope she can lip-read, '– thanks for all you've done for me.'

And I miss Nan, who has mothered me my entire life. Need to stay strong – no tears – and focus, if I'm ever gonna escape Wallulljagun and see my grandmother again.

Silverbird draws a circle in the air with her finger. 'We are like the sun and fat moon.'

If I didn't feel like crying, I'd laugh. No-one's called my scrawny figure a fat moon.

'We are important in each role we play. When I cared for you, I was the knowledge-sharer – this part.' Her finger moves in a semi-circle shape. 'But you were the other half, the supporter.' And she air-draws the other half of the circle. 'No one is more important than the other.'

'A circle,' I say, my pointer finger looping like Silverbird's. And I remember the Elders gather this way.

'A circle is made when two people embrace. Both give and receive equally … to form true connection – show love and respect. One person is not higher or stronger. That would be the shape of a pointy mountain; you'd be alone balancing at its top. When a storm comes, it's a proper long way to fall.'

'Guess we all need to be part of something greater than ourselves,' I say, more determined for Nan and I to be more involved in our community.

'You've taught me much, Little One.' And my kind knowledge-sharer wraps me in a big hug. I hold her tight 'til our circle-time ends.

'I'll take you to N'gian's cave. It's where I defeated the mind-spear and maybe it'll be revealed to you.' Silverbird's speaking fast, and I'm trying to take it all in, let alone understand it.

We've spent hours backtracking, sidetracking, and I'd be lost without her, but eventually we're inside N'gian's cave, sitting around a small fire.

'I'll leave you here. If those men still hunt us, I'll draw them away to keep you and N'gian's cave protected.'

'You're leaving?'

'You won't be alone for long. It's meant to be,' she says, before slipping past the hidden entrance.

The flames capture my attention with its yellow and orange light never staying still. Silverbird's words about my 'lie cloaked as truth' cuts and soothes at the same time. One truth – or lie – taunts me. Tarni could have bolted and left her blind friend asleep. Instead, she sacrificed herself for me. Silverbird did too.

Is there something in me that attracts death? Mum, Wuz, Mrs Drew, Mel, Tarni, Silverbird … either dead or had a mock heat with it.

Maybe I am cursed.

I scan the entrance for the umpteenth time. N'gian is a no-show. So is his message stick. I wiggle my toes to keep awake, but the more I watch the flames, the longer my blinks become.

The green curtain rustles and a gust of wind swirls around. I gawk at the entrance again. A sudden shift in the air snaps me from drowsy to alert, and the static electricity makes the hair rise on my body.

A once-comforting fire roars into a furnace, as if it's been doused with petrol. The inferno shows moving pictures in different dimensions. Translucent golden layers with detailed data. All overlapping with spherical shapes. No noise, just 3D holographic stories. Its intensity dries my mouth, and my heart beats louder and louder. Faster and faster.

There's a pattern. A reoccurring theme in threes: Bad things. Good things. Three things.

Some people I recognise. Others I've never seen before or remain faceless. My eyes and brain twinge with an information overload.

N'gian is here, without moving through the leafy entrance. And there's no loud booming voice. It's happening in a way I'd never expected. In one moment, I see it all: future, past, and things leading to my future truth.

Saving Wallulljagun saves humanity.

One thread glows brighter with a familiar face: Narn.

I focus. It enlarges.

He's on a large grassy field with ochre-painted warriors on either side. The fight is over. The white-painted bodies win. Narn turns and grins. Then his face distorts into a tormented yowl. A thick long spear sticks out of his stomach. Blood gushes out. His hands can't dam the bloody torrent. He gurgles into the ground.

Narn is dead.

And it's not a yellow-tinged Malung mind trick. I can't stop shiver-shaking.

Can I save him? Or is it happening now and I'm too late? The room is hot and suffocating. My mouth is a nuclear wasteland. Head is spinning, I'm losing control. My face hits a hard cold surface, and darkness overpowers me.

A wetness is pulling on my forehead. I touch it and there's white stuff stuck on my fingertips. Then I notice a shadow moving near the mouth of the cave, on the other side of my smouldering fire.

I scramble backwards. My pouch with N'gian's ochre is on the rocky floor, so I grab it and tuck it into my bag. 'Who are you? Why did you take my ochre and smear it across my forehead?'

There's a murmuring and a smaller, child-like shadow dashes out of the entrance. The remaining silhouette moves into the light. '*Jingi wahlu*, Tarni's friend, you finally woke up.'

I blink sporadically, as if it's Morse code and I'm sending a message out there to see if this is real or another vision. Crawling further away from him, I wait for my instincts to confirm if I'm in danger.

'You're not N'gian,' I mumble … unless N'gian has a woven headband and long wavy hair covered with feathers.

'No, I'm Wanjellah, that fella you met with Nyrah.' He chuckles, leaving me curious and confused.

'Why're you here? How can I understand you? Last time, you were running away. What are you smiling at?'

He calms his smile and clears his throat. 'Sorry, you looked funny. I found you lying on the ground. Your eyes were as wide as a *bora* ring.' And he chuckles and snorts. 'You looked dead.' My intruder shuffles closer and gives me an I'm-sussing-you-out look. 'That's how you dream?'

I wrap my arms around my knees. '*Phuufft* – no! Dunno.'

He moves out of the light and his forehead has white ochre on it – it's not glowing.

I study my fingertips. Then cast a net of questions hoping to catch an answer. 'Why are you here? Why did you take my ochre and paint me with it?'

'Silverbird sent us for ochre to heal Nyrah. Didn't take it from your pouch. We used the one mixed in that coolamon. And you looked terrible, so I put that healing ochre on Nyrah's, mine and your forehead.'

There's a rustling. Nyrah and a little girl push past the cave's leafy entrance.

'Kirra, you remember Nyrah, and this is her little cousin Kalinda,' Wanjellah says, ignoring my questions.

Nyrah shuffles over. '*Jingi wahlu*, Kirra,' and she gives me a hug and sits next to Wanjellah.

'*Jingi wahlu*, Nyrah. *Jingi wahlu*, Kalinda,' I say in an upbeat way, though my heart's still thumping out an irregular beat.

The little girl peers out from behind Nyrah, then ducks back into the safety of her cousin's shadow.

'Don't be shy, Kalinda,' Wanjellah says. 'She's a friend of Tarni and your favourite person who calls the dolphin … Uncle Narn.'

Kalinda peeks.

'Narn!' I yell. Kalinda squeals and hides under Nyrah's fur. 'Narn is going to die. I saw too many things – see too many things – to explain.'

Kalinda cries and I hope it's 'cos of the fright I gave her, not that somehow she understands me. Who tells a little kid their uncle's gonna die?

Nyrah wraps Kalinda in her arms and soothes her in their language with the odd 'Narn' thrown in.

'Sorry. Didn't think she'd understand.'

Nyrah gives me a sympathetic grin, patting the small bundle whose cries have stopped.

'What's important about your dreams?' Wanjellah asks.

I gulp – no Tarni to hide behind.

Then I remember Silverbird's lessons. 'They come true,' I say in an unwavering tone. 'It's happened lots of times.'

Wanjellah doesn't pause or give me that 'she's *different*' look. Instead, he asks, 'When you dream, have you ever thought it meant something, but you realised later what you saw was right, only your interpretation was wrong?'

I remember how I dreamt of Mrs Drew being stabbed, which really meant surgery. I'd misunderstood. I nod, a little surprised by Wanjellah's insight.

He picks up a stick, pokes the fire, and burning ash explodes in the air. 'You need a dream-teller,' he says, prodding more of the sleeping embers.

The fire *clacks* and *blitzes* the air again, which triggers me. My mind screams with visual data, and I tuck into a ball. The images flash and whirl at a dizzying speed – a merry-go-round from hell. It feels important, and I'm scared I'll forget. Wish I had my dream journal and a pen. Things I'll never take for granted again.

'Don't try to explain it all. Flow with the images as they come,' Nyrah encourages me.

Words seem too basic to explain my intense vision, and by the time I finish, my voice is scratchy.

'Sounds like you need some tea to help that throat,' Nyrah says.

'Thanks, it's so dry,' I say, and she strolls over to the entrance.

Wanjellah springs to his feet. 'You two drink tea. I'll talk to Nyrah's uncles,' and he dashes away.

Nyrah picks up the coolamon. 'I'll collect water from the creek,' she says with a smile, and swishes through the cave's mouth.

I stretch and yawn, a little jealous of how peaceful Kalinda looks: fast asleep, snuggled in her cosy blanket.

Minutes later, Nyrah shuffles through the entrance, the coolamon brimming with fresh water. She places it beside the fire, then takes two flat cooking rocks and heats them in the hot embers. She swaps out the rocks from the embers into the coolamon, again and again. At first there's steam and a sizzle when the rock touches the water, but within minutes the water's boiling hot.

This girl's got skills. I can't even boil a kettle that fast.

Nyrah unravels her dillybag and pulls out a small stem covered with green leaves. She plucks off the young leaves, scrunches them and chucks them into the hot water.

'Mmm, smells lemony,' I say, and before she hands me my small wooden container, she mixes in a stringy, sticky golden-brown substance gifted by our stingless bees.

'Sip this, Kirra.'

'Thanks.' One slurp and the taste of lemon myrtle with a hint of smoky honey soothes my throat.

Nyrah and I sip from our carved wooden cups, while the fire turns a log into ash. When our second cup of tea warms our bellies, Wanjellah returns.

'The uncles say we should warn Birrabunji. He'll know what to do.'

'Can we save Narn?' I ask.

He nods. I wanna *woohoo* but my throat is still radioactive.

'I'll go see Birrabunji,' he says.

Can't see this plan working, so I ask, 'If Narn dies with a massive spear through him, how will we save him?'

Wanjellah shrugs off my worries. 'I'll tell Birrabunji what you saw. He'll know what to do.'

I stand and tighten Silverbird's cloak around me. 'I'll come with you.'

'No,' he says.

My hands clench into fists, but I don't let the tension reach my voice. 'Why can't you tell Narn not to turn his back or he'll die?'

'Can't tell him.' Wanjellah's jaw muscles twitch.

Nyrah agrees.

'Why not?' I say, my pitch at full throttle.

'Reasons – things we can't control,' he says. 'Birrabunji will know what to do. Silverbird said that Narn needs to save you, so you can save us all. Promise me, you'll tell no-one about Narn's death. Not even Tarni.'

'Fine. I promise.' I shake my head, my ponytail flicks from side to side. 'But why can't we just say, "Don't turn your back"?'

'Why? Why? Why?' He scowls.

I stomp back to the fire and sit in my famous don't-talk-to-me position.

Nyrah nudges him and he mutters, 'Sorry.'

Ignoring him and his gammon apology, I keep my arms crossed, legs crossed, and lips crossed.

Nyrah stays next to her sleeping cousin, while Wanjellah skulks over and sits across from me. 'I'll tell you why … you can't cheat death.'

I uncross myself and give him my full attention.

'I'm not sure how to save Narn,' he says with a shaky voice.

I swallow. 'So what will you do?'

'I'll find Birrabunji. It'll be his decision. He carries his son's fate.'

'Okaaay.'

'I'm Narn's initiation brother. We are united by ceremony, so he'll need to prepare the traditional way. I'll take ochre to him.'

'Wanjellah, don't forget that the world's survival depends on Narn. He's the only one who can send me back, after the next dolphin call. And somehow, I need to work out how to save Wallulljagun.'

He jumps to his feet. 'I'll tell Birrabunji. Are you sure it's after the next dolphin call?'

I walk to the cave's entrance. 'In my vision, I saw a dark hollow place near the headland. And somehow Narn's call to the dolphins will echo me back to my people.'

'N'gian always has a plan,' Wanjellah says.

Nyrah's voice floats over. 'Don't try to understand it. Be obedient and fearless as you follow each sign.'

'Wanjellah?' I give him a long sideward glance. 'I thought you said we needed a dream-teller to explain my visions and dreams?'

'*Yuh-huh*. But you will be the first one –' He stares at Nyrah and both are quiet.

'What?' I look at Wanjellah, then Nyrah, my head shifts like I'm watching a live tennis match. 'Wanjellah, I'll be the first one to … understand dreams?'

Nyrah's gaze eventually rests on mine, but Wanjellah looks everywhere except at me and says, 'No – yes, you will be the first one to know all of N'gian's gifts.'

His statement empties my mind.

Empties my questions.

Empties my mouth, which is now hanging open.

'I need to find Birrabunji.'

The human race becoming extinct prickles my neck and I say, 'Wanjellah, we must save Narn.'

'We will.' He places his hand on my shoulder. 'Tomorrow, Nyrah and her uncles will take you back to the saltwater people to prepare. You will need to get ready.'

And I say without hesitation, 'Ready for when the full moon sets.'

He leaves, and his final words ring through my head: 'Saving Wallulljagun saves us all.'

It's dark. Can't see the fire or Nyrah or Kalinda. I blink a few times and wait for shapes and shadows to appear. Hope it's dawn and not the middle of the night. A dream woke me. The same one I had in Silverbird's hut: I'm sitting on the edge of the rainforest where two ancient trees are intertwined and growing together.

This is the place where I'm eating macadamia nuts and Tarni runs past me. And as unbelievable as it sounds, it might be the only way to find her. Soft light from the embers' death throes give shadows meaning.

Nyrah and Kalinda are asleep. I know what I need to do. I roll up my blanket, collect my water bottle and dillybag. Sneaking past the still shapes, I remember Nyrah's words from last night. And yes, I'm being obedient and fearless as I follow each sign. I tiptoe out of the cave, crouch at the edge of the creek and fill my water container, careful to avoid Nyrah's uncles' camp.

There's a scurry behind me. I turn around and Kalinda's there. I leap into the air and almost tumble into the water. She giggles and I *shoosh* her. Still unsure if she understands me, I say, 'Tell Nyrah I had a dream from N'gian.'

Kalinda rubs her eye and her little pixie face doesn't seem confused, so I add, 'I must find Tarni. I will meet you later at the beach.'

She scampers away.

The sun speeds across the sky today. My legs ache but I plod on, in search of those sacred trees.

I lick my dry lips, desperate to find a creek to refill my container. I'd say I was lost but that would mean I knew where I was to begin with. My brisk walk fizzles to a saunter.

With daylight vanishing, I'll need to find food, water, and shelter. This green jungle must drink from something.

My search for a creek is limited, 'cos I stick to the tracks, which leads further into the pristine rainforest.

A large boulder is perched in an opening. Little green fur hugs the rock and I squish the moss with my fingers. Parrots squawk in the distance. I sit peering at some thick-trunked trees. On the ground are round, hard nuts. We have them every Christmas. Forgetting my tiredness, I collect handfuls of macadamia nuts hidden in their rough casings. I make a small pile on the boulder beside me.

Grabbing the nearest rock, I smash the outer husk and collect the small round shiny brown shells with the creamy nut trapped inside. I find a boulder with a tiny hole in the middle that'll hold one in place. Perfect.

I crack open the shiny brown shell one at a time and gobble each nut. This protein will give me energy. I gulp another and pause. Two large trees tower above me, their main branches have woven and grown into each other. They peer down at me.

My dream ... the macadamias ... the linking trees ... the exact gut-feeling. This is where it happens. Will Tarni run past me today, or do I do this tomorrow or the next day or sometime in the future?

I'm lost. I'm tired. And I'm so thirsty I could lick the sweat off a water dragon.

Silverbird's words wash over me: find the lie cloaked as truth to detach the mind-spear.

I crack another macadamia and hope Tarni will pass me before the creatures of the night emerge. I must believe in my gift.

Then it hits me – hard: a massive emotional thump, which leaves me winded.

The lie wrapped in truth. I thought the truth didn't set you free; it didn't when I told Nan about my dreaming gift. I was forced into weekly counselling sessions. It didn't set Great Nanna Clara free either, they left her in a psychiatric hospital. And it didn't when I had proof in my dream journal.

That's the lie.

The truth does set me free. It sets me free to be myself, to trust myself. All this time I believed that *gunang* lie. Truth isn't about others and what they think or say or believe. It's about being true to myself, and that's what sets me free.

The mind-spear will completely dislodge when I find the centre of who I really am. And when I learn to love that, no matter what others think or say. I smash another shiny brown shell and crunch the light-coloured nut, while swinging my legs, enjoying the green scenery.

My dreaming gift is not a curse. I'm not afraid of it anymore. And being like Great Nanna Clara is more of a blessing than I ever expected. And to prove I won't hide it, or let Tarni or Mel be my voice, I yell it as loud as I can: 'My dreaming gift is not a curse.' Then hoot a long-winded '*Yew*!'. And a flock of galahs screech and fly out of the trees, their feathers matching the pink and grey clouds above.

A cool wind blows. I unroll my red possum fur and wrap it around me. I need to expect more from my gift. Need to believe I can make a difference. And I need to accept that macadamia nuts could be this city girl's only hope for survival.

CHAPTER 23
NARN

Grassy plains surround huge red rock cliffs. In front of those rocks is a group of red-dusted young hunters armed with spears. Clouds kept Dark Emu hidden, which meant two days of losing and finding the right track. Then two more were spent searching for Tarni. It's mid-morning, and the further I'm away from the dolphins, the tighter my throat, chest – everything – gets.

It's this place. It's upside-out and inside-down. They're living at their hot-season place, when it's early winter. They meet in a large circle and make decisions as if they're Elders, but they're my age or younger.

Where are his circle of Elders?

No clan or tribe has one leader, yet all of these fools answer to a loud short fella called 'Jiemba'. He's covered from head to toe with thick red dust, and it's not the way we traditionally wear ochre. I can't see any bare skin. And his hair is muddy and long, piled up like thick brown seaweed, stuck to the middle of his head.

This 'imbalance', as Dad said, affects us all. I'm tempted to rush in and fight. Plan or no plan, I watch. I wait.

Stealth is my best option, just not my strongest weapon. Slowing my breath, I steady the bait ball swirling inside. I edge closer on my stomach, the long grass hiding me.

Jiemba, the man who stands between Tarni and my happiness, begins to pace. He yells and men sprint in all different directions, as if they've stolen an emu egg and are being chased by its angry feathered father. Are they searching for someone?

Maybe the situation isn't as bad as the silver-haired woman believed. I double-check all the faces.

Tarni isn't here.

I'm wiggling back through the grass, when two men arrive dragging a woman.

Tarni. Her name's on my lips, but I don't let it out. They pick her up and slam her down. Jiemba struts.

She kicks, screams, then bolts. The men yank her back, then pummel her body to the ground. I'm ready to fight them all, but I must be smart.

Tarni is slow to get up. If this is how he treats his promised one, I'd hate to be his enemy.

'Look who we found,' a broad-shouldered, fat-necked man says. 'She escaped and set the other women free – forced the guards to move the rock. Speared one in his foot. The other women are gone, but we caught her.'

Jiemba's head flicks to one side. 'How did you escape? You didn't help those women. They'll be recaptured and punished.'

Tarni lurches at him. 'You think you're powerful?' Two red-ochred men pull her back. 'You won't get away with this,' she says, her body hunched over.

He stiffens. 'If it wasn't for your father and our alliance, I'd have killed you already. You're not worth the trouble.'

A man smeared with the same colour dashes out of the scrub and approaches Jiemba. 'The girl, the time-breaker, Kir –'

'Don't say that name!' Jiemba shrieks. Then he regains his composure and signals the fella to talk.

The messenger keeps his eyes on the ground. 'She's been seen on the outer border.'

'You sure she's alive?' Jiemba sneers.

'Yes,' he says, recoiling.

The short leader chucks back his head. '*Arghhhhhhh*!' he hollers and the fella scurries away.

Did Kirra survive the mind-spear or was it her spirit they saw?

N'gian's clay jar weighs heavy on my shoulder and my conscience. What if the ochre healed Kirra? Glowing or not, I should've kept it safe and hidden in N'gian's cave.

'She's alive?' Tarni stands taller. 'This proves Kirra is more powerful than you or your father. And her N'gian gift is strong.'

'The Malung is the only one who's returned,' he snarls. 'Where's your N'gian? Nowhere.'

'So why is there terror in your eyes?'

'Shut her up!' Jiemba bellows and a red-dusted hunter cracks Tarni across the face. Her knees buckle, and she's yanked to her feet by her hair. Tarni glances my way. Does she know I'm here? Cuts and bruises cover her skin. Skin that was silky and smooth and radiant and innocent.

A surge is coming. I can't control it. Wild squalls and tidal shifts shake me. An urge to knock the red dust right off them.

Stop Jiemba. Silence them all.

My heart is banging out death threats.

I shred through the grass with every muscle tense till their sharp spears dig into my face and body and force me to stop.

Jiemba's men surround me.

I speak with authority, as if I were much older and wiser. 'Jiemba. I am Narn, son of Birrabunji from the saltwater clan. I come as a "messenger", unarmed, the way our lore has always been.'

The fool dips his head, and his men pull back their spears. 'Do you carry a message stick?'

I shake my head no.

'Narn, son of Birrabunji?'

'Yes,' I say, amazed that we understand each other. I know enough language from our neighbouring tribes for small interactions but not like Tarni does.

'So that's who's been hiding in the grass,' Jiemba sniggers, and his men join in.

With a smirk, he saunters over to Tarni and tucks a loose curl behind her ear. 'He's not as clever as your father, is he, Tarni?'

Tarni shudders at his touch. She glances at me, then stares straight ahead again.

Jiemba circles behind me, his voice rumbles on, 'And you didn't see the straight column of smoke? We were warned when you first arrived.'

The short-legged lout points behind me towards the creek I'd crossed earlier. How did I miss a smoke message? If only they sent a slender column of dark smoke, it'd mean an invitation to talk about a tribal grievance. Instead, a straight column of smoke without a succeeding cloud must've spiralled into the sky. All our clans and surrounding tribes know its meaning: an enemy is coming. I study his cave-like eyes, unwilling to show any emotion.

His neck tilts back when he returns my stare. 'Narn, do you call the dolphins like your father?'

'Yes. And I challenge you by our lore.' I point at Tarni and say, 'Her little finger shows she's not promised. She's here with no father or mother or aunty – without a chaperone.'

Tarni's mouth tightens, but I keep talking. 'You offend our ways. I challenge you to fight, a *pullen-pullen*, the way our lore has always settled things. If I win, Tarni will leave peacefully with me.'

Jiemba saunters closer. 'She's promised to me. We are to be joined.' The way his eyes roam over Tarni's body makes me want to smack him in the head with a *jabir*. 'The string is just a token,' he says, while he flicks a trivial speck off his arm, and ignores the fact that his whole body is covered with them.

I straighten to my full height and tense my chest. 'No. It's a symbol that seals the deal. And the string is from her female Elder, a granny, to show –'

'Yes, yes, to show they've approved,' he says, the way a mother corrects a *jarjum*.

'No,' I say, in a tone that demands his attention. 'It's not about approval. It's a blessing from your mother's mother or your father's mother ... the life-givers.'

'Yeeeesss,' he whines, 'I know. Without them we wouldn't have survived.'

'No.' I jolt him again. 'Not survival. The reason for our very existence is that they taught us and nurtured us.'

Jiemba scratches the back of his neck, and red powder flies off. 'Not always. Mine didn't. She left me ... didn't attempt to get better ... just died and left my father to raise me. It was survive or die. Choose his yellow stone or be thrown away.' His close-set eyes widen. He's staring at nothing, as though the grassy plains have swallowed us all.

Then one of his men coughs and Jiemba's eye twitches before he snaps back to us. 'Now … survive or die.' He sheds a snake-skin smile. 'We didn't discuss what happens if I win?' Jiemba's voice sounds almost innocent. But I sense it's just another layer of red dirt to hide behind.

I need to get Tarni out of here quick, so I say, 'Tarni becomes yours as promised.'

The woman I love slashes me with a murderous scowl.

'What if I don't want her?' Jiemba responds casually.

I shrug. 'She walks free, and I stay in her place.'

The whites of his eyes roll, reminding me of a shark during its attack.

'Why would I want you when I have Tarni?'

He circles us. The veins in his forehead swell as his creepy-calm intensifies. 'She's been promised to me since she was a girl, and before you mumble on about how the Elders give a few options, I killed those others off years ago.' Jiemba grins. It's been chopped into his cheeks with a blunt, stone axe. 'Did she promise herself to a dolphin boy? You know that's what her father calls you.'

'She's not promised to me,' I respond without thinking.

He throws back his head and laughs. I expected it to be scary. But as it gains speed, he sounds like a kookaburra with a cockatoo stuck in its throat.

'What *do* you want?' I say to regain control.

'I was joining with Tarni to unite our tribes. If you want to fight, I want a real one … one no Elders would approve.' He slinks closer. 'I want a battle to the death.'

His suggestion silences us.

'If I win, you die and I rule all the clans of your tribe. Your Elders would become part of my advisors, of course, but I would lead both tribes. If you win, you win the freedom of Tarni, yourself and your tribe.'

My muscles tense. 'I can't speak for my clan or any of the clans that form our tribe.'

He flicks his hand, and his men lift the spears to our faces. The tips dig into our skin.

'I'll kill you both now. You are trespassing and she's broken her vow.'

I shove the spear away from my face. 'I will do as you say.'

'Narn!' Tarni yells, speaking directly to me for the first time. 'You can't decide for the whole tribe –' then she mumbles, '– or me.'

'He'll kill you if I don't.' Looking into her eyes is my undoing; they fill with fear and my courage crumbles.

Jiemba paces in front of us.

Tarni's voice is calm, and only for my ears. 'What if we were never meant to be together?'

'What if I believe we are?' I shoot back, not thinking to ask if she meant her and Jiemba or, more importantly, us. 'What if my belief can be strong enough for both of us?' I say.

'It doesn't work like that,' she whispers.

'Maybe it does for me.' I shift my position so I can death-stare Jiemba. 'I accept your challenge, but Tarni will need to tell our Elders.'

'Narn – no. Why would you do this?' Tarni's voice trills.

'You know why,' I say, as she bites her bottom lip. 'I care about you more than anything.'

Her head drops.

'A death battle is set!' Jiemba announces and his circle of clansmen cheer and shake their spears. A hooded cloaked man seems to suddenly appear behind Jiemba and they murmur together. His hand slips out when they embrace, and his skin is covered in thick layers of red dirt.

Jiemba faces us again, twisting his lips upwards. 'I will allow Tarni to go and bring back your tribe's Elders as long as she returns with the magic canoe.' He swaggers over. 'The Malung doesn't want to kill a dolphin caller, even if you did conjure that magic canoe with the marking of N'gian, and its long-haired rider.' He's standing over Tarni and pointing at me. 'My father *will* kill him. And if Narn dies by Father's yellow light, there'll be no spirit life for him. Father must have her magic canoe.'

Tarni nods, as if he's said something normal. And I hope he's lying about that evil light stopping me, or anyone, from entering the Dreaming.

'If you – they – don't return in three days with it, on that fourth day, instead of Narn battling me, he will be executed.' Then he creeps behind her. 'Or maybe you enjoy watching me murder, like that dingo pup when we were *jarjum*.' He whispers in her ear, 'You didn't think I saw you. I liked that you watched – proved we were meant to be together.'

She's trembling. I want to whack Jiemba between his puny eyes, wrap Tarni into my chest until she stops shaking. Except there are too many spears.

Jiemba's still hovering around Tarni's slender neck. 'That puppy was nothing. If you don't return with all that I've asked, Narn, you – everyone you know – will end up like that stinkin' mutt.' He slithers back to his father.

Tarni keeps her head down, and says, 'It's a four-day journey, two there, two back.'

I reach out and squeeze her hand.

Jiemba's eyes have a glint in them. 'Then you'll have to run through the night. Let's hope the moon is kind to you and your old people.' He swishes his hand to dismiss us.

Two men grab Tarni and drag her away. When they release her, she looks at me in a way I've never seen before. And I don't know what it means. Then she bolts, disappearing into the scrub.

'You think she loves you?'

The last person I want to talk about love with is Jiemba, but I answer, 'Don't know.'

'Well, we'll see if she returns. Either way, this is where you'll die,' he says, his arm pointing at the grassy plains. Jiemba's men lead me over stony red dirt, then push me into a hole. I free-fall in the dark, thud onto the ground and am trapped in a red rock cavern.

All I can think about is Tarni, though now it's different. Usually, I'd imagine her long curly hair and smiling eyes. Now it's Tarni running for her life, the darkness chasing her, and that haunted look she gave me before she disappeared.

I'll battle to the death. If I win, I win our freedom. If I lose, I enslave our whole tribe and our long ties with the dolphin pod will be finished forever. Worse, our Elders will probably be killed. I'm not that gullible. I saw his eyes, darting back and forth, when he said he'd keep our Elders as advisors. He's a liar. His own advisors look about his age. I don't want my tribe to serve Jiemba, the Malung's tribe. I've failed Birrabunji, Kirra, all my Elders, my whole tribe, and the woman I love.

Night becomes its darkest and I walk around and around inside the cave.

This place is still and quiet and saltless.

'I can beat Jiemba,' I say and tense my muscles to get angry. I've three days to prepare my mind, body, and spirit for the death battle.

CHAPTER 24
TARNI

I sprint across the land, pumping my arms and legs, urging my body onwards. Faster and faster, analysing where to leap, the best route around, over or under. Small decisions now could mean Narn's survival, and light is fading fast.

At the edge of the rainforest, not on our land, nor my mother's country, is a banging sound and a strange yelp. I skid to a stop, scrounge through my dillybag for my knife.

Aack! Why'd I give it away? The possum fur unravels, and I clutch the message stick ready to re-wrap it when galahs screech and swoop above.

I almost drop the ancient stick and a clap of shivers thunder through me. Not because of the screeching birds or darkening skies or whipping wind.

There was a flash. And the trembling hasn't stopped.

Little by little, I uncurl my fist, gripping the message stick. It looks as though it's caught the evening star. Not all of the stick glows, as our fire-time stories told. Not even all of N'gian's symbol. The wave part of his symbol glows.

'Tarni? Tarni!'

This place gets stranger the longer I stay here. 'Kirra?'

She's sitting on a boulder, popping food into her mouth.

Is she a spirit? But spirits don't eat. Those men weren't lying.

'She's not dead,' I say, unable to move.

'No, she's not.'

Her reply unfreezes me. I could understand Jiemba, but this is a better confirmation: I can unweave languages again.

I slip the message stick into my bag and race over to Kirra. 'Jiemba's men said they saw you, but I thought you were dead,' and I give her a quick squeeze. 'I'm happy I'm wrong.'

As we embrace, I think, *Of all the places, why is Kirra feeding her face here?* Narn's facing death, our tribe's in trouble, and she's all cosy in a fur coat, cracking *gumburra*.

I release her. She grins, and stuffs her cheeks with more round nuts.

'What are you doing?' I shrill. 'You know that's stolen food?'

She shakes her head, no.

I breathe in long and slow to remember the lesson from the mountain of bones, except my mind wrestles back: Was she raised by dingoes? Didn't her parents teach her stealing was wrong, or does she ignore parents and Elders and lore? No respectful person would break the lore without remorse. And everyone, everywhere, knows this.

Kirra collects more *gumburra*, ignores my words.

'This is *not* our country! Not that they have welcomed us onto their land. But your host provides your food. You cannot take berries, nuts, or strip bark and build a shelter. These things must be given to you when you are in someone else's boundaries. They cannot be taken. You are stealing!'

I stop and remember to breathe.

She gasps, opens both hands, and *gumburra* tumble to the ground. 'I'm sorry. I didn't know. What should I do?'

'We have to go. Only take the opened ones. You have anything you can leave?'

She tugs the coat off, rolls it up, and murmurs, 'This cloak.' Her voice sounds embarrassed, and when she won't look at me, I realise it's guilt.

'Who gave you this and what happened to mine?' My head pulses as I gawk at Kirra, to the fur and back at her.

'The woman who saved my life said she preferred grey, and wouldn't take "no" for an answer.'

'Who? What?' I say, but I don't care about details. I just want Mum's cloak with all those painted memories back. My last link to Mum is gone. She could be part of that mountain of bones. And her possum cloak with her life story and our early memories are forever lost. I can't waste any more precious time.

'I'm sorry,' Kirra says. She looks as vulnerable as a puggle – a baby echidna – blind and spineless.

'What happened to you?'

'Met a healer. She saved me from the mind-spear and my sight was fixed. The Malung's men burnt her home and chased us through the forest. She sacrificed herself. Left me in N'gian's cave and drew them away. Saved my life twice. I just finished the last part of my training when those birds rioted,' she says, rubbing the fur cloak and mid-stroke, adds, 'I'm sorry about trading your cloak.'

'It's fine,' I lie. Cringe. Then mix in truth to cure it. 'A red possum skin is thicker and warmer, and one square is worth two of the greys. It's a good trade.'

Except I didn't care about the fur colour or quality. It was Mum's.

As Kirra ties it around her waist, I ask, 'Was that woman tall?'

'Yes.'

'Was her name Merindah?'

'No.'

'Are you sure?' My tongue feels numb.

'Her name is Silverbird, and she thought I'd find a message stick. I didn't and she could be dead ... Could've died for nothing.'

My breath catches when she says 'message stick', but it doesn't feel right to tell anyone. Not until I understand it better.

'Do you know her?' Kirra's waiting for my response.

'No, I thought it was my mother. Bring the fur and shelled *gumburra*.'

'Sorry about the cloak and the nuts, that was stu ... pid,' she says, her voice trailing behind her.

I don't have time to pander to her guilt. 'We have to run,' I yell over my shoulder as I bolt ahead. 'Hurry. It's a four-day journey and we only have three.'

Kirra surprises me when she catches up, and asks, 'For what?'

'To gather our Elders and return in time for the death battle.'

'Death battle?'

'It's not our lore, we normally have a *pullen-pullen*. To save our tribe's lives, Narn agreed to battle Jiemba. We have to hurry or he won't get a chance to fight. They'll kill him if we don't return in time. But when we bring our Elders, Narn will battle Jiemba to the death. If he wins, he gets a pardon. If he loses, he is killed.'

Kirra stays quiet for a time. Eventually she says, 'I wish I could do something to help.'

'You can do two things. Don't tell anyone it's a death battle.' Kirra nods and I hope she'll be willing to part with her only possession. 'And give us your magic canoe. The shadow-spirit demands to own your suuuur –'

'Surfboard,' she says, and looks like she's about to cry. 'But that's the only way I can go home. I'll be stuck here forever. Never see Nan and Dad again.'

Our strides slow. 'That's how I felt about Mum's possum-skin cloak.' I glare, hoping it'll nudge her the right way. 'It was my last thing of hers, and if you don't give the shadow-spirit your surfboard, Narn will die. Maybe we could rescue it after Narn wins his battle.'

She thinks for a moment, and nods in agreement. 'Okay, you can have it.' I thought she'd be more upset. If she can part with her surfboard, I guess I can part with Mum's fur.

'Thanks, Kirra. Without your surfboard, the shadow-spirit would've used his yellow power to curse Narn so he'd have no spirit life.'

She's quiet, and without saying anything, we run as fast as our legs can carry us. My heart pounds to the rhythm of my feet.

One thing pushes us.

The death battle.

Darkness slows our pace. We stop at the creek to gulp the cool liquid.

I give Kirra a reluctant smile. 'You're faster now – keeping up with me.'

'Thanks. It's easy without blurry vision and I copy your movements.'

Admiring her willingness, we run until the light disappears.

There's something different about her. I want to ask about her training – if her sight was restored because she conquered the mind-spear – but my want for Narn to live supersedes everything. He may die without knowing I care about him.

Should've told him the truth: I love him.

The sky is beginning to wake. All the stars have stopped twinkling except for one, the morning star, which welcomes the sun's first glow. Kirra and I have rested, eaten, and our water bottles are half full. As the sky brightens, our walking switches to running. Kirra matches me in every way – determined to reach our clan at the beach. We hurry through the outskirts, and it's strange no children play in the creek or along the beach. We jog closer and our rows of *ngumbin* come into view.

'It's too quiet. Where is everyone?' I say, though I'm happy to hear the waves crashing onto the beach again.

'Dunno. Can't see anyone,' Kirra answers.

I race back and forth. Kirra does the same. We don't need to talk to know something is wrong. The tall open shelters – that provide shade and store food away from the dogs – are bare. Their long layers of *wudjuru* have been taken.

Then I see him in the distance.

He's sitting outside his *ngumbin* on the large trunk of a tree, which grew horizontal along the ground before shooting towards the sky. It's the perfect place to sit in the shade. I sat in that same spot every morning as a *jarjum*.

His head is down. I narrow in on him.

Forgiveness and peace are sucked away, and venom seeps in again.

Minjarra, my father, doesn't move.

That was our – my – special place. And him sitting there pretending he's one of us, makes me want to set that tree on fire and watch it burn to ash. He doesn't deserve to be here. Not when he started this whole thing.

Kirra shuffles backwards. 'Um ... might check the headland.' She turns and runs.

'They all left a couple of days ago. Mosquitoes drove them inland, up the big river.' He doesn't bother to look at me when he speaks.

We ran past the swamps. Not one bite. If there were that many to chase the whole clan away, where are those pesky things now?

'It'll be a slow walk. With that many mosquitoes, you know what happens. The younger boys light the grass on each side of the track, so the whole clan walks through the smoke, and the older ones, trailing last, will put it out.' And he mumbles, staring at the ground, 'Don't want a wildfire this close to our winter camp – *ngumbin* have been here for a long time, and will be here for plenty more too.'

'Kirra,' I yell.

She dashes over.

'I need to talk to him.' I nudge my head in Minjarra's direction. 'I know it's bad timing. We need Birrabunji –

well, all the Elders – and our best spear throwers to hurry back here. Oh, and we need your surfboard.'

'Birrabunji or Narn stashed it somewhere,' Kirra says.

I place my hand on her slumped back. 'First, we need Birrabunji.'

Kirra straightens. 'I'll find him and the rest of them.' Then stares right into my eyes and says, 'Tell me where to go.'

'Thanks.' I try not to sound stunned, but this girl has changed. I walk Kirra to the edge of the creek. 'Follow this all the way. It'll widen into a big river. They'll be camping along it. There won't be permanent huts – look for *gunyah*.' I'm about to explain that *gunyah* are simple bark shelters used to camp in for a short time, but Kirra nods and I can tell she knows what to do.

I whisper, 'Find Birrabunji. Tell him these exact words.'

Kirra repeats my words over and over, memorising them and I give her a nod of approval. 'What does it mean?' she asks.

'The future of the tribe is in trouble. Everyone hurry back.' And I know how to get Birrabunji to convince everyone back quick. I check we're out of Father's view, then unwrap the message stick. 'It's N'gian's message stick. I found it.' I shudder. 'Protect it with your life.'

'The wave's glowing,' she says, eyeing off the middle of N'gian's symbol.

'No time to explain. Give this to Birrabunji. Don't tell anyone else.' I wrap the message stick in the fur, place it into the bag and pass it to Kirra, along with the rest of our food. I repeat the words to her.

It feels good to manipulate language again. Kirra speeds away. She moves differently than she used to, almost drifts through the trees.

Now it's time to face the 'traitor'.

Minjarra hasn't moved.

I yell, 'Can't believe you'd show your face here after what you've done!' Our *ngumbin* are empty, but I wouldn't care if they were full. I'd still be this loud. 'I saw you at the ceremony at Jiemba's camp, three nights before full moon.' My simmer turns to rapid boil. 'I heard what the Malung said. I know your evil plans. I'm ashamed to be called your daughter.'

His head drops, as if there's something in the sand more important to stare at.

I step closer and tower over him. 'I can't believe you were forcing me to marry Jiemba. After I told you how evil he is, turns out you knew all along. It proves you and he are the same. Evil befriends evil.'

My words spit down at him like little spears searching for a sensitive spot to wound.

'How can you live with yourself? He almost killed me. Our guest, Kirra, too. We were captured. Did you know we were missing? His father, your friend Coen, is the Malung.'

He doesn't look surprised or shocked at any of these details.

I heave in a deep breath. 'Now Narn is held captive. And faces death. The whole tribe's in big trouble.'

Still no response. His silence fuels my fury.

'We could all die. Don't you care? You did this to your own people! How could you, Minjarra?'

I can't think of him as my father anymore. I scream as loud as I ever have in my life. 'Say something!'

My accusations rumble through the air.

'What – you got nothing to say?'

My throat craves water to wash away this dry repulsion. Lungs burn. Yelling hasn't eased my anger. I want to hurt him. He needs to answer for all the pain he's brought me.

'I hate you! I wish you weren't my father.'

I've lost. Lost the battle where the light had washed away my anger. A big rock wall forms around my heart, and I glare at the wrinkled old man sitting below me.

He leans on the corner of the trunk and slowly meets my gaze, tears flood his cheeks. 'I'm sorry. I know "sorry" doesn't change it. But I am sorry.'

I've only seen him cry once, when his mother, my Granny Yindi, died. Thought I'd feel better knowing he's sorry, but I don't. I'm still angry at him. But I'll listen to what he says.

He rubs his eyes, the wetness smears across his cheeks. 'I had no choice,' he says. 'Didn't know things would turn out this way. When you were little and Jiemba's mother was alive, things were different. Coen was strange – always covered in red dust and a hooded cloak. I heard he covers a terrible scar across his head, but Jiemba's mum was kind. I'd made a vow for you to be promised to her son.'

'What happened?'

'The next time I saw them, his mother had died, Coen had completely changed, and was wearing that thing around his neck.'

Minjarra's voice is crow-like. He pauses to clear his throat. 'Your mother tried to stop it – didn't want us to promise you to be joined. She was carrying your brother –' He makes the pregnant-woman shape over his belly, and his voice tremors, 'You know he threw a mind-spear into her. We lost both of them. Your mum and baby brother.'

'Why didn't you tell me I had a brother?'

202

'You knew ... Everyone stopped talking about it so you wouldn't cry. If we talked about your mum or brother, you cried. So we stopped talking about it long ago.' He stares into the air without blinking. 'Sent your mum to her family in the rainforest – to their sacred birthing site to protect her, but he got her anyway. That mind-spear brought on labour. They both didn't make it. Her people wouldn't let me see their bodies or say goodbye through ceremony. They told me it was a sacred site linked with women's business, and I respected their wishes.'

He grips the trunk with both hands. When I think our talk is over, he says, 'I made a vow with Birrabunji about Coen being the Malung and the mind-spear he threw at your mum. It diminished his power, so we kept it quiet. But that second crystal around Jiemba's neck has increased his control and caused big trouble again.'

I wanted him to speak, but listening is harder than I thought.

'This is the only vow I've broken, because facing the spears is better than losing a daughter. I'll tell Birrabunji and face the consequences. Guess my mum, Yindi, was right. Sometimes a lore can be broken for love.'

Mum, nor my relatives, told me this story. The rock wall inside me crumbles.

'After the Elders were told that Coen went into the forbidden cave, I was asked to stay friends with him. You know, keep an eye on him and let the Elders know if something unusual happens. Somehow, I lost my way. Truths, half-truths – lies to protect a truth – can tangle you up.'

I had no idea the Elders suspected something. Each time my father talks, another part of the wall crumbles.

'Everyone in our tribe would've been killed if I hadn't agreed to Coen's demands. The Malung controls him. So, I joined his tribe and pretended to be one of them. I thought I could save our tribe, save you. But there's nothing left of the man I once called my friend.'

He takes in a deep breath and closes his eyes for a moment. 'I'm sorry, Tarni.'

A ghastly sound heaves out of his body, one after another, the way a fruit bat screeches in the middle of the night while it fights for food. It's getting ugly. Ugly and awkward.

I want to stay angry, but little by little it evaporates. When a strong man like my father, who guards his feelings, finally cries, it's unstoppable. He looks terrible. Sounds terrible.

And the remaining internal rock wall collapses.

I decipher his blubbering. 'Tried to save you, your mother, the tribe. Lost everyone I've loved.'

My legs ache to sit down, but I'm reluctant to give in. 'And Kirra? I know you two hadn't met, but it was like they were searching for her,' I prod.

His eyes confess before his words do. 'Wasn't me. He told me he was looking for a time-breaker, that Kirra arrived during the dolphin call and she'd N'gian's symbol on her magic canoe.'

'It's not a magic canoe. She calls it a surfboard – made from *fibre grass*. Guess it's a smoother fibre-grass tree.'

'I'm sorry, Tarni.' He shoots me his stern fatherly look. 'You were never meant to be on that track. They were searching for Kirra and capturing any women with magical gifts.' The way he stares at me tells me I should confirm his suspicions.

Instead, I shift from one leg to the other and say, 'We have to take the clan back to give Narn a chance to fight for his freedom. His, mine, and the tribe's.'

Minjarra shakes his head. 'Won't work. It's a trap. Tried to fight for you and your mother once too. First, I thought he wanted his son to marry, and we'd unite the tribes the normal way. I was wrong.'

I give into my tiredness and plonk next to him.

'Then, I thought he wanted lots of wives. Heard some men in other tribes have two, sometimes three. They've been collecting women with magical gifts. Thought that could be wise, having wives with healing powers could benefit both tribes.'

My urgency dwindles while I put this information into some sensible order. But when Jiemba or his father is involved, you can't make sense of their spiderweb of deceit.

'This last trip, I thought he wanted power over two tribes. Then I saw the truth. He wants to rule every tribe in Wallulljagun and kill all N'gian magic carriers. I sent your mother away to save her from the Malung, but he threw a mind-spear into her anyway.'

My father has my whole attention. I drink in every word. It tastes a lot like guilt.

'I failed your mother. Tried to save you. Bought us time with the promise of a joining ceremony to Jiemba. I needed a good plan to save you and our people.' He shakes his head. 'I was wrong.'

'You sacrificed being with Mum so she would be safe.'

'Didn't work,' he mumbles.

'You sacrificed the whole tribe, for me.'

'You sacrifice everything for someone you love,' he says with a wobble in his voice.

Narn sacrificing everything for me flits into my thoughts. Then I realise what Dad's saying.

'You really love me?'

He pushes his wet cheeks into an almost-smile. 'I'm sorry I've never said it. My father was tough and strong and strict. It's no excuse, but even when you don't want to be a certain way, you turn out exactly the same ...' He breathes in hard and blows air out. 'Tarni, I'm proud of you and ... I love you.'

I've never heard him say it before. I let the words hang in the air, then wrap them around me like a big warm hug during bedtime stories, and snuggly fur, and all the things a little girl never really grows out of. I stare at this man I've lived with most of my life but don't know at all.

He looks tired ... older.

I should feel sorry for him but he's exhausted because of all his lies, deceit and pride.

I fold my arms. 'This can't be love. It's wrong. This ending doesn't excuse what you did. How could you sacrifice the whole tribe for someone you love? For me?'

I emphasise every word. I want him to feel the full brunt of my accusations.

His handful of words wound me: 'You just did.'

He can't be speaking the truth. I don't realise I'm biting my lip till I taste blood.

'No, I'm nothing like you. I have no choice. We need to save Narn. And we are running out of time.'

I don't want to hear the truth. I hate it as much as his lies. My head thumps with pain, because, deep down, I know he's right.

'What if the time you bought runs out?'

'What do you mean?' I say, scared of what he'll say next.

'That's what happened to me. Time ran out before I could save you from Jiemba and his father's plan.'

I shake my head, not wanting to believe this new truth. And the same way the tide turns, my tears can't be held back. They tumble down my cheeks.

'I was wrong about everything. You. Me. I thought you were evil, selfish and that you never loved me.' I sniff at the end of each sentence.

He drapes his arm around my back, and I rest my head on his shoulder. We sat here, like this, after Granny Yindi died. He hushes my tears with his words, 'I know. I know. And it's all true. I am selfish. I've done too many bad things in my life, but I've always loved you. I always will love you. The only other person that I loved this much was –' There's a glimmer of light in his bloodshot eyes. 'Merindah, your mother. The Malung threw a mind-spear into her. And no-one survives that. Not even N'gian survived the mind-spear.'

'No, Father. That's not true.'

'He threw one into your mother's mind and she left to die.'

'No, not that.' I hope he doesn't notice my rushed tone.

He's staring straight through me when he asks, 'N'gian survived the mind-spear? N'gian is alive?'

'Yes. Kirra did too.'

'You sure?'

'Yes, N'gian gave Kirra gifts and,' I suck in some air before I reveal, 'I have N'gian magic. I speak and understand different languages. It happened when I was little, before Narn had his drowning accident.'

Father doesn't move, like a fish trapped in the creek stunned by the grey-green *worong*.

'You are like your mum,' he says at last. 'She'd be proud of you, if she were –' And a hardness sweeps over his face. 'They tricked me. I believed their lies. They said they had the most powerful magic. The magic that defeated N'gian.'

'N'gian lives and has many followers in lots of different tribes who carry his power,' I say.

'It makes sense. But if N'gian and Kirra survived the Malung's mind-spear, then maybe your mother did too.' He leaps to his feet.

'Where are you going?' I ask, scared he'll confirm my suspicions.

'I need to know if she survived.'

'But what about Narn and the tribe's future?'

He collects his spears and kisses my forehead. 'I'm sorry, Tarni, for all my mistakes. I love you. But something in your face tells me I've been wrong all these years about your mother, and I need to know. For all the things I've done wrong, this doesn't change that, but I can make a good choice now and a chance to make things right. Before I face the consequences of the broken vow.'

'Wait, what should I do? Father?'

He marches away, yelling back over his shoulder. 'You'll know. The tribe will help you. Don't be like me. Don't do it alone.'

He's gone. Running away with the excitement of a young fella. I didn't get a chance to tell him Mum's missing, hasn't been seen for ages and could be dead. I could race to catch up with Kirra but decide to collect and prepare food for our return journey. I hope Birrabunji and our people hurry here, or time, not a battle, will cause Narn's death.

CHAPTER 25
KIRRA

Wish I had sunnies, I think, as our golden fireball hovers over the horizon. The tide has lassoed the moon, and the sea slurps so far back it reveals kilometres and kilometres of footprint-free shoreline.

Nyrah, Alba and I dig for eugarie on the beach closest to our huts. I sway and twist my hips, as waves splosh around my ankles. My feet swish like windscreen-wipers through wet, sloppy sand and expose shells with their juicy meat clamped inside. Another cold hard lump is underfoot. The white water retreats again, and I grab two large eugarie. The purple female one, I toss back into the sea and hand Nyrah a white one, which she pops into her dillybag.

With Tarni busy bossing everyone, Nyrah 'unweaves language' for me. Smearing the ochre from my pouch with Nyrah and others didn't work like it did with Wanjellah in N'gian's cave. No idea why.

'You dig the way we teach little kids,' Nyrah teases, fanning her feet the way I do but clumsier and more exaggerated.

'Ha!' I keep my duck-feet stance, stick my bum in the air, waddle over to her and say, 'What? You reckon the experts are as deadly as me?'

And the two of them giggle, a welcome change from shadow-spirits, death battles and dreams predicting a gloomy unavoidable future.

'Tarni's the best at it,' Alba says.

'With feet *that* big she should be,' Nyrah adds, and a fresh batch of giggles fills the salty air. 'Kirra, don't ever tell her she's got big feet or she's too tall, unless you want her to be wild with you until the next fat moon.'

And Alba agrees.

When all the laughter and teasing is taken out with the tide, Nyrah walks along the beach to a divot in the wet sand. 'This is how the grown-ups do it,' she says, then digs in her big toe, flicks it up and pops out a palm-sized clam.

Alba copies, equally as skilful.

'Hey, my nan taught me this way when I was a kid,' and I'm alone in the sandy slop while they walk and flick, walk and flick, proving their method is quicker and cooler.

'Well, you're not a *jarjum* anymore,' Nyrah says, as she strolls over to me, then kinda pull-shoves me onto the firmer sand.

With Alba on a seafood mission, Nyrah steers our conversation back to Narn and the *pullen-pullen*. Since that dream, we've snatched moments to discuss it. Never when anyone's within earshot, especially the tallest woman in the tribe.

'Birrabunji gave Wanjellah permission to prepare him with ceremony before he –'

'Kirra, Nyrah, Alba, *jingi wahlu*.' It's Tarni. Her words ring out across the beach as she marches over.

We hide our surprise with a simultaneous *jingi wahlu*, and our smiles stretch wider than the bay.

'We're collecting eugarie to cook a big feed for your journey,' Nyrah says in a rush. Hope Tarni doesn't feel the weird vibe.

'You mean *our* journey. And we should've left already. Why is everyone moving so slow?' Tarni waves Alba over, who's halfway down the beach. Her younger cousin is quick to respond.

'Just because you got in late last night doesn't mean we leave later today,' Tarni says.

'*Uh-huh,*' is all Nyrah huffs out.

Although Tarni's bossiness isn't helping, our secret keeps us stand-offish.

'Is everything alright?' Tarni asks Nyrah.

'Yeah,' she says, and her face lights up. 'I was telling Kirra about the mosquitoes.'

Tarni seems to accept this, so Nyrah continues as we stroll across the empty beach towards the dunes. 'Birrabunji said they heard them from afar – an annoying hum – in the air from the direction of the swamps. Something was wrong. Everyone said they'd never seen them this thick.' Nyrah, taking on Wanjellah's dramatic persona, makes a *zizzing* noise, scratches her arms, and watching her makes my skin itch.

'But it didn't rain much,' Tarni says. 'We've had bigger wet seasons. It's early winter and we've never had swarms of mozzies near this beach.'

'Well,' Nyrah nods at the dunes, and we sit down on the sandy mounds, 'Birrabunji and the Elders said it's linked. If the spiritual realm is out of balance, it'll show up in the physical.'

'With mosquitoes?' I ask.

Nyrah nods. We listen as her voice switches gears to neck-breaking speed. 'The whole clan squeezed the juice from the *nyulli* and rubbed it all over their skin. It usually stops them; this time it didn't.'

Tarni bounces her leg up-down-up-down, pauses to frown at Alba, who's still collecting eugarie as she dawdles back. Then our tall, agitated friend glares behind us at the huts and mutters, 'Is Birrabunji ready yet? Why hasn't he moved?' She's jigging her leg again and asking Nyrah, 'Where are the mozzies now?'

'Tarni.' Nyrah frowns at her. 'If you skip ahead, you'll ruin the story … A couple of days ago, the leaves hung limp.'

She looks ready to leave when Nyrah says, 'Birrabunji and the Elders thought something bad was coming, not that they'd tell the *jarjum* that. They'd planned to camp at the inland river until the onshore winds picked up, hopefully in a day or two, to chase away those mozzies. But Wanjellah found Birrabunji and … and …' Nyrah's eyes are wide – satellite-dish wide.

'You're getting more and more like Wanjellah,' Tarni whinges. 'Hurry up.'

I elbow Nyrah and say, 'I gave Birrabunji the message stick like you asked.'

Tarni doesn't smile. I'm glass or invisible 'cos she's staring right through me.

'I told you not to tell anyone or show anyone but Birrabunji,' she says with clenched teeth, and even seated, Tarni seems pro-basketball tall.

I move my lips and cower a little. Words won't obey and spring out.

Nyrah tries to rescue me by continuing her story, this time at turbo speed. 'When Uncle Koa, Uncle Yarrin, Kalinda and I found the clan, they were already walking back. We went to watch over those who don't go to the *pullen-pullen*. Wanjellah said when Kirra gave Birrabunji the message stick, a big breeze whipped around and all the mosquitoes were blown away and the Elders decided to return. Must be a powerful message stick.'

'It's N –' I begin to say, but Tarni jabs my side and knocks the air out of me.

'Where's Wanjellah?' she asks Nyrah.

Alba finally arrives and plops next to us. 'What's happening?'

Nyrah's staring at the sand when she replies, and I'm not sure if she's avoiding Tarni's question, ignoring Alba or actually worrying about her husband. 'Wanjellah's gone to Narn to perform ceremony … ready him for the *pullen-pullen*.'

When Nyrah says *pullen-pullen*, Tarni cringes.

She jigs her knee, this time with punk-rock drummer aggression, and claws the back of her neck. Does Tarni know we're hiding Narn's death from her? Or is she too busy covering up her own secrets?

'Nyrah?' Alba says, with Nyrah interpreting. 'How did you, Wanjellah and your uncles know to come and care for the clan before that message stick was sent? Did you already know about Narn?'

Tarni's head snaps to Nyrah and growls something.

Nyrah doesn't move. I stiffen too. And Tarni psycho-stares at us.

We're caught in an emotional rip.

Tarni springs to her feet. 'Kirra, what aren't you telling me?' She towers over me. I'm small and unimportant and right back at high school trying not to get bullied.

Nyrah steps in front of me. We're standing in an unfriendly huddle.

'Don't tell her, Kirra. You promised Wanjellah. It'll make it worse if she knows.'

'Let her talk, Nyrah. Kirra doesn't need you to be her voice,' Tarni snarls.

And I'm winded by her words. Can't breathe. Can't hide behind Tarni's confidence anymore, and she's right: I have my own voice. I choose who and when I share my dreams with. And there's no way I'm telling Tarni about Narn's death.

'Whaaaat?' Alba's pushes past and takes a gun-slinger stance opposite Tarni.

'Keep out of this, Alba,' Tarni says, then motors right through her personal space. 'This has nothing to do with you.'

Alba isn't fazed by the height difference. She scowls up at Tarni. 'You're a hypocrite. If Kirra can't hide behind Nyrah, you can't hide behind me anymore. You face the cousins and aunties and everyone by yourself. Don't use me to smooth things over or stick up for you again.'

Tarni and Alba are still facing off, while Nyrah translates everything the cousins say.

Alba, with a hand on her hip, shakes her finger at Tarni. 'Nyrah's your cousin. Look at her face. You know she wants to tell you but it's obvious she can't. No good keeping people happy because you're scared of what they'll say or do. It seems an easier way to live, but it's not true oneness.'

She sucks in a lungful of air, like after a two-wave hold-down, then adds, 'True oneness is keeping people safe because you're ready to sacrifice everything, willing to be humble, admitting you're wrong, saying "sorry", and using wisdom – not to make yourself powerful, but to use the power of selfless love.'

I can imagine Alba as an Elder one day.

'Tarni, you're my closest cousin – like a sister to me, but you're not perfect. I know you're angry, and some things are too hard to hear. When you want to talk more and move on from this, I'm here and ready.'

Tarni looks wounded. She ignores Alba, and her eyes narrow on me. 'Where's the surfboard you promised me? Are you coming to Narn's *pullen-pullen*?' She enunciates *pullen-pullen* to test me, see if I'll snitch on her about the death battle.

'No,' I say, 'What's the point? Without my surfboard, I can't go home whether Narn wins or loses the *pullen-pullen*,' and I accentuate the phrase, the way Tarni did. But something terrible strangles my conscience: I don't want Narn or anyone to die. And I can't admit I'm too scared to face the Malung again. Last time, he slammed death's door in my face. Locked it, deadbolted it, nailed it shut, and with Silverbird's help and N'gian's glowing ochre, I barely squeezed through death's doggy door.

Tarni drops her shoulder into mine and bulldozes past. At the top of the dunes, she says, 'If something bad happens to Narn and your secret could've saved him, you two will be sorry. And, Kirra, you *are* right, you could be stuck in this place for the rest of your life. Nyrah will go home with Wanjellah. And don't ask me to translate. With your skills, how will you get food, water, shelter, fire?' And she stomps away.

I wander back to my briny playground. If by some miracle Narn lives, there's no way he'll want to help me get home. Not after he finds out I dreamt about him dying and didn't warn him or Tarni. Anyway, I agreed to give the Malung my ticket out of here. Where did Narn stash my surfboard? I'm tempted to grab it and escape, or at least surf away my stress before Tarni takes it.

But the sea laps the shore with teeny unbroken crests, then stumbles backwards, tripping over pebbles and pumice and pipi shells. It, too, is not my ally today. Something blue is bobbing in the shallows. I wade out and scoop it up. The sea taunts me, a reminder that I'm from a different time. I wring out my slimy shredded rashie. Competing in a surf comp feels as useless as a teenager believing her dreams come true or that she's been chosen by an ancient spirit to save the world.

Weird, but I no longer feel like a surfer. It's not because I don't have a board. Or that there are no waves … Deep inside where intuition lives, I think, *What's the point of it all? Why did N'gian pick me or bring me here?*

Ignoring Tarni's threats and the growing guilt, I sit in the dry sand and scowl at the sea. It's flatter than a mirror. And the sky is an insipid blue – so empty of clouds and planes and hope, it's a country song waiting to be written. I know its title: 'Stoke comes in waves … unless ya got no surfboard'.

What I thought was rock bottom disintegrates, and I plummet to a new low: missing guitars and cowboy hats and sad, dog-howling songs.

CHAPTER 26
NARN

Sitting around a small fire, I gaze at the stars through a large hole in the cavern's ceiling – the one they threw me into – and prepare my mind for tomorrow's fight … if Tarni and the Elders arrive in time. And if Birrabunji gets Kirra's buoyant canoe out of the sea cave. If they don't, this is my last night alive.

My captors gave me flint rocks, wood, and every now and then, food scraps. They went through my bag, stole my pot of ochre, but left everything else. And I'm hoping that ochre isn't N'gian's glowing one. So with water in my roo-skin carrier, the food Silverbird shared with me, and the insects and lizards in the cave, I've enough to survive. As each day passes, I'm weaker. Wish I had Aunty's flat bread, berries or food from the sea.

Tomorrow is my first solo spear fight. I've fought plenty of times at tournaments, competitions and side by side in *pullen-pullens* against other tribes.

But a death fight? No-one fights to the death.

If there's an offense, the spear fight ends it. You aim for the thigh of the other man. He throws spears. I throw spears. We dodge and move till someone is hit. Simple. Efficient. And it'll stop a feud from even starting. The idea is to maim, never kill. If someone deserves death, it's their Elders' decision. Never heard of a death battle before.

I sneak along a narrow passage to the cave's mouth. Spears, ends stuck in the ground, tips all face me, which is useless because not even a kid could fit through that gap. Four men sit around a fire supposedly keeping guard. Two are asleep and the last two are nodding off. They're predictable: they'll talk late into the night, then drop off one at a time.

Everyone's behaviour is odd, I think, and wriggle back to my fire. It's not just the death fight. No-one captures and traps people. When my flames slow into embers, the cave's entrance is silent.

'Brudder, put out your fire.' A head leans into the hole above.

'Wanjellah?' I whisper-shout.

Then I snuff out the flames, leaving dying embers. He passes me spears, stands on my shoulders, slips down, and we forego our usual greeting of a forearm embrace coupled with noisy back slaps.

'What are you doing here?' I say, with a magpie-like warble.

He flashes a boyish grin. 'You know you're my brudder for life and death.'

'You have a wife. Can't run to help me each time I'm in trouble. Thought challenging Jiemba will get me the respect of our clans, Minjarrah ... Tarni. No good thinking that way now.'

'The lore is serious business,' he says, followed by another you'll-get-through-this smile.

'You sound like Birrabunji.'

Wanjellah's cheerfulness is snuffed out the same way my fire was. 'No-one has ever tried to take over a tribe or land before.'

I rub the back of my neck and exhale. 'I know.'

'By accepting this death battle, you gave Jiemba permission to live outside the lore. And so do you.' My brother chucks me a look that says I'm in deep *gunang*. 'We should kill you both.'

I drop my head. 'You're right,' scrapes past the thickness in my throat. I hand him a spear. 'If this is what the Elders and Dad want, I accept.'

'No.' His face scrunches like dry old fruit, and he shoves the spear back into my hands. 'I'm here to help you prepare for ceremony. Silverbird said you have N'gian's glowing ochre – can't believe it revealed itself to you. She gave us some, but she must be confused because it didn't glow. Can't wait to see the real stuff.'

He plonks beside the embers. I join him. Wanjellah's digging around his bag pulling out tiny parcels wrapped in *wudjuru* and string. He's brought all kinds of different food. I lick my lips and calm myself, because I'm tempted to gobble it all. He passes me roasted wallaby meat, bread, some roasted yam and water.

'Where did you get this?' I say, as I stuff in mouthfuls. 'You ran with all this?'

My brother chuckles.

I try to share the food, but Wanjellah insists I eat most of it. When my belly's full, I ask, 'How's Tarni? Is Kirra …' I stare at my feet. Feels like I've made the wrong decision by the looks of where it led.

'Kirra is alive. Overcame the mind-spear. Now let's see this glowing ochre.'

'And Tarni?'

He grins with the same glint that's got me in plenty of trouble. 'She's good. On her way here with Birrabunji.'

For the first time since she left, my tense body eases a bit. Tarni's coming. So is Dad. Kirra's alive and well. Could my choice be the right one after all? 'Wanjellah,' I say, as he's emptying everything out of my dillybag, 'the ochre's not there. They stole it.'

He stops rummaging, drops his head and closes his eyes for a moment. 'We can't use any old ochre – not that I have any – this is serious business, you know. Why does Silverbird believe it's N'gian's?'

At first he isn't convinced, but by the end of my glowing-symbols-and-clay-pot story, he's keen to apply my special – even though it's non-glowing – ochre.

'Did you try it?' he asks, his scepticism seeping through.

'Yep.'

'And?'

'As far as I can tell, it's ordinary ochre.'

'Well, it'd be hard to be stealthy with glowing ochre; you'd have to run through the night like this.' Wanjellah covers his limbs and pretends to run.

A chuckle spills out. When it's quiet again, I confess, 'I've messed up.'

He gives my shoulder a little shake. 'It'll work out. We'll be ready.'

For all the trouble Wanjellah got me in when I was younger, he's always been there for me. 'Thanks for coming. I've missed you since your joining.'

Before he was joined, Wanjellah was rarely serious. Now, his eyes lose that muck-around gleam and he asks, 'Why were you in N'gian's cave?'

'Looking for Tarni. It's when I was given the unseen gift.' I pinch my lips together before more secrets escape.

'When?'

'Before I came here,' I mumble. 'Too dangerous. We shouldn't talk about it.'

My brother shuffles closer. 'What gift?'

I trust him so I answer, 'Not sure what it's called. It's linked to the dolphin calling.' I ignore Silverbird's warnings. 'It calls in the unseen when we need them, and they come. It strengthens others' gifts. Silverbird said this ochre is supposed to protect others from a mind-spear, but it doesn't glow. Looks like it ran out of magic.'

'No, it didn't.' Wanjellah bounces to his knees. 'Did you mix it in a small coolamon in N'gian's cave?'

I nod.

'Did you give it to Silverbird to heal Kirra's mind-spear?'

I nod again.

'We used the ochre mixed in the coolamon.' Wanjellah is talking fast, and his legs and arms are twitching. 'You joined me to Kirra and Nyrah.'

'Wanjellah, slow down. What are you talking about?'

'Kirra had a dream-vision thing. She saw you get captured and fight Jiemba.'

Something flickers across his face, but before I can question him, he races on with his story. The way Wanjellah can't sit still, you'd think he were the younger brother.

'Your special ochre made Nyrah's gift so strong I could talk with Kirra in her language.'

'Wait.' I rub my forehead, clay flakes off. 'I was wearing that ochre. Is that how I could understand Jiemba's language so easily? Did it link me to Silverbird and her language gift?'

'Figure it only works when you're involved. Tried mixing it with Kirra, Nyrah and me back on the beach, but it didn't work.'

'Don't know how, but I sense you're right,' I say. 'When I get out of here, I'll need to steal it back.' Then we coax the embers into a fire, and talk about everything and anything, like we used to when we were younger.

'Saw Tarni the other day.'

I don't answer. It won't matter what I say, when Wanjellah has a point to make, he'll stab you in the eye with it … Might as well let him speak his mind.

'Why didn't you tell her?'

Wanjellah assumes I didn't. It annoys me, though he's sort of right.

I shrug. 'I did, but I messed up when I accidentally lied to her. Might die tomorrow without making it right and never knowing how she feels about me.' I let out a husky breath. 'Or any chance of being joined.'

Wanjellah rolls onto his side with his arm tucked under his head. 'So ask her tomorrow.' His words escape with the smoke into the starry night. 'Won't be the best timing or the perfect place.' Wanjellah's voice is cheery, one of his positively annoying traits. 'You didn't get those two long scars on your chest for nothing. It's simple. Tell her you love her again. Then ask her if she loves you.'

'Is that what you did with Nyrah?'

'Eventually.'

'Ha – you're giving me advice.'

'Well, I *am* the one who's had a joining ceremony,' he gloats, so I slap his back – hard – like I've always done, and he tries to force my face under his smelly armpit.

Once we settle, I ask again, 'So how did you do it?'

'Well, the worst job turned into the best one. I had to keep an eye on the shared corridor and make sure no-one went into the forbidden mountain area.'

I wiggle onto my back and smile at my brother's dramatic voice. This could be our last fireside yarn.

'Every day I watched. Still did my other duties, hunted with our dingoes and nets in that area, but protected our outer boundary.' He pauses, rubs his hands over the fire, then says, 'I met Nyrah's dad, from the southern rainforest clan, who pulled back the boundary line after he started getting lumps on his arms and legs. He thought it was a warning that evil has grown inside that cave. He said he only saw one person enter. And,' Wanjellah leans in, 'he's still alive.'

I sit up, 'Who was it?'

'Jiemba's father.'

'Is that why they call him "the Malung"?'

'Well, somehow, the shadow-spirit tricked Coen into wearing his glowing bone-string, so that ole evil thing could control his mind, body, and spirit,' my brother says in a soulless voice.

The flames glide over the embers. 'Good thing I'm fighting Jiemba, not his father. How would you fight a spirit-man? Jiemba blabbered on about the Malung. That his yellow-light curse can stop your spirit entering the Dreaming.'

'Nah, he's got no power over the fight. It'll be fair with no magic.'

'What makes you so sure?' I say. My voice rises to a bat-screech pitch.

'You know as well as me, he can only control the minds of those who let them.'

'No wonder Dad tells me to keep my mind strong, that it's my greatest weapon.'

'Birrabunji is a wise ole fella.'

'So –' I need to change the subject from Dad and battles and death, '– how did you get to know Nyrah?'

'Her father got too sick to guard that rainforest side of the mountain, so Nyrah did it and we'd chat every day.' Wanjellah yarns and yarns, tells me every detail and by the end my patience has vanished.

I interrupt, 'Then you told her you love her, right?'

He looks uncomfortable. 'Actually, she told me. Then we had our joining ceremony.'

I bust out laughing. 'So you didn't live up to your two initiation scars, eh?'

'What? I still asked her father's, mother's, grandparents', and her Elders' permission – almost everyone in her clan.'

'Must've been so hard.' I hurl sarcasm at him.

'Well, everyone's joining is different,' he says, blocking my jabs at his sides.

Wanjellah may be older than me and no longer single, but he's still the same ole fella. He always makes me feel better, even if tomorrow, there's a chance I'll die.

'Time to live up to them scars now,' he says with a smile, and when I realise he's not mucking around, we wriggle to the narrow cave's mouth.

Wanjellah's behind me. 'Is that it there?'

I'm about to ask 'Where?', because how can he spot a clay pot in the dark? N'gian's symbol, on the outside of the pot, is glowing, even though it's inside a dillybag that's attached to the toughest huntsman.

'Yep … heard them say they weren't giving it to Jiemba but planning to gift it to the Malung when he returns, to gain his favour.'

'I'm getting it,' Wanjellah says in his don't-care-what-anyone-thinks voice.

He's squirming backwards, thumping out the fire, hanging his dillybag across his chest, standing on my shoulders, and climbing out through the hole he'd entered.

'I can pull you up. You can escape.'

'No,' I say. 'They'd kill everyone if I don't fight tomorrow.'

He doesn't answer, just disappears.

I scoot back to the blocked entrance to watch. Wanjellah's already there. A dillybag's wrapped around the hand of the fat-throated hunter.

He stirs. Wanjellah stops. One hand's in the bag, and he's balancing the weight of the bag in his other hand, so it doesn't wake its owner.

Wanjellah has the pot. What's he doing? Wasting time – they could wake any moment. He pops the lid off and is scooping handfuls into his leather pouch. Maybe our grandparent's grandparent's stories were wrong. Or this ochre is so old, it's lost its glowing power.

A dingo howls. Another does too.

The fat-necked man's eyes pop open. He's staring at Wanjellah.

I want to yell and warn him, but I don't want to wake the other three louts. This one's already bigger, taller, thicker.

'Wake up! Intruder!' he bellows, launches at Wanjellah and grabs his ankle. Wanjellah's fast. He snaps on the lid, grabs the pouch, and slips out of Tubby's grip. Four men chase my brother. And I can't see anything.

I squirm back to the main cave. The scurrying noises stop. There's movement above.

'Narn?' It's not my brother's voice.

'Yes,' I answer, trying to hide my disappointment.

'You're lucky you're here. If you'd disappeared, we'd kill everyone tomorrow.'

My heart is swimming in an ocean surrounded by sharks.

Is Wanjellah dead?

How will I have ceremony and prepare tomorrow without any ochre?

Then I spot a small leather pouch and smirk. He must've thrown it in.

Kookaburras *ka-ka-ka-ka* a long-winded call. They're probably enjoying the morning sun on some thick shaggy branch of a nearby *wudjuru*.

Paint drips off my fingers as I prepare for my fight without my brother, father or uncles. If I'd waited to be welcomed to this land or came as a true messenger carrying our Elders' message stick, I would be able to challenge Jiemba in the normal way, not this disrespectful battle to the death. If I'd talked to our Elders, I wouldn't have journeyed alone and wouldn't have put the fate of the whole tribe in my hands. And if I'd yarned with our Elders, Tarni and I may've had a chance at becoming joined and we wouldn't be in this mess.

I tie the small leather pouch around my waist, hidden under my *tabbi-tabbi*.

Will they forgive me?

The noises above grow louder, and my paint has been dry for ages. They are coming. I stand to face my fate.

Will I die at their hands now or battle to the death against Jiemba? I'm hoisted out of the cave. Four of Jiemba's men surround me. All are covered with red dust and carry spears. Deep scowls crease their foreheads.

The fella with battle scars seared across his face shoves me forwards.

'It is time.'

CHAPTER 27
TARNI

Darkness hobbled away while slow-gathering light entered our beachside camp. Narn's chance to fight for his life is shrinking. I've had little sleep, my mind obsessed with saving Narn. My people skills aren't the best. Interpreting, explaining, communicating what others are saying – I'm clever at that. Been told it since I was young. But using words or ways to convince people – I'm rubbish ... fit for the midden.

This morning, I spoke with Nyrah, Alba and Kirra while they dug for eugarie. Did it turn out the way I expected?

No, it was a failure, an ancient midden-sized failure, piled high since the Dreaming.

And I've tasted Alba's 'straight talk'. She's more skilful than me at delivering a message without destroying friendships or family bonds. As for Kirra refusing to journey with us and support Narn – no real loss. It's not like she can save Narn or our tribe. What can she do? I know her skills: can't make fires, hunt, gather, walk up hills in the rain. Out of every man or woman, why did N'gian send her?

I uncover a coolamon in the shade and use the large shell in there to scoop out a cool drink. I guzzle mouthfuls but can't quench the fever within, so I return to our *ngumbin*. Most people are sleeping or moving slower than a sea turtle walking over quicksand. Haven't seen the dolphin pod today. Narn would want to know they're fine, but there's no time.

'We only got two days left,' I say to a huddle of aunties. They gawk at me with no intention of moving. I use a stronger voice: 'We're out of time, might have to walk through the night if we leave any later.'

It's obvious I have no authority. Birrabunji's near the *jambinbin* grove, and I need him to tell everyone to get moving, but something important is still gnawing at me.

'Birrabunji. I'm sorry, I've some bad news.'

He nods at a shady spot.

We sit cross-legged and he gives me his full attention. 'I've led your son into a trap. I didn't know.' I swallow hard, not wanting to disappoint one of my favourite Elders. 'Now I know the whole story. Jiemba and his father are trying to kill all N'gian followers.'

The more he listens, the more I speak. And the more I tell him, the lighter my shoulders feel. So in one long breath, I reveal everything, and my worries and the responsibility of the tribe pass to him.

'Women with N'gian magic were forced to live in a large cave, a gigantic human trap. If you didn't choose to follow the Malung, you were murdered. And if he kills you with his death-curse, there's no spiritual life, no Dreaming, no being with the ancestors or loved ones who'll pass on later. I'm sorry, Birrabunji. I need your forgiveness for Narn and our tribe.'

Birrabunji looks weary, yet peaceful. 'I would forgive you but it's bigger than you, me, Narn, or our tribe. This is a battle between two powers.'

I force a thank-you-and-that's-why-you're-my-favourite-Elder smile, and although I'm relieved he isn't annoyed at me, Narn still faces the death battle with the Malung's heir.

Rubbing his snowy beard, Birrabunji says, 'That explains how he's getting stronger, because he should've weakened if Kirra defeated his mind-spear just like your –' and he shifts position and his line of thought, even though he was about to say my mother. 'He's gathering strength by gathering more people to choose him, eh? Even if it seems forced, it's their choice.'

Narn's dad – my future father if Narn survives and we become joined – tightens his mouth. Then he breathes in and out of his nose with a deliberate slow steadiness. 'Thank you for telling me. I'll go and think until I know what I should recommend to our circle of Elders. We have a third step.'

'What's one and two?' Birrabunji often says things that need further explanation.

'Have I told you about three things to change your path from wrong to right?'

I nod, remembering his steps as a *jarjum*, but I get ready to hear them again. Birrabunji doesn't say much. When he does, it's clever to pay attention.

'First is *light*. When you saw you were wrong, it lit up your mind.'

He waits for me to nod before he continues.

'Second is *right*. You saw something broken and made it right by asking forgiveness. And third is what we need now – *sight* – to find peace and a new way forward.'

He pats my shoulder, walks past me and heads towards the sea.

I dawdle behind him. Birrabunji sits on the beach, eyes closed with the sun on his face. He doesn't move, not even distracted by the *jarjum* playing along the beach or by two squawking seagulls fighting over a smelly fish carcass.

We don't have time for this. Everyone needs food, water, and we should be walking already. We must form a plan to defeat Jiemba's tribe or at least outsmart them. N'gian, or the unskilled helper he sent, has given us no strategy to defeat our joint enemy.

Fears about Narn quicken from worry to frantic worry, and my trembling hands won't stop shaking, even after I clench them into fists. It was easy to make decisions before I talked with Father. I used to see one right path. One good option. And reasoned it to be the best choice for me and everyone. Now I don't feel confident.

Moments later, worry is cocooned, and instead of transforming into a peaceful butterfly, its fiery wings flap and flutter in my belly and head. I'm marching and screeching at everyone sitting or cooking or dawdling. 'You're killing Narn … You're slow and selfish … Go on, feed your face – you're murdering him.'

Aunty Marlee stuffs more food in her mouth and shouts, 'Being a bit dramatic, Tarni. It's only a *pullen-pullen*.'

'Narn's *only* fighting the Malung's heir,' I mutter, and with nothing to lose, I do something shocking.

Birrabunji said he was going to find answers … needed time alone.

Well, I need to interrupt him. His son and everyone's life depends on it. I stomp down the dunes and place my shadow over his face. He squints with one eye.

I crouch beside him, my voice quivers and head sizzles. 'I'm sorry, Birrabunji. There's no time for this.'

'I disagree,' he says with one eye still closed. 'We make time for this, and time will render itself to us later.'

'What does that even *mean*?' I snarl, and that good girl who once pleased Elders disappears.

'You claim you want to change,' he says in his usual calm tone. 'You make decisions too quickly. Rushed to save Kirra, then got captured. Now you rush to save Narn, who's also captured. I'm finding peace right now – a way forwards. You should try it.'

Thinking he doesn't understand, I mutter, 'We don't have time.'

His eyes lock onto mine. 'No, but we need to make time.'

I sit next to him. Closing my eyes, the sun floods my face and thoughts.

'I'll help you get started,' he says.

I agree, not wanting to ruin the search for peace. And secretly hoping peace can be hurried.

'Your mind has great power.' His slow, steady voice is soothing. 'It controls your body. It controls your feelings, if you learn how to master it. You must practise. Push away your thoughts. Let the sun fill your mind, your body, your spirit. Forget rushing. Clear your head of worries. Be here, right now. I'll do the same, and we'll stay until peace fills us.'

I let the warm sun soak in. My shoulders relax and a tingle spreads from the base of my neck outwards. Is this peace? There's a brighter light in the middle of the sunlight. I know it's N'gian and he's talking to me, except it's so quiet I feel, rather than hear, what he says.

I battle for you, with you. I am a part of you. The magic in me is already in you. Time cannot stop me. For me, it does not exist.

Calmness circles, then flows through me. It's a balance of emotion and thought, and I drink in the silence a little longer.

I peel back my eyelids. Birrabunji's smiling at me. Kirra's surfboard is on the sand next to him, and he's completely wet. How or when this happened, I don't know.

He passes me N'gian's message stick. 'Granny Alkira wants to talk to you. We've gathered the Elders. Now we're ready.'

'Shouldn't you or one of the Elders keep this?' I say, holding the message stick out to him.

'No. It revealed itself to you. For now, you're its custodian, its speaker. Keep it safe.'

The waves in our bay are calming: gliding over the golden sand and out to the green-blue sea, in and out, an ocean lullaby. And I'm amazed my frustrations have disappeared. After checking nothing had changed with N'gian's message stick, I tuck it into my dillybag. Then meet Granny Alkira in a shady spot away from *jarjum* or other listening ears. No doubt, the aunties and cousins would've told her about my outburst, if she hadn't heard me carrying on earlier.

'Tarni-love, sit.' Granny Alkira's weathered hand pats the *wudjuru* mat.

I plant myself next to her, still lulled by the waves.

'The Elders met. Everyone agreed this is different. Things have been done outside of lore, and it doesn't seem fair to thrust lore onto you in these unusual circumstances.' She snuffs in a breath and says, 'Tarni, share your truth.'

I hesitate, steady my resolve by telling myself never to lie again to please the Elders. But how can I know my truth after the mountain of bones and my conversation with my father?

'Imagine your heart and head and fear and failings form your truth,' Granny Alkira continues. 'Now wrap all those things inside a possum-skin fur and tie it around with string. Now picture the string is made from instinct: a deep knowing.'

Her words remind me of N'gian's message stick and in this moment, I know what I must do: for me, Narn, our clan, our tribe. My sacrifice will restore lore. Lore started with love. Not as a set of rules to control each other, but as a set of rules to love each other properly … in a selfless way. And I remember Alba's words and Nyrah and Kirra's faces when I yelled at them this morning.

'Granny, can you let Alba, Nyrah and Kirra know I'm really sorry. Please tell the circle of Elders I will give Kirra's surfboard to the Malung, and I'll promise to join with Jiemba to unite our tribes as agreed by our Elders. I will be the calm centre of this cyclonic storm.'

Before I finish, she kisses my head and whispers into my ear, 'Follow your Granny Yindi's way. I think she told you about growing old for this reason.'

I nod, then finish my explanation. 'Before, I wasn't, but now I am ready to do whatever it takes, Granny Alkira.' Tiny lightning zaps inside me: in my guts, in my hands, through my bag that's draped across my chest.

We yarn about me growing up and not being perfect or pleasing Elders and that relationships – bloodlines – are like language, which go beyond our physical time here. Our stories are told and passed on and woven in a way with no clear beginning or end.

Two things happen: when my words stop, her tears start. She hugs me and I understand it's not a 'thank you, granddaughter' hug or 'I'm sorry'. It's much sadder. One that says 'goodbye' when our tribe only believes in saying 'until we meet again'.

Secondly, bats screech and fly out of every tree in the scrub surrounding our *ngumbin*. They soar into one thick, black mass. There's so many, they block the sun.

'This is a sign – either a good one because they've left or –' Granny Alkira gulps, '– a bad one, because they were here and we didn't know. Never seen bats behave like that in the daytime.'

There's an uproar near our large *bora* and I sprint over. Uncle Jarli has been speared in his leg, and our armed young men are chasing two or three red-dusted hunters.

'They know about that message stick,' Uncle Jarli says between groans. 'I'm good,' he adds, pulls out the spear and limps to the small huddle of Elders.

'Someone's sharing our secrets,' one of them says. 'Better leave more men here.'

The traitor. Is it Dad?

What if Dad's crying and confessions were just an act to get me to tell him about N'gian's magic and Mum? I'm gullible. I've put more people in danger. Time to find Birrabunji and leave.

We've been walking a day and a half and Granny Alkira's final words ring through my mind: 'Don't tell Narn your decision. Give him the best chance to win.'

One by one, we ant-trail behind Birrabunji as the sun sets. Tonight is the last night. We must arrive tomorrow to give Narn a chance.

Our hunters carry their spears. Except for Birri's eldest brother, Bahloo, who's responsible for Kirra's surfboard. It's tucked under his arm, and the long stretchy leg-rope's wrapped around it, the way Kirra had taught him back at the beach before we left. Our children and elderly have stayed behind with helpers, including Kirra and Nyrah. We also left behind the female Elders and mothers; those, who don't need to battle, and ten or fifteen skilful hunters to protect them.

There're fifty or more of us. Men of all ages: Elders, men with greying hair, lanky youths, and lads with fresh initiation scars. Then there're women, young ones like me or older mothers whose children are fully grown. Our role has always been the same. Not as spectators, but we pass the spears to our men during the *pullen-pullen*. Kirra is the only one I've told about the death battle, and the pain in my stomach makes me question if it's another mistake I'll regret. Didn't get a chance to tell the Elders about where I found N'gian's message stick, at 'the end of light'. Guess I was too busy hugging loved ones and saying silent goodbyes.

We journey inland. There's no yarning or laughter. Our thoughts are our own and can make us powerful if we stay focused. The sky shifts from emu-egg blue to charcoal black. It's easier when Birrabunji leads; some hold hands and we all follow the person in front. One step at a time. A single line. Birrabunji, leading us on.

It's too dark to see, even for Birrabunji, who has the best night vision. Or maybe he remembers how the land falls and the trees stand. We stop to rest. A fire burns brightly and most of us sleep around its warmth. We take turns keeping watch and stoking the fire. Kirra's surfboard lies next to me, the N'gian symbol faces the stars. It's Bahloo's turn to keep watch, and sleep overcomes us, one by one.

My heart thumps – eyes snap open.

There's a sound of a woman screaming.

I hear it again and my nerves burn. But I know it's no woman being slayed. And no person shrieking. It's the call of a feathered brown bird, the *booangun*.

It calls again, a murderous cry. No, more like the sound of ten hundred dying victims releasing one long hectic screech. If that mountain of bones could scream, this is how it'd sound.

I jolt upright and hold my breath. Bahloo, who's supposed to be on watch, is snoozing. Something Narn would never do. Everyone's asleep. How can they not hear it? It screams again, the sound that gives *jarjum* nightmares and freezes adults with fear. *Booangun* is known by many tribes as the death bird.

It calls its next victim. I shudder.

Someone will die tomorrow.

I grab my dillybag and fumble for the fur. Then unravel the string. The message stick glows with the wave and … I blink a few times to make sure I'm seeing its truth.

The circle, surrounding the wave and sun, is glowing.

What made it glow: the *booangun*'s call? What's happened since talking with Birrabunji and now? I wrap N'gian's glowing message stick away and tuck it into my bag.

In the darkness, the death bird calls three more times. Will it be Narn or Jiemba? N'gian can't be ready. If he were, his whole symbol would glow.

An earthquake stampedes through me. It destroys my confidence. And another high-pitched scream ricochets through the cool night.

The echo of death.

CHAPTER 28
KIRRA

It's midday, the sun's position is my daily indicator, and if I were at home, Nan would call out, 'Lunch time, Bub.' 'Cept I'm not hungry, probably won't ever be. Can't enjoy the clear skies and warm weather. Not with hunters on duty gripping spears, while their backup wooden clubs are stashed nearby. Not with knowing Narn will battle to the death today, while I chose to hide here. Not without a plan or hope of returning home to Nan and Dad and surfing and showers and toilets and TV and cars and chocolate … and my real life. The real me.

Nyrah stayed behind with me. I'm grateful 'cos Tarni, my designated interpreter, left to save Narn. No-one negotiates with death. If Wanjellah is right, death will not leave empty-handed. Even if we could save Narn, who takes his place? Tarni? Me?

The remaining Elders, led by Granny Alkira, have organised us into small groups, assigning daily tasks to each team. It distracts us from the Narn saga. We're gathering herbs, checking fish traps, taking leftover eugarie shells to the midden, collecting water and firewood, planting and harvesting yam-like roots, turning seeds into flour, making damper – all the things necessary to meet our everyday needs, including taking care of our older people, pregnant mothers, and little ones. Young hunters stand guard while mothers, older children and most of the elderly work together.

Nyrah is with her younger cousin Kalinda. Everyone calls her Kali. Now that I've seen her during the day, not tucked behind Nyrah or sneaking in the dark, she looks about seven or eight. I'm in their group, and Kali's shyness is short-lived.

'Coming, Kirra?' Whenever Nyrah calls, Kali copies in a piercing voice, which'd shatter glass or set off car alarms if they existed.

I trudge behind.

'It'll work out,' Nyrah coos. Her sweet-syruped smiles create cavities in my teeth. 'Tarni said "sorry". Narn will return soon. They'll all come back. Might even bring your flat canoe with them.'

Gritting my teeth stops me from talking or gammon-smiling or remembering who I was. This place has changed me. Not for the better either. Been playing my part: collecting piccabeen baskets from the elderly, so we can fill those palm-frond vessels with sweet water and return them to their owners.

It's obvious now. No matter the time or place, the whole world is flawed. In my time, the competitive culture of greed and power strangles happiness. Here, the culture of custodianship is about cooperation, connection and giving everyone a place and purpose. Still, good people die for no good reason.

The world is broken. I'm broken. We all face loss eventually. A memory stirs ... Intertwining sacred trees.

It's the place I realised my dreaming gift was not a curse. Two separate trees, once-wounded, have healed by growing together.

Is that how it's meant to work?

Our small broken pieces match the wounded shape of others. Oneness: is that what Alba was talking about? Which means, oneness isn't perfect. The shadows of doubt shrink away and my shoulders straighten.

We pass the rows of *ngumbin*, meander along a well-worn sandy track towards the shared space where we gather at night. Three older women, crowned with silver hair, sit under a large shady pandanus. They huddle over square-cut pieces of possum-skin fur. One woman uses a mussel shell to scrape and cut her design into the leather skin. Another paints with yellow and brown ochre. And the youngest, guessing from the least amount of grey hair, is sewing pieces of fur together.

I stop to watch. Kali bumps into me, her head just missing my butt. She giggles so loud a flock of crimson rosellas dart out of the trees, swoop past Nyrah, and zoom into the forest ahead. A squadron of fighter pilots, turning sharply to avoid missiles hitting their crimson jets. Even with my lighter skin, I know I belong. Knowledge is passed down. Wisdom is learned by mistakes, or if you're smart, learned through someone else's. But culture, connection to country, is in our bloodlines. It's in me and no-one can take that away.

The woman who's sewing the fur pieces together is punching a hole with a sharp tool. 'What's she using?' I ask.

'A kangaroo bone, you can use an echidna quill too,' Nyrah explains, then faces the forest track.

'Wow, looks hard. I can't even use a sewing machine,' and I ignore the strange look Nyrah gives me. I sigh to free the tightness wrapped 'round my rib cage. Nan wanted to teach me to sew with her machine. Should've let her. Wish I had my phone, 'cos Nan would've loved a clip of this.

Kali sits next to the woman who's holding the leather punching tool. Nyrah adjusts her dillybag on her shoulder. She seems keen to get our work done, but there'll be plenty of time for chores.

A brick-like heaviness lifts off my chest as I admire the women. Their hands sew and sway in a peaceful dance. This cloak-making task is a thread of truth stitching my head-knowledge with the understandings of my heart. School taught 'Aborigines' – ignorant colonial term – were *only* hunter-gatherers who didn't sew clothing. I always knew we weren't savages, like they assumed.

Nyrah introduces Granny Jidda, who passes her the end of a long, stringy substance.

'It's kangaroo tail sinew.' Nyrah holds it out.

I rub it between my fingertips. It's spaghetti-thick dental floss, just softer and stretchier.

She hands it to Granny Jidda, who moistens it with her mouth. She has her own rhythm: pierce the hole, take the sinew, moisten and chew, push, pull, and tighten the stitch. Her hands move with expert precision. Slowly the pieces merge together, one--neat--stitch--at--a--time.

Crouching next to Granny Jidda, I say, 'It's beautiful,' and Nyrah tells the seamstress my message. I tuck away this memory with a warm thread of hope that one day I'll tell Nan about this.

The three of us stroll along the sandy path, away from the beach homes and head to the grevillea grove, next to the freshwater swimming hole with our empty water carriers. We collect big bright grevillea flowers – red, yellow and pink. The water containers are full with the flowers soaking in them.

Something shifts in the air. The grevillea groves rattle. A funny tingling whips across my skin and my tummy tightens. I press my hands into my stomach and wish I'd brought my fur cloak.

'I feel it too,' Nyrah whispers.

She beckons Kali. Without saying a word, we collect the water, flowers and head back to the beach. Dirt changes into sand as the village of *ngumbin* comes into view. Our scattered bark shelters are shielded between the dunes and the bush.

'Kirra. Nyrah.' Birri's a blustering windmill of arms and legs. He stops in front of me and speaks so fast, it's obvious he's forgotten I've no clue what he's saying.

Nyrah grabs my arm and the more Birri talks, the harder she grips.

I want to understand but my tummy cranks tighter 'til I can't move.

Birri stops. He's smiling.

Nyrah's not. 'He said he was down at the bay near the headland.'

She hesitates. Birri sprints off to the next cluster of people and natters at them. Kali races after him.

'Birri said he saw the dolphin caller swimming with the dolphins.' Nyrah rubs the little bumps forming on her arms.

'Are they back? It's too soon, they can't be back yet. Where's everyone else?' And more questions form in my throat, but Nyrah squeezes my arm again.

'Birri said the dolphin caller told him he's going back to the water.' Her voice is quieter. 'Where he belongs.'

And I can't contain the secret: acid hurls from my gut to my throat. 'It wasn't a *pullen-pullen*,' I blurt. 'It was a battle to the death. Narn's dead. Call it a gift. Call it a curse. My dreams come true.'

Nyrah doesn't say anything. Neither do I.

I wander to the ocean. The arvo sun warms everything 'cept my frostbitten hope.

CHAPTER 29
NARN

I follow the four red-dusted men over granite platforms and paths. They carry my spears as well as theirs. As we leave the shadow of the red rocky cliffs, light warms my face, and I lick my cracked lips. The sun's too bright, shining from the highest point of its arc. I'm stumbling across a rocky terrain, searching around each corner, aching to see my people.

Is anyone ready for their life to end?

Each time I fall, they hoist me to my feet. 'You will die soon enough,' the scar-faced fella says, and the butt of his spear prods me along.

Patches of white ochre are tinged pink from the blood oozing out of my scraped knees. At full strength, it'd be a difficult battle to win. And I hope this ochre is N'gian's, because if I ever needed saving, it's now. At least Kirra, N'gian's helper, will be here.

Birrabunji taught me to have a strong mind: I stretch my frame to its full height and imagine I'm Wollumbin, our sacred mountain – the first place along our coast that receives the sun's rays. Determined to look strong and fearless, even though my terror could fill the deepest valley,

I am led by Jiemba's men to the wide-open plain similar to many other fighting grounds. This is not the usual ritual, where two tribes of combatants line up on each side and launch spears at each other.

I scan the grassland as I pass angry red-painted men with sharp spears and patterned shields. They growl and bang their weapons. A few women are scattered among them and no old people. The rowdy crowd parts, and the other side of the field is teeming with white-painted men and women, ochre matching mine. My initial worry disappears. The hunter with the scarred face passes me my spears and motions me to the other side.

I race across the battleground.

Tarni and Dad rush towards me. Placing my spears on the ground, my hands tremble and I struggle to speak. With them, I don't need to be a towering mountain, instead I throw my arms around Tarni. She stiffens. I ignore it and drag Dad into our shared hug. Gripping them tight, I don't let go.

Wanjellah is here. He and others slap my back and I soak up the encouragement. The huddle disperses; my smile doesn't. I receive more embraces and back slaps from the rest of our clan. This is my family. It's who I am. I greet each one, thanking them for their support. One face is missing. She's meant to save our future.

'Where's Kirra?' I squint at Tarni and Birrabunji.

Tarni turns to Birrabunji.

He clears his throat. 'She couldn't be here.'

'She didn't come?' My voice reaches heights I didn't know existed.

'They would kill her,' Tarni says, and there's an undercurrent in her voice. 'Kirra's back at the beach with

Nyrah, Alba and the others looking after the young ones and our old people ... where she can be useful.'

I wince. Tarni doesn't get how important Kirra is.

Dad's eyes bore holes in me. I'm a pumice stone tumbling in the shore break. Both tribes grab shields and spears and form lines on either side of the wide grasslands.

'Dad, Tarni, I can't fight if things are wrong between us. I can't battle ... can't die if –' I lick my lips, except they shrivel up again.

Tarni's face softens. Her eyes fill with an incoming tide.

There's no time to comfort her. I continue. 'I need your forgiveness. I should never have spoken for the tribe and put my needs, and Tarni's life, above the rest of the whole tribe's. I'm outside the lore ... I'm sorry.'

Tarni's lips are quivering. A slight smile forms, fades, re-forms.

I lean in and hug her, though every part of me wants to kiss her – the kind of kiss she'll never forget. Wanjellah jumps into view, waves his arms around, and signals me to make my move. He's as subtle as a murder of crows squabbling over a carcass. It'd be cruel to ask her again to be mine when death could be moments away. I squeeze Tarni tighter and twist us around, so Wanjellah disappears.

'Narn.' Tarni's voice pulls us apart. 'This won't make sense now, but I understand why you're here. We sacrifice for our tribe.'

'Tarni, I did it for you. I love you ... always have.'

She says nothing.

I turn to Dad. Tarni's silence wounds me.

He plants a hand on my shoulder. 'All will be made right, son. The lore will bring you back. What happens today is meant to be.'

Dad hooks his arms around me, a python-squeeze, and the weight of my wrongs whip away.

One of Jiemba's men hollers. It booms across the plains. Tarni passes me my spear and scampers up the grassy slope to stand with the women and our Elders. Everyone except Dad shakes their spears in the air and yells and howls and roars. Power rushes through me.

Jiemba marches down the slope and steps onto the grassy field. The scar-faced man who started the battle cry is by his side, and he throws his head back and shouts, 'It is time!'

Dad steps in front of me and raises his arms to silence the crowd. I shouldn't be surprised, but it works straight away.

'I am Birrabunji, father of Narn, from the saltwater clan. I have permission to speak on behalf of our Elders.' He points back at our small circle of Elders, who stand behind our huntsmen.

They all haven't come, and in a lightning flash, I understand the wisdom behind this decision. Without me realising, they've influenced most of the important things in my life. Always quiet. Always together. Never one person big-noting a victory or left carrying the guilt.

Jiemba's men murmur among themselves. Their women have gone and there are still no old people either, except that cloaked being. The Malung stands behind rows of red-ochred men on higher ground: the best and safest view of the fight.

Dad stands with his shoulders back, chest out and chin held high. 'I vouch for Narn. If Narn loses, he will take responsibility of what happens here today.'

Jiemba's a spotted quoll, elusive and starving. He snarls, 'Birrabunji, I accept.'

Ignoring my short opponent, Dad's authority floats past Jiemba and all his painted men. 'How will we know the challenger, Jiemba, will keep his word at the end of this battle? Who is the Elder vouching for him?' He searches the faces opposite us. 'I see no circle of Elders here.'

Dust swishes into the air around the cloaked man. He's transported from high on the hill to the valley, a few steps in front of his son. His cloak covers everything, except those glowing bones rattling around his neck.

'I can vouch for Jiemba, heir of my tribe.'

No introduction ... So self-important, he assumes everyone knows he's the Malung.

'Where is the magic canoe?' the shadow-spirit rasps.

As I stare at him, shivers armed with sharp edges slice down my spine.

Birrabunji whistles and Kirra's flat canoe is held high in the air.

We wait. No more is said. Then, someone races through the field with the magic canoe. I recognise that run. Tarni passes it to the Malung. Though their words are muffled, the longer she speaks with our enemy, the stronger the fire burns in my belly.

Tarni sprints back to our women – won't look at me as she passes. Has she made a choice that'll ruin our lives? Another whirl of dust and the cloaked shadow returns to his initial position.

Jiemba's confidence returns. With his chest out and frame stretched to full height (which doesn't make him a sand-grain taller), he struts forward. 'Today we use spears. No shields. No *jabir*.'

I stomp closer and shout, 'Agreed.'

It's custom for the challenged to choose the weapon we'll both use, and the challenger must comply. Though it's a little strange we're not using shields.

'And there's a new rule.'

My jaw tightens.

Jiemba's lips twist. 'Once the spear leaves the hand of its thrower, the other combatant can't move. It must fly in the air and land, even if it's through your throat.'

A murmuring spreads through both tribes, then he adds, 'If you move, you lose and die.'

Ignoring the uneasiness building around me, I growl, 'Agreed.' But it's the most wombat-headed idea I've ever heard. He's the kind of fella that'd dishonour our custom and maim your left shoulder so the scarred pattern would be ruined.

I shuffle back to Dad. He whispers to me and I repeat it to Jiemba, 'And are the rules still the same for how this ends or are you changing every custom?'

Jiemba sniggers. 'Didn't think a death battle needed explaining. The battle will stop when someone is mortally wounded.'

His clan roar. Mine gasp.

'Agreed,' I shout, though every fibre of me doesn't.

Birrabunji leans into my ear once again. 'Use everything you have. Unleash the huntsman within. Patience. Timing.' And he leaves the field.

Jiemba throws back his head and howls.

I yell too. The battle begins with our loud cries.

Red-painted hunters wearing different ochre designs form a line behind him at the edge of the open grasslands. Mine do too. Our tribesmen wear curved lines of white ochre on their chests and faces. Stamping, shouting and banging spears onto shields; all need to release anger, power – whatever is necessary to win.

Jiemba nods to his offsider, who grabs a spear, dusts its tip and passes it to his leader.

No doubt it's powdered with a grounded root that makes the blood flow out faster. But I won't let fear or anger poison my mind. Such disrespect for our lore will boomerang him. It always does.

Patience. Timing. These are my allies. I search for stillness within me. Use it to block out the ruckus. All other thoughts and doubts, I push out of my mind.

'We kill for pleasure.' Jiemba tries to break my focus. 'Animals. Birds. People. It's all the same.'

Closer and closer, he's circling and sneering. 'Death ends all life. It's the stronger of the two.'

Each time he opens his mouth, it's like a river of diarrhoea runs out. And he reeks of it. 'Death is the most powerful force. No-one can run from it. No-one can hide from it.'

I watch his spear, his steps, and mirror them, ready for his first throw.

'The more I kill, the more life I gain,' and when he yells, his neck bulges.

'No. You're wrong.' I talk in tiny simple phrases so his thick ugly head will understand. 'The more you give … the more life you receive. Happiness. Love. Respect. Peace. These give life value.'

Our tribes quieten. Jiemba and I battle with words.

'What has death given you, Jiemba? Nothing.'

'Respect.'

My voice is softer, more controlled. 'No.'

And with eyes locked on his, I wave around at his tribe. 'They fear you. It's not the same thing.'

He squints, his small eyes disappear further into his thick head.

'They may be loyal now … in the end, they'll follow whoever has the most power. True respect is love. They'll never love you.'

'*P-hah*!' Spit flies from his mouth. 'I don't need love.'

We step side to side – two mud crabs – and thrust our spears in the air like huge sharp claws.

'You think killing satisfies? You'll crave more and more. It's sucking the life out of you.'

Jiemba grimaces, cracks form in his face paint. 'For you, winning would be far worse than losing,' he hollers.

'Jiemba, know your place,' the Malung's voice thunders through the air.

'Sorry, Father,' and the spear jitters in Jiemba's hand.

A tiny rancid-yellow light dangles around his neck. I can't let his words or that crystal distract me. So I attack him in the cruellest way.

'Jiemba, you weren't strong enough to save your mother.' He stiffens and I flex my chest. 'Heard what happened to her … how she died. Wasn't she a keeper of N'gian's magic? Which makes her your enemy.'

He throws back his long hair, lets out a deep violent howl and launches his spear. It's flying through the air aiming towards my heart. In our normal ritual, he's supposed to aim for my thigh, and by the gleam on his face, this was his plan all along.

Jiemba grabs another spear from the warrior near him. My reflexes are primed and urge me to duck, twist, run – but with his new rule I stand still. I refuse to break our agreement or the honour of my bloodlines.

The spear spins in the air, almost slowing its motion.

I think of my people and lock my muscles.

Sucking in my last breath, I wait for the poison to pierce my life-beater. A gust of wind blows, turning into a small narrow *boulmung*. It picks up dirt and leaves and spins around and around between our tribes. All fall silent.

The *boulmung* swishes the spear past me – doesn't even scratch my skin. Its powdered tip moves away from my chest, past the white ochre, which looks like it glows. And words push into my mind: *This ochre has a protective magical power.*

I never believed it till now.

Clenching my fist tighter around my wooden spear, I scowl at Jiemba. Then I run and use my fiercest power to launch my spear high into the air. It's a good throw, soaring at a perfect angle. I shade my eyes and watch it veer towards its target.

My clan chant, banging their spears on their shields, or using their hands to clap three beats after my name.

'Narn.' *Clat-clat-clat* … 'Narn.' *Clat-clat-clat* … 'Narn.'

We sense it. Feel it. If there's no gust of wind, we know it will land in the middle of Jiemba's right thigh. A sign confirming victory with honour.

It gets nearer. And nearer.

The spearhead closes in on Jiemba. I steady my breath. Just before it pierces his skin, Jiemba pulls the red-painted offsider in front of the spear.

It lodges in the scarred-faced man's stomach, and he thuds on the ground.

Our clan's cheers are silenced. My breathing is loud and fast. The truth stands before us, an uncovering that cannot be hidden.

Jiemba is a coward.

Both tribes know he's lost more than this fight. He has no honour. No respect.

Jiemba's men are summoned over to their shadow-spirit Elder. The bones rattle around his neck, activated by the yellow glow. His face remains hidden. The red-painted men form a circle around Jiemba.

We watch and wait until the cloaked man blasts his verdict for all to hear: 'Our alliance is broken. Jiemba and Tarni cannot be joined. He has no honour. You are free to go *without* the magic canoe. Leave now. Never return. You are trespassing on Malung country. Go before I change my mind.'

Jiemba's father, who's still hidden beneath his hooded cloak, hugs Kirra's canoe. His laugh is worse than a curlew shrieking in the night.

'Father!' Jiemba pushes past the circle of young men.

'No coward calls me that.' He spins around, his back facing Jiemba.

The Malung flicks his hand, and his men re-form a circle around Jiemba, their backs face him with spears gripped tightly.

Jiemba shrieks, 'Father. Father. Please.' He punches at their backs and can't break through.

The cloaked shadow retreats. And the men release Jiemba from the circle. Not one of them acknowledge him.

Jiemba throws himself to the ground next to his fallen clansman. Yelling and pounding the earth with both fists, he doesn't even remove my spear from the body of his faithful friend.

I almost feel sorry for the Malung's heir.

He'll never see his father again, his tribe or this country. A silent death: penalty by banishment. He'll have no choice but to enter someone else's country without permission. The circles of Elders may be lenient. But for an exiled murderer, the penalty is clear.

Death.

At first I don't move ... It doesn't feel like victory. Eventually I turn my back. Dad is weaving through our white-painted clansmen.

'You did well, son.' He pulls me into a hug. When he releases me, he says, 'Remember, the right choice can be seen clearer from many eyes, not just yours. Next time, talk with the Elders or with me or someone who'll give you another perspective.'

'I won't make this mistake again, Dad.'

Then he steps aside. His eyes are on Tarni, who's racing through the long grass.

'You did it, Narn,' the most beautiful woman I know says and plants a kiss on my cheek, which makes me want to spin her around and around so her feet lift off the ground.

But I don't.

I stay as still as a billabong in case she'll plant those warm soft lips on me again.

'Let's go home,' Tarni says, and I reach to wrap my arms around her, but Dad shoves Tarni aside, and she thuds to the ground.

'Noooooooooo!' His cry blasts through me, and we land in an awkward heap.

Dad's full weight squashes my airways. Then I see why.

A spear protrudes from his stomach.

It's the death spear. The barbs remain in him, and blood is gushing out. I can't think or breathe. Cradling Dad in my lap, I'm torn between retaliating and caring for him.

Then through the masses of red- and white-painted men with their spears flying and shields banging, I see him. Jiemba's ugly smugness taunts me.

I hate him.

It fills every part of me.

I slide Birrabunji onto Tarni's lap. She tugs at my arm and yells something. But her words have no meaning.

Snatching a spear, I power towards my enemy. His eyes are wider than an animal of the night. This time I'm not aiming to maim.

A leg for a leg.

A life for a life.

I close in. He falls back and scrambles to his feet. His eyes glancing around. No-one is coming to help. Terror spreads across his face. A kind of pus-filled panic.

There's no mercy. No compassion. One thing will give me satisfaction. With a ferocious instinctive roar, I grip the long wooden handle with both hands, so I can launch it into Jiemba's body. I'm not risking a throw in case the wind, or other launched spears, re-direct it. He seems smaller, insignificant. A new feeling prickles over me. It ignores my conscience and feeds my hatred.

I arch my back, every muscle tenses, and drive the spear towards him.

With no time to blink, Wanjellah swings his spear to slam mine away.

'No, not like this, Brudder.'

It's a blur. Jiemba's quick to his feet. He rips the spear out of his dead friend, slams Wanjellah in the back of his head, then stabs me in my shoulder. Jiemba thrusts it again. This time aiming for my heart, and I can't remember picking up a spear or wanting to defend myself. But I'm

256

standing over Jiemba. My spear sticks out of his gut, and he's sprawled on the ground.

Wanjellah pulls me away.

Up on the ridge, the hooded man reappears, his fur-covering flaps in the breeze. The yellowy-green light around Jiemba's throat is diminishing; its glow arcing back to the Malung's necklace. One pulsing brighter, as the other turns to ash. The Malung swishes his cloak and vanishes.

'Tried telling you winning would be worse,' Jiemba says. He's calm and a strange innocence surrounds him, as if his innards haven't spilled over the grass. 'Him letting you all go means he's sick of people, and he's decided to destroy it all.' The puddle of blood soaks up the rest of his words.

But I understand. We won't be able to avoid the imbalance much longer, which means one thing. We'll have to destroy the shadow-spirit.

A spear swoops my head, almost clipping my ear, and Wanjellah yells, 'Birrabunji needs you!'

I sprint to Dad and Tarni, weave all over the field while spears fly through the air. I glance over my shoulder; two unpainted men drag Jiemba away. The rest of his tribe retreat.

Call it self-defence: he tried to kill me. But I accept the truth.

I'd wanted to kill Jiemba.

The coward tried to kill Tarni. He speared my dad after his Elder's verdict. Who spears someone in the back? I drop to my knees and cradle Dad's head in my lap.

'Proud of you, son.' His voice floats to me.

'Dad, I'm sorry. *Why* – why did you do that?'

Every breath scrapes his throat. 'You're my son.'

He coughs, blood splutters out of his mouth. 'Nothing to be sorry for.' His eyes struggle to stay open. 'Proud of you. Always have been. Always will be.'

Tarni rubs my back, and slips her other hand into my dad's. I look at her, back at Dad, and don't have to ask.

His smile is weak. 'Was wrong. You have my blessing.'

He's holding both our hands now. I feel something soft in his. His eyes are narrow and his breathing, shallower.

'Good. Bad. Both – important in life.' He's too quiet, so I drop my ear to his lips. 'Use this.' His whisper is muffled. The rest of his message is for me alone.

He places a short piece of brown string in my hand. Woven from the fine bark fibres of *mungulli*, its strong bond won't break and is useful for fishing lines, hunting nets, but this time, an important, delicate purpose. I tie it around Tarni's little finger on her left hand above her second joint.

Now, she's promised to me.

We squeeze Birrabunji's hand and I can tell he's pleased. His hand feels cooler. Chest is shallower.

I'm staring at his mouth. Each breath he takes, I think, *Is this his last? How do you fit a lifetime of moments into final breaths?*

Not sure, but I can't let them be silent. An 'I love you, Dad' flows out … So do my tears.

Dad's mouth doesn't move. His hands are cold. His chest concave. Then I realise his last breath is lost – carried away on the wind – and I'm scared my memories of him and everything he's taught me will be sucked away too.

My shaky fingertips brush Dad's eyelids closed, and a long, miserable sound echoes through the field.

It's coming from me.

A long line of saltwater people trudge home. Me and Wanjellah are the last two. We're walking at the same speed. It's mid-afternoon and we're getting slower as the day progresses. My brother gave me N'gian's pot of 'magical' ochre, but what's the use – it can't bring my father back.

I'm in front, Wanjellah's behind. We're balancing two long branches on our shoulders. And I ignore my wound: pain, numbness – it's the same kind of uselessness. Our sturdy branches carry a precious body wrapped in layers of *wudjuru*, firmly secured with string. Dad's possum-skin cloak drapes over his cocooned body. His painted stories are displayed, the way we've always worn them.

Without Dad, there's an ache the size of a giant cave.

Some Elders walk ahead of us to make sure the body of our loved one is properly respected.

My shoulders and back press heavily on my legs. As we shuffle around a corner, I wobble and grip tightly onto the branches. We'll swap carriers at the southern rainforest corridor and two other young men will bear this weight.

Wanjellah probably senses I'm struggling. 'Almost there, Brudder.'

My hands are sweaty and my injured shoulder bleeds, but I don't care. I plod along, one trembling leg at a time.

'Must be close to that track. You tell me if you need to stop. Narn?'

'No.' I can't get enough air and suck in more. 'I'm fine.' I know I'm not, but we carry my father, and it's my responsibility to take him home to the land where he was born.

Tarni's ahead. The Elders stroll past her.

'Narn, Wanjellah, you want a drink?'

'No,' I grunt.

'Can't stop yet, Tarni,' Wanjellah says. 'Narn and I got to get to that rainforest track.'

'We're nearly there.' Tarni's voice sounds half-chirpy, half-hesitant.

'Yeah,' I mumble, 'the further away from that evil place, the better.' Carrying my father's body changes me: I'll never muck around again.

Her brows bunch together. 'It's worse than you think. They hunt N'gian's gifted ones and kill them. I saw their open graves, no proper ceremonies, just piles and piles of dry bones. Never seen anything like it. They call it "the end of light".'

I can't talk. Not about dry bones, not yet, not ever.

'You alright, Narn?' Tarni says, her feet step to the rhythm of mine. 'Some water might help.'

'Water won't fix all the trouble you've caused,' I say, and as soon as the words leave my mouth, I wish I'd held onto them. Even though it's true. Because of Tarni, Dad is dead, the Malung has Kirra's surfboard, and Tarni doesn't respect that Kirra will save us all.

With the trouble she's caused, I'm not telling her about my N'gian's gift or his ochre. Anyway, Tarni's always acted so clever with her language gift. She doesn't need it strengthened anymore.

I keep my eyes on the terrain ahead.

'I'm sorry,' she says, her tone begging for forgiveness. 'You want me to go ahead again?'

A small headshake keeps her here. I can't blame it all on Tarni. We walk in silence. My worries feel heavier than this cherished body Wanjellah and I carry.

Will everything I love be snatched away?

Dad.

Tarni. I've freed her, but my sourness will soon chase her away.

I adjust my shoulder, and check the *wudjuru* bark cocooning Dad. He needs to remain covered until the burial ceremony is performed when we farewell his body, while his spirit lives on.

For me to attend depends on what the Elders decide. A verdict without my father's influence.

I've no doubt Dad loved me. I know who I am, or who I was: a valued member of the clan. My dad may have forgiven me, but now I face our lore. After getting Dad killed, I deserve to be banished.

I'm the dolphin caller. Dad will join our past Elders, and past dolphin callers too. He said the dolphin caller is the heart of the tribe. Who will be its pulse if I'm cast out?

I chew the inside of my cheek and think about the sun, the sky, the sea – anything else. There'll be time for tears but, right now, I need to get our great loreman to his sacred site. I know nothing compared to what Dad knew, and I wish I'd more time with him.

But my greatest wish isn't escaping exile. It's to bury Dad properly, with two burials, the way our forefathers have always done with dolphin callers.

One now, one later.

CHAPTER 30
TARNI

People gather from near and far for the Old Dolphin Caller's ceremony, under the careful watch of our clansmen who guard our boundaries. Spears and weapons are carried around, a disturbing reminder of how he was murdered by a coward and that coward's father is alive and hungry for power.

With no peace, our land will suffer, because more time will be spent guarding boundaries than caring for country: our totems, fire-stick farming, waterways and animals. Our minds are heavy. There's no dancing, singing or trading amusing stories till the imbalance is mended.

Narn's a fistful of dry sand. The firmer I hold, the quicker he slips through my fingers. And N'gian's message stick hasn't changed: not after the battle, not after the death. Why isn't the whole symbol glowing? Have we taken the wrong track? Has N'gian abandoned us? I'm tempted to unwrap it – haven't checked it today, but I'm helping Granny Alkira make *kalmuhran* bread.

We're in a small open area of the rainforest, next to the creek not far from N'gian's cave. I'm too sad to be hungry, but Granny Alkira says taking care of yourself means keeping your tummy full, so there's enough strength to see the day through. We'd collected, soaked and roasted the *kalmuhran* roots, a fern from our swamplands. I've ground them into flour and we're cooking little cakes.

Granny Alkira turns over a flat stone heating in the glowing embers. 'Heard your father's back.'

'Mmm-hmm,' is all I say, and shape more clumps of dough.

'He went looking for your mother. Did he forget she died when you were little?' She pauses, peers at me – waits for my response, before she continues. 'And he won't talk to me about it, even though I'm his mother's sister.'

I answer with another, *'Mmm-hmm.'*

My father hasn't given up hope, even though he returned for the burial ceremony, along with all the clans of our tribe who responded to our message: a heavy column of white smoke, made from a big pile of dry grass, was sent high into the sky. So people far away would know someone has died.

If Narn's father hadn't passed, mine would've been speared in his thigh. He broke a vow to the Old Dolphin Caller. Now death has closed the matter.

I press the paste into a flat cake. My eyes follow Narn as he walks up the track towards N'gian's cave.

Granny Alkira snatches the odd-shaped dough from me and places it on the hot flat rock. 'You know he met with the Elders this morning?'

My eyes snap from Narn to breadmaking. 'Who?'

'The one you can't stop staring at.' She muffles a chortle and her eyes twinkle.

My cheeks warm and I hide an I've-just-got-busted grin with my sticky hand. Today isn't the day for smiles or laughter. But grannies have a way of knowing which rules to keep or break. She pulls off the toasted bread, tosses it to me and cooks another one. 'The Elders decided that old evil spirit tricked him into the death battle.'

I nod, scoffing down the hot bread, eager for Granny Alkira to tell me more.

She wraps her cooked bread inside a soft sheet of *wudjuru*, tucks it in her dillybag and puts out the fire. 'And you know his father's death is punishment enough. There's no need for him or the tribe to avenge, as he already retaliated when he speared Jiemba.'

I'm relieved, though unsure of our future – if Narn and I even have one.

Granny Alkira talks while we follow the line of people up the track. 'Everyone decided the matter is closed after Narn apologised to the Elders and made his promise.'

'What promise?' I feel it in my heart, hear it in my voice. 'Please, what promise?'

'May not be what you want to hear.'

I don't take my eyes off her.

This time there's no teasing twinkle in Granny Alkira's eyes. 'He will still be our dolphin caller, but promises to be joined with the right woman and raise the next dolphin caller – one of the Elders' choosing … even if it's not you.'

Not you, echoes in my head, and a slow-rolling numbness takes control. What's wrong with me? Is this a sign of the Malung undermining us so he can destroy everything? Or part of N'gian's plan to save us?

Love is meant to be the answer, the beginning and the end,

I think, as I rub the string Narn tied around my pinkie. It shouldn't be this hard.

'Now we can have the ceremony with a clear conscience,' Granny Alkira says.

The longer I listen, the further my shoulders curl; a browning palm leaf reaching the end of its usefulness. After a lifetime of obedience and pleasing the Elders, it's clear my hard work was for nothing. And I can't believe Narn met with them to decide his fate without telling me. He could've been banished.

Then again, I haven't told him about N'gian's message stick. No point if it's for N'gian's magic carriers or ones who knew N'gian, as Birrabunji obviously did when he took Narn to be healed in N'gian's cave.

I dust my hands, sneak a peek inside my bag at the message stick and drop it immediately. The meeting place symbol, which is used as a sun, is shining. What can it mean? The whole of N'gian's symbol glows.

'Granny Alkira?'

'Yep, Tarni. I see it. Time to go.'

She's not looking at my dillybag with the glowing stick though. The ceremony smoke wafts out of N'gian's cave. It's time for us to paint our skin with red ochre and say goodbye to the Old Dolphin Caller, to weep and wail and comfort each other.

I follow the line of people into the vast cavern. A rock platform holds a human-shaped mound covered in paper bark. Birrabunji's fur, with the symbols and stories of his whole life, is draped over him. Tales he shared around our big fire, which warmed our spirits during cold winter nights. Two faded pieces of possum skin are in the middle of his cloak. They would've been painted by his mum or granny and swaddled him as a baby. Then, as he grew, more painted fur skins were added. A personal record of special celebrations, totems, and clan stories were passed down since the beginning of time. But we thought he'd be around long enough for new ones to be added.

I rub the string he gave to Narn before he passed. 'I'm sorry you died because of me.' And I hope no-one hears me. 'Sorry you won't be with us when Narn and I become family.' And Granny Alkira's earlier conversation stings.

If Narn still wants me. And the Elders allow it.

I want to say more but the person behind me shuffles closer and her intrusion chokes my words. Cupping the smoke, I scoop it towards the Old Dolphin Caller's body. The grey rising swirls, his gum-scented send-off.

The woman behind me steps closer again. She's urging me on – edging nearer and nearer. I don't want to end my one-sided conversation, so I speak with false boldness. 'Go join our old people. Say *jingeri* to Granny Yindi for me. Though your spirit lives, we will miss you.'

I follow the aunty in front and tears roll one after another. I can't wipe them away, because my arms, like the rest of me, are numb with grief. I wait for Aunty to finish, embracing Narn and speaking her well-chosen words. She kisses his cheek and follows the line of mourners out of the cave.

It's my turn. I wrap my arms around Narn. He smells so good. I want to tell him I'm sorry about his father dying. Or say something encouraging or meaningful. Instead, I drop my chin to my chest, and the first thing that pops into my head springs out of my mouth. It's the same phrase I've heard many times – the kind of words people told me when Granny Yindi died.

'I'm sorry. We will miss him.'

I mean it, but I wanted it to mean so much more.

He nods, his red-rimmed eyes not quite able to hold my gaze. I don't know what to do next. If we were joined, I'd be standing next to him as part of his immediate family receiving embraces, holding his hand. I hug Narn's Aunty Lowanna and repeat my condolences. I'm unable to think – breathe – let alone have meaningful words to say.

Following the line outside the crowded cave, I give Narn time to grieve with the string of people behind me. It's a slow process. I wait outside the cave's entrance, as each member of our clans slip out and edge past me to the more open area of the rainforest.

People cry. Some with silent wet faces. Others wail loudly. Many are in small groups hugging. All mourn our wise loreman: a kind man who looked after the *jarjum* and helped the old people. I sway side to side to stop my legs from being restless. Everyone must be out by now.

Narn doesn't emerge.

Two more people slip around me. Then I go and stand with our clans in the small opening of rainforest near the creek, in full view of the cave's entrance. Some men pat my back and the women hug me goodbye, before they return to our home by the sea.

About five or six aunties and cousins form a small yarning circle around me. They whisper among themselves. I know they have something to say, so I wait, preparing myself for the brewing storm.

Aunty Marlee speaks first. 'Tarni, the grieving time is a long time and we think the joining should wait out of respect to Narn and his father.'

I rub the string wound tight around my pinkie. There's no point talking if they have more to say. And by their expressions, there's plenty.

My older cousin Lia rushes to fill the silence. 'Yes, what Aunty says. Maybe Narn needs time to grieve.'

Lia's sister, Arika, adds, 'Feels wrong to have a joining ceremony. How can he be happy when his heart is sad?'

Aunty Marlee wraps her arm around my back. 'Don't worry, it may not be as long as the second burial. My Aunty – your Granny Tarni, who you're named after – had to wait a couple of whale migrations. But you know grief takes what it takes. There's no rush. You can't control these things.'

Somehow the circle has turned into a walk-Tarni-home routine. An aunt is on either side in a sideward-sort-of-awkward hug. My cousins follow close behind. They lead me away from N'gian's cave. Away from Narn. I've no choice but to meander along with them. Wish I'd taken Alba up on her offer to walk back with her and Kirra. Or even with Wanjellah and Nyrah, who left earlier to organise the earthen oven for tonight's special meal. Instead, I'm walking back to camp with the swarming women who haven't stopped yabbering about what I should do or, more to the point, not do.

Aunty Marlee pulls my left hand and lifts it to her face. She stares at the string. 'Your joining was rushed,' she says.

Her words infect me, a rash spreading from limb to limb.

'First it was Jiemba. Now Narn. And your older female relative, your granny, should have woven that string.'

She drops my hand.

I drop my head … Tears storm my face. I breathe in through my nose and out through my mouth to gain control.

Maybe they're right. About the string and his dad. I've never lost a father or had one like Narn's. Almost did, if he hadn't died. If Narn wasn't fighting Jiemba … if I hadn't led him there.

I listen and nod – curl the end of my lips and hope they'll believe it's a genuine smile. Inwardly, I retreat to rebuild those invisible walls and guard my heart by shutting everyone out. I'll let Narn grieve, but who would want to be joined with the woman responsible for his father's death?

Yesterday I said goodbye to one of my favourite Elders. Last night, there was a big dinner with our clan and the clans who'd travelled here to pay their respects. Wanjellah and the young men cooked loads of meat, eggs, fish and yams in an underground oven. I gave Wanjellah and Nyrah the message stick to take to our language experts in the rainforest clan to help decipher it. Without new information, what's the point of discussing those glowing symbols with our saltwater Elders?

I'm collecting late-fruiting *midyims* near N'gian's cave, because it makes me feel closer to Narn. Alba hasn't changed a bit: I hear her before I see her. If I were hunting, I'd be annoyed. The animals would've already bolted.

'Tarni.' Her hands grip her hips. There's no greeting. 'You shouldn't be out here alone. Since his death, it's not safe. Why aren't you with Narn? Haven't seen him around.'

I ignore her reprimand about being safe, and keep picking the speckled white berries. 'After the smoking ceremony, the aunties and cousins said Narn needed some time to grieve and the joining can come later.'

'Well, have you checked on him? He is your promised one.'

There's a sting in her voice. It makes me drop my head before I look at her again. 'I'm sorry I didn't get to tell you about Narn and …'

I struggle to finish my apology; she cuts in: 'It's all good. I knew ages ago you both liked each other.'

'Really? But –'

She rolls her eyes so deliberately, her head topples from one side to the other. 'Everyone knew!'

Alba reaches up, picks off an overripe berry, and pops it into her mouth. She's thoughtful. We're taught to eat the overripe ones first and leave the ripe fruit for the next person coming after us, so they'll have food tomorrow or the next day.

She swallows and says, 'He's still your friend, and stop worrying about what people say. You never used to. What happened to *that* Tarni?'

'What are you talking about?' Does Alba walk around with ochre stuck in her eyes? 'You know I've always worried about what other people say. Keeping the Elders and cousins happy helps me do my language-expert job. It's why you used to stand up for me, isn't it?'

'I guess, and like I said before, I'm not doing it anymore.'

'You're right. I shouldn't have let you.' I stop collecting berries and peer into my cousin's eyes. 'After talking to Father and Jiemba and the burial, things I thought were right ended up being wrong. Bad things happened because of me.'

'Well,' Alba says, eyeing a berry out of her reach.

I tippytoe to pick the *midyim*, and hand it to her.

She pops it in her mouth. 'What if the aunties or cousins hadn't said anything? What would you do?'

'Find Narn.'

'There you go, follow your instincts,' she says with a hint of eucalyptus on her breath. 'Don't think he's left N'gian's cave since the smoking ceremony.'

'What?' Then I remember. 'No, he came out for the big feed with our clans.'

He sat next to Wanjellah and Nyrah. I sat with Granny Alkira and kept stealing glances all night. Narn didn't look at me once.

'Well, he must've gone back.'

'He's probably not eating either.'

'I better go rescue Kirra,' Alba says, and she walks back to the track, yelling over her shoulder, 'Left her making *kalmuhran* bread with Aunty Marlee and you know when Aunty's hungry, she gets real bossy.'

'Thanks,' I say, then run as fast as my long legs can manage. This time, I'm hunting Narn. It doesn't take me long to get to N'gian's cave. Collecting berries nearby has paid off.

I reach the narrow entrance – shouldn't be here, but I cup my hands around my mouth and yell into the cave. 'Narn, are you there?'

No answer. Smoke is drifting out.

'Narn, it's Tarni. I'm coming in.' I step inside and wait for my eyes to adjust. The cave is thick with smoke. Odd. He must keep smoking the cave over and over again.

The smell is overbearing, more putrid than rotten eggs and it's worse the closer I get. I cover my nose. There's an outline of a shape on top of the rock platform and a shadow at its base. Squinting to see, I edge closer.

Narn slumps against the rock that holds the remains of his father.

'Are you alright?'

He doesn't move.

'I've been worried about you,' I whisper, though it's just the two of us.

He shifts his position – doesn't look in my direction.

I crouch next to him and speak soft and slow. 'Narn, I've been wondering where you were.' I touch his leg with my fingertips.

He stiffens and I move my hand away.

'Now you know how I feel. Always had to hunt you down.' His voice sounds cold, as if it belongs to someone else, not my carefree Narn. Even during our arguments, I've never heard him use this tone. He mustn't love me anymore.

I'm not sure what to say or do, so I sit next to him, as close as I can without touching. The smoking ceremony should have finished. Then our Elder's body stays here until all that remains are bones.

Only then will Narn enter the cave and the second burial begin. Dry bones will be placed into a hollow log and taken to the sacred Elders' burial site ... so sacred I don't even know where it is.

I know this custom. Narn knows this custom. Everyone knows this custom.

I'm confused.

Why is Narn still here?

If it were someone else's death and someone else's son, Narn's father would've already interceded. He'd help them out of the cave after the ceremony. The smoke would have stopped, and he'd have made sure the cave was sealed. Then he would've taken him home, fed him, and cared for his immediate family.

I glance at the shape on the rock platform. *We miss you. You did little things that made us all feel important.* I don't know how to help Narn. And I don't want to make things worse either.

'I'm worried about you. Thought I'd give you time, but you never came back.'

'Did you even ask me if I wanted to be by myself?' It's like he's speaking to the air, not me.

He sits stiffly. I shift and shuffle so we sit opposite each other. I make it easier for him to look into my eyes.

'You know everyone grieves differently.' He sounds angry. But it's better than sharing the silent stench. I hug my knees and listen as he continues. 'Not everyone wants to be alone. If everyone leaves, I'm alone. And it makes the emptiness too big to carry. But what else can I do?'

'I'm sorry, Narn, never thought of it that way. I wanted you to do what I would've done.'

'Didn't I do that already? I fought your shark and won. Except I don't feel like a winner. He killed my dad. I killed him. We may have got what we wanted, but to get it meant we lost so much more. And this hollow shell.' He pokes his chest. 'This is all that's left. I'm no killer. But now I've killed, how can I be anything else? I can't go back to being Narn, the dolphin caller. Don't know who I am anymore.'

I wait a few moments before I speak. 'Feelings are just feelings. Your mind chooses how you feel.'

Narn laughs hard, mockingly. '*Pffttt*! Who said?'

'Your father.' I scowl.

His head drops.

I place my hand on his slumped back. 'I'm sorry. That came out wrong,' I say, but he stays hunched, unresponsive to my touch. 'I've made everything worse. I shouldn't have come.'

'Why did you?' he snaps. 'Am I the next useful choice? First you wanted me so you didn't have to be joined with that coward. Then you were going to be joined with him when you handed over the surfboard. Yes, I heard about it at the Elders' circle. Now he's dead and you're back here.'

My confidence disappears into the smoky air. He's right about it all – and wrong as well. Love wears all kinds of cloaks. But how do I explain that to someone sitting next to their cloaked dead father?

'I didn't tell the Malung what they or you think. Granny Alkira reminded me about Granny Yindi. So, when I handed over Kirra's surfboard I finally understood. My granny would say, "The best thing about getting old is you know which rules to keep or break." And I must be getting older like Granny Yindi, because I knew in my heart to break a rule – for the right reason – can sometimes be not to *please* yourself but to *be* yourself.'

Narn doesn't respond.

The smoke and stench is overpowering and I'm ready to bolt, but he looks as if someone has poisoned his body, soul and mind. I don't want to leave him again, especially when he doesn't want to be alone. So I make one more attempt.

'I'll make this easy. Do you want me to leave or stay?'

I wait.

He doesn't move.

I stand. Facing the cave's entrance, I'm longing to breathe fresh air and feel warm sunshine on my skin. I want Narn to want me, but it's his choice so I shuffle towards the light.

'Stay.'

I turn and face him. 'You once said I was confident. I'm not. When we were young, everyone thought I was clever. It was my gift. And if I lost that magic completely, would I still be me?' I swallow a lifetime of fear. 'I know the Elders will choose who you'll be joined with. I need to know.' I play with the ends of my string skirt, then peek at Narn. He's watching and waiting. 'Could you love me – no magical gift – just me?'

I'm unable to move. His answer can't come quick enough. 'Yes.'

I let out my worries and breathe in again, not caring if it's stale air with the stench of death. It feels great to breathe knowing he loves me.

'Can you love –' his voice breaks and I wait for him to finish, '– love me as I am now?'

'Yes!' I rush to him and pull him to his feet so we can be in each other's arms. It's a big never-going-to-leave-you-again embrace.

'I love you.' I sob the words into his strong chest.

His 'I love you' rumbles through my body.

Narn loves me. Just. As. I. Am. And I love him more than I thought was possible.

I don't want this hug to end. When it does, I hold his hand and lead him to clean air and warm light.

We stand outside the entrance. My head tucks under his chin; we're a perfect fit. He kisses my forehead. I gaze into his eyes. It's clear how we feel.

I copy the way he kisses me. Gentle at first, then deeper and stronger, not wanting the moment to – I pull away.

'Narn. I need to talk to you about something else.'

We lean against the rock. Narn's holding my hand, and the smoke coming from the cave confirms my unfinished business.

We sit together against the granite slabs. The sun peeps through the canopy of the rainforest, its filtered light beams into the undergrowth. I want to be rid of the guilty ugliness.

For the second time today, I'm about to risk it all. 'I'm responsible for your father's death. If I hadn't taken Kirra to the healer or been promised to Jiemba, he would be alive.'

Narn rubs my hand. 'I'm sorry I blamed you. It's not your fault. Not my fault either. He saved me and gave me another chance at life. A life with you.'

I bite my lower lip. 'What about the Elders? My aunties and cousins said we should wait to be joined out of respect for your father.'

'What do you want? Do you want to become my wife, my family?'

'Yes,' I say, and my head and tummy feel woozy.

'I think we respect the life Dad sacrificed so we can live ours together.'

Aunty Marlee's words drag through my mind. 'What if they say something?' I ask.

'We talk with them. Listen to them. I'll explain what Dad said before he died. That it was his dying hope we become joined.'

'You never worry what people will say. Alba doesn't worry either.'

'Tarni, you don't always worry what people think and say. You were friends with me even though your father disapproved. You wore an emu-feathery thing around your neck and didn't care then.' He chuckles, low and soft. And it warms every part of me. Love hearing his laugh, and having him tease me again.

'You said I looked like an emu.'

'Well, I'm *not* sorry,' he says, wrapping me into his chest. 'Emus are my favourite bird. I loved that feathery thing and wanted your attention, even if it was you getting annoyed at me.' He plays with my hair while I listen to his voice rumbling through his strong chest.

'Tarni, you've forgotten. Sometimes, you, me, we all need help to remember: we are plenty.'

He kisses my hand and pulls me to my feet. 'That's part of being together. I can help you love who you are and you can help me. Just because I grieve for my dad doesn't mean I don't love you, even though I treated you like I didn't. And you were right. It's true what Dad said: love is a feeling. Love is a choice too. And I will choose to love you every day.'

Tears, not sad or angry ones, slip down my face. And Narn, my broad-shouldered man, leans forward and gently wipes them away. I wish I could force out more so he could stroke my cheeks and lips again.

'I choose to love you every day too,' I whisper back. 'I think N'gian's special magic is fading in me.'

Narn kisses my forehead. 'Magic or no magic, you've always been the one.'

He holds my hands and gazes into my eyes. 'I have something to tell you, and a couple of important details I can't, till we've defeated the Malung and get a chance to talk to the Elders.'

'I understand,' I say, ignoring a twinge of dread.

He rubs the string on my finger. 'Dad told me Granny Yindi wove this for your promising and that he – she – both of them – always hoped we'd be joined.'

I stare at Narn's thumb caressing the string wrapped around my little finger. This time I reach up and pull him into a kiss, which becomes a steady stream of them. Warm, deep and almost frantic. Love is on our lips without uttering a word. This time, we don't pull away until we run out of breath.

Side by side, Narn and I pant. My lips tingle. They understand loneliness for the first time.

Our hands are woven together and between heavy breaths I ask, 'What were you going to tell me?'

'It's about my past,' he whispers and hot air tickles my ear. 'I remembered something Dad called "dangerous".'

CHAPTER 31
KIRRA

As surfers are drawn to swell, the whole clan has been drawn to the shared fire on the edge of the large *bora*. Everyone, 'cept the hunters on guard duty. Those little fires outside the *ngumbin* have been left unlit since the Old Dolphin Caller's funeral.

Tarni sits next to me in her interpreter's role again. Since the cave burial, she's friendlier. Maybe that string tied around her pinkie has softened her tough-girl attitude. Narn and Tarni will make a cute couple. But the Malung must be defeated before we make any other plans.

I check the moon: its half-hearted light reflects my chances of returning home. The rounder its circle, the sooner I leave. That's if I can steal my board from a bone-pointing, death-cursing shadow-spirit. Or convince someone to carve me a wooden one – an *alaia* – like the original surfers, the Hawaiians, use. But there are no koa trees or surfboard shapers here. I slink under my fur blanket.

Tarni boomerangs a smile to Narn. He catches it and returns one back.

'Look at you two love birds.' I giggle, as they send not-so-secret messages.

Tarni nudges me; she's shame but tries to hide it with conversation. 'See those stars sparkling up there?' She points and lounges back. 'Granny Yindi used to say when they twinkle, they're talking to each other.'

I lean back too. 'Can you hear what they're saying?'

'Not really … The old language experts in my mother's clan could. The night sky tells us when certain food on land was ready. Dark Emu nesting up there meant time to hunt eggs down here. And when we were little, we'd follow them on journeys through the night and never get lost.'

We lie gazing at the chattering stars.

Tarni speaks softly with the lull of the sea. 'They can tap into their gift and block out noisy distractions … fuzziness becomes sharp. For them a whisper can be as loud as a shout, it's about clarity.'

I glance at Tarni, her face hidden by the darkness, and ask, 'Could you, with practise?'

'Maybe, one day. Strange thing is Granny Yindi never had that gift, but taught me all kinds of things can speak to us if you listen hard enough. It's like she knew I would get this magic.'

'Did she talk about your mum?'

'She didn't say much about her because of my father. Granny said Mum was kind and Father changed after she disappeared.'

'She said *disappeared*, not *died*,' I say, still staring at the billions of stars, filling the unpolluted sky.

'Never thought about that, maybe she knew –'

A noise thunders along the edge of the bush. It rushes towards us, like a mob of kangaroos. Everyone freezes for a second. Men and women, young and old, grab spears, shields, axes, *jabir*, or whatever they have near. Then Tarni and I scramble to our feet and scamper to the fire to join the rest of the women. We form a human shield and tuck the *jarjum* behind us. We've been ready for that Malung and his men to attack, but our guard system has failed.

'What is it?' I say to Tarni, my eyes glued on the southern edge of the camp.

'*Who* is it?' she replies and adds, 'Not sure. But they're in a real hurry.'

The thumping becomes louder and closer 'til shadows move from the outskirts of camp, right into our shared space.

Our clan drop their weapons, then signal the guards who'd chased Wanjellah and his mates from the outer track to return.

I shake Tarni's arm. 'What are they saying?'

'Narn's telling Wanjellah he's lucky he's so fast – could've speared him and his friends. And he asks why Wanjellah didn't *cooee*.'

Narn grabs his brother. There's a flurry of back slaps … The bromance is strong.

Wanjellah speaks between heavy breaths. Then a whooshing sound of muffled chatter swoops 'round the crowd. Its volume builds, and one word is repeated over and over: 'N'gian'.

I hear my name and my heart revs.

Tarni responds. 'Wanjellah says there's no time. He needs to see you. The rainforest Elders sent them to return N'gian's message stick. And they need N'gian's glowing ochre.' Tarni stares, no, kinda flinches at Narn. Those earlier smiles and giggles have mutated.

Narn unties the pouch from his waist and passes it to Wanjellah.

Everyone else huddles around the message stick, its carrier and his friends.

Seconds later, the swarm switches from Wanjellah to me. 'Tarni?' Her eyes flick my way. 'Are you sure he meant me?'

'Yes.'

My cardiac muscle kicks into overdrive. Our clan launches grenade-like questions. Tarni scrambles to keep up.

'Are we in danger?'

'Who found it?'

'Why bring it here?'

'When was it found?'

'How did you make it glow?'

One of the older men, Uncle Gukuji, steps through the people. Tarni keeps interpreting.

'Give him space,' Uncle Gukuji says, and passes Wanjellah some water. 'Here. Sit, rest for a bit.'

Wanjellah nods in thanks, guzzles the water and passes it to his friends. But they don't sit.

There's a haunted look in Wanjellah's eyes when he holds the message stick in the air. The glow radiates in the dark night. 'When Tarni gave me N'gian's message stick, after our ceremony for the Old Dolphin Caller, the N'gian's symbol was glowing.'

Narn gawks at Tarni – not in a lovesick way. 'You found N'gian's message stick and never told me,' he says.

She mirrors his rigid stance and pre-fight boxer attitude. 'You mean the same way you told me about N'gian's ochre.' Tarni's slower to translate this.

Uncle Gukuji shooshes the crowd and Wanjellah says, 'Our translators say, "N'gian will answer when we call. As the Malung disrupts the balance, N'gian is already moving his clever ones into place." They told me to return. Only its finder can translate its message.'

The process is slow. Someone talks. Tarni translates. More talk. More translation.

'Tarni, where did you find N'gian's message stick?' Uncle Gukuji asks.

'In a mountain of bones made from N'gian's followers, the place they call "the end of light",' she says. 'Above the pile of bones was a large rock with N'gian's symbol painted on it. The symbol on the rock glowed – not straight away – but it glowed as if it called me. The message stick was in a crevice there. Once I had it, the rock stopped glowing.'

'Did N'gian's message stick glow?' someone else asks.

'No.'

'When did it glow?' Another question is thrown from the darkness.

'When I found Kirra … galahs screeched and the wave part of N'gian's symbol glowed.'

It's quiet. Tarni stares at me.

'That's when I was fully released from the mind-spear,' I say. 'I found my truth and believed in myself: that I have a gift, not a curse.'

'Makes sense,' Uncle Gukuji says. 'Without knowing yourself, you cannot find your purpose.'

'Tarni, when did the next bit glow?' Granny Alkira asks.

'The woven circle lit up after I talked to you. At first, I thought it was when I was willing to be joined to Jiemba. Now I know it's because of Granny Yindi and understanding lore isn't about rights or wrongs but our ancestors based it in love. Not a set of rules to power over each other or to get our own way but so we can learn to love and respect each other properly … in a selfless way.'

'And the meeting symbol?' Granny Alkira asks.

'Don't you mean the sun?' Uncle Gukuji adds.

'It's the same symbol,' Tarni explains. 'I think it happened when Narn talked to the Elders, came back under lore, and showed them respect by being willing to be joined to a woman of their choosing.'

Narn frowns at Tarni.

Granny Alkira fires another question. 'How will you defeat the Malung with N'gian's message stick and ochre?'

Tarni shrugs.

'Not sure,' Narn says.

I stand there – got nothin'.

Narn clears his throat. 'Don't think we're meant to know,' he says. 'When I got N'gian's gifts, I accepted only some things will be revealed, and we must believe we'll know what to do as it happens.'

Tarni's eyes are the size of Mars' moons. I'm guessing she didn't know about Narn's gifts either.

'You saying the best plan is *not* having one?' Granny Alkira asks.

'Something like that,' he says. 'One thing is clear: N'gian doesn't do things or use people the way we expect.'

'This one lit up last night,' Wanjellah says with Tarni explaining. 'Our language experts say it's Kirra's symbol and she'll need to do something.'

Everyone gawks at me. Some wave me to come closer. I step nearer to the weird stick. Tarni stays by my side, the perfect translator. I stare at one of the glowing symbols, the one I drew onto my surfboard.

'This isn't my symbol. It's N'gian's,' I say with stroke-of-genius confidence.

Wanjellah shakes his head and Tarni explains, 'No, see, this one.' His finger hovers over a different glowing shape near the bottom of the stick. 'We thought it was a strange-shaped shield.'

People press in close to see the glowing symbol, and Wanjellah continues, 'But it's the thing that carried you across the waves.'

It *is* the shape of my surfboard, even has the pointy nose and swallowtail. The glowing message stick is mesmerising. I can't take my eyes off it. He tries to pass it to me.

I step backwards. 'I'm not touching that thing.' I glare at Wanjellah, unsure of his next move.

Wanjellah overcooks his smile. He speaks, Tarni translates. 'Narn called in the dolphins and you arrived, right?'

'I guess,' I mumble, avoiding his eyes.

Before I have time to say anything else, he drags Narn and Tarni closer, scoops up white ochre, pours water into Narn's cupped hand and babbles at Narn, who plasters ochre across his own brow, mine, and Tarni's. A murmuring races through the crowd, faster than a Mexican wave at a footy final.

'What?' I say, and I'm tempted to ask if I've grown three heads.

'Your ochre is glowing,' Tarni answers.

'Yours too,' I reply, then we stare at Narn. From temple to temple, his ochre shines.

Wanjellah thrusts the message stick into Tarni's hands.

'Do you see this?' she shrills.

'Nothing's happening,' I whisper.

'Different symbols are glowing one at a time,' Tarni says. 'It's language I can unweave.'

As she reads the symbols on the message stick, each word fills my mind with familiar pictures. Her words, those symbols, seem to stitch my dream fragments together.

'Half-moon bright, half-moon dead,' Tarni says.

I don't know if she's speaking English or Yugambeh or N'gian's language because pictures surround me. And these dream-like visions form one ginormous nightmare. My legs give out. I'm lying on my back, eyes forced open with strange imagery swirling above me.

Tarni finishes decoding the symbols.

Still sprawled out, surrounded by the clan, I say without a trace of fear, 'I know what my dreams mean.' I leap to my feet, grab the message stick out of Tarni's hand, and thrust it into the air. 'I know what this means.'

'How?' Tarni's voice jumps a few octaves.

'When you spoke, I saw pictures.'

Her mouth flings open like a Pez candy dispenser.

I clutch Tarni's hand. 'We must work together. The Malung is gonna destroy everything.'

'Everything?' she says, and the crowd goes quiet.

'Yes. All life, people, everything.' I talk in clear, short words. Wanjellah gives me an approving nod and suddenly his cave rantings – weeks ago – make sense.

Saving Wallulljagun saves us all.

I need everyone to understand if we don't stop the Malung, that evil shadow-spirit will destroy the whole world. And will end humanity.

As the sky lightens, our shadowy surroundings come into focus. Our small cluster of paperbark homes are quiet. But this time the silence isn't because of the one we buried. Wanjellah, Tarni, Narn and I are sitting with the circle of Elders again. I gulp more water, but my throat stays hoarse. Our foreheads are smeared with N'gian's ochre; there's no need for Tarni to translate.

Uncle Jarli speaks. 'Kirra, I know you told us last night. Please, we need to hear it again, so we can understand how you know Wallulljagun and your world will end.'

'I've been having these dreams from before I came here.' I pick up a stick next to me and break it into small pieces. 'My dreams were like this: fragments.'

I smooth out the sand in front of me. 'I got bits of dreams. They didn't make sense,' and I scatter the broken sticks over the smooth sand.

'But when Tarni translated those symbols, the images I saw made those dream fragments join together in the right order. I can see what is going to happen and what we can do to stop it.' I pick up the pieces and place the original stick-shape in front of me.

Granny Alkira says, 'Those dream fragments are your dreams that come true, eh?'

I nod.

'Like when you dreamt of Narn dying and warned Wanjellah, who told Narn's father before the *pullen-pullen*.'

Tarni and Narn scowl at me. It'd melt the wax off my surfboard. I focus on the twigs in front of me, while the Elders chat in ripples of whispers.

How will we join together to fight the Malung, when Narn had a secret stash of N'gian's glowing ochre, and if he applied it, I didn't need an interpreter? Or when the message stick has been evolving and glowing and Tarni didn't tell us. And neither of them knew about my dream of Narn dying. If we don't trust each other, how can we overcome a powerful shadow-spirit?

'You knew he'd die and you hid it?' Tarni whisper-snarls at me.

'It wasn't my choice … but you chose to hide those other glowing symbols on N'gian's message stick and their meanings,' I retort.

'You two, stop squabbling. What are you, *jarjum*?' Narn chips both of us.

'*Jarjum*?' Tarni says and springs to her feet. Narn does too, kinda tugs her arm to stop her leaving, and Tarni's trying to yank away.

I catapult to my feet. 'Leave her alone,' I yell, struggling to pull him off her.

'Stay out of this, Kirra,' he says and shoves me. Losing balance, I thud on my butt and exhale steam.

Tarni helps me up, glaring at Narn. 'You had N'gian's glowing ochre and didn't tell me, but worse, you kept your N'gian gifts secret. So don't pretend you've done nothing wrong.'

'Tarni. Narn. Kirra.' Granny Alkira is suddenly in the middle of us. 'You are meant to work together.'

Some team, I think. But we stop bickering and focus on the small persuasive Elder in front of us.

'Tarni had the message stick. Narn had the ochre. Kirra had the dream. Will you choose to forgive, so you can work with oneness?'

'Yes, Granny Alkira,' Tarni mumbles. 'I'm sorry, Narn and Kirra,' she says with a louder voice and sits down.

'I'm sorry too,' I mutter, and plonk beside Tarni.

'Tarni and Kirra, I'm sorry.' Then Narn turns to the Elders and apologises to them before he sits.

Granny Alkira seems to accept our regrets, returns to her seat and waves her hand in the air. 'I think it wise to use N'gian's ochre sparingly. It isn't an endless supply. Now, Kirra, do you believe you answered Narn's call?'

'I do now,' I say, my voice a little shaky from our spat. 'I arrived here when Narn called the dolphins.' I don't say I plan to return home after the next full moonset, 'cos until the Malung is stopped, there'll be no home to go to.

Uncle Gukuji clears his throat and asks, 'What do you think we need to do, Kirra, to stop this evil spirit?'

'Narn needs to call the dolphins. Tarni needs to translate and help Narn communicate with them in their language.'

The Elders lock their eyes on mine.

'We need a pod of hundreds, maybe thousands of dolphins to stop the Malung. It's what I saw.' Then I turn to Narn. 'And glowing white ochre – we need lots to fill our pouches for protection.'

Narn and Tarni watch me; it's neither friendly nor feisty.

'How will that stop him?' Uncle Jarli asks, 'And how does he destroy Wallulljagun and "the world"?'

I pause before answering. 'Jiemba's father is a man. He broke the lore and went to a forbidden cave, one that holds uranium.'

There's frowning, chin rubbing – every face is telling me the same thing, so I add, 'It's a place that holds great energy, a sleeping power. Remember the story about a powerful spirit, as bright as the sun. N'gian loved all life and gave out magic to heal and help his people.'

Aunty Marlee nods, which encourages me to continue.

'A shadow-spirit, the Malung, became jealous because the people loved N'gian and gave him food, ochre, tools and other gifts. The Malung wanted the people to love him, bring *him* presents, and thought they would accept him if he took human form.'

'Yes, we know what happened,' Uncle Gukuji's voice booms. 'Before N'gian banished him, the Malung grabbed inner bark fibres from *mungulli* and wove a strong string that would never break and was short enough to tie around a person's neck.'

Uncle Gukuji is a knowledge-holder; his story confirms my vision.

He has an even mix of seriousness and steeze. 'The Malung found small rock-like bones embedded in the cave wall, an ancient life-form from the beginning of time, and attached it to the string. Then he took all his spiritual powers and hid inside the rock-like bones,' he says, rubbing his greying beard. 'And the Malung beckoned the young man, planting small seed-thoughts inside his head, telling him he'll be clever, stronger, wiser.'

Granny Alkira's eyes are bright and intense. 'And it worked,' she says. 'The moment that fella placed the string with the dangling bones around his neck, the Malung could control his every thought and action. Problem was, the shadow-spirit was not good at being good. He used the young man's body to destroy giant ancient trees, even tricked the man to eat his own totem – his sacred animal that he must never harm.'

'Then the Malung got bored and killed people,' an Elder with a long, flowing white beard adds to the story. 'He became the most famous bone-pointer. He'd curse a person, holding that string of ancient rock-like bones and they'd wander away and die. He took great pleasure in destroying everything N'gian loved.'

There's silence, then Granny Alkira picks up the story thread. 'Our people were terrified. They begged N'gian to save them from the shadow-spirit. N'gian answered them. He removed the string of ancient rock-bones from the man's neck and trapped the Malung deep in the belly of a mountain.'

It's quiet again. Even the sound of the ocean can't soothe us tonight.

Tarni's Uncle Gukuji takes a deep breath. 'Like I said, we know this, so how did Jiemba's father become the Malung?'

I gulp, those images clog my mind. 'When N'gian banished the Malung to the mountain, a great energy lived in it. In my world, we call it "uranium". As that energy changed – from crystal to crystal – the Malung did too … until gems grew up out of the belly of the mountain and formed a cave. It looked beautiful, like a coral garden of glowing light. It was a crystal rockery of different colours: pinks, yellows and whites. The Malung called – no, lured – Coen to the cave.'

'Who's Coen?' an Elder asks.

'Jiemba's dad,' Tarni says.

'All he needs is someone to freely wear the crystal,' I continue. 'The Malung stayed hidden in those glowing crystals. Coen crawled deep into the cave with his axe tied to his waist. He ignored all the painted lores that warned him not to enter. Coen eyed off the biggest crystal and swung his axe at it with all his might. It didn't budge. He smashed at every crystal until sweat poured out of him. Not one broke.'

The circle is quiet and still, and not in a peaceful way.

'Coen saw a thin tiny crystal with two prongs sticking out. It glimmered brighter than the sun. And it felt warm. When he pulled it out of the wall, fossils – small bone-like things – were attached to it. He strung it around his neck, obsessed with its yellow light, and didn't realise the lights in all the other crystals went dark. The energy of all that uranium was taken by the Malung's energy force and transferred into that yellow crystal.'

I'm out of breath and wish this was a fable and not a vision burning with truth, but I push on. 'The cave turned cold. Icicles formed over the ground and up the cave walls. Coen crawled out of the hollow, the warm crystal and rock-bones dangled from his neck.'

Minjarra, sitting in the Elders' circle, says, 'I remember when I first saw Jiemba's father wearing that crystal. It glowed in the middle of those tiny bones, strung tightly around his neck. He's always hidden under that long cloak, but I heard he lost all his hair.'

Some of the older women chuckle.

'And,' I say, 'from that first moment, the Malung controlled his mind, his thoughts, his actions. He is under the shadow-spirit's every influence.'

Narn clears his throat; flicks his hand up for all to see. 'Jiemba said to me that winning would be far worse than losing. It would mean death for all.'

'He planned to destroy all people gifted with N'gian magic,' Tarni says, 'and when that didn't work, he decided to destroy all here. Those that die from his mind-spear won't go to the Dreaming.'

It's colder, quieter, and more depressive than ever.

'But how can he do that with one man and a crystal?' Minjarra asks.

Tarni nudges me to answer.

Without hesitation, I say, 'I'm not sure about the afterlife stuff, but if that powerful energy – the concentrated uranium – is dropped into a dormant volcano, and not just any volcano but a supersized one, it's hot enough to melt that massive magma chamber. And all that liquid rock beneath the Earth's surface in that supervolcano … becomes super lethal.'

My words seem to confuse them, so I rephrase: 'A giant sleeping volcano can be woken with his crystal. It will explode. Ash blocks the sun, covers most of Australia – I mean, Wallulljagun – and blankets everything. Plants die, most of the ocean will freeze over. There'll be cracks in the Earth's crust that'll cause tsunamis and earthquakes. A supervolcano will blow up the land, sea life, air life – everything.'

There's gunpowder in my gut and stench in my sweat. My adrenaline is pumping – it needs to – so I can do whatever it takes to defeat the evil shadow-spirit. 'If all the powerful energy in that crystal is ignited, it'll kill everyone. And if we don't stop him, the world will end!'

'Well.' Granny Alkira stands. 'We'd better start by giving each of you pouches with N'gian's ochre. Does that feel right to you, Narn?'

'Yes, the clay pot's in my *ngumbin*. I'll go get it now.'

'Great, 'cos I used the last of mine this morning,' I say, 'and we need to protect our minds.'

Minutes later, Narn sprints into the Elders' circle, out of breath. 'I searched everywhere,' he says gulping in air. 'N'gian's ochre – my pouch and clay pot – are gone.'

The circle disperses with Uncle Gukuji's spine-shattering words: 'It must have been stolen by the traitor.'

CHAPTER 32
NARN

News of N'gian's message stick has reached our neighbouring clans, as it did in our grandfather's grandfather's time. In the last couple of days, tribes have united to fight against the Malung. We're here for one reason: to save everything and everyone – plants, people, animals, sacred sites, land and sea.

My vow with Dad surfaces; by lore, I'm allowed to talk about it, but I submerge those thoughts so I can focus on our important task. Plus, everyone knows a shadow sneaks up from behind. The rainforest clans, saltwater clans and our neighbouring coastal clans have been watching for that shadow-spirit to attack a sleepy, fire-bellied mountain. We're protecting our loved ones.

Every day at sunrise, we gather with a large circle of Elders who represent the clans willing to fight the Malung. N'gian's ochre would be useful so we could speak easily with Kirra. It's still missing. And Kirra and Tarni keep empty pouches tied around their waists. The circle is packed and expands each time we gather. Kirra's seated and searches the crowd. She sees me and seems relieved. Tarni's not here – strange, because she's never late.

Uncle Gukuji stands. A hush settles the rabble. 'Thank you, friends and family, for coming. Narn, Tarni, Kirra and our hunters are keen to replace the night watch and defend our borders.' He pauses, looks around. 'Where's Tarni and the message stick?'

'I'm here,' she says a little breathless, and her skin glows with sweat. 'It's gone.'

The crowd erupts. Some with cries of disbelief. A few go silent. While others throw question after question, and I can't hear what Tarni is saying.

Uncle Gukuji slips fingers in his mouth to give an ear-piercing whistle, which stuns the lot of us.

'We must remain calm,' he says. 'One person talks at a time. We don't have the message stick to keep order, so can everyone sit except the speaker? Tarni, when did you last see it?'

She remains standing while people crouch around her. 'I sleep with it next to me, after someone stole N'gian's ochre. I keep it in my bag – even took it to the women's creek this morning when I collected water.'

Tarni's Aunty Marlee stands. 'I growled Birri for going near the women's area at first light.'

'Marlee, you don't think it's him? He's the most helpful *jarjum*. A good boy,' Tarni's Granny Alkira says.

'I'm not saying that. Maybe Birri saw someone near the creek? I'll send Lia and Arika to find and ask him.' Marlee hurries towards the *ngumbin*.

'I'll snap his skinny legs,' I snarl. And other men mutter similar threats.

'Wait,' Granny Alkira yells. 'We never even talked to him. This is Birri. Let's find him first and hear what he has to say.'

Moments later, Marlee hurries into the middle of the circle. 'Birri's gone. Look!' She points to a smoke signal burning into the sky coming from the track to Wollumbin.

'It's wrong. I know it's wrong,' says Kirra, using Tarni to explain.

Ignoring her, a group of young men race past the circle with spears and *jabir* towards the signal.

'It's a trick. Don't go,' Kirra yells, with Tarni echoing her concern.

The Elders' conversation switches from composed to chaotic. No-one moves. If it was sent by our men, there'd be more than one lit.

Uncle Gukuji looks around, his eyes pause on me. 'Let's focus on our task … Anything to report today? How is the dolphin pod going? Has Wanjellah or those who watch Wollumbin sent any messages?'

I stand in the middle of the circle. 'No messages. We've been communicating with our dolphins with Tarni's help and dolphins are swimming into our bay, making our pod the biggest it's been.'

I want all Elders to know how hard and well our clans work together, and that they can trust us younger ones to protect our tribe. 'Our best huntsmen are guarding Wollumbin, the old volcanic mountain. We have strong men protecting every mountain in all of our boundaries and, so far, there's been no enemy movement on our lands,' I say with certainty.

The more I think of the Malung, the more I wish we had N'gian's message stick and ochre. 'We'll know if the enemy comes. There are unlit stacks of wood ready along our seashores and inland. If that evil spirit comes anywhere near our lands, fires will be lit or smoke signals sent. And Wanjellah's returning today to help search the coastline.'

'Why?' Nyrah's Uncle Koa asks. 'There are no mountains here,' and he points to our beach.

'Kirra?' Tarni and I say together.

Kirra stands, and Tarni interprets her words. 'In my vision, the Malung's always on the water with hundreds – maybe thousands – of dolphins. I don't know why. He drops the crystal in the ocean. Are there any dormant – I mean, sleeping – underwater volcanoes?'

Granny Alkira waves her hand in the air and the crowd falls silent. 'My grandfather used to say, "You sneeze too much, you'll make an island."'

No-one responds. And she's not worried. 'It was an old joke he told from the northern coastal clan. He said *his* grandfather made him laugh when he was a young fella – told a tale about a sneezing creation spirit who tried to make an island at the edge of our bay, far out in the deep sea.'

Granny Alkira stares at Kirra and says, 'It'd sneeze and spray into the air like a whale's blowhole, but bigger. It tried and tried to make a little island; there was too much water and the land never formed. Maybe at the edge of the bay right over the other side, that volcano is sleeping.'

'Alkira,' says Burnum, an Elder from the northern coastal clan, 'we had that same joke. If we were on the beach and anyone sneezed, Dad would point to the outer sea boundary between our borders. It could be there.'

The circle goes quiet.

Three prominent hunter-Elders from our tribe stand, then honour us with their *jabir*. We won't use them to club animals but as paddles. We'll replace our simple *jabir* with their elaborately decorated ones. I thank them with a nod.

A whining noise rises from the track. Wanjellah, followed by a small group, is pulling Birri by his earlobe. He jostles him into the middle of our gathering.

'Tell them!' he demands.

'Wanjellah! What's this about?' Granny Alkira asks, 'Birri, why you crying – what happened?'

Birri throws himself on the ground, wailing louder, and Wanjellah hoists him up again. 'Tell them!'

Tears stream down Birri's face. 'I did something bad,' he bawls. 'But I didn't know. I just wanted *gumburra*.'

'Tell them what you did,' Wanjellah barks.

Birri's head drops. 'I told them about Kirra when she first came. Where to find her on the rainforest track.'

'Who did you tell, Birri?' Granny Alkira asks, her voice sounds more kind than angry, and I'm confused.

Birri is the traitor.

Fresh tears are added to his stained face. 'He said he was my uncle. I didn't know he belonged to the Malung.' His sobs are interrupted with hiccups. 'I'm so-rr-y.'

Wanjellah releases his grip. Birri sinks to the ground with more hiccups and loud cries and 'I'm sorry's'.

Then my angry brother hauls him to his feet. 'Tell everyone about the fire you set.'

Birri says nothing, stands hunched over and stares at the sand.

Wanjellah digs through his bag, then passes me my clay pot and missing leather pouch. He gives the message stick to Tarni, which she hands to Uncle Gukuji.

'Anyone who wants to talk holds N'gian's message stick,' Uncle Gukuji says with the stick held above his head. 'But first, we hear from Birri.' But Uncle doesn't pass it to him.

Kirra and Tarni hand me their empty pouches. It takes the rest of N'gian's ochre to fill them. We tie them around our waists.

Birri's small shoulders shudder. 'He's got Mum and my little brothers too.' He kind of chokes on each word. 'For me to see them again, I had to get that message stick and special ochre.'

'Birri-love,' Granny Alkira soothes, 'it'll work out. We'll get them back. Did that uncle wear ochre or anything unusual?'

'He doesn't wear it like us. They use tree sap to glue red dust over their skin. He used to be nice, pretended to be my friend. He'd play a game, ask me questions about Kirra or other stuff, and if he liked my answers, he'd give me *gumburra*.'

Birri's scrawny legs give way, and I regret saying earlier that I'd snap them. He's in a tiny huddle on the ground, blubbering into his arms. And the aunties and grannies move in to comfort him.

They prop him up, rub his back, and persuade him to talk. 'He needed three things to beat N'gian: message stick, special ochre and Kirra's flat canoe ... those things N'gian gave the clever ones,' he says from his huddle.

'And then what?' Wanjellah growls, but the aunties give him a look and my brother's face softens. 'I'm sorry, Birri, why did you light that fire?'

'I was meant to light the fire along the track to Wollumbin, so that mountain's smoke signals would be sent and call everyone away from the coast.'

One aunty's still rubbing Birri's back, while the other one's passing him food from her dillybag.

Birds screech, cluster in huge groups as they leave the protection of the forest. Every feather flaps away in a disorganised flurry. Me and most of the men jump to our feet – listen in all directions. Animals – snakes, wallabies, bandicoots – leave their hidden homes in a hectic hurry.

'They're coming,' bellows one of our white-painted watchmen, as he races over the dunes. 'Need to stop them.'

Along the beach, as far as the eye can see, a swarm of red human locusts carrying spears are consuming our land. Swift and intimidating, they stampede towards us. Out of nowhere, spears with balls of fire attached to their tips hail down around us. *Ngumbin* after *ngumbin* bursts into flames. Our beachside home is obliterated.

Men, women, and fellas with fresh initiation scars grab *jabir*, spears – anything that could stop the Malung's men – and sprint to the beach to defend our families. Women search our camp to collect *jarjum* and hide them at the edge of our large *bora*. Grannies, aunties, mums, even the childless, rally together to check no sleeping child or resting Elder is trapped inside our flaming homes. Younger women bang out the fires, so they can dash in and snatch up precious possum blankets.

A bolt of fire flies through the air above a scared young fella. I scoop up the terrified *jarjum* in one arm, collect another bawling one on the way, and hide them with other tear-streaked faces under the *bilang*, the babysitting tree, near the edge of the *bora*. With uncontrolled fires, snakes will be scampering to safety and ready to attack any threatening predator.

I'm racing through camp ready to collect more *jarjum* when Wanjellah grabs my arm. He is with Tarni and Kirra. Tarni hands me N'gian's message stick. I attach it to my waist, next to my ochre-filled pouch. Armed with a *jabir*, my brother leads us towards the bay. We dodge flames and spears and men battling along the beach.

'We'll light big fires along the beach if we see the Malung on the ocean,' Wanjellah says. 'And we'll light the fire on the headland if he's on the land to signal you to return. Search the bay and stop him. If you need help, light the fire – drop!' He shouts and we duck as a red-dusted hunter swings a *jabir* at our heads.

Two more are charging at us.

'Go,' Wanjellah yells, as he fights them off.

The rest of the tribesmen and women battle the red-dusted men, while we slide the bark canoe into the bay and paddle away.

My muscles burn and I yell, 'Pull. Pull. Pull.' We stroke together, my arms beg me to ease, but I embrace the pain and search the sea for that cloaked creature.

When we reach the middle of the bay, we stop to smear the white ceremonial clay I mixed over our faces and arms and legs. This is no time for skimping. I hope it'll protect us from the shadow-spirit. And that N'gian will answer our call.

Back at our saltwater home, a crowd is sprawled along the dunes and water's edge. Dark clouds crowd the horizon. There's no lightning or thunder that a normal storm brings. Yet, it traps the sun behind it, and we're in the shadows.

We paddle over small, murky waves, heading to the northern coastal clan's boundary. I'm in the front of the canoe, and check the message stick is tightly secured.

'What's all this seaweed for?' Kirra asks, sitting in the middle of the canoe on a sheet of *wudjuru* and avoiding a mound of wet seaweed, piled with dry wood.

Tarni, at the back of the canoe, leans forward. 'So we can send a message.'

'Never thought fires and wooden canoes would go together,' she says, her once-chirpy voice now shaky and low.

As we paddle, a strange prickling covers me, as though ten thousand sea urchins jab my body. How could there be a volcano underwater? What if Kirra's dreams are wrong?

'Tarni, Kirra, look.' I point my paddle towards the horizon. Then slap the water's surface with it as I sing. The bay fills with thousands of dolphins. Their smooth bodies dive over and under the sea with trails of splashes behind them.

'It's a superpod,' Kirra says.

'Tarni. Kirra. Pull.' And we dig our *jabir* into the water.

'Pull,' I say again. 'Pull,' and there's a powerful rhythm to our strokes.

We paddle together, drawing nearer to the northern boundary.

Smoke rises from the beaches to our north. Then every warning signal is lit. All have a straight column of grey smoke. The message is clear: An enemy approaches ... from the water. A large crowd gathers on the beach behind us. We search everywhere for the Malung.

I shield my eyes and point north. 'There.'

A cloaked man is paddling a canoe. Yellow mist forms around him. He turns, spots us, then paddles away faster.

'Do we turn back?' Tarni's voice is trembling. 'We could fill every canoe with men who can fight.'

I glance at the beach. 'They're already fighting.'

'This isn't just physical warfare,' Kirra says, 'it's spiritual too.'

I look at Tarni. 'Kirra's right. And if he drops that crystal in the volcano, it won't matter if we have ten thousand men with us. We'll all be dead.'

'What about the fire?' Kirra points to the seaweed and wood under her feet. 'Do we send a smoke message?'

'No time,' I say. 'Paddle hard.'

We grip our *jabir*. I jam my paddle deep in the water and pull hard, long strokes. There's power in my arms and our canoe glides across the sea.

'*Whoa*. You two seeing this?' Kirra gawks at the message stick hanging from my hip.

Not only does it glow but it's pulsing.

'Does this mean the Malung and the end of the world are coming closer?' Kirra asks, but there's no time to talk.

We paddle with an urgent rhythm. There's a shift and the waves are smoother. Our enemy is three or four canoe-lengths away.

His necklace glows with a pukey yellow. Inside his canoe is Kirra's flat one.

We stop paddling.

Tarni yells, 'Pass me the message stick. Sing your song.'

I untie N'gian's stick and hand it to Tarni. She places it on her lap. We sit holding hands, and I feel the hum brew. I sing the words that Tarni says to the hum's tune. My voice carries across the sea. The shining symbols change and glow and turn and spin on her lap. She speaks it and I sing. The dark blue waters don't change.

'There. That's gotta be it.' Kirra drops our hands and points at a patch of light blue. She peers into the shallow waters. The ocean floor rises. It's the top of an enormous underwater mountain and is the colour of pumice stone. Most of it is covered in sand.

'See that giant grey dome with a long funnel pointing to the surface? There's no bubbles or steam escaping,' Kirra says.

'Kirra, the message stick has stopped.' Tarni grabs our hands, squeezes it hard and the symbols change again.

We're all needed. More and more dolphins propel themselves towards us. Dorsal fins launch and smooth bodies slap the water. All keep their own rhythm.

Tarni presses both palms on her temples. 'They communicate by slapping the water, whistling – so many things at once; it's hard for me to translate.'

'Tell the superpod to block the volcano,' Kirra says. 'They need to swarm his canoe, so there's no way the Malung can access it.'

The pod crowds the water: a huge dolphin bait ball. We clutch hands. The cloaked killer grips his crystal with the bones dangling around it. He points it at the dolphins and spews out vile sounds.

Kirra grabs her head with both hands and screams, 'I know who I am. I know who I am.' Then shrieks louder, 'I know who I AM!'

His necklace shakes; every bone in her body does too. Are they linked in some way? Does a mind-spear leave barbs after the weapon's removed?

Tarni's biting her lip and gawking at Kirra.

My body feels heavy, anchored in one place. Forcing my arms through the dense air, I shake N'gian's helper. 'Kirra! Kirra!' And I remember my gift.

She shudders, trapped in a daze. I dip my hand in the sea then into my leather pouch. I sing and smear glowing ochre across her face, ears, hair, neck until she settles. This N'gian power works in a quiet, calm way. I coat Tarni and myself with sea-blended ochre, and the vibrating babble can't penetrate anymore.

'Tarni, what's he saying?' I ask.

'I can't repeat it.' In a flat voice, she adds, 'It's the death conjuring – the curse of the mind-spear.'

Each dolphin the shadow-spirit points to – chants at – swims away. More of them fill the gaps, but eventually he'll be able to access the volcano. The Malung stands; the canoe doesn't topple and his yell-curse changes. The crystal's bright yellow light grows bigger and bolder around him.

Then I spot my life-long friend.

'Noooooooooooooo!' My throat is sore, but I can't stop screeching.

Tears drench my cheeks, as I stare at the dolphin with the pointy dorsal fin. She's drifting in the water. Dead.

Kirra shrieks.

Tarni wails.

I'm still yelling, 'Nooooooooooooo!'

Hundreds and hundreds of dolphin bodies float to the surface. Slaughtered.

'W-what's happening?' I stammer.

'He's killing them all,' Tarni says, unable to take her eyes off the bobbing bodies.

'How?' Kirra cries.

Tears tumble down Tarni's ochre-streaked face. 'They believe the lie of the mind-spear. He's telling them they are fish and can breathe underwater. Somehow they are drowning.'

The bloated bodies of our precious friends thud into our canoe. And fill our bay.

Tarni grabs Kirra's arm and shakes her. 'Do something.' Then she says to me, 'N'gian sent her to help us, she's got to do something.'

Tarni rattles Kirra until she shudders, 'Don't ... know ... what ... to ... do ...'

The Malung's glow creeps to us. Wherever the strange light is, death follows. Stiff fish appear. Turtles and other lifeless deep-sea creatures join the carcasses. All float on the surface of the sea. Will we die too, if the yellow reaches us? Is he destroying the track to the Dreaming?

'N'gian, is this who you sent to stop me?' The Malung sniggers and his hooded cloak jolts. 'Three children. Not so clever now.' He throws his arms to the heavens, one fist clenches the crystal. 'I will defeat you and all that you love!'

'That's it,' Kirra says.

'What?' Tarni and I yell.

'We call on N'gian.'

'How?' Tarni asks.

'Not sure,' Kirra says. 'Any ideas?' she asks me.

I shake my head.

His poisonous fog edges closer. We struggle to breathe.

'Tarni, you've got to know N'gian's language. Just try,' Kirra splutters, then grabs our hands.

Tarni chants the symbols from the message stick. We copy her. Say it together. Then, sing with all our minds, bodies, souls and might. The message stick leaves Tarni's hands and spins in mid-air. A breeze is on our face, and the more authority we chant with, the stronger the wind gets.

We sing with our eyes closed to concentrate, and call on N'gian. There's a yellow-like presence and, distracted, I open my eyes. The enemy's canoe is next to ours. The shadow-spirit hovers above us. His yellow stench presses in.

I want to thump him but I'm scared of his putrid fog. The Malung swipes at the message stick.

I dive at it. I'm too late.

His claw-like fingers clench the stick, then he chucks it into the sea. It sinks. The quicker it drops, the faster the flashing symbols pulse. He flings off his long fur cape and there's no hair on his body. Red ochre covers him and his ribs protrude so much that his skin seems strange. The Malung's bald head has a huge ugly scar, and his eyes shift from the surfboard to the water. Then, he lurches out of the canoe and dives into the sea. His splash pushes the floating carcasses away.

We peer over the canoe. The Malung's yellow glow goes deeper. Its eerie light flickers above the underwater mountain top. . My heart has tripled in size, and my chest can't contain the intense pounding.

'Tarni, he's almost there. We need N'gian's chant, we need the symbols,' Kirra yells.

I'm on my knees and singing again. And the littlest dorsal fin approaches.

'Echo. Echo.' I tap the side of the canoe and the tiniest dolphin in the pod pushes past the bodies and swims to the canoe. The mind-spear mustn't influence the young ones.

'I've got it. Tarni, we need to convince the dolphin calf to dive down to the message stick and tell us N'gian's symbols,' Kirra says.

Tarni's voice quivers. 'It's too late. He's already at the volcano.'

'Tarni, you can hear their language from a long way – like your old people and the stars: it's about clarity. If you can hear it, we can say it,' Kirra yells and snaps her into action.

'I'll try,' Tarni says, and she tells me the words.

I sing to Echo.

And our fate seems to lie with one of our smallest sea friends. Echo dives, her tail wiggles frantically.

Seconds later, Tarni sings and Kirra joins in.

We link hands, pressing tightly, and we sing with full force. Wind whips around us, faster and stronger.

Kirra's grip tightens. 'Narn. Tarni. Do you trust me?'

'Yes,' we yell over the strong breeze that's spraying around and around like a giant watery *boulmung*.

'Do you trust N'gian?' Kirra says with such conviction, I can't believe she was that quiet girl who wandered onto our beach.

'On the count of three, we throw all of our ochre into the air,' she says.

'But it's the last of N'gian's ochre,' Tarni screeches, 'and if it doesn't work, we'll have no protection from the Malung.'

Kirra has a fistful ready. 'I know it's what we must do,' she says. 'Okay?'

I know she's right. We have one hand in our leather pouch.

'One. Two. Three,' we chant.

Handful after handful, we throw glowing ochre into the air until our pouches are empty. Then we bellow out his song. A blustering wind swirls from our sides. From our hands, off our faces and legs and arms, the magical ochre turns into a N'gian spirit force and whips around us. It spins into the water, towards the yellow glow beneath.

The sea is spiralling, a huge waterspout, lifting everything into the air. We're at its edge, gripping the sides of our canoe. The dry sea floor is below. There's a grey mound with a silent pointy thing that looks like an emu caller. N'gian has parted the sea and land, and the Malung is trapped in the middle of the enormous ocean *boulmung*. He's spinning around and around, arms and legs floundering. His mouth is wide open; the howling wind muffles his shrieks.

Faster and faster he spins and the walls of water rise higher and higher. The yellow colour and the human body that holds the Malung separate. A limp figure flings out of the *boulmung* and crashes onto the dry seabed. His head smacks a large rock and blood floats from his head, drawn up into the spiralling windstorm. The yellow-coloured water in the centre of the *boulmung* shrinks. There's a thundering explosion of crashing seas, and a blinding light makes the yellow glow disappear.

The barrier of water plunges; the ocean floor is hidden once again. We hold on tight as the bark canoe thuds and thrashes around. I search the dark waters. Has N'gian defeated the Malung?

Sunlight breaks through the clouds. Streams of light warm our skin. There's no watery *boulmung*. No strange yellow glow. And a breeze gushes around. Still clinging to both sides of our canoe, I shut my eyes as the wind whips my face and we speed across the water, faster than any animal I've ever seen. A few breaths later, we thump onto the beach.

'Maybe it really is a magic sled.' When I hear Kirra's voice, I pry my eyes open.

'My shaper will be stoked, not that I'll ever tell her any of this,' she says, and I follow her gaze.

Next to our canoe is Kirra's undamaged 'sled'.

When the whipping white-ochred wind stops, my pouch pulls at my side. I open it and it's full of glowing ochre dust again. The Malung's crystal, Jiemba's father and his canoe have vanished. And there's no sign of N'gian or his glowing message stick – hope we won't need it again. The waves disappear and the three of us stumble onto the beach. I hug Tarni and Kirra. All our allies – from the north, south and inland – are gathering around, yipping and whistling and cheering.

Wanjellah races in. He hoots and swings his arms into the air. 'Brudder!' he yells, slaps my back, and we chest-slam into an embrace. Then Wanjellah scoops Tarni and Kirra into a giant stumbling squeeze and they squeal. Nyrah arrives. She laughs at Wanjellah's antics.

My brother picks her up, spins her around and shouts, 'Saving Wallulljagun saves us all. Kirra, looks like Wallulljagun and our connection to the Dreaming are saved, right?'

Kirra smiles, but I'm not sure she's convinced.

He places Nyrah down and hoots and races around again, yelling, '*Yuh-huh. Yuh-huh. Yuh-huuuuuuh.*'

I ruffle Kirra's hair. 'We did it.' Then I pick up her surfboard. 'I'll keep it in Dad's secret spot till you need it.' She agrees, so I tuck it under my arm and ask, 'Have we saved your world?'

'I'll know when I return, if –'

'If what?' Tarni asks. 'Kirra? You'll know when you return if what?'

Kirra's answer is weak and wobbly, gawking at the lake-like sea and says, 'If the time-tube hasn't been destroyed.'

CHAPTER 33
TARNI

It's mid-morning and the sun is hidden behind a cloak of murky clouds. But this gloomy weather won't slow my excitement. Narn and I are meeting with the Elders. In the grassy area at the edge of our largest *bora*, our grey-haired men and women sit cross-legged, wrapped in fur. Granny Alkira and Narn's Aunty Lowanna is among them.

We sit side by side in the gap that's waiting for us.

Uncle Gukuji waves his hand in the air. The catch-ups stop.

'Minjarra?' he says, and my father emerges from the *jambinbin* grove.

He came? Thought he'd be searching for Mum again.

'If the Elders decide in their favour, do you give Narn permission to be joined with your daughter?'

Father's eyes are as dark as the basalt rock on the headland. His beard scoops into a smile. 'Yes.'

Uncle Gukuji nods at my father, who blends back into the grove's shadow. Then Uncle addresses us again. 'Narn, Tarni, I'm nominated to speak on behalf of the circle today. Are you willing to hear what the Elders have to say?'

'Yes,' we chime.

'In the past, the Elders agreed that two people with N'gian gifts cannot be joined.' Uncle's seriousness softens. 'Is there good reason to dispute this?'

Narn whips out a warm smile before he speaks. 'Yes, I'd like to share my dad's wishes before a decision is reached. But we will honour the Elders' choosing.'

'Tarni,' Granny Alkira says, her tone and posture oozing with confidence. 'Anything you want to say about the joining?'

Though I tremble inside, I copy her conduct. 'We ask permission to be joined on the next full moon. And,' I add in a stronger voice, 'invite my mother's clan.'

'A full moon means we can dance and sing all night. But,' Uncle rubs his chin, 'after driving out the red-dusted men who followed the shadow-spirit, we must be diligent.'

'N'gian has steadied our physical realm, and we must maintain it,' Granny Alkira says.

It's so quiet you could hear a Currumbin pine needle flutter and fall.

After a few stifled breaths, our meeting is interrupted by a small group: Aunty Marlee and the same cousins who talked to me after the burial ceremony. Squishing between people, they make the circle bigger and uncomfortable.

Aunty Marlee clears her throat. 'I'm sorry to come uninvited but we have something to say about this joining. It's disrespectful to the Old Dolphin Caller. We, but especially Narn, should be grieving, not singing, dancing and watching comedy performances with other tribes.'

'Lowanna.' She searches for Narn's aunty. 'He was your big brother. You agree with us, don't you?'

Narn's Aunty Lowanna crosses her arms. 'I came to hear what Narn has to say.'

Heads swing to Narn. He leans forward. 'Thanks, Aunty Lowanna. I love my dad. He was a wise loreman. I need to tell you what he said before … the light left him.'

Around the whole circle, pairs of compassionate eyes rest on Narn, and I'm proud of this man.

'Dad gave us his blessing to be joined – gave his life so we could live. Gave this string,' and he holds up my hand for all to see.

Before Aunty Marlee can interrupt, I say, 'Granny Yindi wove this when we were *jarjum*.' Narn's warm hand remains wrapped around mine, and a tingle travels all the way to my toes.

'Dad left an emptiness that aches.' Narn falters, his jaw clamps so tight a eugarie tool wouldn't be able to pry it open, so I give his hand an encouraging squeeze. His husky voice carries on, 'But it will ache whether I join with Tarni or not, now or later.'

Aunty Lowanna and Granny Alkira nod. The other Elders listen intently.

'Tarni could help me while this pain shapes who I am now. I need her – love her. If the battle with the Malung has taught us anything, it's that life is precious. Dad spent the last of his strength to tell me …' The tremors increase in Narn's voice, but he pushes through: 'He said, "If N'gian thought Tarni and I work best together, why should anyone prevent us from joining?"'

Narn smiles at me; it's small and sweet and sad. And I'm too jittery to share it with him.

A murmur, starting at one end of the circle, ends with Uncle Gukuji saying, 'Some Elders remember the Old

Dolphin Caller was worried: two people with N'gian gifts should not be joined because they would be too powerful.'

'N'gian's gifts don't make us powerful,' I almost yell to cut through my nervousness, and my leg can't stop twitching.

Narn says in a softer way. 'It takes trust and confidence that those gifts work when you ask N'gian for help. If anything, it makes you more humble.'

I wish I could kiss this clever-headed man, but we wait for a decision, which will seal our future: together or apart.

The Elders talk among themselves for a bit, then Uncle Gukuji speaks. 'Narn, Tarni, we can't ignore that N'gian chose you to work together. The *wudjuru* are flowering, the mullet will soon fill our seas and our big gathering with all our clans and surrounding tribes will be held. A joining ceremony could be part of that, as all the families will be here. We'll send word.'

'But-but-but …' Aunty Marlee waves her hand to the rhythm of her disapproving reply. 'How will we feed *all* the tribes?' she asks. 'This is before the dolphin song. Maybe they can't have a full-moon celebration. But if they wait till after Narn calls the dolphins, there'll be plenty of fish for a joining ceremony.'

When the chatter eases, I say, 'A full-moon celebration is good, but Narn and I living under one *ngumbin* is better.'

Granny Alkira nods at Uncle Gukuji, and he says, 'Well, let's ask our best hunter. Minjarra, do you agree?'

Father steps out of the shadows. 'Not enough food? From the beginning of time, our old people have said there's so many fish in our creek, we could cross it by walking on their backs. Have you forgotten our Dreaming beliefs?' he asks, staring straight at Aunty Marlee.

'Long before the dolphins chased in the fish, the way Gowonda, our ancestor, taught them, we worked with our dingoes. Still do. I'll light some patches of fire near the mountain creek.'

Father's voice seems to sing.

'Only takes a couple of days for the grass to grow green and sweet. We'll set up our big nets and the dingoes will herd the wallabies into them. And,' he smiles at his mother's sister, 'Aunty Alkira, like most of you women, has sealed clay pots full of plums, figs, seed for breadmaking – traded at the last big gathering.'

Father pats his belly. 'There's always plenty of food.'

Granny Alkira and Uncle Gukuji chuckle. A few others join them. The troublemakers seem satisfied. The Elders seem satisfied. *Satisfied*? I could cheer and scream and hug everyone, even snarky Aunty Marlee.

Soon, Narn and I will be joined.

The wind has been wild since the Malung's defeat. Jellyfish and bluebottles with their trailing thin stingers were swept onto our beaches. But late last night, the breeze shifted. I stroll along the foreshore. The tireder my legs get, the clearer my mind becomes. A wave glides onto the beach and over my feet. I leap out of the chilly water, away from the shiny wet sand into its warm powdery form.

Since our victory, the saltwater people, rainforest people and our other coastal allies north and south of us chased the Malung's followers out of our lands. Many Elders and their families, from the red-rock inland nation, had sought refuge with neighbouring tribes. They've returned home to their sacred sites. Any imprisoned women, those captured after I left, have been set free. Smoking ceremonies were performed by Elders from all of the surrounding areas, as those unidentified bodies and bones could be from any tribe. They've been meeting and discussing how to honour the mountain of bones called 'the end of light'. It will be the beginning of a long process.

Lore and the Elders' circle of the plains country are strong again.

Kirra's sitting on a mound of sand alone, with silvery-green tufts of grass around her. I walk in her direction humming a song I learned last night at our *bora*, where we've gathered with other clans to celebrate the mullet migration. We'll harvest those tasty fish at their fattest. Kirra wears N'gian's ochre across her forehead, so it links to Narn, me and the Elders. It's the easiest way to communicate.

Clanswomen search the rockpools at low tide to collect all kinds of shellfish. The sea has blessed us: our fish traps are full, and there's been plenty of crabs, prawns and stingray. Smoke whirls from beyond the dunes. Earthen ovens are being prepared for tonight's feast.

Over the last few days, old grievances between clans have been dealt with according to our customs. With the serious fighting aside, ceremonial ones have begun. Trading is done, new dances are learned and Dreaming stories are performed. The new favourite is the defeat of the Malung. That and, of course, Gowonda Dreaming. Tonight, our dolphin caller beckons me.

And I'll answer: *yes*.

I scurry up the dune. 'Kirra, the winds have changed in time for tonight. Look at our beautiful bay.'

She says nothing, her arms are woven around her legs, so I keep chatting, 'A flat stone could skip across its surface many times.' I crouch next to her. 'Looks like your smile's been sucked out to sea. Are you alright?'

'I'm fine.' She sighs the words out. 'It's flat. There needs to be waves by tomorrow.'

I ease into the sand. We stare at the salt water, and I say, 'It looks beautiful, don't you think?'

'Looks better with waves.' She picks up a pumice stone and pegs it over the dune.

'Don't worry, the waves always come back,' I say in an extra-bouncy tone. 'They never stay away for long.'

Her emotional tide shifts. A frown lifts into the teeniest smile.

'There it is. Got to smile, because tonight Narn and I have our joining ceremony.' I nudge her with my shoulder. 'You better dance with us women.'

'I will,' and she bumps me back. 'I'm going for a swim. You coming?' She throws off the string skirt I gave her and races down the dunes in what she calls her 'Bik. Inies'.

'No, it's too dangerous.' She's halfway there, so I yell, 'Well, stay in the shallows.' Then mumble, 'That nice warm water was chased away by those wild winds.'

Later that day, when the women's waterhole is in full sun, Nyrah and a few younger cousins keep me company. I've used crushed wattle leaves to soap my body. And Granny Alkira gave me some carpet-snake fat. It'll make my skin soft, smooth and shiny.

'Can't wait for tonight,' I say aloud, splashing Nyrah.

'Me too,' she agrees, and flashes her dimples at me. 'Knew you and Narn would be joined. Got to go, girls,' Nyrah calls out to our cousins. 'Not you, Tarni,' she adds, and they leave to prepare for tonight.

After I'm dried, dressed in my string skirt, and my skin is glowing, I rub some of the leftover oil into the decorated side of my fur cloak. I apply it carefully over the centre piece – the first design that Mum and Granny Yindi did together to honour my name: waves in the ocean. Its meaning comes from Mum's Granny's language. After tonight, I'll add another possum skin and paint the story of Narn and I joined under the full moon.

I'm wearing my emu-feather decoration. A river of feathers flows over my chest and dangles at my waist. Haven't worn it since Narn had teased me. So much has changed since then.

Someone's in a hurry. A *thud, thud, thud* echoes from the track. Alba's puffing and hunched over.

'Where'd you come from?'

'Rainforest track,' she says between breaths.

'Did you run the whole way?'

She nods. When her breathing steadies, she wanders to the upper pool and drinks.

'Did you see Mum?' I ask.

'No-one's seen your mother since the healer was killed.'

My heart sags in the middle.

Alba plonks on a boulder, and I settle next to her. 'I left word about your mum, and the rainforest clan passed it on to their surrounding clans. Maybe they'll find her. I'm sorry about Aunty Merindah. All these years, we kept it secret that your mum didn't die.'

'I know.'

319

My cousin gives me a big squeeze. 'Hope nothing's happened to her.'

'Me too,' I say, then we dawdle along the beach track.

More and more people arrive from all our surrounding clans and tribes. Extra *ngumbin* were set up for our guests, including one for Narn and me. He's talking with Wanjellah, near the underground ovens. I rub the string on my pinkie. My heart goes from skipping to a chased-by-an-emu sprint. Tonight a 'promise' becomes a 'joining'.

Jarjum have tripled in numbers; a group of eager boys and girls race along the track. Nattering non-stop, they share the same tale: the sun sinking at the exact moment the fat-bellied moon rises. When the afterglow fades, a low drone begins.

The sound is fluid and uninhibited; it rolls in and out. About a hundred men thrum the calming tune. It flows from *ngumbin* to *ngumbin*, passes along our tracks, and leads everyone to the *bora* … a male *whirr* of a wave rolling onto our sacred ground.

The stage is lit by a circle of little fires, which the women who are not involved in the performances will maintain. A stack of wood awaits. The rest of the females sit in a semi-circle, row after row, behind the dancing flames and wait for the custodians of the sacred drums. Our female Elders arrive last with their *bunngunn*: the possum skins are stretched over laps and ready to drum. Women who've had a joining ceremony also beat their *bunngunn* with their open palms. The rest keep rhythm on the tops of their legs, all linked to the beat. Kirra is among them with glowing ochre on her face. She's holding the left wrist of Alba, while drumming her thigh.

The low drone sweeps over the large ceremonial mound and swarms our giant tree at the edge of our *bora*. Men in feathered headdresses scale it. The higher the men swing and climb, the more men clamber onto the trunk. Over thirty scurry up the tree. The moon highlights their decorative feathers and ochre-painted bodies, as the tuneful bellow crescendos into a song. Now we sing with all our might, and the air *buzzes* and *pops*.

Two senior men, Uncle Jarli and Uncle Gukuji, each have a set of boomerangs. They clap them together to keep rhythm and start each song. Another two men hold fire torches in the air, so each detail of the performance is visible.

Moving from the shadows, I sit at the furthest edge. Narn saunters towards me. Fresh ochre covers his body; curved white lines define his muscular chest and accentuate his jawline. Emu feathers sway in his hair.

Narn's leg brushes mine when he sits next to me. Though we're excited about our new life together, it's tinged with sadness. His father isn't here in person, because for one life to be saved, one was taken. I stare at my emu feathers. Mum isn't here either. Maybe, they watch from a distance in spirit form.

Songs flow from one clan to the next. In the end, everyone has a chance to dance. Outstretched arms, fingers kept stiff – showing skill and magnificence – while legs shake in rhythm. All ages. Everyone enjoying the celebration.

The possum lap-drums slow and the singing stops.

Narn jumps to his feet, beaming at me as he struts and puffs out his bare chest. He enters the centre of the circle and dances in front of me with the bright orange fires burning around him. It's the brolga mating dance. His legs and arms move fast with power, matching the tempo of the possum lap-drums. Brolgas choose a mate, one they keep their whole life. Even if their mate dies, they never leave their side.

It's a beautiful choice. I want this moment to be a memory I never forget. Narn's muscles tense. His injured shoulder, with the scarring patterns of a man, has healed. And I can't take my eyes off the fella I love. My cheeks burn and ache because my smile doesn't wilt.

My father and every man who's not 'too young' – those who've had their own joining ceremonies – perform with Narn. Wanjellah is among them. Legs move to the beat. Bodies flex. All imitate the elaborate courtship displays of the spectacular leaping birds. Narn's eyes lock on mine. The rhythm vibrates through the earth. Strong. Powerful. Passed down from generation to generation. The brolga courtship performance ends with Narn stopping right in front of me. Even the wind favours us tonight; it blows the dust and smoke away.

Narn sits beside me again. His strong scent makes me giddy. Beads of sweat cover his ochred body. 'I was going to do the emu, but I thought the brolga courtship was the right dance to do, because the male emu sits on the eggs and raises the chicks. Don't want you to get the wrong idea. You know brolgas, both the mum and dad build the nest, hatch the eggs, and feed and guard the young.'

He puffs out his chest and grins. I giggle, so do some of the aunties.

Someone is moving in the shadows on the other side of the fire. It's a woman. Streaks of flowing white-grey hair reflect the moon beams. As she passes each person, the murmurs grow louder. She's wearing a similar neck-covering of feathers to mine and is smiling at me.

'*Waijung*!' I can't get to her fast enough. 'I knew you weren't dead.'

Mum wraps her arms around me. I cling to her, and the ache of our time apart disappears.

'Your father found me,' she says and releases me. 'We've talked. Only wished we'd that courage when you were little, but we can chat about that later. Love you, Tarni.' Her eyes glisten, then she glances around. 'Now, where's Narn? There he is.'

'How did you recognise him?'

'I've kept watch over you your whole life. And I may have met him before.'

Narn walks over and embraces my mum. She smiles so hard, tears squeeze from her eyes.

Kirra races into an overly familiar full hug.

When they finish, I say, 'You know my mum, Merindah?'

'I know her as Silverbird. Didn't know she was your mother.'

It's then I notice Mum's grey possum-skin cloak.

'I met your mum as Silverbird too,' Narn says. 'But I should've worked it out, now that I look at you both. You have the same emu neck thing. I mean "emu-feather thing", not "neck thing".' There's a glimmer in his eyes that dances about, and this time I know what he's saying.

I slip my hand into his and he squeezes it.

Father strolls over, and it's not strange, even though he won't stop staring and grinning at Mum. We sit, yarn, laugh and the feasting begins.

Father takes charge of the food. The men carefully scrape away the sand and leaves until they uncover the huge pit lined with *wudjuru*. All gather around them, eager to unwrap the food that's been cooking for hours. The volcanic rocks are moved so the parcels of food can keep warm on them. The smaller parcels on top are filled with damper, tomatoes, yams and eggs. Then there's fish and scrub turkey. And huge pieces of tender roasted roo are the last to be taken from the enormous earthen oven. Coolamon are filled with *karum* spinach, roasted yams, flat cakes, roasted crabs, *gumburra*, finger limes, *nyulli* (Kirra calls them 'pigface', and their old flower bulbs, 'salted strawberries'). So many different foods are passed around: to children, old people, guests, and lastly our clan. Each person places handfuls of food on a big flat leaf.

The *wudjuru* parcels of roasted kangaroo and bush turkey have peppery lemon flavours. We eat *nyulli* leaves with the meat to give it a hint of salt. And there's plenty more food warming on the hot rocks.

I sniff in the smoky fragrance of meat marinated in bush herbs. The meat melts in my mouth. 'Father, this is the best *marba juwi balay jagan* I've ever had.'

'Thanks, my girl,' he says, then flashes me the biggest grin I've ever seen him wear.

'Did you use lemon myrtle and something spicy?' Narn says, in between mouthfuls.

'Yes. That spiciness is pepperleaf. I traded for it long ago,' Father answers Narn. Then he swishes down some sweet water, wipes his mouth with the back of his hand and says, 'It's been a good night.'

'The best,' I agree. 'And my belly is as full as that moon.'

'Yep.' Narn tickles me. 'But we're not finished yet.' He stands, pulls me to my feet and leads me into the circle of small fires. The laughter and talking fizzles.

Narn wraps one arm around me. 'Thank you, Elders, for giving me – us – permission to speak now and honour a custom from my first tribe, the old one I came from before my dad saved me in the bay. My dad's passing means my vow with him ends, and I can share my past with you.'

Everything is still. Only the fire and the ocean can be heard.

Narn pauses for a moment too; his father's passing affects us all.

'The place where I was born has a tradition to thank everyone during the joining ceremony. I'm not sure how I know this, because after my drowning accident, I don't remember much about my old tribe except two main things, which Tarni will share later.'

The thought of talking to all these people at once, makes my tummy feel it's spent days in a canoe on large rough seas.

'Thanks, Minjarra and Merindah, Elders, family and friends from Tarni's mother's clan for coming and our family and friends from here and all the other clans too.'

He turns to me. 'I've always loved you, Tarni. From the beginning, it was a friendship-love that grew and grew ... until I knew I wanted to spend the rest of my life with you.'

My knees knock together and won't stand strong.

'You make me want to be a better man', he says, tucking a curl behind my ear. 'And because of you, every day I will try. Thank you for agreeing to be joined with me. We are no longer two flames burning alone ... but one. And maybe soon, we'll have a little dolphin caller of our own, for me to train.'

There's giggling and hooting. That twinkle returns to his eyes, and he answers my smile with a kiss. We don't usually kiss in front of anyone, especially not all the clans of our tribe.

Everyone laughs again. I stare at my toes wiggling in the sand.

Narn nudges me. 'Your turn.'

I take a deep breath. 'I claim this man to be mine for the rest of my life. He has more than one name. Our tribe calls him Narn. But his first tribe calls him –' I pause to make sure I have his names in the right order. 'Byron Wuz Anthony Wallace.'

I search for Kirra. Her mouth opens so wide, a camp of bats could fly in.

Gripping Narn's hand, I focus on Kirra. 'I claim his kin as my kin. His sister Kirra, known by her tribe as Kirra Wonda Wallace, is now my sister.'

I give my best big sisterly smile, but Kirra doesn't move. Her eyebrows are two non-returning boomerangs thrown high into the sky … an expression I know well, just like her big brother.

Everyone stares at Kirra. She hasn't blinked. Narn smiles and winks at his sister, and I want to wrap her in a huge hug. Narn's prediction was wrong.

Kirra hadn't realised he was her brother.

I move towards her, but Narn tugs me back and kisses me again. A long kiss that makes me forget about sisters and clans and sends my head spinning. I ignore the clapping and cheering. Instead, I enjoy Narn's strength and gentleness and every detail of this moment.

Then there're back slaps and hugs from family and friends, and the big gathering under the bright moon disperses. Little ones are already sleeping in their mum's or granny's arms. The older *jarjum* games have stopped.

They've joined the adults in smaller groups, yarning and yawning.

Narn is with Mum – feels strange to say it.

I hug Kirra. 'Narn said to tell you he'll have a long yarn with you tomorrow.'

She nods, and I want to stay and talk, but Mum and Narn motion me over. The older women, led by Mum, wave *jambinbin* leaves from both sides of the sandy path. The pathway to our new *ngumbin*. No longer will I sleep in the one with all the single girls.

Narn takes my hand as we walk past the waving *jambinbin* leaves and singing women. His eyes are intense: the sun, moon and all the stars shine from them. It's my Narn. My happy, joking, dolphin-obsessed tormenter.

We follow the tunnel of *jambinbin* leaves along the well-walked path and enter a new home – the first thing that's ours.

A deep voice yells from the crowd, I recognise it as Wanjellah's. *'Gowonda kunga neubungunn.'*

I beam. It's true. I'm now the dolphin caller's wife. Tomorrow, I will stand with him on the rocky headland, as he calls our grey-skinned friends.

The cool season is not so bad when I nuzzle into Narn's bare chest under his fur blanket.

I sit up. 'I thought you said Kirra knew?'

'Thought she did.' His strong arms pull me into his warm embrace. 'We were meant for each other,' he says nibbling down my neck.

'Mmm-hmm,' is all I can say between giggles.

'Our names mean *wave* and *sea*. We belong together.'

And he kisses all over my bare skin, making me squirm and laugh and breathless. Never knew life could be this great. And we have the rest of our lives here together … *if* he doesn't remember.

I shouldn't think it. These are not the thoughts of a loving, caring wife. I'm happy he remembered his name and that Kirra is his sister. But I hope he doesn't regain his memory, because we will never visit his tribe with their curious ways. And he can't find out that I'll do anything to stop him from leaving ours.

I snuggle into his embrace, with my first secret as the dolphin caller's wife.

CHAPTER 34
KIRRA

Instinct tells me it's time to leave, yet my thoughts and feelings wrestle. How do you bury a brother, mourn his loss for ten years, finally move on, then on his wedding night, discover he's alive and happily stuck in the past? And hours later, I need to say goodbye. Forever. Or convince him or both newlyweds to time-travel with me during their honeymoon on a six-foot surfboard.

'*Jingi wahlu*,' I say to Tarni and Narn, kinda surprised to see them on the beach this early.

'*Jingi wahlu*,' they reply, as if last night's ceremony joined their voices too.

I dig my toe in the sand, not willing to see disappointment in their faces. 'I wish we had more time,' I say to Tarni, waiting for her to tell Narn my message or for Narn to smear N'gian's ochre on our foreheads.

'What?' my brother asks.

'Wait – you understand me. You speak English!' My head's spinning faster than a ride at a theme park.

'I'm sorry, Kirra. Dad made me promise a long time ago. Tarni was my interpreter after the drowning accident.

329

And she convinced everyone I wasn't empty-headed just because I didn't understand.'

I don't wanna argue or waste precious time.

'It's okay. I get it,' I say. 'Just don't wanna lose you again.'

'What do you mean?' my brother says in a tone too off-key for a singer.

'I've found my big bro, nabbed a sister, and I've got to leave today.'

I try to imagine him without his thick beard or long hair, wearing boardies and a tee, and speaking in modern Aussie slang. But I was six when he disappeared. Anyway, Nan said he was a 'late-developer' for a twelve-year-old. Now he's a tall, solid man with a deep booming voice. Still, I thought I'd recognise something about him.

Tarni gives Narn the well-do-something face, and he looks awkward. Guess he really doesn't remember how close we were.

'Why go today?' He sounds unconvincing and insincere.

'I dreamt about it in N'gian's cave. Tarni's mum took me there. Then Wanjellah arrived after my dream. Threads of time became a single moment. I'd focus on one thread and see everything: what happened, what's happening, and what will happen. That's why Wanjellah and your father saved you. You were meant to die. I saw Jiemba thrust a spear through your stomach ... Wait a minute.'

I'm staring out to sea, but my dream-vision is dancing around me.

'Kirra?' Narn taps my shoulder.

'Sorry, I'm remembering the vision: I saw your face and Jiemba throw a spear. It went through the middle of someone. Then blood poured out, but it was from a different perspective.'

I'm holding my palms out in front of me. 'There was blood over both hands. I thought you were gonna die. Glad it wasn't you.' Then I bite my inner cheek. 'Sorry, Narn. Didn't mean it that way. I'm sorry it was your dad.'

'Narn – you alright?' Tarni clings to Narn's arm like he's a life jacket and she's shipwrecked. 'I promise I didn't know about Kirra's dream,' she says to him. 'I found out at the Elder's gathering when you did or I would've told you.'

Narn's mouth falls open, then widens further. 'You didn't get it wrong,' he says, frowning at me. 'Dad's hands were like this,' and he holds his hands in front of him.

'Yeah, they weren't your hands,' I say, tripping over guilt, its baggage, then easing to my feet again.

'It wasn't me you saw,' he says, emphasising each word. 'You saw the dream. You just didn't know how to interpret it properly.'

'Sorry,' I say, even though I thought we'd already dealt with this before we defeated the Malung. 'Wanjellah made me keep it a secret. He said it could make things worse. Should've kept my mouth shut.'

'Wanjellah knew and didn't warn me either,' he mutters. 'Why *did* you bring it up?'

'Because it's when I saw today happen,' I snap. 'Everything looks and feels exactly the same as that dream. You. Tarni. The small groups of people gathering. You'll call in the dolphins, and Tarni will stand next to you.' I rub the ends of my string skirt. It's hard enough leaving, let alone telling them something that'll make them drown in disappointment. 'Today is when I catch a barrel back to my time.'

'Your time?' he asks.

I stare right through him. 'You know I'm from the future, right? I caught a time-tube. It's a wave tunnel that sent me here. I need to go back to my time … in the future.'

'What future?' My brother scratches his head, the emu feathers from last night's ceremony bounce up and down.

And I'm a little surprised he doesn't get it … that his memories are actually lost. 'When I go back, I'll see your grandchildren's grandchildren or their grandchildren.'

'*Uhhhh*,' is all he can say.

Our two paths are separating. Why would he leave his family here, when he's got no connection with ours?

Time's ticking away and he's avoiding my eyes.

'I know I need to leave today,' I say.

Tarni wraps the large fur blanket around them.

Narn gives her a gentle squeeze, then turns to me and says, 'I thought you'd be here longer, *Yilgahn*.'

I love him calling me 'little sister' in Yugambeh language.

'Me too, *Kagohn*. It's not gonna be easy to get back. I need a decent wave. One sucky enough to barrel and the sun shining through it. Tough, when the swell has dropped since yesterday, and the tide has just started going out.'

As if he can read my mind, Narn says, 'Your best chance is at the lowest point of the tide. That's if the swell picks up.'

Tarni stares at him. I do too.

'What? Don't ask how I know,' he says, flicking from Tarni to me. 'Some things click. Others stay stuck in a night-fog.' Narn blinks a few times too many and mumbles, 'Got sand in my eyes.'

Tarni nestles into him, and in one shared glance, we know his sandy cover-up.

'Dad talks about the swell like you,' I say to refocus on the waves. 'Wait 'til I tell him and Nan.'

Will Narn's eyes light up with memories of our family? Nope.

'And even your mum – do you remember you and I have different mums?'

He shakes his head.

'Well, she was at your funeral. They all think you're dead!'

Tarni ducks out of the blanket and gives me a quick hug. 'It's a lot to think about,' she says.

'I had a funeral? Without my body?'

'Yeah,' I sigh. 'Hated that empty coffin. Made it sadder.'

'That's because I didn't die. I came here.'

'Wuz – Narn – I have to know, will you come back with me?'

Tarni bites her lower lip, so I rush to add, 'You *and* Tarni. Dad and Nan will never believe me if I tell them you're alive and living somewhere in the past.'

'If you can fight a mind-spear and the Malung, I'm sure you'll handle Nan and Dad. You're stronger than your feelings.' He ruffles my hair, and I screw up my face at him.

'It's more than just feelings,' I say. 'Our great-grandmother had this dreaming gift, and she was admitted to a psych ward. Don't want that to happen to me.'

'Did she wear his ochre?'

I shake my head.

'When you go back, you'll need to find N'gian's cave and collect his glowing ochre. I'll leave the sealed clay jar with his symbol on it ... I'm sorry I can't go with you, Sis.'

He's never said 'Sis' before. Is he trying to soften the blow?

Narn wraps his arm around Tarni. 'I have a wife now. This is where I'm meant to be.'

I expect his answer and nod towards the sea. 'I'll need my surfboard. The tide is getting lower.'

'I'll get it after the dolphins gather our breakfast,' he says.

'I almost forgot,' Tarni chirps. 'Told Mum I'd help her this morning. I'll meet you on the headland, Dolphin Caller, and see you after we collect fish, Little Sis.' And she races along the beach.

When Tarni's out of view, I say, 'There's so much I haven't told you about our family, about Dad, about Nan.'

'Things happen for a reason, even if we don't always know why,' Narn says.

'How are you sure?'

'Don't really understand but the magic N'gian gave me means there are things I know: I know the right wave will take you back. I sense it. I feel it.'

'I hope so,' I say.

'Tarni's mum said I have the "unseen gift". It strengthens other people's gifts too.'

'Okaaaay.'

'My gift called you here. My belief joins yours and strengthens it. Actually I don't really get it, I just know my gift is real.'

'But how do you know you have it?'

'I feel it, like a strong belief in my gut. It's not up here.' He taps his temple and says, 'It's not knowledge or reasoning, and it's more than thinking everything will be bright and cheery. It's "belief" mixed with a strong sense of "knowing". Just like I know you're right: it is time for you to go back to your tribe.'

'Don't you mean *our* tribe?' The tears are coming and there's nothin' I can do.

'Yes. You're my sister, my family. You always will be, and Dad, Nan – they're my family with or without memories. They are my blood. But here is where I need to be, and where I want to be. I'm sorry.'

We hug and I squeeze him tight. 'I love you, Wuz – I mean, Narn.' I pull away and wipe my eyes. 'What should I call you?'

'Narn. It's what the Old Dolphin Caller named me, and he was my dad here. It's who I am and what I remember.'

Don't cry. Stay strong, I coach myself.

'But I don't mind if you call me Wuz. I *Wuz* your brother before I *Wuz* Narn.' He grins and elbows me.

I shake my head; a giggle escapes. And Narn is obviously happy with his dad-joke wit, 'cos he does this weird swagger and wink. For the first time, it's the brother I remember. And I blink away more tears.

The vibe switches.

'I know you have what it takes without a doubt. Choose moment by moment, bit by bit. Do what you can at each step without worrying about the next one.'

'I'm only sixteen and life in the future is very different.'

'Doesn't matter. It takes belief in unseen things.' Narn sits in the sand.

I sink beside him, hug my knees under my chin and say, 'Believing my dreams come true is easy. I see them unfold. But believing in unseen things is ludicrous – no, more like impossible. I like facts ... knowledge.'

'You want proof? You want to see the unseen gift?'

'Sure.'

My brother points at the beach behind us. 'See that tree with those funny-looking roots?'

'The pandanus?'

'Yeah, we call it *jambinbin*.'

I break it into three smaller chunks: '*Jam-bin-bin*.'

'Look all the way from the roots up to its branches. High in that branch there's a start of a root. That pandanus root starts growing, knowing it'll reach the ground.'

I run my fingers through the sand. Never heard him talk this way before.

'It can't see the ground. But one day it'll reach it and be able to draw up food and water. Kirra, that's called believing in an unseen thing.'

I listen hard, not to reply but to understand.

'Believe that if you start, it will happen. You let those *jambinbin* roots grow. And even when days, weeks, months pass and those roots don't touch the ground, you still grow and believe one day they will.'

'Thanks, Bro. I needed to hear that.'

'I believe in you, Sis, your gift and your future.'

The silhouette of a tall woman is waving from the headland.

'We'll say a proper goodbye after we gather fish,' he says, and he jumps to his feet. 'Kirra?'

I stand – wait for him to speak.

'Thanks for coming when I called. I never knew we needed you.' And my brother nods towards the sun and says, 'But that old fella did. Do what is right and good, even when you have no strength. Believe, even if there's no proof or evidence. Persist, even if you feel alone. Promise?'

I nod even though it's confusing.

'I'm trying to say, I believe you can do whatever needs to be done.'

'Why didn't you just say that in the first place? For someone who usually doesn't say much, once you get started you're an old philosopher.'

He chuckles. I'm gonna miss him.

CHAPTER 35
NARN

The moon and sun fight for attention. On one side, the silvery light sinks into its dark bed, while a golden one rises from its watery slumber. Tarni slips under my possum-skin cloak. Blood pumps around me like an oncoming southerly swell. I wrap my arms around her and pull her closer, as we stand high on the headland. My beautiful wife rubs her hands over my chest and back. And I realise I'm warm with happiness and love. Life has given me all I'll need ... or want.

A group of women and *jarjum* gather on the beach below. My sister is with them. I'll call our dolphins, grab her surfboard, then send her home. Our clansmen, carrying spears and *arabin*, walk down the dunes, ready to haul in masses of mullet. We've let the first large bait ball travel down the coast, so tomorrow's children can carry this tradition.

Tarni snuggles closer. 'It's cold this morning.'

'You just want an excuse to steal my blanket.' Releasing my grip, I let her take it all.

Her smile is playful, dancing up and down her lips.

A look reserved for husbands with long fur cloaks. I spin her to face me. 'How did I catch a wife as beautiful as you?'

She chuckles; it's my favourite sound. I tighten my muscles, one powerful squeeze at a time, and say, 'Maybe it was the right kind of bait, huh?'

She giggles as I flex my arms and chest and turn around and tense my *kumo*. I do it over and over, anything to hear her laugh.

Tarni presses her palms on her cheeks. 'My face hurts. I don't want to laugh anymore. Stop.' She heaves in a breath. 'Please stop.'

I flex my body once more, then wrap her in a massive hug.

There's a glimmer in her eyes. No longer the eyes of an innocent girl but of a woman. And not just any woman, she's my wife and this is the first time she's stood next to me on the headland while I call the dolphins. Still can't believe she fell for me and became my wife.

The superpod has scattered. I squeeze Tarni's hand to help me ignore the ache in my chest. It's the first time I'll call the dolphins without Dad. Spinner, my favourite pointy-finned friend and her little calf, Echo, won't be here today either – or ever again. The sea drowned too many that day, and when Spinner died, it determined Echo's life too. No mother's milk. No survival.

I pick the spot Dad taught me that'll send my voice across the headland and further out to sea. Cupping my hands around my mouth, I sing one long, low sound. The spears slap the water to the beat. My voice rises and falls louder and faster. I close my eyes and feel every word and every note. I sing with all I have and all I am. I call the unseen when we need them, and they always answer our call.

Tarni points out to sea. 'There. A white fin.' Her voice is the sound of a small frothy wave rolling onto the beach. 'Big Boi, the boss of the pod, is coming.'

It doesn't take long for our smooth-skinned friends to jump and splash into our bay. They chase a black cloud of fish towards the shallow shores. And turn hard work into fun. I spot the white-tipped *gowonda* leaping out of the water, and my heart dips and dives with him. His white fin reminds me of my sister's surfboard and her reaction last night. When she found out I was her brother, her eyes were wide and her mouth had no words.

Big Boi splashes above the waves again. After all these years, I never tire of this. Dad loved it too. And with him gone, it means more.

Tarni yells into the air. 'I'm going down to help!' And she springs from rock to rock until she lands on the thick sand below.

My wife joins the women and *jarjum* on the beach to collect fish from the shallows or off the men's spears. They scramble in calf-deep water, while the waves wash in more flapping fish. The dolphins brought in plenty. Guests, from our surrounding clans, have wandered down the dunes to join us in our full-moonset tradition. Some have danced all night.

Our senior *arabin* experts, Gunggin and Nunnjahli, stand in the waist-deep water with their fine-meshed net attached to its cane frames. Each hand grips the curved cane handle and they stand side by side, stretching out the cane, so their fine woven nets form a wall to trap the fish. More mullet, chased by our dolphin friends, zoom towards the beach. Our skilful fishermen use slow movements to scoop the nets through the water. They tilt the open nets so the fish swim towards them. Then a quick snap, the two cane handles close together, trapping the mullet in the handheld net. Each hauls their load out of the water and up the beach. Their wrists bear the scars of previous heavy catches.

Everyone is eager to play a part in our dolphin-fishing custom.

I rock-hop to the beach and wrangle a mullet that washed in with the last wave. The water temperature has plummeted over the last couple of days, but I wade out until the cold water creeps over my legs and reaches my middle. Gukuji holds his spear out to Big Boi; a flapping fish is speared through its middle. Big Boi's round teeth tug the fish off the spear, then he disappears out to sea.

Spinner's mum swims around me. I hold out the fish by its tail, and she swallows it whole. She stays by my side so I chat to her: 'I miss them too. Sorry about your daughter and her –'

As if she understands me, she lets out a high whistle. Moments later, a young dolphin zips in. And a large protective mother, who has a chunk missing from her dorsal fin, follows the little one's every move.

The tiny tail swims in closer and splashes water on my face.

It's Echo.

She's been adopted by a nursing mother who must've been part of the superpod.

Echo jumps and splashes, her tail wiggles up and down. Bubbles fizz around me and it's exactly how I feel inside. I no longer care about shivering in the cold water or how many fish fill our dillybags.

Echo is here. Alive and active as ever. She chomps at a leaf floating on the surface.

'That's it, Echo. Practise catching your fish. You won't be on mother's milk forever.'

I haven't seen her since the battle in the ocean. And since then, the tip of her dorsal fin has whitened … maybe she'll be the next leader. I'm thankful she's been adopted and our bond deepens. A generous man raised me as his own, and I'm grateful he gave me a place in this clan.

Spinner's mum retreats to the deep. The pod of dolphins, including Echo, jumps over the crest of waves. We cheer and clap as they vanish into the horizon.

White froth tumbles in and out on the shore while *jarjum* squeal and hold the flapping fish that're trying to escape back into the grey-blue sea. Dillybags are filled and pull down their owners' shoulders.

I sprint to Tarni and Kirra. It's a great start to the mullet season. I sneak behind my wife and wrap my dripping arms around her.

'*Eeeek.* Narn, you're wet and cold.' She chucks the long fur cloak over my head.

Kirra turns to me and says, 'Your dolphin call is amazing. I love dolphins.'

'*Gowonda*,' Tarni interjects. 'That means "dolphin".'

'I remember,' Kirra says. The way her eyes stare makes me think her thoughts are carried far away.

I dry my face on the fur and shake the water out of my hair. 'Did you see Echo?'

Both Tarni and Kirra throw smiles my way, and my wife gives me a big squeeze. 'I can't believe she's alive.'

'Kirra, did you collect fish?' I ask with Tarni tucked under my arm.

'Yep … Helped Birri carry a big bag over the dunes for

the aunties to cook. But when we came back, the rest had been collected. There's plenty of people helping today.'

I agree. Then the three of us stand there, not sure what else to say. Silence seems easier.

Minjarra's walking down from camp and stands at the top of a sand dune. I can tell he wants to talk to me, and I still need to get Kirra's surfboard from the sea cave, so I need to hurry this conversation along.

'You know, I only remembered my name because I scratched it on a cave wall, before I lost my memory,' I say to Kirra.

She tilts her head. 'So, how did you know I was your sister?'

'Didn't ... not till I saw the glowing symbols in N'gian's cave.' I shrug. 'Like I told you this morning, the Old Dolphin Caller made me vow. Even if I'd remembered everything about my past, I was under lore to keep silent. Dad said that it was for my safety.'

My shoulders stiffen. I try to relax them, but they tighten back up.

Tarni gives me an everything-will-all-work-out smile, and says, 'We should paint Kirra with N'gian's ochre before she leaves.'

'Good idea,' I say, and pull the fur across my wife's shoulder.

'Come back with me, please,' Kirra pleads.

Tarni tightens her grip.

'Nan and Dad will absolutely love you, Tarni.' Kirra talks faster as if talking faster will convince us more.

My wife's lips pinch together. There's nothing more to say. Minjarra is pacing along the sand dunes. And I want to keep my wife and her father happy.

'Sorry, Kirra, Minjarra's waiting for me. Better go see him. Then I'll get your surfboard. Be back soon.'

'You need help?' Tarni asks.

'No, I'll be quick.' I leave her with my cloak and race through the deep, loose sand to Minjarra.

Thought Kirra and I would have much longer to talk. I didn't expect her to stay forever, but now I know how she felt last night. One surprise deserves another.

The wind's blowing on my face. And with the water temperature having already dropped, I know she's right. She must leave soon. The *dugan djulung waring gwong* has already begun. This may be her only chance.

'Minjarra. Father,' I say, keeping my eyes averted to show my father-in-law respect.

'The catch was good today.' He chuckles. 'You must sing better as a married man, *uh*?'

'Or they saw Tarni standing beside me and they're worried my dolphin-calling days may be over, now that I have a wife.' It's the first time we've joked together. It's a new awkwardness, but a good one.

'You know, Narn.' His tone is serious. 'I was hard on you because it's an important custom. A privilege.'

'Yes. I love her and promise I'll take care of her, her whole life.'

He says nothing.

'You talking about Tarni?' I ask.

'No. I was talking about being the dolphin caller.'

I'm eager for more, because he's never discussed this.

'Used to think it was a big mistake,' he says. 'Now I see the Old Dolphin Caller made the right choice.' We sit in the sand, our elbows resting on our knees. The sound of the ocean keeps our conversation private.

'The dolphin caller is an honoured place,' he says, and I know he's right.

I listen as we watch the waves roll onto the beach and back out to sea. The sun climbs further away from the horizon. Kirra still has time, and this talk with Minjarra won't happen again.

'You know, I hoped for that role as a boy, after – you know – the Old Dolphin Caller lost his first son.'

'Never knew that.' The more today goes on, the more surprises I get, and it's still hard hearing my dad's name changed to the 'Old Dolphin Caller'.

Minjarra wriggles deeper in the sand. 'My father made me practise diving and holding my breath underwater. I think he knew being the dolphin caller had something to do with that ... not that you call the dolphins from underwater.'

As soon as he says that, I think of the sea cave Dad made me vow never to reveal.

'My father hoped I'd be picked as the next dolphin caller. But no-one was chosen for a long time. Dad made me train in the sea every day. But that father of yours didn't choose anyone, just called the dolphins himself.'

I savour every word.

'And I grew up, got joined to Merindah, had Tarni, and lost a son of my own. Losing a child changes you.'

He clears his throat and I don't move. Tarni's never mentioned this.

Then his eyes rest on the ocean again. 'I can see why he took so long to train another.'

I'd no idea he wanted my job. Doubt Tarni's heard this story either.

'Have you worked it out yet?' Minjarra asks.

'Worked out what?'

'Where the dolphin callers get buried. Ya know, the second burial in the special place. His bones won't be buried in the large sacred site with the scarred trees. Dolphin callers have their own sacred site. But you already know that. He would've trained you in that secret business.'

'He never told me.' A sickness swirls around and around in my stomach the way a shark circles its next victim.

My father-in-law slaps my back twice. 'You'll work it out. It's your duty. You have to take him there by yourself.'

I can solve that problem another day, today has enough of its own. I stand and dust the sand off my hands. 'I've got to help Kirra; she's going back to her time and people.'

'She's really from a different time?'

'From the future … our grandchildren's grandchildren's grandchildren's time.'

Minjarra's quiet for a moment, then says, 'Merindah, Wanjellah, Nyrah – everyone – will want to see Kirra before she leaves.'

'I'll grab Kirra's surfboard.'

'Well, I better check those fish are cooking – that Kirra and everyone has a feed before she leaves.' And he hurries up the dunes.

Tarni scoots over, hands me my grey cloak and says, 'I'm going to get the glowing ochre and a *waalum* pod for Kirra.' She walks away calling over her shoulder, 'I'll bring Mum to say goodbye. You get that surfboard.'

A few kids play on the headland, the place where I sang earlier. When the beach empties and all the fish are taken to the big communal area, I make my move. There's a long lull between the sets of small waves. I swim out into the black soup of mullet. We never swim this time of year for one sharp-toothed, killer reason.

Control my fear or my heartbeat becomes a loud drum, a shark caller. I push away my fear and dive deep into the underwater cave.

Once inside, I scan the sea cave walls. This time I enter as a man armed with knowledge and understanding of what my future holds. On a rock shelf near the top of the sea cave, shadows of similar shapes rest high above the tidelines. Dad knew I would realise what this place really is: a sacred burial site.

I'll return one more time to this cave, in a year or two, to lay the bones of my father, the Old Dolphin Caller, after I've cocooned them in a hollow log. And, one day, the next dolphin caller will be responsible for my remains. This is where my future lies: a link to tides and swell. A burial of both land and water. A constant connection to saltwater country.

It's a part of me. Always will be.

In Kirra's time, will this still be the sacred site of the *gowonda* callers?

I pick up my sister's board and hear children yelling far above me, from the spot on the headland where I call the dolphins. My knowledge deepens. This sea cave is an underwater echo chamber, sending loud sound vibrations out to the sea to our dolphin allies. It connects us.

I swim out of the cave and the surfboard pops to the surface. I lay on the board and paddle-swim to shore with familiar ease. Then race along the beach with Kirra's surfboard tucked under my arm. I hand it to my sister.

She places it beside her and scoffs the rest of the food Minjarra has sent her.

Tarni runs over, passes Kirra the *waalum* pod and puts the coolamon holding N'gian's ochre next to the surfboard. She pulls Kirra into a hug, and I wrap my arms around them both.

'Goodbye, Tarni and Narn.'

'There are no goodbyes,' I say.

'Until we meet again,' Tarni says with a soft, heartfelt tone.

Kirra nods and I wait to see if she'll burst into tears. She doesn't.

I dip my hand in the coolamon and smear glowing white ochre across her forehead and mine at the same time. 'This will help me strengthen your gift. It'll protect you.' Then, I tap N'gian's symbol on her surfboard and add, 'The sea brought us together.'

Kirra hunches over her board and scratches the *waalum* pod along its top. 'This will make the wax more grippy.' Then she says to Tarni, 'Sorry for ruining your banksia pod. Don't brush your hair with this one. Wax takes ages to get out.'

'Nah, there's plenty of old flower spikes. It's their flowering season,' Tarni says, looking at the groves of *waalum* along our beaches.

'Nature's hairbrush,' my sister says. She's on the tips of her toes, squeezing those scrawny arms around me again. 'The upwelling is here.'

I stoop to make our embrace less awkward. 'Time doesn't separate us; it connects us,' I say. And when our hug finishes, an 'I love you, Sis,' escapes from my tight throat.

Aunty Lowanna, Granny Alkira, Merindah, Minjarra, Wanjellah, Nyrah, Alba, Birri – everyone – is on the beach to say 'until we meet again' to Kirra.

The tide drops to its lowest point, and tiny waves roll into our bay. Tarni and I watch from the shore with the rest of the clans, as Kirra fastens her leg-rope to her ankle then paddles past the rocky headland into our deep black squid-inked bay. Shimmery mullet swarm the sea for as far as the eye can see. Man-eating sharks trawl our coast this time of year.

Kirra turns her board to face the beach, lies on her belly and strokes hard and fast like a goanna, arms at full speed. The wave rolls past her, and she punches the water. Another wave forms. Kirra's paddling hard and picking up speed. She catches it but it's not big enough to form a wave tunnel. Neither is the next one. Or the one after it. She's sitting on her board. The ochre has washed from her face.

My body feels hot, and I'm itchy all over. So I bolt to the headland and clamber up the rocks. Tarni follows me.

'You all right, Narn?' she asks.

'I can call dolphins in with my song. But I've never done anything to send them home,' I say, scratching the back of my neck.

She takes my hand, and we stare at Kirra bobbing on her surfboard. An enormous black ball of fish tumbles towards her.

A crowd gathers on the beach. Most of our clan scamper up the headland. The circling fish are mesmerising. They form a massive bait ball – a span of twelve canoes – beneath my sister's dangling legs, seeking protection. Because it's being herded by a huge pointy-noised shark with a stark white underbelly. The beast is five to six spear-lengths long, and it charges through thousands of fish.

'Kirra. Shark!' We yell it again and again.

She can't hear us. We scream louder.

It's too late.

The large jagged-toothed monster picks up speed in full feeding-frenzy mode. My sister's unaware of it approaching from below. Its powerful tail flicks side to side as it strikes.

Kirra's surfboard flips upright like a shield or burial marker.

The bait ball swarms and swirls.

Concealing Kirra and the shark.

CHAPTER 36
TARNI

'Naaarn,' Mum bellows as she scales the headland. 'You need to sing Kirra back to her time.'

Once she's by our side, he answers, 'I don't have N'gian's song. It starts as a hum, which grows into a powerful tune. The words come after.' And Narn's eyes haven't strayed from his little sister, who surfaces and scrambles onto her surfboard.

Kirra paddles towards shore. She's a long way out, and the waves have lost their power. Sparse ankle-slappers trickle onto the beach.

At the edge of the fish swarm, that mountainous grey fin surfaces then disappears.

'Paddle, Kirra!'

'Faster!'

We shout in helpless support. Fear is a wide-mouthed killer swallowing us whole.

Kirra's smashing her arms into the rippling water. She isn't moving. A strong narrow current washing out to sea is preventing her from paddling in.

'Sing your dolphin song,' Mum orders my husband.

'Them gathering more fish is not gonna help Kirra,' Narn mutters, but he sings – hesitant and helpless.

It's all rushed and wrong. Mum's out of control: her wind-messed hair bounces up and down as she marches along the shore, organising men and women into two lines. From the beach all the way to the headland, each man's right hand is placed on the shoulder in front of them, until Wanjellah touches Narn's back. It's same for the women, ending with Granny Alkira's hand on mine.

The shark hasn't resurfaced. Maybe it's gone?

Mum carries a coolamon over to us, then interrupts Narn's dolphin song.

'N'gian's gifts are for the benefit of the whole tribe, never for an individual,' she says, then leans in closer. 'I learned that when you two and Kirra defeated the Malung.'

'I don't know how to send her back,' Narn admits.

'You're not alone in this,' Mum says with such gentleness, it makes me a little teary.

I grip Narn's shaky hand.

A cavernous '*hmmmm*' begins at the beach. Each male joins the deep-voiced warble as it sweeps through their line, up to Narn. It sounds like last night – how the men start off every mullet festival. Women keep the rhythm, the way we always have with our possum-skin-drum technique.

The beat passes from me to my husband, and he sings again. Rich song-like vibrations saturate the air, and we welcome the shivers they send. Narn's song seems strengthened, so does his stance.

'Faster, Kirra, faster,' someone yells from behind.

Kirra's arms haven't stopped. The black sea heaves, the shark fin emerges and speeds across the surface. It's charging her.

Narn's dolphin call intensifies.

The shark's vicious head launches out of the water; serrated teeth crowd its gaping mouth. Eyes roll to white terror. And the largest member of the shark family breaches. As it lunges towards Kirra's floundering legs, its grey body jolts to one side.

And misses her by a tooth-width. But its wake knocks Kirra into the sea. This time she launches back on her board, and her arms paddle faster than I could run.

Out of nowhere, eight or ten dolphins are ramming the shark with their blunt snouts. Every direction the grey beast moves, it's jabbed multiple times from the strongest dolphins in our pod. They herd the shark away from Kirra. And the giant grey fin leaves our bay.

We yell our thanks to our saltwater helpers. The celebration is short-lived.

'The tide is shifting,' Narn says peering over the cliff edge. 'Kirra's out of time.'

Mum walks over to Narn and passes him N'gian's ochre. 'The community will support N'gian's gifts,' she says with practical, no-fuss tact. 'You have to sing without knowing how to send her back. When you call the dolphins, you don't wait to see a dolphin first. You sing believing they'll come. This is the same.'

'I'll try,' he says, and he smears ochre on his face and mine at the same time.

'No need to try,' Mum calls after him. 'N'gian will give you the power.'

He paints Mum's forehead with ochre, then walks through our linked clans and applies it to everyone. When my husband returns, he holds my hand tight.

The men's drone rumbles through the air and ground. The women's beat brings life to the sound. And we anticipate Narn will receive N'gian's song.

He sings his normal call, then something switches in his tone.

Bumps cover his skin, and there's a tingling across my back. Warm ripples spread from Narn to me and along our human chain.

'This happened when my sister first arrived.' He's breathy. 'Can't think or talk. Must use my instinct to sing.'

My fingers tighten around his.

A low hum echoes and expands from Narn. It flows and the men's voices surge with it. It's powerful and beautiful as well as humble and raw. Then Narn bursts into a new song with words that make me tingle and tears stream.

Kirra's flat against her surfboard paddling away from the bait ball.

Arms blur with speed.

And a peak, full of fury, grows behind her. Kirra's arms spin faster, and she's drawn deeper into the crest's shadow. Its presence makes her ant-like; her board, a white speck.

A sea-god force is toying with the end of Kirra's board, dangling her over its life-threatening cliff. Then in a blink, she switches from belly to feet and zooms down the watery mountain, which changes as it picks up speed. The whole wave plummets and sidesteps and spins, before the coiling crest breaks into two green curling parts. Its middle spews out angry white rapids. Rapids that would trample bones and airways.

Kirra's on the side furthest from the headland. Slightly crouched, her legs are glued to the board, and she's powering along the unbroken part of the wave. She tucks in close to the spiralling wall, and a giant waterfall buckets over her, while she's hopefully in its air pocket. But it looks like a monster of the great deep has swallowed her whole.

'She's in the wave's cave,' Mum yells, and the tribes cheer and clap the same way we send off our dolphin friends.

'Did the sun pierce through it?' I shout over the thundering sea.

'Dunno,' Narn says, and we can't see Kirra or her surfboard.

The dark wave explodes. Thick white froth sprays into the air.

'She's gone,' I say, with tears threatening to surge. 'That's what she needed to do, right?'

Narn swallows. 'Probably won't see her again.'

His watery eyes are my undoing. I cry into his chest for the loss of our little sister.

'I hope she was pulled back to her time.' Narn's voice has an edge that could sharpen spear tips. 'Hope that the time-tube hasn't closed and Kirra's sinking to the bottom of the sharky sea.'

'We must believe N'gian sent the right wave and summoned the *dugan djulung waring gwong* to take her back to where she belongs,' I say, wiping my face with the back of my hand. 'We'll keep Gowonda's story alive, so in years to come, it'll be passed down to your sister's time.'

Narn and I watch the pod splashing in the distance. A tiny dolphin with a white fin plays in the rolling waves.

'Knowing where you're from is a part of knowing who you are,' he says, wrapping his arms around me. 'The more you know yourself, the more you'll know your purpose.'

And Granny Yindi's words return, along with Narn's dad and my mum's: it takes confidence to know your place and purpose, so you can choose which rules to break or keep. But it takes a community to help you know and grow.

Birrabunji would be proud of Narn. He's become a respected man. But it was never Narn that needed to change; it was me. Gifts aren't to promote an individual or make them seem clever. They are to connect a community. Each person has an individual way of applying talents and skill, seeing them grow, doing it according to their uniqueness. Who they are now and are becoming is their responsibility. But it's also our tribes' duty to maintain oneness.

'I love you, Narn,' I say, knowing I can't translate the whirr of emotion into words. And I peck my husband on the cheek. 'Always have. Always will.'

'Me too,' he says, scooping me into his arms. 'Even if my memories return, nothing will change, 'cos I love you more than anything or anyone.'

Then my tall dolphin caller kisses me the way he sings: slow and soft until it builds and peaks. The song must reach its full potential to be complete. It's like N'gian's symbol. The circle, which surrounds the meeting place and wave, is now complete.

Kirra's time here has finished.

CHAPTER 37
KIRRA

A mechanical *beep-beep* ... *beep-beep* ... *beep-beep* ... matches the rise and fall of my breath. Someone's here. *Where am I?* I want to ask. My mouth won't move.

I half-open my eyes, but the pain in my head squeezes them shut.

Crisp sheets, soft pillow, faint bleachy smell.

Am I in hospital? Those high-tech sounds mean I can't be in Wallulljagun. Happiness floats upwards – not strong enough to make me smile. *I'm back!*

'Kirra, ya 'wake?'

I ease my eyes open, and a face comes into focus: Nan.

She lurches from her chair and hovers over me. 'Thank God you're awake!' Nan smothers me in a mumma-koala hug. She presses a red 'call' button, then holds my hand.

'I should wait for the nurse or doctor. They said to wait for them if ya woke.' There's a quiver in her voice. 'But ya just got out of four weeks in the ICU, and 'cos of that white rash and yer brain being bumped and swelling and their anti-contagion policy, this is the first time ya dad and I could be in the room with ya.'

Her worry-lines are deeper. Nan's eyes superglue to mine, as though she'll never let me out of her sight. Makes sense, I am the remaining grandchild. Wait – Narn, Tarni – if I'm here, are their lives over? I gulp. Our ancient burial sites protecting their precious remains would've been bulldozed to make way for high-rises and highways and houses.

Nan eases into her chair. 'Ya dad'll be back soon. Oh, he's gonna get a big surprise ya finally woke up. He's ducked out to get coffee. He too good for instant. Reckon he'll get the good stuff while he's back in town.' She chuckles, her shoulders bounce up and down. 'Spent a lotta time at this hospital waitin' for ya to wake up. Maybe it's why they gave ya yer own room, a real flash one.'

I've missed her song-like voice and how she carries the conversation when I'm quiet.

'And you told me ya got no friends. Looks like plenty to me.' Nan scans the large room. A bunch of freshly cut flowers stand tall in a vase on my bedside table. Foil balloons float towards the stark-white ceiling. There are 'get well' cards arranged like framed pictures in a pop-up art gallery, fighting for space with bunches of bright-coloured flowers, which cover every surface in my hospital room. Nan's commentary of who sent them hums in the background: '... Mr Harris, yer surf coach; Mel and yer other surf friends; yer shaper, and ...'

I'm real grateful for family and friends. At school, it's easy to forget you have them, but it wouldn't worry me if there were no flowers, balloons or 'get well' cards. My mind's stronger now. And I'm not afraid of being alone on this overcrowded planet.

'Sorry, Nan ... couldn't get back sooner,' I try to say but unfamiliar noises escape, and I hope she can decode them.

Nan scoops up my hand and strokes it, pet-guinea-pig style. 'Don't talk, Bub. There'll be plenty of time for a proper catch up. I'm glad yer awake … frightened us real good.'

Before I can respond, a nurse whirrs in, armed with a computer on wheels. 'Good morning, Kirra. You had us worried there for a bit. Glad to see you're awake. Doctor Conner will be here soon. How are you feeling?'

The nurse's hair and make-up are start-of-the-shift perfect. She natters in a cheery voice while checking her gadgets. But my brain's quicksand, and her questions are lost in it.

'My head hurts.' And instead of my voice, an old man with a smoker's cough splutters. There's a tightness around my head and my fingers rub over a thick bandage.

'Sorry, what was that, dear?'

'She said her head hurts,' Nan jumps in before I can mouth anything to the nurse.

'I'll give you something for that right now. Then I'll check your stitches and bandage before the doctor pops in. Fingers crossed that those stitches have held this time and are healing nicely.'

I wince as I wash down the two tiny tablets she gives me. The water tastes bitter and smells like a public pool. Thought I'd miss a soft mattress, but my body rejects its comfort. Everything is different. Was it always like this? Well, comfy bedding ain't gonna cut it when I tell my time-travel tale to Nan and Dad and whichever doc they'll send for after I freak them out.

Days (and many awkward Wallulljagun time-travelling conversations) later, Nan is out buying the next round of coffee, while Dad sits in a chair beside my bed. His eyes have lost their sparkle, haircut is overdue, and once-black curls are covered in grey – more salt than pepper.

I haven't told them about Narn being Wuz, yet. If Narn shaved, would he look like Dad? Both are tall, not fat or skinny, but solid with dark brown eyes and thick hair. Nah, I reckon my half-brother takes after his mum's side, and I haven't seen her since Wuz's funeral.

'Hey, Dad, you okay?'

Nowadays, he's not one to initiate conversation. When I was little, we used to yarn. I loved when we'd sit around the dining table and share funny stories.

'Thought we were gonna lose you.' Dad's mouth clamps so hard, his jaw sticks out. He turns his head away, but it's too late. I saw his glassy eyes.

Dad wears sunnies at funerals to hide his tears. Now they spill over his grey-stubbled cheeks. His chin trembles, and I feel close to him again.

'I was so worried – couldn't lose you too. Not after your mum and Wuz.' He pauses, his voice quieter. 'I could never call him Byron, even when he was in trouble,' and he wipes his cheek with the back of his sleeve.

Our conversation stops. Not in an uncomfortable way. We're used to silence. It's an old friend that sits with us, 'til we're ready to talk and listen.

The clock on the far wall *tick-tick-ticks*.

'Dad, will you go back to the mines?' I don't wanna sound desperate but I'm tired. Tired of forcing myself to be brave. Brave words use too much energy. Energy I no longer have.

'I was thinking of staying here, so we could all live together again: you, me, Nan … if you want.'

I grin. And his eyes brighten. 'I wanna make the most of our time together,' he says.

Just like his silence summoned my silence, his words conjure mine.

'Why did you go away? Did I remind you too much of Wuz?'

'No.' His voice is firm, then he shakes his head and adds, 'Dunno. Maybe.'

'Dad, tell me. Please.'

He shifts in his chair. 'You grew so fast – weren't a little girl anymore. Needed more than I could give you … a mum, and Nan was the closest thing. Didn't think …'

His lips move but no words come out.

I wait.

Then, his dam wall crashes.

He's sobbing, shaky, and snotty.

I pass him a box of tissues from my side table.

After a loud blow, he says, 'I had nothing left to give … knew I couldn't be happy, so leaving was the best thing I could do for you. Maybe you could find happiness without me dragging you down.'

I place my hand on Dad's arm, but instead of soothing him, more sobs hurdle out. He heaves in another big breath. 'I was wrong. You needed a dad, not the money I sent. So I'm here for as long as you need me.'

My head aches from his words. I've lugged hurt and anger around for years. And paid too much for its excess baggage. Hot tears tumble. 'I don't want you to *ever* go away.'

Dad leans over my bed. He bear-hugs me. My head hurts, but I don't care. Dad and I are together. A real family and nothing can change that.

He sits again. 'I'm sorry, Bub. You know I love you.'

'Love you too. I missed you. And I will always need you, Dad.'

He squeezes my arm, our smiles confirm the worst is over.

Maybe Dad would be happier if he knew that Wuz, now called Narn, is alive in the past. But this is the first time we've been close in ten years, and I don't want to ruin it. Especially 'cos Dad's gonna live with us.

'We'll get you out of here,' he says with a wink, as if it's an exclamation mark to his deadly plan.

I prop up a nothing-is-bothering-me smile 'cos I have two choices. One is to lie, a get-out-of-jail-free card, so I can play happy families and ignore my dreams. Or two, I tell the truth and face the consequences, like Great Nanna Clara, and I know how that ends. I'm whirling, wanting a win-win outcome, when Doc Conner opens the door for Nan.

She's juggling muffins and coffees. 'Look who I found. Did you know Doc Conner specialises in comas?'

I stare past his neat brown hair, black-rimmed glasses and into his unwavering blue eyes. The way Nan said 'specialises' and 'comas' makes me think 'Doc' is code for a psychiatrist or psychologist or a kind of hit-man who eliminates the irrational part of your mind.

Doc sits on a chair, opposite Nan and Dad, on the other side of my bed.

'Isn't the truth a funny thing, Kirra? I believe there are many versions of the truth. What do you believe?'

Truth isn't funny at all. It's a minefield and not as black or white as I'd thought. I wiggle further into my propped-up pillows. Remembering Silverbird's lessons about mind-spears and lies, I spill everything.

A hundred heartbeats later, Doc asks, 'So Narn is Byron, your brother?' He sounds like he believes me.

Dad and Nan stiffen while I answer the doc's question. 'Yes, I didn't find out until the night before I returned here. I know it sounds absurd.' I look at my stunned family and say, 'Wuz says hello. He's happy – just married Tarni.'

I hadn't planned to tell them that way. Though Dad says nothing, which isn't unusual, his eyes bulge in a cartoonish way.

And I'm on my own again. Right when I need Dad, he's missing in the mines, 'cept he hasn't left my room.

Nan avoids eye contact.

Doc Conner stands. 'Kirra, thanks so much for telling us your experience. I believe it's very real for you. Do you mind if I tell you why?'

It's not like I have a choice, so I nod.

'Well, Kirra, you are not the first person to have this experience. There's a lot of research on this. People have woken from comas, or a brain injury, and they've had – I'm going to call them *experiences* – because they are far too real and detailed to call them dreams.'

He gives me his charming-prince-saves-the-day smile.

Perfect teeth. Perfect timing. Perfect mess.

The hairs on the back of my neck become as hard as needles, and I want to use Doc Conner as a pin-cushion.

'A patient of mine had a similar experience. She'd hit her head and, like you, was in a coma for almost four weeks. I believe you're so creative and young, your brain produced weeks of experiences to keep it active while it was recovering. It can be part of the way a brain heals itself. There are so many more examples of this.'

A numbness stops my thoughts. I'm a puzzle piece, swollen with water, unable to fit back into place.

There's a knock on my door, and Doc opens it.

'Sorry to intrude.' I recognise Furroway's voice straightaway. 'Kirra, I was dropping off flowers for you, and the nurse said you were awake.'

She flashes her red-lippie smile at Nan. 'Hello, Mrs Wallace.' Then she turns to Dad. 'You must be Kirra's father. I'm Imelda Furroway. I'll just put these here and be on my way.' She glides to the nearest bench, shuffles a few cards, then places the box of rainbow-coloured gerberas down.

'Imelda?' Doc says to Furroway, as she grabs the door handle.

'Wait. You two know each other?' I say, and hunt for confirmation on my doctor's or Furroway's face.

'Yes, I was just a grom when Imelda's brother was the president of our boardriders club.'

Mrs F looks awkward.

'How is Coen?' he asks.

And I'm interested how she'll answer about the brother she's 'not very close to'.

'He's fine, David.'

'I'll never forget Coen's gnarliest scar. He was always –'

'Sorry, David, I'd better go,' Furroway says, rushing to open the door. 'Hope you feel better, Kirra. Goodbye, everyone,' and she bustles away.

I'm surprised she brought me flowers, and can't believe I've been here four weeks. None of this makes sense.

But Doc Conner has answers for every question.

And I'll be on strong medication or kept here longer with more tests if I don't agree. My words, not theirs. The 'what-ifs' deflate me: What if it was a dream? What if truth, not just beauty, is in the eye of the beholder?

What if Wuz is dead and this all happened when I was unconscious?

A tear is coming. I wipe my eye before it escapes. More of them surge past their high-tide mark, and I must let Wuz go – again. Time to leave this place and live my life.

The next morning Nan arrives, as chirpy as a magpie's morning call, and I miss nature's long-beaked alarm clock that woke the girls in our *ngumbin*. No longer caged by worry, Nan delivers my clothes, then shuffles into the corridor, and I get out of the faded blue hospital gown and into shorts and a tee.

I know my truth.

I'm the great-granddaughter of a dreamer. I'll find that glowing ochre and protect my mind. Wish I could've gifted it to Great Nanna Clara and given her a different ending.

N'gian – your spirit or light or whatever you are – I don't mean to sound disrespectful, just don't understand how you work. But if you are real, please give me a sign.

Nan knocks, opens the door and pokes her head in. 'Come on, Bub. Yer dad's got the van ready out front. Wanna leave this place and go home?'

Her head disappears and she tells someone, 'She's dressed but still in bed.'

Dad comes in. 'Hey, I got permission to park the car in a loading zone for five minutes. Better hurry up.'

The door swings open. They're frothin' like groms heading on their first road trip.

I think it before I feel it. *Believe in yourself. Don't be afraid.*

Then perch on the edge of the bed. 'Nan. Dad. I need to tell you something. Can you please close the door? This won't take long.'

Dad shuts the door. They stand side by side.

'I love you both and must do what I believe. We fear things we don't understand. You can judge me. The doctor can judge me. But I won't come under the judgement of others. I'm not a *jarjum* anymore.'

I gulp in sweaty air, thick with tension. 'I said what I had to, so I could leave today. I believe in Wallulljagun, that Narn is Wuz, and I went back in time to our people and learned our ancestors' ways. I've a gift given to me by N'gian, our greatest cleverman. I have dreams that come true 'cos I take after Great Nanna, and I'm fine with that. The difference is I was taught how to protect my mind.'

Is Nan gonna cry?

I power on. 'You can believe me or you can treat me like Great Nanna Clara. Or you –' I stand and grab their hands to form a family ring. 'Or you can love me, no matter what I believe. I want your support. But I'll find the strength to do it without you if I have to.'

Nan is first to speak. 'I love you too, Bub. I won't make the same mistake twice. You're right, I don't understand. It was the hardest thing staring at you through a tiny glass window these past four weeks.' Nan shudders. Her tears leave glossy trails. 'It's my fault me mum, your great nanna, went to a psychiatric hospital.'

Dad side-hugs Nan. 'It's not your fault. You were just a kid. You didn't know they'd take your words and use them against Nanna.'

I offer Nan the tissue box, she tugs out two and dries her cheeks. 'One day, maybe I'll understand too,' she says, and a tight-rope kind of smile wobbles across her face.

Nan gives me a hug, a long one, and Dad joins in. Then she's back to business.

'Bub, why aren't you wearing your glasses? I brought them in here when you first came to hospital. Do you have contacts in? Tony, did you bring her contacts from home?'

Dad frowns at Nan. 'No, Mum.'

The talking stops. There's that *tick-tick-ticking* sound.

How could I forget N'gian's power? A warm energy starts from the tips of my toes, moves through my body, arcs past the hospital ceiling and into the sun. My smile launches to the same height.

Dad's eyes flick from mine to Nan's and back again in pinball-machine motion. 'What?'

'I'm not wearing contacts. It's twenty past eleven, Dad. You got here at a quarter past. So we better motor.'

Nan checks the clock, hanging on the wall furthest from us, then looks at my eyes.

She gasps and grabs Dad's arm. 'Well, how? Your eyes are fixed.'

'N'gian,' I say, and a chuckle spills out.

When we walk out the hospital doors, the sun warms my skin. I'd missed it. I'm gazing into it, feeling a small voice – not audible, more like it's speaking from the sun and in my heart at the same time. It reminds me of how a dolphin hears. Instead of the vibration of sound echoing along my jaw, feeling the words, it echoes in my heart.

Don't be afraid. I'll send you a helper. Every dreamer needs a dream-teller.

I squint at the sun, my heart rattles in my ears while my mind searches for answers. What's that old fella, N'gian, up to now?

We all jump into Dad's old '76 V-Dub Kombi. The three of us squish together in the cabin with Nan in the middle.

Dad turns the key and the motor coughs and splutters. 'Isn't it high tide we leave?' he says, and Nan and I chant our usual response: 'Foreshore. Foreshore.'

Windows are down, salt spices the air, and my surfboard bounces 'round in the back, as we rumble down the coast towards Jellurgal Point. The smell of wetsuits and surfboard wax fills the van. It's like I've gobbled a packet of popcorn kernels and they're exploding in my tummy. I've missed the GC: the people and the place.

'I'm gonna join Yugambeh Choir,' I say. 'Nan, you could come, sit and yarn with all the aunties.'

'Good idea, Bub. Never too late to get involved. That reminds me of what Mum used to say: "Culture is within us. We're born with the lore of this land."'

'I love that, Nan.'

We chug around a corner, hit a bump, and a necklace pops out of Dad's shirt.

'Daaad!' I scream and point to the tiny bones swinging around his throat. 'Where did you get that?'

The relic rattles. His voice is graveyard calm. 'The nurses gave me your surfboard when they discharged you. This was wrapped around your leggie.' Dad strokes the fossil-like bones, the way a percussionist plays the chimes.

My throat slams shut, as if I've swallowed one of them. I'm choking.

A smile slithers over Dad's face. 'They're not real bones, Kirra. It's your necklace.'

Shivers shoot across my back: a sting of a thousand blue bottles.

I've seen that smile.

Haunting my dreams.

Has my world been breached?

GLOSSARY

Languages of Australian Aboriginal and Torres Strait Islander peoples are oral, not traditionally in a written form. Therefore, the spelling has many variations.

Words are listed with pronunciation* in parentheses, followed by other spelling variations in Yugambeh [or neighbouring languages], then its English definition.

arabin (nga-ra-bin), also known as *g'narrabin, ngarravunn, ngarbany, dawur, tow row*: fishing net attached to two cane frames, which were woven by Aboriginal women and used by Aboriginal men to trap and scoop fish.

bilang (bihl-lung), also known as *bilung, nyugal*: casuarina tree, she-oak, oak.

booangun (boo-ahn-gahn), also known as *buwangan, booiurragun*: bush stone curlew

bora (boh-rah) is a common Aboriginal word from many tribes, also known as *boul, buhl, buwul, bule*: sacred gathering ring or place.

boulmung (boouhl-muhng), also known as *buluhlmang*, *bulwang*, *buhwulmang*: whirlwind or willy-willy.

buhnyi buhnyi (buhn-yee buhn-yee), also known as *bonyi bonyi* [Jinibara]: bunya pine tree.

bunngunn (bahn-gahn), also known as *bungun*, *bangan*: possum-skin drum.

cleverman or **cleverwoman**: an Aboriginal healer who's highly respected and is a keeper of sacred knowledge, songlines, culture, places, spiritual beliefs and lore; has secret supernatural power.

coolamon (cool-ah-mon) or *gulaman* is a Gamilaraay word, commonly used by many Aboriginal people: a shallow wooden or bark dish that carries food, water and babies.

Dark Emu or 'Emu in the Sky' is part of 'skylore' or Australian Aboriginal Astronomy and is used by many Aboriginal communities: the dark patches of the night sky and its dust trails, found behind a cluster of bright stars (known as the Milky Way).

deadly (dead-lee): a term used by many Aboriginal communities to mean 'great' or 'cool'.

dillybag (dihl-lee-bag) is a common Aboriginal word from many tribes, also known as *dugul-duguhl*, *gulay*: bag or net, woven out of vine or string made from bark, reeds or pandanus leaves.

Dreaming or **the Dreaming** is a common term used in many Aboriginal communities: a foundational part of Australian Aboriginal culture and spirituality, which tells how Earth was created and how these Aboriginal ancestral spirits shaped lore. Dreaming stories and rituals are different (though sometimes shared) in tribal nations across Australia and form part of stories, songs, dances, art and customs. A lot of Aboriginal people believe their spirit returns to the Dreaming when they die. Dreaming is a complex spiritual concept that exists outside of time and can be accessed in the present 'living' culture.

duck-dive: a surfing technique where a surfer uses both hands and a foot to push a surfboard nose-first under a wave that has broken or is about to break.

dugan djulung waring gwong (do-gahn dju-lung wah-ring gwong): the upwelling, or in this Yugambeh phrase of up-push-cold-water, is a weather phenomenon where wind-swept motion drives cooler and nutrient-rich water from the deep towards the sea's surface.

Elder/s: a highly respected Aboriginal man or woman in their older age who is a custodian of a clan's knowledge and lore. They are given this role by their community in which they advise, settle disputes, arrange marriages, etc., according to the clan's lore.

eugarie (you-gah-ree), also known as *yugari, yugiri, ugari, ugarie*: a common pipi; a triangular bi-valve mollusc shell found in saltwater.

gammon (gah-mon) is a common Aboriginal word from many tribes, also known as *gagum* (gah-goom): a term used to say you're 'joking' or 'mucking around' or something is fake or pretend.

gnarly (nah-lee): a surfing term for 'good', 'heavy' or 'tough'.

Goories (goo-rees), also known as *Guri, Goori*: Aboriginal Australians from the coastal area of far northern

New South Wales and South East Queensland. The same goes for Murries or Murri (from Queensland), Koories or Koori (from New South Wales and Victoria). These are expressions that Indigenous peoples call themselves.

gowonda (gaw-an-deh), also known as *gawandeh*, *kawandeh*, *gowondo*: dolphin; the giant dolphin (mythical).

gowonda kunga neubungunn (gaw-an-deh koon-ga new-bun-goon): this Yugambeh composite phrase of dolphin-call-wife is used to describe the dolphin caller's wife.

grom/s: short form of grommet; a surfing term for a young surfer who is often enthusiastic.

gudje (*goo-djah*), also known as *kujei*, *gudja*: honey of the larger native stingless bees.

gumburra (goom-burr-ah), also known as, *bumburra*, *gumbar*, *gambar*: macadamia or Queensland nut.

gunang (goo-nang), also known as *gundang*, *gunyim*, or *goona/guna* [Pama-Nyungan]: faeces, poo, crap.

gunyah (guhn-yah), also known as *guhn*, *kudjen*: a humpy or small temporary shelter made from bark and branches.

jabir (dja-bihr), also known as *jab'eri*, *dha'biri*: a carved wooden club, nulla-nulla or waddy, used for fighting, digging, hunting and as paddles.

jagun (dja-goon), also known as *jalay*, *dha'gun*: country, ground, earth.

jambinbin (jahm-bin-bin), also known as *jumpinpin,* or *winnem* [Jandai]: root sucker of the pandanus palm; pandanus.

jarjum (jah-djam), also known as *jahdjam*, *jahgam*, *djahdjam*: child, children.

Jellurgal Point (yell-er-gull), also known as *jalinggul, jaling, jalurgul, yalurgul*: Burleigh Heads in the southern Gold Coast, Queensland, Australia.

jingi (jing-gih) or ***jingeri*** (jing-gah-ree), also known as *jinggi, jingeri, jinggeri*: greeting, hello. So, '*jingi wahlu*' means 'hello, how are you?'

kagohn (kah-goon), also known as *gaguhng, kagon, kagong, kagoon*: elder brother.

kalmuhran (kahl-muh-ran), also known as *yugay, galmuhran, kamiru*: swampland fern or root of bungwall fern; used to make a biscuit-type of bread.

karum (kah-ruhm), also known as *garum*: wild.

kook: a surfing term for someone who can't surf and is often uneducated about surfing protocols, terms, place in the lineup, etc.

kumo (kuh-moh), also known as *kumu, bandang*: backside, butt.

kurrajong string (car-rah-jong): the bark fibre of the kurrajong or bottle tree is used traditionally by many Aboriginal tribes along the east coast to make strong twine for nets and fishing lines.

leggie (leg-ee): an abbreviated surfing term for leg-rope or legrope, which attaches a surfer's leg to the surfboard.

line-up or **lineup**: a surfing term for the area where surfers sit and wait to catch unbroken waves.

Malung (mah-lung), also known as *malong*: shady, shadow, or evil spirit.

marba juwi balay jagan (mahr-bah jew-ee bahl-ay dja-goon): this Yugambeh phrase of roast-down-beneath-earth means to roast or cook meat and vegetables in ashes underground; earth oven.

midyim (mid-jum), also known as *midgen*: a native shrub grown in coastal South East Queensland and northern New South Wales area with small sweet, tangy berries.

migaloo (mi-guh-lu) or *migalu* is used in many Aboriginal communities, also known as *duggai*: a white person or white fella.

mind-spear: 'bone-pointing' is a curse that executes someone without leaving any trace.

mungulli (muhn-gul-li), also known as *talwalpin* [Jandai]: Australia's native hibiscus tree with bright yellow flowers; coastal cotton tree or beach hibiscus.

N'gian (ngih-ahn), also known as *yelgun, yalnun, nyunga, or ngayan* [in Gumbaynggirr]: sun.

Ngulungmal waringan gahla (new-lung-mahl wah-rin-gahn gah-lah): It will get cool.

ngumbin (nguhm-bihn), also known as *nguhmbiny*: house or hut.

ngurun (ngur-ahn), also known as *nguran, jurginy, kurgany, nalgal*: dingo, a wild medium-sized dog native to Australia.

nyulli (nyuel-lee), also known as *yuli, babracowie* or *babragowi* [Jandai]: pigface is an edible succulent with bright pink flowers, endemic to eastern Australia.

piccabeen basket (pic-cah-been): traditionally produced from the folded frond of the piccabeen or bangalow palm.

pullen-pullen (pool-lehn pool-lehn), also known as *bullen bullen, nabullen,* or *bumalen*: fighting using a spear, boomerang and shield; fighting ground or battle.

shame is a common word used in many Indigenous communities, also used as 'shame job' or 'that's so shame': to feel embarrassed or an embarrassing situation.

shaper is an abbreviated surfing term for surfboard shaper: person who takes a 'foam blank' and uses a machine or planer to shape the foam into a surfboard ready for laminating (glassing) and sanding.

steamer: a surfing term for a full-length wetsuit, that is, a long-sleeved and long-legged wetsuit.

steeze is a term used in surf, skate, wake, snow – all of those board sports: it's a combination of 'style' and 'ease'.

tabbi-tabbi (djah-bi dja-bi), also known as *jahbi-jahbi* [Bundjalung], lap-lap or traditional belt: a customary covering over the groin or loin cloth using animal skins or woven plant fibres.

waalum (wahl-loom), also known as *wallum* [Kabi Kabi]: an autumn flowering shrub found in coastal heath areas; banksia.

wahlu (wah-lu), also known as *wallo*: you.

Waijung (why-dja-ung), also known as *wadjung, wadjung, wayung*: mother, mum, used also for mother's sister.

Wallulljagun (wahl-luhl dja-goon), also known as *Jagun wahlul, Jalay wahlul*: many country, used as a Yugambeh composite word for 'Australia'.

waring (wah-ring), also known as *waringgal, wahgaru*: very cold, cold season, winter.

wettie: surfing slang; abbreviation for wetsuit.

Wollumbin (wool-lum-bihn), also known as *Walum, wulambiny*: a sacred mountain; Mount Warning.

worong (woh-rong), also known as *wurang, wurahng, wulang*: leaf, leaves.

wudjuru (woo-dju-ru), also known as *balbul, bulam*, or *oodgeroo* [Jandai]: melaleuca or paperbark tea tree, ti-tree, has a light-yellow flower and thick papery bark.

yilgahn (yihl-gahn), also known as *yirgahng*: younger sister.

Yugambeh (you-guhm-bear) or *Yugambir*: an Australian Aboriginal language; ancestors of the Traditional Custodians of South East Queensland and north-eastern New South Wales (Gold Coast, Scenic Rim, Logan City, and Tweed City) spoke one or more dialects of Yugambeh.

*For more on pronunciation ('oo' as in 'book', 'u' as in 'you'), see the Yugambeh Language resources below.

Allen, J., *The Language of Wangerriburra and Neighbouring Groups in the Yugambeh region*, from the works of John Allen and John Lane during 1850–1931, edited and published by The Kombumerri Aboriginal Corporation for Culture.

Allen, J. & Lane, J., *The Modern Yugambeh Language Dictionary,* First Edition Orthography, Yugambeh Museum Language and Heritage Research Centre, 2013.

Sharpe, M., *Dictionary of Yugambeh (including neighbouring dialects)*, The Australian National University, 1998.

Sharpe, M., *Gurgun Mibinyah: Yugambeh, Ngarahngwal, Ngahnduwal: A dictionary and grammar of Mibiny language varieties from the Logan to the Tweed rivers,* Aboriginal Studies Press, 2020

Watson, F.J., *1946 Vocabularies of Four Representative Tribes of South Eastern Queensland,* Royal Geographical Society of Australasia (Queensland).

AUTHOR'S NOTE AND ACKNOWLEDGEMENTS

I respectfully acknowledge Elders past and present, Traditional Custodians of Yugambeh-speaking country, and all Aboriginal and Torres Strait Islander peoples. Thank you to my old people who proudly passed on our Indigenous heritage and connection to Country.

I'd also like to honour your/our non-Indigenous ancestors who travelled across vast oceans from faraway nations. They intertwine our pasts and weave our futures together as we share this ancient land, stories and culture. Though *The Upwelling* began with me, it ends with you. For that I'm grateful. You are the reason why I put pen to paper.

In the beginning, but long after the Dreaming, my parents (and all their scruffy kids) would visit Aunty Averil (Dad's sister), Uncle Irwin (Dad's brother) and cousins on the Gold Coast ... since I was a baby. So when my husband and I moved to the GC with our two groms almost ten years ago, we immediately felt at home.

As a family, we love visiting our briny playground. Five years ago, I was surfing Kirra Point and thought, *What did this place look like before the highways and high-rises?*

Then I had this idea: What if an Indigenous girl raised in the Western way could somehow experience life before colonisation? So I'm waiting for waves and wondering, *Can I write a novel?* One year later, I was surprised to win the 2018 black&write! Fellowship and hear the judges praise *The Upwelling* as a highly original coming-of-age story, unlike anything they had ever read. Without that comp, I don't think I would've had the guts to write a novel. So I'm thankful to the State Library of Queensland, CEO Vicki McDonald, and the SLQ's black&write! editing team: Grace Lucas-Pennington and Caitlin Murphy.

You've probably guessed that Kirra, my protagonist, is named after the surf break where it all began. I couldn't base this novel on any of my Countries where my Indigenous bloodlines are from because there's no surf (and lots of crocs!).

I'm incredibly blessed to have the support of many families and community members who are Traditional Custodians of this beautiful place I call home, with its long stretches of golden beaches, rainforests and some of the best surf breaks in the world. I'm humbled to be part of this community.

The characters, events and places in *The Upwelling* are fictional. Any likeness to real persons, incidents or locales is purely coincidental. What I love most about reading (and writing) novels is it's the only place you can see/ read what someone really thinks. Aboriginal and Torres Strait Islander 'culture' can be mistaken as only art, dance and song. Yet, reading characters' thoughts, which an Indigenous person writes, makes you privy to our culture's intricacies. This way, you get to participate – not just be a spectator.

I love researching but also wrote from my lived experiences, like when Dad took us on Country with wait-a-while, collecting bushtucker, etc., as kids. Over the past five years, I researched everything about dolphins. We had a family trip to Tin Can Bay and handfed the humpback dolphins. It's where I saw the six-week-old dolphin calf that I based Echo on. I also made piccabeen baskets, fires using firesticks, did string-making from *mungulli*, made knives the traditional way, and learned possum-skin cloakmaking, smoke signals, ochre painting, bushtucker, and so much more.

Dreaming stories are real beliefs, and it's an honour to be given permission from Elders, Traditional Custodians and Indigenous knowledge-holders to use these knowledges in this novel. I'm humbled by Ysola Best, her research and knowledges she shared. She (and other Indigenous research pioneers) paved the way for the next generations of writers. If there are any mistakes in this fictional book, it is due to my misunderstandings and not the Indigenous knowledge-holders or any of the following experts I have received the information from.

As we say in Torres Strait Islander language, my grandfather's language, a big *eso* (thanks) to the members of the Yugambeh Youth Aboriginal Corporation, who permitted me to use the following traditional Indigenous knowledges in *The Upwelling*:

- Yugambeh language words/phrases
- possum-skin drum and music customs (found in the Ysola Best and Candace Kruger's research and academic publications)
- Gowonda, the Dolphin Dreaming story

- Burleigh Headland Dreaming story: the giant and bush honey
- burial and marriage ceremonies
- other Indigenous knowledges and cultural references used in this region: possum-skin cloaks, fire-making, bushtucker, songs and dance ceremonies.

I couldn't have written *The Upwelling* without the following Traditional Custodians (TCs), whom I've met with or contacted since February 2019, including Yugambeh Elders – Elder John Graham (Yugambeh-language region TC) and Elder Ian Levinge (Yugambeh-language region TC), Hague Best (Yugambeh-language region TC), Shannon Best (Yugambeh-language region TC), Dr Candace Kruger (Yugambeh-language region TC), Tracy Ritson (Mingungbal – Yugambeh-language region TC), special thanks to 'Uncle' Mark Cora and his Elders for permission to use Wollumbin (Mingungbal – Yugambeh-language region TC), Lann Levinge (Yugambeh-language region TC), Justine Dillon (Ngarahngwal TC) and Joel Slabb (Bundjalung/Yugambeh-language region TC). As well as Ysola Best's granddaughter, Laura Stable (Yugambeh-language advocate).

And *eso* to Indigenous community members along the South East Queensland and Northern New South Wales coastline who generously shared their traditional knowledges, including Rick Roser (Picambul people; weaponry/Emu egg/fire-making/weaving knowledge-holder), Dr Carol McGregor (Kulin Nation; PhD possum-skin cloaks/cultural protocol consultant), Julie Carey (Bundjalung/Gumbaynggirr Nation; dolphin caller/ocean totem knowledge-holder/cultural protocol consultant),

Paula Nihot (Gamilaraay language region; bushtucker/ Yugambeh language advocate/cultural protocol consultant), the late Laurie Nilsen (Mandandanji people; bora rings/ Aboriginal spirituality), Jo-Anne Driessens (Guwa/ Koa, Guugu Yimithirr, Yalanji Nation; Arts & Cultural worker), Leanne Fisher (Bundjalung Nation; casuarina tree knowledge-holder/cultural protocol consultant), Kieron Anderson (Quandamooka/Kullilli/Wakka Wakka people; bushtucker/Jandai-language advocate), BJ Murphy (Jinibara Country; *bonyi bonyi* festival/cultural protocol consultant), Libby Harward (Quandamooka/Ngugi people; Jandai-language advocate/cultural protocol consultant), and Stephanie Parkin (Quandamooka people; cultural protocol consultant/Parallax Legal).

A percentage of royalties from *The Upwelling* will be donated to Indigenous not-for-profit organisations, including (but not limited to) Yugambeh Youth Choir, where Yugambeh language and culture continue to be passed to *jarjum* of the Gold Coast region. Massive thanks to choirmaster/maestro Candace Kruger for your support with the glossary, Yugambeh pronunciation and for being such a positive ambassador of Indigenous culture.

I am so thankful for Suzanne Derry (Arts Law) and her legal knowledge, for Jack Howard (Paralegal) and Jo-Anne Driessens (Artists in the Black Coordinator) who all understand the importance in the protection and respect of Indigenous 'shared' knowledges within communities.

Thanks, Dr Chris Yule (geophysicist) — not wanting to paint you as a villain, but few people can tell you how to destroy the world using rocks and energy!

Thanks to snake (and venom) experts Luke Cheyne and Dr Bryan G. Fry.

To my amazing writing critique partner, Andrea Grigg: there is no problem, big or small, that I don't discuss with you. *Thankyouthankyouthankyou!* Everyone should have a writing friend like you because *iron sharpens iron*, and you are sharp in wit, editing and fresh writing. My other writing allies include Zoe Bisschop (13 and already a fantastic editor!), Cat Hudson, and editor extraordinaire Margie Lawson.

A big thanks to the hardworking team at Hachette Australia: Robert Watkins, Brigid Mullane, Vanessa Pellatt, Chris Kunz, Lesley Halm, Ailie Springall, Emma Rafferty and Kate Stevens.

To these wonderful wordsmiths: Dr Bronwyn Bancroft (Bundjalung artist, author and anything she puts her mind to), Tim Baker (bestselling surf author and former *Surfing Life* magazine editor), Amie Kaufman (*New York Times*-bestselling, award-winning author – love your writing style, humour – everything!) and Bern Young (award-winning radio presenter on ABC Gold Coast and journo with a personality-plus-plus-plus) – thanks for taking time from your busy schedules to endorse my book. I am humbled by your words, encouragement and strength.

Thank you to my family and friends for your support. Your enthusiasm and understanding (with deadlines) have been overwhelming.

To my parents: Dad, thanks for the plant information/ discussion for a traditional headache remedy, the word 'Wanjellah', and for raising me to be a proud blue-eyed, blonde-haired Murri. Mum, you married into an Indigenous family and encouraged us to walk confidently in both worlds – thanks for all you do.

And to my husband, Ray (the surfing/ocean authority and perpetual frothing grom), this book would not have happened without you taking care of everyone and everything so I could write and meet deadlines. Finally, to my *jarjum*, Zoe and Bob – my upbeat encouragers (who also never hold back when it comes to honesty). I can write thousands of words daily, yet you three often leave me so full of emotion that words become sparse and fleeting.

Indigenous stories are shared stories. It's how we learn, have two-way conversations and weave our past, present and future. Now, it's time to release my grip so that you can hold these fresh-printed pages ... and I can finish Book 2: *The Upwarping*.

In **Wallulljagun** (the Yugambeh conglomeration of words I used for Australia), the earth beneath your feet taps into the oldest living culture in the world. I hope you enjoy reading *The Upwelling* as much as I loved writing it.

Lystra Rose, a descendant of the Guugu Yimithirr, Birri Gubba, Erub and Scottish nations, is an award-winning writer and editor who lives in a land where the rainforest meets the sea ... Yugambeh-speaking country (Gold Coast), Australia. When she's not catching waves with her husband and their two groms, Lystra is editing *Surfing Life* magazine and is the executive producer of *Surfing Life TV* (globally broadcasted on Fuel TV). She is the first female editor-in-chief of a mainstream surf magazine in the world. Surfing is Lystra's daily reminder to 'let fear be your friend, not your foe, and use it to do the things you love or were meant to do'. It's also her creativity generator.

The Upwelling is Lystra's debut novel.

hachette
AUSTRALIA

If you would like to find out more about
Hachette Australia, our authors, upcoming events
and new releases, you can visit our website or our
social media channels:

hachette.com.au

HachetteAustralia

HachetteAus